LONE JUSTICE

The Virginian held himself perfectly still. When he responded, each word was clipped and precise and seemed to hang in the air of its own accord. "If you want to die—*try*!"

Killebrew did. He went for his six-gun with all the speed he could muster, but the barrel had not yet cleared the holster when the room thundered to two shots spaced so closely together they sounded like one, and twin holes blossomed high on his chest. The impact hurled him rearward into a card table that gave way under his momentum and weight. Both hit the floor with a tremendous crash.

Now the room became deathly still again. Everyone there stared breathlessly at the limp corpse.

"Anyone else want to play his hand?"

To the Virginian's surprise, there was. The sound of gunmetal clearing leather filled the air, and an instant later came the deafening roar of gunfire. . . .

THE RETURN OF THE VIRGINIAN

David Robbins

BANTAM BOOKS
New York • Toronto • London • Sydney • Auckland

THE RETURN OF THE VIRGINIAN
A Bantam Domain Book / June 1994

The Return of the Virginian *is a creation of Siegel & Siegel, Ltd.*

DOMAIN and the portrayal of a boxed "d" are trademarks of Bantam Books, a division of Bantam Doubleday Dell Publishing Group, Inc.

ISBN 0-553-56321-1

Published simultaneously in the United States and Canada

Bantam Books are published by Bantam Books, a division of Bantam Doubleday Dell Publishing Group, Inc. Its trademark, consisting of the words "Bantam Books" and the portrayal of a rooster, is Registered in U.S. Patent and Trademark Office and in other countries. Marca Registrada. Bantam Books, 1540 Broadway, New York, New York 10036.

PRINTED IN THE UNITED STATES OF AMERICA

OPM   0 9 8 7 6 5 4 3 2 1

Dedication

There is only one person to whom this book can rightfully be dedicated.

To the man who defined the raw character of a growing nation; to the romantic who captured the romance lurking
in all souls; to the poet who saw ennobling truth where others
saw only mundane facts; to the adventurer who dared to tread
where few had gone before; to the wealthy aristocrat who perceived the genuine worth in all; to the concerned citizen who
so loved his country that he penned an ardent appeal and an
impassioned warning; to the eloquent writer who wrote one of
America's favorite novels: *Owen Wister*.

To him, and him alone, is *The Return of the Virginian*
dedicated. And may those who enjoy the sequel see reflected
in its pages the high esteem in which the original is held.

Acknowledgments

A writer owes thanks to so many when a work of this size and scope has been finished that they can't all be listed, or the list would rival the length of the work itself. So I will concentrate on a few while offering a general heartfelt "thank you" to the many.

First to be mentioned is my wife, who honors me with her continued love and devotion.

Next are my two sons, who sacrificed time with me so that the novel could be completed.

I must also extend my gratitude to Stephanie Lile of the American Morgan Horse Association, whose research into the history of the Morgan in Texas and Arizona proved invaluable.

A very special thanks goes to Ben T. Traywick of Tombstone, Arizona, whose excellent research into the life of a certain notorious gunman set the record straight at last. To Ben and others who will wonder why, when I knew the facts, I chose to wed the romantic myth to the historical myth, I can only plead artistic license. It was aesthetically pleasing to do so; the circle is now complete. I hope I can be forgiven.

And to the good people of Wyoming, whose stalwart natures embrace elements citified "book riders" can but marvel at, my sincerest regards.

To the Reader

Certain of the newspapers, when Owen Wister's *The Virginian* was published, branded it a "historical novel." Wister himself called it a "colonial romance."

The sequel is a bit of both and more. It is historical in the sense that the plot relates directly to the Johnson County War, a conflict between ranchers, rustlers, and homesteaders that actually occurred. It is a romance in the sense that the relationship between the Southerner and the Schoolmarm continues to unfold, and we get to share the full depth of their love, to experience their many heartbreaks and their personal triumphs.

Foremost, however, *The Return of the Virginian* is intended to be an entertaining Western from the first page to the last. It is the story of a Wyoming cowboy, a tale of a man coming to grips with his past, his present, and his future. It is a stirring account of frontier times when this great nation of ours had not yet succumbed to the enticing lures of self-indulgence.

If, along the way, this book has anything of note to say about the state of our country, or the nature of politics, or the never-ending war between the "haves" and the "have-nots," it is entirely incidental to the story itself.

Out of respect to Owen Wister, I have adhered diligently

to the style and tone of his original classic. The Professor's journal entries, for instance, are related as first person accounts—as well they should be—since part of our fascination comes from viewing the West through his inexperienced eyes. The Virginian's adventures, however, are related in the only manner they can be told, through straightforward narrative. Quintessential Mystery Man that he is, the Southerner's thoughts and insights are reflected by his actions. We are rarely permitted to see the world through his eyes, as we do with his good friend. The Virginian, unfortunately, did not leave a detailed journal for posterity.

Some might say that mixing the two narrative styles is confusing. But not in this case, where the two points of view so perfectly complement one another as to give us an indelible portrait of a man unique in the annals of the American West and perhaps in all of American literature: The Virginian.

This one last note, and then I will let you read in peace. For those who will regard the main character's proficiency with six-shooters as unduly exaggerated, I would refer you to an article written by Robert A. Kane, an editor of *Outdoor Life*, concerning the marksmanship of one James Butler Hickok, better known as "Wild Bill," near Milwaukee during the latter half of the last century. A critical observer, Mr. Kane wound up being so impressed that he later wrote he would be "prepared to believe any story of his skill or prowess that does not conflict with the laws of gravitation and physics."

Now read on, and may you enjoy the time you spend between the covers of this novel. If, when you are done, you set the book down and smile, I will have been amply rewarded for all the effort.

Oregon
October 1993

1

Back to the Primitive

I was so excited at being back in Medicine Bow for the first time in over a year that I bounded from the Pullman car onto the platform without thinking. In my eagerness to see my old friends again I failed to look both ways to make certain no one was approaching from either direction. A small blunder, you might think, but in this instance it was to play a big part in the ever-escalating series of turbulent events that eventually led to the most terrible bloodshed and appalling violence ever recorded in Wyoming.

For just as I sprang onto the platform, at the very moment when both of my feet were in midair, a stocky man stepped directly into my path. There was no hope of avoiding him. There was no time to swerve to the right or the left. All I could do was exactly what I did, namely, to reach out and grab his arm as we collided and to hold tight as the two of us stumbled a few feet. We nearly went down. Somehow I managed to keep both of us upright, and as we came to a stop, I hastily blurted,

"My humblest apologies, sir! I didn't mean to run into you."

The man recovered quickly from his initial shock. He angrily looked at my hand on his arm, then brushed it off with a sharp gesture. "The hell yu' say, yu' yack!" he snapped, his dark, beady eyes critically raking me from head to toe. "I should've knowed you'd be a tenderfoot."

"I'm truly sorry," I stressed, controlling my temper at being branded a rank Easterner. The many months I'd spent in the company of my Southern friend and his cow-puncher associates had convinced me that I'd pass for one of their wild and carefree fraternity anywhere in the West, and now to learn otherwise was quite upsetting. Hefting my valise, I went to go around the offended citizen. But he wasn't about to let me. Nor were his friends.

Two men closed in, one on each side, and between the three of them they effectively hemmed me in. On my left stood a grizzled puncher distinguished by a large wad of chewing tobacco that made his cheek bulge. On my right was another cowhand—or so, in my abysmal igno-rance, I believed him to be—dressed all in black, a tall, wiry man whose striking green eyes for some reason re-minded me of the eerie unblinking orbs of a coiled rattler.

"I beg your pardon!" I declared.

"Do yu' really, pilgrim?" responded the offended cit-izen.

"What's the problem here, Killebrew?" asked the grizzled puncher. "Is this Monkey-Ward cowboy givin' yu' a hard time?"

The man in black snorted. "He surely does look like a mail-order catalog on foot, don't he?"

Their mocking tones fueled my growing resentment. I was about to give them a piece of my mind when I hap-pened to notice that all three were armed and that their hands dangled dangerously close to their hardware. Killebrew and the grizzled puncher both wore Colts on their right hips. The man in black, however, went them one better. He was a genuine rarity in my experience: a two-gun man, sporting a matched set of ivory-handled six-shooters in tied-down holsters. At the sight of them my sharp retort died on my lips. To cover my embarrassment I coughed and said, "Listen here. I meant no offense. It was an accident, plain and simple."

"There ain't no such animal," stated the grizzled puncher. "Only fools and foolishness." He cocked his head and gave me a withering stare of sheer contempt. "My pard and me saw what happened. Seems to me yu' ought to get down on your knees and beg Killebrew here for forgiveness."

I saw the wicked smiles that curled the mouths of all three men, and I knew I was in trouble. Many a tenderfoot had been made to dance to the tune of whistling bullets for sins real or imagined, and frankly, I didn't fancy becoming one of them. Since I've never been much of a fighter, diplomacy seemed my best bet to avoid further trouble. "I've already apologized to your friend," I told the grizzled puncher. "But if it will make you feel better, I'll do so again."

"How thoughtful of yu', pilgrim," said the grizzled hand. Then he unaccountably cackled.

There are certain vivid moments in our lives that we never, ever forget: our first horse ride, our first passionate kiss, the death of a loved one. You must have some you will always remember no matter how many years go by. This was one of mine. It was an instant in time when time itself was encased in ice, when all the universe had ground to a halt except for my racing blood. The three strangers hemming me in were like sinister statues while I was more alive than I could ever recall being. My senses were extraordinarily acute. I could hear my own rapid breathing. I could feel my temples pounding. And I swore I could smell the sweat that dampened my collar. I was, in short, vibrant with expectancy, certain I would be soundly thrashed if I didn't give in to their request to kneel.

At that juncture, with my manhood hanging in the balance, a firm hand fell on my shoulder, and I was pulled backward as a gruff voice interjected, "So here yu' are, Professor! Yu' ought to know better than to keep us waitin'."

Suddenly I found myself being propelled toward the station. Twisting, I gazed fondly into the bleached-blue eyes of Scipio le Moyne and opened my mouth to thank him for the timely rescue when he whispered urgently in my ear.

"Shush, yu' darned yearlin'! We ain't out of the woods yet."

Accenting his comment, the three men who had accosted me swiftly caught up with us.

"Whoa there, le Moyne," Killebrew said. "You're not cuttin' that calf out until we've done put our brand on him."

Scipio halted, and as he did, he pushed me to one side and behind him so that he alone squarely confronted the trio. "What's the problem, gents?" he asked amiably.

"The problem is that your friend don't have no manners," said the man in black, his eyes hard as flint. "We figured we'd teach him some."

"That's right obliging of yu', Brazos," Scipio responded, still as friendly as could be. "But yu' wouldn't want word to get around that you're beatin' on foals, would yu'?"

"What are yu' on about?" Brazos growled.

"Why, just this. If a grown horse acts up, sometimes a man has to give the contrary critter a smack or three to make it behave. But no man in his right mind would do the same to a foal, 'cause the animal is too ignorant to know better. The Professor here," Scipio said, jerking a thumb at me, "is a foal at heart. He just doesn't know no better about anything. Why, I remember one time he forgot to cinch up proper when we went for a ride in the mountains, and about an hour out from the ranch I heard a yelp and turned to see him hangin' from his horse, saddle and all, like one of them bats in a cave—"

"Ignorance is no excuse," the grizzled puncher interrupted. "It's just a fancy word for bein' a fool."

Once again Scipio refused to be offended. "We should thank the Lord for the fools of this world, Santee. They make the rest of us look like we know what we're doin'."

I could see Scipio was getting nowhere.. These three were determined to put me in my place, and I feared my friend had put himself in jeopardy by coming to my aid. Scipio and I went back a long ways; I'd known him almost as long as I'd known my Southern friend, and I was honored to be included in their intimate circle of boon companions. So to spare him from having to intercede in my behalf, I took a step into the open, resolved to take my own medicine. As I did, the one called Brazos glared at me with an expression I can only describe as malignant in the extreme. Which puzzled me greatly, since my alleged crime hardly warranted such intense hatred. Then his gaze shifted, going over my shoulder, and he tensed and took a half step backward.

I twisted to see why, and the wave of relief that washed over me was more delicious than words can convey. Crossing the platform toward us were more men I knew—all, like Scipio, hands from the Sunk Creek outfit. There was Chalkeye and Dollar Bill and Honey Wiggin and the Toothpick Kid. At their forefront strode Lin McLean with that slight limp he has, his short curly hair jutting from under his broad hat. His hazel eyes, ordinarily alight with the fire of playful deviltry, now glittered with a different, harder light.

Scipio had also noticed the timely arrival of the cavalry, and he now chuckled as he turned to Killebrew. "Appears to me that school's out for the day. Unless, of course, yu' figure on teachin' a bigger class than yu' was countin' on?"

The Sunk Creek punchers formed a solid wall behind us, all except for Lin McLean, who stepped up next to Scipio and nonchalantly hooked his thumbs in his cartridge belt. So natural an act, it seemed, yet it put his right hand within inches of his pistol. "Howdy, Brazos," he said.

That individual merely nodded.

"You'll have to come up with another brainstorm," Lin said. "This one is nipped in the bud."

"Crow while yu' can, cowboy," Brazos retorted, and

spun on his heels. Santee and Killebrew flanked him as they stalked off into the crowd.

And such a crowd! Not until that moment did I realize how many people were bustling about the usually tranquil train station. In the past the Union Pacific would have let off four or five travelers at the most on an infrequent busy day, and there might have been a few souls on hand to greet them. Today there were close to two dozen either stepping off or boarding, most doing the former. In addition, a busy crowd covered the small platform and milled about in the dusty street. Men in suits both shabby and fine, men in homespun farm clothes, men in the typical attire of cowpunchers, were all moving to and fro, either greeting new arrivals, bidding loved ones and friends good-bye, checking freight, or whatever. I was amazed at such an unexpected sight, even more so when I saw all the women who were present, wives and daughters and sweethearts and spinsters in their pretty dresses and gaily decorated hats.

You must understand how unusual this was. Women were as scarce as hen's teeth on the frontier. For every one hundred men there were four women—if that many. Every eligible female, whether she shone with radiant charm or not, could count on more ardent suitors than she had ever imagined in her wildest romantic fantasies. Men would ride a hundred miles or better for the privilege of calling on her, and they would treat her like royalty in the bargain since in their rough-hewn estimation every member of the opposite gender was as precious as a priceless diamond.

On my last trip to Medicine Bow the fairer sex had numbered not quite a dozen. Now I marveled at beholding a score or more right here at the station, and I wondered what had produced so drastic a change. My musing was cut short, though, when Scipio suddenly grasped my elbow and hastened me away from the slowly puffing train. The Sunk Creek hands promptly followed.

"We've got to get yu' to somewhere safe pronto," he stated.

"But my trunk!" I protested.

"We'll send someone to fetch it," Scipio said as he adroitly steered me through the crowd. "Right now savin' your hide is more important."

"What do you mean?"

He squinted at me, studying my features as if he were a scientist and I a new form of microbe he'd just discovered. "Sometimes yu' plumb scare me." Sighing, he sadly shook his head. "I told yu' before and I'll tell you again, Professor. Yu' really oughtn't to be let to travel around alone the way yu' do. How you've lived this long is a mystery to me."

"Are you referring to those three characters? Why, they wouldn't have done more than make me do a jig."

"Pitiful," Scipio moralized. "Downright pitiful." He came to the sidewalk and paused, glancing both ways. "What *he* sees in yu' I'll never know."

I didn't need to ask whom he meant, but I was in a quandary over his unusual attitude. He knew I wasn't as helpless as he made out. Why, last year I'd assisted in the roundup and performed more than my fair share of the grueling work. I'd done so well that the punchers had all come to accept me as one of their own. Or so I'd thought.

Lin McLean spoke up. "He was over to the store the last I saw."

"It wouldn't do to make smoke there. Too many womenfolk and younguns about," Scipio said, scratching his pointed chin.

"We have them buffaloed. They wouldn't dare."

"Don't put nothin' past that Brazos. A sidewinder like him is liable to strike anytime, anywhere."

"They're outnumbered."

"Are they? Do yu' know for a fact that more of their bunch didn't hit town this mornin'?"

"No," Lin admitted.

"So we play it safe. You find him and we'll treat the Professor to a drink," Scipio said, then added meaningfully, "And don't dawdle."

I keenly desired to know what was going on, but before I could pose a question, I was hustled along past a row of buildings I had never seen before. Looking around, I realized Medicine Bow had grown in my absence. The old water tank was still there, and so was the general store, the billiard hall, the two eating-houses, the feed stable, and others I remembered from the early days, but now there were many others, including not one but two hotels, several new saloons, and a lawyer's office. Prosperity had struck Medicine Bow and brought with it the earmarks of decadent civilization.

So much was happening so fast that I had barely collected my wits when we entered the very saloon where my Southern friend had first tangled with the late Trampas. In my mind's eye I saw them as they were, playing cards at the corner table, and heard once again my friend's awful challenge.

"Why, if it ain't the Prince of Wales!" exclaimed the bartender upon spying me.

"Ain't yu' heard?" Scipio addressed him. "We done gave him a new handle."

"Do tell. I suppose it was overdue, since he doesn't wear those fancy duds anymore. Is it Owen now?"

"No."

"Grizzly Killer?"

"He ain't no Indian."

"Ducky, then?"

Scipio beamed. "You, seh, have a memory like an elephant's. But no. We call him the Professor."

"Pleased to see you again, Professor," the bartender said, shaking heartily. "Name your poison. I've got some tonsil varnish here that'll tingle your toes."

"That will be fine," I mumbled, uncertain whether I should be humiliated by the treatment I was receiving or pleased by the fact the bartender remembered my name. The whiskey was everything he promised, and I broke into a fit of coughing.

"Been a while, has it?" Scipio asked.

I nodded. Composing myself, I leaned close to him. "Will you please tell me what is going on? Why did you bring me here? Who were those three men? And what in the world has happened to Medicine Bow? It used to be such a pleasant, peaceful town."

"That it did," Scipio said wistfully. "But times are changin', and not for the better." He scoured the faces of the patrons, then went on. "We have enemies hereabouts. None of us are safe, not even you."

"Enemies?" I repeated in disbelief. "You're exaggerating, surely. Is this one of your put-ons? All I did was bump into some cowhand with the disposition of a bronco. It was a trifling mistake on my part, nothing more."

"Triflin' mistakes can lead to big bullets." Scipio lowered his voice even more. "Yu' worry me turrible. Are yu' out of diapers yet? You don't think your run-in with those three was an accident?"

"It wasn't?"

"Hell, no! For one thing, those three ain't punchers. They like to style themselves range detectives, but the truth is they're paid killers. Gun-hands who'd shoot their own kin for pocket change."

My skepticism must have shown because his temper flared and he waded into me with both eyes flashing.

"You've been back east for pretty near a year, so don't stand there so high and mighty and act like yu' know better than me what's what. Yu' weren't here to see all the nesters swoop into the territory like a flock of buzzards, spreadin' out every which way and squattin' on the best land they could find. Yu' haven't seen all the fences they've put up and the water holes they've taken over. Yu' haven't heard about all the cattle bein' rustled from every outfit from here to Montana. And I'll bet a month's wages you ain't heard about all the shootin' and the lynchin'. Why, even a woman has been hung!"

His sincere outburst startled me more than anything else so far. I rested my elbows on the bar and tried to comprehend the full scope of what he had told me. The serpent, apparently, was once again loose in Eden. I felt a strange sense of foreboding, a premonition if you will, a most disturbing sensation that caused me to take another swallow of whiskey. As I did, I heard a commotion at the entrance.

Brazos, Killebrew, Santee, and five or six others of their ilk were entering the saloon. The man in black spotted me instantly and came straight toward me.

2

"If You Want to Die—*Try*!"

I barely felt Scipio's restraining hand on my wrist. Not that he need have worried. I was too stunned to do more than gape as the newcomers advanced. At tables nearby, the Sunk Creek hands were rising: Chalkeye, Honey Wiggin, and the rest, all as grim as the Reaper. I set down my glass and did my best to appear unruffled, although inwardly my stomach was churning.

Scipio stepped in front of me. "Care for a drink, boys?" he greeted Brazos and company. "I'm buying."

"We're not here to socialize," Brazos declared flatly. "The tenderfoot owes us and we aim to collect."

"How much?" Scipio said, smiling. He started to reach into his shirt pocket. "My money is as good as his."

"Yu' know damn well it's not money we're after," Brazos said smugly, doing as McLean had done earlier and hooking his thumbs in his cartridge belt. "Stand aside so we can learn this tenderfoot to be more careful about how he gets off trains."

"I reckon I can't oblige yu'."

"You're feedin' off your range. This is between him and us."

Chairs scraped the floor as men quickly got up and moved to the sides of the room. Anxious muttering broke out. All the hands from Sunk Creek and Brazos's bunch were warily regarding each other, most with their hands poised. The bartender began to ease his hands under the counter when a stern warning from Brazos froze him in place.

"I wouldn't if I was yu', Quince. Buckshot might be final, but your scattergun is heavier than both my pistols put together."

I could scarcely accept the reality of what was happening. Tension crackled in the saloon like lightning during a thunderstorm. Fierce, lethal gunplay was on the verge of exploding all around me, and all because of a stupid moment of carelessness on my part. Despite Scipio's revelations I firmly believed I was the cause. Such being the case, defusing the situation was entirely up to me. "Gentlemen!" I declared, stepping into the open space between the two sides. "There's no need for this. I've apologized twice already to Mr. Killebrew, and I'm doing so again publicly to show my good intentions. What more do you want of me? Can't we shake and let bygones be bygones?"

It was Killebrew who answered me as he strode forward until the brim of his hat nearly touched my nose. "Yu' know what I think, mister? I think all your words are hidin' the fact you're cold-footed." He sneered and touched his palm to my chest. "Did yu' hear me? I say you're a no-account yellow-belly."

It all seemed so senseless. So stupid. Grown men behaving more like immature schoolboys. For in the light of my rigidly liberal Eastern upbringing, that was how I viewed their behavior. My civilized sensibilities were more intact than I'd imagined, and rather than feel indignation at the insults Killebrew so lavishly bestowed, I felt sorry for him. He was, after all, as much a product of his rough-and-tumble environment as I was of the refined culture in which I had been reared and nurtured. From an early age

I'd been taught that fighting was the last resort of simpletons. Gentlemen were above such bestial displays. "Listen to me, friend—" I began in an earnest effort to pacify him.

"I ain't your friend, tinhorn!" Killebrew snarled, and gave me a shove with all his might.

I went flying back against the bar, jarring my spine and rattling glasses when I struck. Wincing in pain, I instinctively went to reach behind me.

"Keep your hands where I can see 'em, tinhorn."

There was a wild gleam animating Killebrew's beady eyes, and his face shone with blood lust. I saw his fingers twitch as they hovered above his Colt. He was looking for an excuse to shoot. Any excuse. It didn't matter to him that I wasn't wearing a gun. A slight ripple of raw fear coursed through me as I belatedly perceived he was going to kill me no matter what I did.

A terrible silence pervaded the saloon. Not a man there so much as twitched. All eyes were on Killebrew and me, awaiting the inevitable outcome.

Then, as I saw the stocky gun-hand grin in feral anticipation, two figures moved swiftly through the doorway, pushed past the threatening ring of Brazos's companions, and halted close to me. One of them gave me a fleeting look of tender sympathy for my plight, a look that instantly transformed itself into one of dark, simmering rage as he faced Killebrew.

The Virginian had arrived. With him was Lin McLean, but I had eyes only for the slim young giant who now dominated the room. His broad-brimmed hat, flannel shirt, overalls, and boots were no different from those worn by the majority of men present. Nor was his scarlet handkerchief unique, except in the way it complemented his burning red cheeks and brow. No, his singular commanding presence was due to one thing and one thing alone—the force of his potent personality. He was one of that rare breed blessed with an indefinable essence so overflowing with magnetic vitality as to attract the attention of all who saw him.

Killebrew reacted to that potent force as if to a physical blow. He retreated a full stride and blinked in alarm, then scowled, visibly girded himself, and barked, "Good! It might as well be me."

I had no idea what he meant, but I did know what was about to happen unless I intervened. I would have, too, if not for Scipio, who unexpectedly grabbed my arm and held me fast at the selfsame moment that Lin McLean's revolver flashed out and Lin shouted, "No one butts in! The first man to touch a six-shooter is lookin' to visit boot-hill!"

I saw Brazos turn toward McLean and go to lower his hands, but evidently he thought better of the notion and stopped. He, like everyone else, had been watching the Virginian. McLean's move caught him completely by surprise, and his contorted features betrayed his fury at the development.

Killebrew was also taken aback. He glanced at Lin, then at the Virginian. He licked his lips and flexed his fingers, but he made no move to draw his steel.

The Virginian stood relaxed and easy, his hands loose at his sides, the flush of anger gradually fading as the seconds ticked by. When he spoke a minute later, he did so in his distinctive gentle drawl, a legacy of his early days in old Virginia. "I reckon yu've had your fun. No real harm's been done, so yu' can leave without any fuss."

Everyone there realized the Southerner was trying to avoid bloodshed. Everyone present saw he was giving Killebrew a way to back out gracefully. All Killebrew had to do was turn and go. Twenty paces would take him out into the sunlight and the fresh air. A mere twenty paces and he could go on enjoying life as he saw fit. But he spurned the offer. His mind and his heart were closed to salvation, and his reply sealed his fate as surely as if it had been carved in stone.

"You've got it to do, you big son of a bitch."

A great sigh escaped the Virginian. He held himself perfectly still. When he responded, each word was clipped and precise and seemed to hang in the air of its own accord. "If you want to die—*try!*"

Killebrew did. He went for his six-gun with all the speed he could muster, but the barrel had not yet cleared the holster when the room thundered to two shots spaced so close together they sounded like one, and twin holes blossomed high on his chest. The impact hurled him rearward into a card table, which gave way under his momentum and weight. Both hit the floor with a tremendous crash.

Now the room became deathly still again. Everyone there stared breathlessly at the limp corpse. Everyone, that is, except me. I was watching the Virginian, who in turn gazed forlornly at the smoke curling upward from the end of his pistol barrel. What was he thinking? I wondered. I wanted to go to him, to put my hand on his shoulder and say something, say anything that would soothe the emotional torment I believed he must be feeling. But my mouth wouldn't work. Nor would my legs. Truth to tell, I was an utter wreck myself, in total shock from having seen a human life extinguished right before my eyes.

This was my first such experience, a nightmare made real, and I could barely cope. You might say I'd lived a sheltered existence up to that moment, and you would be correct. In all the time I'd spent in the unruly West, the worst I had been party to was a lynching, and even then I'd hid under my blankets in a stable while the grisly deed was done. I'd heard about dozens of "shootin' scrapes," as Scipio usually referred to them, since they were a common topic of discussion around campfires at night and avidly talked about in saloons and taverns from the Mississippi River to the Pacific Ocean. I'd also memorized every detail of the showdown between the Virginian and Trampas. To satisfy my innate curiosity, I'd gone so far as to seek out those who had been there when it took place so I could get their firsthand accounts of what transpired. But *hearing* about death in no way adequately prepares a person for *witnessing* the dreaded event itself.

"Any more of yu' polecats want to play your hand?" Lin McLean broke the silence, his six-shooter still leveled.

None of those who had entered with Brazos and Santee appeared eager to try their luck. All of them made it a point to lift their hands away from their hardware. Santee, rigid with astonishment, was gaping wide-eyed at the Vir-

ginian. By contrast, Brazos was as calm as could be. He
reached up to adjust his white handkerchief, smoothed his
brown mustache once, then pivoted and walked out without so much as a farewell glance at his slain partner.

"Hey!" Santee found his voice. "What should we do
with Killebrew?"

Framed in the entrance, Brazos twisted and said
sternly, "Feed him to the worms." A second later he was
gone.

"Well, that's that," Lin declared, grinning. He twirled
his revolver on the end of one finger and chuckled.

"No it ain't," Scipio disagreed. "It's just the beginning."

At these words the Virginian turned and slowly eased
his Colt into his holster. There was a haunted aspect to his
eyes that evaporated when he saw me watching him. "I'm
right sorry yu' were involved," he said softly, amiably re-
verting to his Southern drawl.

"It was my own doing," I responded, and briefly related my encounter with the trio at the train station.

"If I'd knowed they was on the prod, I'd o' met yu'
myself," the Virginian said. Taking my right hand in both
of his, he shook warmly. "It's a pleasure to have yu'
hyeh."

"The pleasure is all mine. I've looked forward to this
trip for months, ever since you wrote and so kindly invited
me to pay you a visit. I can't wait to see your new house."

He smiled. "I'm afeared the Judge will be downright
jealous. He's grown accustomed to havin' yu' stay at the
ranch."

The saloon came alive while we made our small talk.
Men hustled to the bar for refills. Others resumed the
games of chance interrupted by the gunfight. Santee and
company had picked up Killebrew and were carting him
outside, leaving a trail of large drops of blood in their
wake.

"Does Medicine Bow have a lawman yet?" I inquired
as another drop splattered down.

"Not yet," the Virginian said. "But if folks keep

flockin' in the way they are, it won't be long before a man will have to follow his horse around with a shovel."

At this there was general laughter from the Sunk Creek punchers, who had gathered around us.

"What'll we do now?" Honey Wiggin asked. "Stay the night or head on back?"

"I vote we head back," Lin said.

"Yu' would. Yu' and the big cock-a-doodle-doo have a wife and a full pot of hot coffee waitin' for yu' to home, but what about the rest of us?" Honey said. "We don't get to town all that often, and I was lookin' forward to gettin' my claws clipped by the new filly over at Salter's."

Scipio noticed my knit brow and elaborated. "Salter brought in a man-ee-cure-ist all the way from Denver, and the menfolk hereabouts have been keepin' her busy day in and day out. Why, if we was to hold a clean-fingernail contest with the folks in New York City, we'd win hands down." Winking, he nodded at his fellow punchers. "Some of these boys didn't have no idea there was skin under their nails until that filly hit town."

The Virginian became the focus of attention. As half partner in the Sunk Creek ranch and their boss, the decision was his to make. He hesitated, and I caught him appraising me out of the corner of his eye.

"Don't head back right away on my account," I said, endearing myself to the hopeful single cowhands. "I wouldn't mind taking in the town before we go." I faced my friend. "Besides, someone owes me an explanation for the ordeal I've been through this afternoon."

"We'll stay, then," the Virginian announced, and whoops raised the ceiling. "Gentlemen, hush! I expect yu' to be on your guard the whole time. Go everywhere in pairs or groups. And whatever yu' do, don't let any of Brazos's bunch get yu' riled. We'll meet at the stable in the mawnin'."

Joking and laughing, the cowhands duly filed off. With two exceptions.

"What are yu' waitin' on?" the Virginian demanded.

"We figured we'd stay with yu'," Scipio said.

"Yep," Lin threw in. "We like your company better."

"You're poor excuses for mother hens."

"My feathers don't ruffle so easily," Scipio declared in mock indignation. "If they did, the Professor would've been filled with lead long before you showed. As things stand, your back'll need watchin' from now until the matter's settled." He rubbed his stomach. "Now what say we fill up before we make the rounds? I could go for a thick steak and fresh biscuits."

I stared at the drops of blood and marveled at his constitution.

The four of us hiked to the eating-house, passing through a large crowd that had gathered in front of the saloon. Killebrew's body had been placed on the back of a buckboard, and the gawkers were having a grand old time pointing and wagging their tongues. When the Virginian appeared, their fingers and tongues did double duty until we rounded a corner.

The biscuit-shooter, a stout brunette, was all business. She took our orders, grunted, and waddled off to the kitchen.

"What happened to Mrs. Glen?" I wondered aloud.

"Ain't yu' heard?" Lin answered. "She done grabbed her warbag and lit out with the wrangler from the Bar-Circle-L about a year or so ago. I recollect it so well 'cause it was about the same time the schoolmarm put her brand on a certain persistent puncher." He grinned at the Virginian.

"How did her husband take it?"

"The freight conductor? How else could he take it? He's been tryin' real hard to pickle his innards, but so far the bug juice ain't done the job." Lin ruefully shook his head. "Plumb sad to see a man go all to pieces like that. And he was a good provider, too. Makes yu' think."

"Don't strain yourself," Scipio said. "Glen is half-bald, and the wrangler has the blackest head of hair in this country. It's as simple as that."

"Not quite the blackest," Lin said, with an innocent bob of his chin at the Southerner.

The Virginian said nothing.

"Now then," I said to change the subject while thinking of that day years ago, long before the Virginian met the schoolmarm, when I'd seen one of Mrs. Glen's blond hairs on the Virginian's flannel shirt, "who will fill me in on everything that has happened since my last visit to this country and why those men wanted to do me harm? Scipio started to explain, but he never got to finish."

They took turns, and the story they told depressed me to such an extent that I barely touched my coffee. Paradise, I learned, was on the brink of ruin. Those who made their living in the cattle trade were embroiled in a fight for their very existence.

The big ranches, including Sunk Creek, were under assault on several fronts. There had always been a problem with rustlers, although prior to the disastrous blizzard three years ago when the huge herds were virtually wiped out, the ranchers had begrudgingly tolerated the disappearance of a few head now and then. After the blizzard their attitude changed. Since every cow was of critical importance to the rebuilding of their herds, the ranchers took a dim view of having their stock stolen. They were determined to wipe out the practice.

As if having the source of their livelihood threatened wasn't enough, the big ranchers also had to contend with the shrinking of the open range as more and more farmers, sheepmen, and small ranchers moved in, often claiming choice land on which to settle, land desperately needed by the bigger outfits if they were to have any hope of surviving.

The big ranchers naturally resented the arrival of the newcomers, who naturally despised the attitude of the cattle barons. It was a vicious circle of mutual hatred, and like mercury on a hot summer's day the intensity of that hatred had shot ever higher and higher until it now threatened to erupt in open warfare.

"That's it in a nutshell," Scipio remarked, "but it don't hardly tell all there is to know." He crammed a succulent piece of steak into his mouth before going on. "There's been killin' galore and lynchings—"

"You mentioned a woman," I said, and all three of them frowned.

"Her name was Ella Watson," Scipio disclosed. "She and Jim Averell were strung up side by side in Spring Canyon on the Sweetwater. Regulators hung them as a warnin' to other maverickers."

Here was a new one on me. "Regulators?"

"Vigilantes, some call 'em."

The Virginian, who had contributed the least of the three of them, spoke up, his dialect strong. "It didn't work, though. Afteh the repawt was circulated, the whole country got riled. Instead o' scarin' the rustlers off, it made 'em madder. Now they're stealin' more beeves than ever." He stopped, lowered his fork, and said so softly we could barely hear him, "Lynchin' never works. It's a fool's proposition."

"How do Brazos and his friend fit in?" I inquired.

A cloud marred the Virginian's handsome features. "Do yu' remember Balaam?"

How could I ever forget him? Balaam was Judge Henry's nearest neighbor, and as arrogant a man as any who ever drew breath. Balaam's huge spread, a three-day ride from Sunk Creek, was famous for two things: the quality of its horseflesh and the temper of its owner. "Yes," I said.

"Well, Balaam hired Brazos, Santee, and the late Mr. Killebrew to be his detectives, as he calls 'em. Their job is to keep nesters from gettin' ideas about settling on Balaam's spread and to run off any rustlers who take a particular interest in Balaam's stock."

"I still don't understand," I said, resting my elbows on either side of my saucer and contemplating the Southerner. "None of this has anything to do with me. I'm no rustler. Why did Brazos and his friends rake me over the coals? Scipio gave me the impression they deliberately sought me out."

"They did," the Virginian said.

"But why?" I persisted.

"To get at me, I reckon."

"Once again—why?"

"There have been rumors," the Virginian said, but went no further.

My impatience caused me to half rise up off the bench. Scipio put his hand on mine and shook his head. As I sat down, he cleared his throat.

"There's been talk that Balaam wants him dead."

"For what possible reason?"

"No one rightly knows."

I stared at the Virginian, whose face was an impenetrable mask.

"Yes, seh," Scipio continued. "Yu' picked a hell of a time to come for a visit, Professor. There's goin' to be a heap o' killin' before this is done."

3

Into the Heart of Darkness

attle Land had changed. How much became evident the moment our wagon rattled out of Medicine Bow at first light the next morning. The fields lying around the town had been divided into an irrigated quilt work of neatly arranged plots stretching in three directions for as far as the eye could see. To the west the scourge of cultivated tracts had been stopped by an imposing barrier resistant to all change, the Bow Leg Mountains.

I kept expecting the homesteads to come to an end, but an hour went by, and still we passed dwelling after dwelling, attended by the yapping of sharp-eyed dogs, the bawling of penned cattle, and the occasional faint squeals of playing children. Two hours passed. I shifted on the seat and looked at the melancholy Southerner, who had not uttered a word since bidding me good morning. "Is the whole state in this condition?"

"Goodness gracious, no. Though it seems that way."

"If it's this bad at Sunk Creek, it's fortunate your wife has given up teaching. She'd be inundated."

A polite grin rewarded my effort.

Encouraged, I braced myself to ask a question that would violate the cardinal unwritten rule in the unique code of conduct practiced by cowhands from Montana to the Rio Grande: a man must never, ever pry into the personal affairs of another. Punchers were as touchy as agitated hornets where their privacy was concerned. So ingrained was this notion that breaking the taboo was considered not merely rude but a grave insult to the integrity of the one imposed on, and more than enough justification for the offended party to resort to his hardware if he felt so inclined. Yet I couldn't keep silent. I was concerned for him. No, it was more than that. I was as deeply worried as if the rumor about Balaam's intentions centered on me instead of him.

There would never be a better opportunity. I was alone with him at last. Strung out behind the wagon were the Sunk Creek hands, but they wouldn't overhear if I spoke softly.

Then I heard the drum of approaching hooves.

"Company comin'," Lin McLean warned us.

The Virginian hauled on the reins and brought Buck and Muggins, our team, to a quick halt. His right hand drifted to his Colt and loosened it as he turned.

A single lanky rider mounted on a fine zebra dun was hurrying to overtake us. He paid no attention to the punchers, some of whom exchanged glances on seeing the color of his skin. Right up to the wagon he came, where he reined up and tipped back his white hat to expose his thick curly hair. Ceremony evidently was not his strong suit, because he immediately addressed the Virginian with, "I'm lookin' for a job, seh, and I hear you're a fair man. Just missed yu' in town. They call me Dapper."

I could see why. His white hat, blue bandanna, green shirt, and overalls were all freshly cleaned and ironed. His boots and saddle had been polished to a sheen. Every loop in his cartridge belt was filled, and the smooth ivory grips of his six-shooter glistened in the bright sunlight.

Lips pursed, the Virginian scrutinized the man from top to bottom. "Texas?" he said at length.

"Texas."

"Can yu' bust broncs?"

"There ain't a horse been made that I can't ride."

"Or a man been made that can't be throwed."

Dapper's teeth flashed. "If he's a man, he gets back up and tries again. Try me, seh. It's all I ask. I'll be your broncbuster, wrangler, ride drag till the cows come home, yu' name it."

"Quality speaks for itself. Thirty a month is startin' wage."

I wish I'd had a camera to record the sparkling delight that momentarily lit up the black cowboy's face.

"I'm obliged. When do I report?"

"This is Thursday. I don't rightly need yu' until next Wednesday."

"I'll be ready for work when the cock crows."

"Yu' need directions to Sunk Creek?"

"No, thank yu'. I been askin' around."

The Virginian nodded and raised the reins. "See yu' then. Repawt to Mr. McLean, here," he said, pointing. "He's foreman."

After touching his hat, Dapper wheeled the dun and galloped off toward Medicine Bow.

"I reckon he'll do to ride the river with," the Virginian commented as he clucked Buck and Muggins into motion.

"A few of the men might not think like yu' do," Lin McLean mentioned with his customary twang, which was almost as pronounced at times as the Virginian's own accent.

"Just so long as they keep their feelings to themselves," said the half partner. "If a man does his work and does it well, I don't give a tinker's damn about his background, his religion, his politics, the color of his skin, or his eating habits. The particulars don't matter if the spirit's there." His hawkish eyes swooped on McLean. "And I don't need to tell you it's your job to keep order. If someone feels he can't live with it, that's his right. Send him to me and I'll have his wages drawn."

The drawl, I couldn't help but notice, was completely absent. This was a surprising new window into the Southerner's soul, a window I never suspected existed, given his early days in the Deep South.

"Don't fret there," Lin said. "I always hold up my end, don't I? Have I ever given yu' cause to regret makin' me foreman? If I have, say the word, and yu' can go hunt yourself a new one."

"Pull in your horns, yu' boxhead joker," the Virginian responded in an easygoing fashion. "You're bein' plumb ridiculous. Yu've made me proud of my decision, and Judge Henry himself told me you're doin' as fine a job as I ever did."

McLean perked up. "Really? Yu' never told me that."

"Only because I didn't want yu' makin' chests at yourself in the mirror every chance yu' get."

I listened in fascination while Lin aired his lungs, exhibiting a protean knowledge of curse words. The Virginian took the abuse in stride. For the next hour Lin stayed beside us, the two of them making small talk about affairs at Judge Henry's ranch and comparing notes on how their own homesteads were progressing. Both of them had taken up land, built homes and stables and corrals, and started their own small herds, the Virginian on pristine Aspen Creek, Lin on picturesque Box Elder Creek. From what I gathered, their wives had become fast friends, which pleased the two men immensely, but the women had also been telling tales out of school, which sorely upset the two cowboys. They speculated on how they might remedy the situation but reached no firm conclusion before Scipio called Lin back to discuss something or other.

At last I had my chance. "Do you think it's true that Balaam wants to see you dead?"

Those broad shoulders shrugged. "It could just be saloon gossip. When punchers get to drinkin' too much, they're apt to start chirpin' away like a flock of sparrows."

"Perhaps. But I flatter myself that I know you fairly well, and I could tell in Medicine Bow you were holding something back," I said, hastily adding, "Not that I mean to meddle."

A goodly distance was covered before the Virginian replied. "I reckon there might be a kernel of truth in the tale."

"What does he have against you?"

"We had a disagreement once."

"Who got the upper hand?"

"I pretty near beat him to a pulp," the Virginian said softly. "There was this hawss, yu' see, and Balaam took to mistreatin' it just like he does most every hawss he owns, and I took as much o' the abuse as I could stand, but then something snapped inside o' me and I went after Balaam tooth and claw."

"Were there witnesses?"

"Just the hawsses. I've never told a soul, not even her."

"Was this recently?"

"No, it was a quite a spell ago. Before ever I got married."

"That long?" I rested my elbows on my legs and my chin in my hands. "I can't see him waiting so long to get his revenge. If patience was gold, he'd be the poorest man on the planet."

"I take it yu' ain't heard about Mrs. Balaam? She was the one who invited my Mary out here, yu' know. If not for her, Mary and me would never have met." He ran a finger along his mustache. "Six months ago she went to meet her maker. Consumption, the sawbones figured. She never let it weigh her down, though. There was a true Christian woman. Some say she tried to her dyin' day to convert her husband, but he laughed her to scorn."

There was no need for him to spell out the implications. With Mrs. Balaam dead, all constraints on Balaam to toe the line of human decency were gone. He could do as he damn well pleased and hang the consequences.

This gave me a lot to ponder as we drove ever deeper into Cattle Land. After a while I realized we were on the open prairie at last, and I eagerly sought my first glimpse of roving cattle. I saw them, but I also saw many more homesteads than there had ever been before. Wherever there was good grass and ample water, there stood a new farm or ranch, and quite often they were rawhide outfits a strong gust of wind might reduce to rubble in a moment. Like a plague of locusts, the squatters were spreading across Wyoming in all directions. Cattle Land, which had withstood the determined resistance of Indians and the fury of the elements, was succumbing to the plow, the pitchfork, and the parlor.

We passed some of the new inhabitants, and by and large they were as hostile as the Sioux and the Blackfeet used to be. Farmers and sheepmen openly glared once they recognized us as a cow crowd, and their women were no less brazen.

"Whatever will I tell her?"

The Virginian's sorrowful declaration took several seconds to register. I glanced around and my heart went out to him at the torment I saw. "Tell her the truth," I advised. "Killebrew didn't give you any choice."

"The last time she could forgive," he went on, talking to himself. "She understood about Trampas. How he never did think much of me, and how he wasn't one to let any man show him up for the four-flusher he was. So he had to challenge me. He had to prove himself in his eyes and the eyes of his friends." A flick of the reins goaded Buck and Muggins into picking up the pace. "She understood why I had to stand up to him. Leastways, she claimed she did."

"And she'll understand this time," I assured him. "So you've had to shoot two men. Does that make you a killer? I should say not. It's not like you're another Hardin or Bonney or Slade. Compared to them, shooting two men is nothing."

"The total is four."

If he had told me he was giving up the cattle trade to become a monk, I would not have been more flabbergasted. "Four?" I blurted. "But I thought Trampas was the first?"

"It don't pay to advertise if yu' can shoot as well as yu' ride and handle a rope. Next thing yu' know, some

pimple-faced kid is temptin' yu' to prove it," the Virginian
said. "Since yu' know this much, I might as well tell yu'
that Trampas was number three. Once a fool in the John
Day Valley had to try me, and there was another by Canada de Oro. The rest don't hardly count."

"The rest?"

"A few who saw the light afteh they came down with
a bad case o' slow and a sawbones patched them up
again."

"I had no idea."

We drove in silence thereafter. The day lengthened, as
did the shadows. We would not reach Sunk Creek until the
fourth day of our journey, which was to be expected, since
by the time we got to Judge Henry's ranch, we would have
covered two hundred and sixty-three miles. That night I
lay on my blankets and listened to the punchers try to
outdo one another in telling stories so outrageous that a
confirmed liar would have found them embarrassing.

Morning found me in better spirits. I was back in Wyoming, after all, back in the country I loved. A sea of
shimmering grass and sagebrush enveloped us now, a
splendid, tranquil vastness humbling in its magnitude, and
soon enough we would be among majestic peaks capped
with crowns of year-round snow. Plains and mountains.
Valleys and plateaus. Gorges and glaciers. Wyoming was a
virgin land of startling contrasts, a land where nature had
painted the landscape in bold, vivid strokes. The water was
pure, the air as invigorating as a dip in a frigid mountain
stream.

Wildlife was everywhere. Antelope watched us go by
from a safe distance. Deer peered at us from thickets. Coyotes gave us a wide berth or observed our passing from
convenient knolls and occasional hills. Jackrabbits and cot-
tontails bounded from our path. To right and left we often
saw prairie dogs, ground squirrels, gophers, and ferrets.

Sage hens winged off at our approach, while blue-
winged teals, lark sparrows, and brown thrashers all
showed themselves at one point or another. Overhead
soared hungry hawks, adroitly banking with the air cur-
rents.

My Southern friend was in one of his quiet moods, keeping his thoughts to himself until the day was half-done. As was often the case, he left me at the hitching post when he remarked, "It's mighty interestin' how women are strong in their ways and we're strong in ours."

"How's that?" I said, sitting up.

"Anyone who reckons men and women are the same in all ways is a right puny thinker. Our bodies are different, our minds are different, and some might allow our souls are different, but there I expect they're mixin' things. Only women can have babies, cert'nly, but does that mean they can't ride a hawss or shoot or chop wood as good as men do? Of course not. Few do, 'cause of their motherin' instincts and all, but they could if they put their minds to it. Just look at Calamity Jane and Cattle Kate."

I was anxious to learn where this byway would lead, so I made no comment.

"No, seh. Women are our equals. Didn't we give 'em the right to vote? And before any other state, too? Everyone laughed at poor ol' Wyoming, but we knew what we were doin'." He nodded in confirmation. "Yes, indeed. Women are strong. They can take bad news as well as we can. And they're not apt to turn their backs on the men they love just because the men don't measure up to their expectations."

At last I saw where he was drifting, and I regarded him critically. "You're still fretting over how she'll take the news? Trust her. Mary possesses more fortitude than many men I know."

His pride was obvious. "She cert'nly does. That woman has so much grit, it spills out o' her ears when she bends sideways. Do you recollect how she saved me that time the Injuns were afteh my scalp?"

"I remember."

"Mark my words. If yu' find a woman willin' to die for yu', yu've found the treasure of a lifetime." He clucked at Buck and Muggins, then gave me the most peculiar look. "Yu' might figure I'm actin' the fool, but I love her so. I can't bear to hurt her. It's worse than hurtin' myself."

My envy knew no bounds. I stared out over the sprawling vista before us and reflected on whether I would ever be as blessed. That was when I spied a formation of dark clouds on the western horizon. "Rain on the way," I said.

"By nightfall we'll see a storm," the Virginian responded. He pursed his lips and shifted his legs, then said gravely, out of the blue, "About that incident at the train station."

"Yes?" I said, all attention.

In his seriousness he neglected his drawl. "I figure they were counting on me being on hand to meet you myself. They'd heard that we're pards, and they aimed to prod me into a fight then and there by abusing you."

"Three against one," I muttered.

"Polecats like to have the decks rigged in their favor. It was dumb luck I got tied up ordering supplies and sent Scipio in my place."

"But how did they know I'd be coming in on that particular train?"

"I didn't keep your visit a secret. Any of the hands could have let it slip while they were in town." He put a hand on my arm and was his old friendly self. "The important thing is their scheme failed, so I reckon yu' have nothin' to worry about for the rest o' your stay. The next time they'll be more direct."

"Why not put an end to this sordid business before it goes any further? Ride over to Balaam's and confront him."

"I don't have any proof," the Virginian said. "Saloon gossip is hardly cause to hang a—" He suddenly broke off, straightened, and stared to the northwest. "Here now. What do yu' make of the proposition yondeh?"

I looked, and circling low in the sky were a dozen or more great, horrid, ugly buzzards. In the effete East, where the cultured class likes to mask anything unsavory behind refined words that spare their sensitive sensibilities from the harsher aspects of life, such scavengers are referred to as "vultures." But when you think about it, when you roll the two words on the tip of your tongue and savor their respective sounds, you readily see that the Western term fits the nature of the ungainly birds far better. It has always been this way. Those who live closest to nature are more in tune to the truth of things both great and small.

Lin McLean and Scipio trotted up. "Want us to go have a look-see?" the former asked.

"I figure it's less than half a mile," the Virginian answered. He gave me an odd, thoughtful look. "We'll all go." So saying, he abruptly cut the team to the left, leaving the dusty ribbon of road for the sage dotted plain.

I had to hold on to the side to keep from being spilled overboard as the wheels bounced and shook. The Sunk Creek riders fanned out on either side of the wagon, and I couldn't help but wonder why all this concern over a few buzzards. It wasn't uncommon to see a score or more on an extended trip, feasting on everything from deer and antelope to small game.

We were still several hundred feet off when, squinting in the bright sunlight, I made out a bulky form lying in the open. A half-dozen buzzards were perched on the carcass, some stripping off ragged chucks of flesh with their big beaks. Even from that distance I could tell it wasn't a deer or any other wild animal, and my stomach tightened in grim expectation of what we would find. Nor was my dread unjustified.

As we drew near, the buzzards took wing, some protesting our intrusion by hissing like enraged vipers or uttering their peculiar groaning cries.

The cow had recently given birth. She had been shot once through the head; then her killers, out of sadistic glee, had slashed her throat wide-open and gouged out both her eyes. The eyeballs lay beside her in a dry pool of reeking blood that swarmed thick with flies. A foul odor permeated the warm air.

I feared I might be sick. My stomach tossed and churned, and I had to turn away so I could breathe again. None of the many stories I had heard about the rustler's activities had prepared me for the gory sight of their vicious handiwork. In my estimation only the worst sort of savage brute would perpetrate so vile a deed against such a defenseless, dumb animal.

"I'm right sorry," the Virginian remarked softly, "but I wanted yu' to see for yourself what we're up against."

"You knew what we would find?"

"I had a hunch," the Southerner said.

"We've been findin' a heap of beeves like this lately," Scipio bitterly threw in. "They ain't content just to take the calves that ain't been branded yet. No, they have to rub our noses in it, too." His normally peaceful features were aglow with wrath. "Rustlers should be treated like the treasures they are and be buried where no man will ever find them again."

It was Lin McLean who rode close to the carcass, dismounted, and walked over to check for the brand. Nose scrunched up, a hand over his mouth, he squatted low to see it. "The Lazy S," he announced.

"Dixon's outfit over on the Sweetwater," the Virginian said. "We'll have to get word to him." His face inscrutable, he goaded Buck and Muggins into a walk and turned the wagon around.

I said nothing. The shock had given way to a cold fury, which must have been as nothing to the bitter feelings the cowboys were experiencing. Cattle were their livelihood; they lived, breathed, and literally ate cows. And while none of them regarded cattle as God's supreme gift to the animal kingdom, they were rightfully protective of the innocent creatures routinely placed in their care. In their eyes the only thing worse than someone who would steal cattle was someone who would steal horses, and they took both heinous crimes very personally.

"How long, do yu' reckon?" The Virginian now asked Lin McLean.

"A day. Likely less," the foreman said.

"They wanted us to find it," Scipio said. "The rotten sons of bitches."

"Who did?" I inquired. "What are you talking about?" But not a one of them answered me. I speculated on this as we resumed our journey, and that night I reflected long and hard on the many changes I had witnessed in Cattle Land. The storm had passed over us earlier, just as we made camp in a stand of cottonwoods. Now, lying there under a myriad of twinkling stars, breathing in the cool, invigorating air, I had the impression I was in the eye of another storm that threatened to turn the land I cherished into a veritable battlefield and paint the tranquil prairie and the regal mountains red with blood. Perhaps I was being overly dramatic; writers have a tendency to do that. Yet little did I realize at the time how accurate my prediction would be.

4

Mountain Majesty

Judge Henry was a remarkable man in more ways than one. His hospitality, for instance, was legendary. Many weary travelers would go twenty miles or better out of their way just to spend the night at Sunk Creek, where they knew they would always meet with a kindly reception. No small part of the appeal was the food, due in part to Mrs. Henry's foresight in having fresh eggs, butter, and milk constantly on hand. The eggs were as rare as hen's teeth in Wyoming, and as delicious as any fare Delmonico's had to offer.

Another aspect that qualified Sunk Creek as an oasis in the midst of the wilderness was the orderly atmosphere of the ranch and the many trees, flowers, and shrubs that had been planted around the enormous ranch house. After countless miles of sagebrush, the sight of so much verdant growth and neatly tilled ranks of red and blue and yellow blossoms was enough to make the most obtuse soul wax poetic.

So visitors came from all around to spend the night

with the Judge. Often friends and relatives from the States would stay for weeks at a time, enjoying brief excursions into the Wyoming wilds, as I had done on previous occasions. One never knew who would be there.

I mention this because of what occurred the morning after our arrival. We had gotten there late, after most of the guests had retired, intending to leave at dawn for the Virginian's own spread. The Judge and his wife had welcomed me as cordially as ever, and insisted that I try to find time to spend with them, if only a day or two, before my eventual return to civilization. I had promised to do what I could.

Because my friend was eager to reach home, we were both up at first light and at the corral saddling our horses when a young woman of twenty or so, attired in a riding habit that was the height of fashion back east, approached from the house. She came up to the rails and said in a pronounced Eastern accent, "Excuse me. Are you two of the cowfellows who work for my uncle?"

I was all set to enlighten her as to the Virginian's true status at the ranch and my own standing as an old friend of the Judge's when he answered her, his drawl in fine form.

"Well, yes, ma'am, I expect as how we are."

"Oh, excellent. I'm Madeline Henry, and this is my first time here. I understand that you cowfellows often take peculiar delight in teasing tenderhoofs like myself. Please be advised that I won't tolerate such inconsiderate behavior, and kindly inform all your friends."

How he ever kept a straight face, I will never know. For my own part, I pretended to be working on my cinch while listening in delighted rapture to yet another demonstration of his native genius.

"Why, ma'am, I'm plumb shocked. I'd never try to buffalo a tenderhoof, and most of the cowfellows I work with wouldn't, neither. Who's been fillin' your pretty head with such turrible notions?"

Madeline Henry was as susceptible to that dazzling smile and rich black hair as any other mortal woman, so she can be forgiven for blinking in surprise, then grinning

as if she were a cat about to devour an unsuspecting ca-
nary and leaning on the top rail to flutter her eyelids at the
Virginian. "Oh, friends, mainly. It's not important." Pausing, she tilted her head and brushed at her hair. "My uncle
has been after me to come out here for years, but I never
saw much appeal to the idea of vacationing in a land inhabited by bloodthirsty Indians and prowling bears and the
like, not after all I'd heard about it."

"Yu' should never believe more than a quarter of
what yu' hear, ma'am, and only half o' what yu' see. This
country is plumb full of interestin' sights."

"So I'm beginning to believe." She stared at the Virginian's horse, Monte, for a moment. "My uncle did promise me I could learn to ride while I'm here. Do you
suppose you could teach me?"

"No, ma'am. I dassent. That there is a job for the regular horse instructor. Me, I'm just the saddler."

"Oh. Dear me. I didn't realize you cowfellows have
such a strict division of labor."

"Oh, sugar. Yes. This ranch would be a mighty confusing affair if we were all allowed to do as we pleased.
Everybody would be forever gettin' in everyone else's
way. So to make things easy, we each have our own jobs
to do and we're not allowed to do anything else."

Madeline deigned to bob her head in my direction.
"Is he a horse instructor?"

"Him? He's my helper, ma'am. Just the assistant saddler. One day, though, he hopes to be a singer."

"A singer?"

"Yes, ma'am. Cows have to be sung to at night while
they're sleepin' or they get quite contrary. A singer is the
man who rides around them from sunset until dawn to
keep them happy." The Virginian pointed at me. "My
friend here has been practicin' every chance he gets. He
has to know pretty near fifty songs before he can qualify
for the job. Cows are particular that way. They don't like
to hear the same song sung more than once a night or they
might up and stampede."

"My word!"

"There's a lot more to being cowfellows than most

folks appreciate," the Virginian informed her. "Let's see now." He elevated a callused hand and counted off on his fingers. "There are the saddlers and the singers and the ropers and the branders and the drovers and the wrestlers and—"

"Wrestlers?" Madeline interrupted quizzically.

"Yes, ma'am. You might have heard we have to brand our stock once a year, and it's the job of the wrestlers to wrestle the critters to the ground so the branders can slap a brand on their mangy hides. Some cows don't take to that too well, and they've learned how to fight back. I tell yu', they can be as slippery as snakes, and there are those who swear the cows wrestle almost as good as the wrestlers themselves. Why, I've seen some scraps that lasted the better part of a day."

The Judge's niece rocked to peals of laughter. "How quaint! This is marvelous. Tell me more. I can't wait to share all these tidbits with my New York friends."

Before the Southerner could display the full extent of his devilish streak, the call to breakfast was heralded by the clanging of the triangle.

"Off yu' go, ma'am," the Virginian advised, "or you'll miss the mawnin' meal. Your uncle is mighty punctual about fillin' his belly."

"Will I see you again?"

"Probably. But the hombre you most want to see is a jasper named Scipio le Moyne. He does all the horse instructin' at Sunk Creek. You look him up after breakfast and tell him Jeff sent you around, and I figure he'll learn you the ropes in no time."

"Why, thank you for your kindness. I'll also mention you to my uncle." She gave him a conspiratorial wink. "Perhaps he'll see fit to advance *you* to whatever job you would like to have."

"Thank yu', Madeline. This saddlin' business does get a mite boring at times."

She scampered off as if she were walking on air, while the Virginian and I hurriedly mounted, took our single packhorse in tow, and headed westward at a brisk clip.

"What will you do when she learns the truth?" I inquired.

"Just pray she knows as much about handlin' six-shooters as she does about cows," said he, and I roared.

But the Virginian's good humor soon evaporated with the morning dew, and I knew the reason why. He would shortly have to face *her*, and there is no more heartrending chore for a man to perform than to have to be the bearer of bad tidings to the woman he loves.

To be frank, I half wished I had taken the Henrys up on their gracious offer and agreed to stay with them for a while before venturing to my friend's. Knowing how zealously he and his ilk guarded their private lives, I felt as if I would be intruding once we got there. I imagined he would much prefer to explain to her in private, and then, if there was to be a row, settle the issue on the spot. But he could hardly talk freely with me around, so I resolved to make myself scarce somehow for as many hours as I could until I ascertained they had come to some sort of understanding.

The ride to their remote valley stirred vivid memories of our previous jaunts in the rugged mountains: of the elk and mountain-sheep hunts, of dizzying heights and vast vistas, of frigid streams and cold nights, of glorious days amidst the raw grandeur of the Garden of Eden. I thrilled to be back, and when we came to the top of the first rise and paused to admire the sweeping spectacle behind us, I actually tingled from head to toe.

Onward and upward we rode. Here were chattering squirrels and scampering chipmunks by the bushel. Jays and ravens frolicked in the treetops or soared overhead on throbbing wings. Occasionally we would see black-tailed deer, and once I had the good fortune to spy a magnificent bald eagle circling high above the earth.

The regal mountains were as resplendent as ever, clothed in emerald-green vegetation on their lower slopes and a sea-green covering higher up. Some were crowned by caps of scintillating snow. Among them wound verdant high-country valleys, and it was toward one of these that we made our determined way.

We talked about everything *except* the incidents in Medicine Bow and the finding of the slain cow. Trampas and Shorty were still much on our minds, and although we knew it was pointless, we indulged in the wishful fancy of imagining how events might have turned out had only this or that happened differently. The conclusions we reached were no different from those of the year before: Trampas had been wicked through and through, the only genuinely bad man I had encountered in all my wide-flung travels, although now that I had met the gentleman calling himself Brazos, I could up the sum by one. My Southern friend had not had the luxury of choice; if he hadn't killed Trampas, Trampas certainly would have killed him.

As for Shorty, what need be said of sheep? They meekly follow their varied masters, and if those masters are treachery personified, they suffer the same fate Shorty did. He made his big mistake when he turned his back on the Virginian's helping hand and embraced the false appeal of easy money and carefree adventure promised by Trampas. Too late, Shorty learned the pitfalls to be found on the owlhoot trail. Better for him if he had never strayed from the straight and narrow.

I wasn't surprised in the least to learn that Steve's passing still bothered the Virginian, as well it should. It isn't every day one hangs one's best friend. The experience had firmed his resolve to thwart the rustlers any way he could, but he confessed to me that their predations had become so widespread as to make the chore of stamping them out virtually impossible. When I pressed him on how best to combat their thievery, he said he had an idea and he'd tell me more at the proper time.

That night, under a canopy of stars, while being serenaded by the howling of wolves and the yipping of coyotes, the Virginian told me about his plans for his ranch. Unknown to all but a few close friends, there was a promising deposit of coal on his land, and if the railroad continued on as it was doing, he figured to reap a tidy sum selling to them one day.

"If I do, it will all be for her," he remarked. "Lord knows, in the old days I lived pretty much hand to mouth.

It wasn't until afteh I got mature enough to stop havin' *feelings* about women and havin' *thoughts* instead that I saw I needed to squirrel some away." He chuckled. "I reckon marriage has done more to make capitalists out of men than all other institutions combined."

And there was another prime example of why I loved him so. Only from a nature endowed with uncommon innocence could such delightfully profound insights flow.

"I hope yu' find the right one for yourself sooner or later," the Virginian said softly as he was on the verge of dozing off. "Until a man does, he keeps on wanderin', always almighty curious about what's lyin' over the next horizon, never satisfied with what he finds, but not quite knowing what he's lookin' for."

My dreams that night were of buxom Amazons.

Aspen Creek is nestled in a lush valley rimmed by the slender trees from which the waterway derives its name. To the west rears a peak rivaling Olympus. To the north and south sit imposing walls of mountains, guarding the valley in phalanx formation.

I had never been there before, and I confess my first sight of the virgin landscape quite took my breath away. It was a moment comparable to when you first see a great work of art and are struck by the ennobling sublimity of the artist's vision.

The Virginian was watching me, and a slow smile curled his lips in satisfaction. "I felt the same way," he said, and sighed contentedly. "So did she."

We rode along the gurgling creek until the house appeared. In the back of my mind I must have been expecting a rustic cabin, because I was quite taken aback by the two-story stone-and-log structure that dominated the center of the valley. Beyond it sat a stable, and between the two a corral filled with stock. To the south squatted a chicken coop, and I didn't need any great deductive insight to know where his wife had obtained the chickens.

Two huge dogs of uncertain ancestry were reclining

at the base of the stone steps. Upon spying us, they leaped erect and bayed ferociously.

"Gentlemen, hush," the Virginian called. At the sound of his familiar voice they bounded forward with typical canine glee, causing Monte to shy at their antics. "Allow me to introduce Old Hickory and Lavender," he said, pointing out the respective dogs.

I was mystified as to how he could tell them apart, since they were like two peas in a pod to me, but of more interest were their names. "Whose idea was Lavender?"

"Need yu' ask? We thought it'd be fairest to divide up the namin'."

Shifting in the saddle, I glanced absently at the porch, and there she stood, bathed in sunshine, her creamy complexion glowing with vitality, her tender gaze fixed on the man she adored. Mountain living agreed with the former Miss Mary Stark Wood of Bennington, Vermont. She was every bit as lovely as the last time I had seen her; indeed, if it was at all possible, she was lovelier. But it was not her physical attributes that I would use to sum up Molly's character. Rather would I stress the two qualities that she possessed in abundance, and which in no small measure accounted for her presence on that porch. Those qualities? Pride and pluck.

If Molly had not possessed pluck, she never would have mustered the courage to leave the security of Vermont for the uncertainties of the dangerous frontier. If she had not possessed pride—and by this I mean proper pride in herself and her ability, not perverse pride in her appearance—she would never have accepted the challenge to teach untamed ragamuffins the essentials of English and democracy.

No one in Medicine Bow knew the source of her unique traits. They stemmed in large measure from a distant ancestor, the original Molly Stark, devoted wife of the famous Captain John. Had Molly wanted, she could have belonged to the most prestigious social clubs in the East. The Boston Tea Party, the Green Mountain Daughters, the Ethan Allen Ticonderogas, the Saratoga Sacred Circle, they all would have gladly accepted her into their reclusive folds. But despite numerous invitations she had never joined a one.

Back in prim Bennington, many had regarded her aloofness as a temperamental quirk. Molly always had been a strange one, they said, and looked askance when she deigned to give music lessons and to embroider for money upon the reversal of her father's fortune. Their narrow vision prevented them from realizing the most important fact of all about Molly Wood: She was a *doer*, not a dreamer or a schemer, and whatever she did, she did with all her might.

Upon seeing her I blurted out, "Molly!" while at the selfsame instant the Virginian declared happily, "Mary!"

And here an explanation is due. Mary Stark Wood had never been fond of her first name. Until the day she met the Virginian, she had always preferred to be known by the same name as her fiery ancestress. Then a curious thing happened. The love of her life liked "Mary" better, and when spoken by his lips, the word became a tender endearment. So to him and him alone she was known as Mary. To the rest of us, Molly must do.

Smiling broadly, Molly hastened down the steps to meet us, brushing aside one of the dogs that tried to jump up against her dress. Hands clasped at her waist, she addressed me serenely. "How fitting you should arrive today of all days."

"Is there a significance I've missed?" I responded as I rode up to the rail.

"One of which you are completely unaware," Molly said, and nodded at her husband, who was in the act of dismounting. "*He* has always wanted to name our first boy Owen."

In all the time of my acquaintance with the Virginian, I had never seen him totally thunderstruck. Now I did. He gaped, his mustache drooping, and he took a faltering stride, as if his knees threatened to buckle. At her light laughter he marshaled and in a twinkling had her in his embrace. I looked away, my cheeks uncomfortably warm.

"There's no doubt?" he asked excitedly.

"None whatsoever."

"I reckon I'd best get the sawbones up here pronto."

Molly's mirth tinkled on the wind. "There's no need to hurry. We have eight months."

He responded not with words, and I found myself studiously assessing the geology of the nearby mountains when a hand touched my boot.

"Are you planning to sit up there all day admiring the view? Or do I get to greet you properly?"

I swung stiffly out of the saddle, then envied my friend again as I inhaled the minty fragrance of her hair and received a peck on the chin. Her eyes danced with unbridled joy. I could see he was equally thrilled, floating on air, as it were. Then I remembered Killebrew, and my features must have betrayed the cloud that passed over my soul.

"Is something wrong?" Molly asked. "Are you ill?'

"It was a long ride," I said lamely. "And it's been a while since I've spent so much time in the saddle. I fear I won't be able to sit for a day or two."

"Well, come inside. A spot of tea will freshen your spirits, and we have plenty of soft pillows," Molly said. Hiking her hem, she led the way.

The Virginian and I walked side by side to the porch. We exchanged glances, and by the haunted aspect in his eyes I knew he was thinking the same thing I was. He silently mouthed two words: "Not yet." I nodded my understanding while wondering when, if ever, would be the appropriate time.

If the outside of the house was a wonder, the inside was a marvel. I could not begin to guess the number of wagon trips needed to haul so much fine furniture to their remote haven. A mahogany table and chairs adorned the sitting room. The dinette set was of polished maple. Colorful draperies and dainty doilies lent charm to the arrangements. By way of a joke, I commented, "Your partnership with the Judge must be quite profitable."

Molly's eyes misted. "Most of our effects came from my great-aunt in Dunbarton."

I misunderstood and responded, "I'm sorry. I know the two of you were close."

"Oh, mercy!' Molly declared, brightening again. "She hasn't gone to meet her Maker. She merely felt I was most entitled to them and sent them along without a word to me that they were coming."

"If ever there was a genu-wine lady, it's her," the Virginian declared.

"And what am I?" Molly playful baited him.

"Yu' happen to be a genu-wine angel," he countered. "Leastways, that's what I figured the first time I laid eyes on yu'." He smiled smugly, thinking he had prevailed, but her next words dispelled his mood.

"Now then, why don't the two of you sit down, I'll fix refreshments, and you can tell me all the latest news from Medicine Bow."

5

Sue

He told her. Not that afternoon when we were all together, but that night when they were alone in their room. I knew because I was awakened by low sobs, and the next morning, when I arose before daybreak and tiptoed downstairs to fix myself some Arbuckles, she was already in the kitchen, standing forlornly in front of the window, her face wreathed in shadows that concealed her sad countenance but couldn't smother her fluttering sighs.

I was in the doorway before I spotted her, so there was no chance to retreat. She whirled in surprise, and I, plastering a grin on my reddening face, boldly entered and quipped, "What? No coffee yet? I suppose I'll have to run out and take a dip in that freezing creek to wake myself up."

Molly self-consciously dabbed a hand at the corner of her eye and said in a husky tone, as if she were coming down with a cold, "Don't be silly. I was just about to make some. Have a seat."

I fiddled with my fingers while the lamp was lit, then strategically avoided meeting her gaze while she puttered about the kitchen. Every so often she would mutter something, and half the time I never caught a word until, while the coffee was briskly percolating and the delicious aroma filled the room, I heard the following distinctly.

"You think you know someone!"

"Pardon?"

"Nothing," Molly said. A strained silence lasted for not more than five seconds, then, "Oh, who am I trying to deceive? You know perfectly well why I'm so flustered, because you were there when it happened. He said so." She leaned on the end of the table, her next words beseeching. "Why in heaven's name didn't you *stop* him?"

"Evidently he hasn't revealed everything, or you would know that if not for him, I wouldn't be seated here. Killebrew was going to murder me right there in front of everyone, and he didn't care a whit who saw it happen."

"Surely there was—"

"There wasn't," I cut her off, rather severely too. "Perhaps you weren't listening. Killebrew was set to *murder* me. I have no doubt he would have claimed self-defense if a law officer later came around making inquiries, and I'm certain his friends would have substantiated whatever wild assertions he made. It would have been their word against the word of the Sunk Creek outfit. The law would have been helpless to prosecute. Killebrew would have gone free, adding to his unsavory reputation at my expense."

"Reputations," Molly said sourly. "Do you also know all about his? I finally learned last night. After all this time! Four men!"

"And I'd wager my entire fortune that every last one of them deserved their fate."

"Does anyone deserve to be shot down in cold blood?"

"Cold?" I repeated sarcastically. "Do you really believe he killed Trampas in cold blood? There was more passion in their clash than there is in most marriages." Leaning back, I drummed my fingers on the tabletop. "I can't say much about the cartridge occasion, as he would call it, in the John Day Valley, because the only fact I have is that he killed his first man there. But I do know a little more about the Canada de Oro affair. Were you aware the man he shot put a bullet into him first?"

"He didn't tell me."

"Making excuses isn't his way, is it?" I saw the confusion in her moist eyes, so I leaned across the table to place my hand on hers. "I'm almost done," I said, and continued hastily. "Then along came Trampas, and we both saw what he was like. Now Killebrew, another of Trampas's breed. Men who think no more of taking a human life than you or I would think of squashing an annoying insect. Even then, knowing him as you do, do you truly believe he shot them in cold blood? Never! Each one cut him to the quick and undoubtedly took a little piece of humanity out of him in the bargain. But he had it to do, as the cowboys are so fond of proclaiming. And he did it without complaint, without asking for pity, without groveling in remorse afterward." I was about spent. "I tell you, Molly, there's more inner strength in that man of yours than in most ten men we know."

There. I had defended him the best I could. And why shouldn't I, in light of all he had done for me? I knew if he had overheard, he would be rightfully furious at my violation of the unspoken Western code: I had meddled. But I felt better for the meddling, and I flattered myself, judging by the composing of her fair features, that she felt better also.

Molly sat pensively for the longest while, seemingly oblivious to my presence. Since I was reluctant to break the spell, I sat still, awaiting her verdict, which was expressed in a most roundabout manner.

"I wonder if I will ever truly know him."

"If you don't, who does? I'd say you know him better than you think you do."

"This time you're wrong. I thought I did. Several times I've thought I did. But just when I have him figured out, he commits an unspeakable or unpredictable act that leaves me gasping for breath."

"Would you want a predictable husband? Your life would be so boring."

"My life would be stable."

Whatever riposte I might have made was forestalled by a horrendous crashing sound from outside the back door. In my alarm I so forgot myself as to utter an oath and leap to my feet, which in turn sent Molly into a fit of hilarity. There came a resounding thump against the outer surface of the door. Suspecting a bear to be the culprit, I dashed over and moved aside the small curtain.

So near to the pane was my face that my nose scraped the glass. Where I expected to see the stretch of grass between the house and the corral, I saw instead what appeared to be a great, slimy, clinging red mass stuck to the other side of the window, a hideous mass that writhed as if alive, and in sheer horror I recoiled and exclaimed, "What the devil!"

Molly was positively in hysterics.

The drooling mass withdrew, sliding off the pane and up into the mouth of its owner, which, on seeing me, let out with a long, "Mooooooo!"

I gawked stupidly at the face of an ordinary cow, a short-aged yearling by the looks of her. She, in turn, cocked her head as if examining me, moving first one big, dull eye and then the other up to the window. This was one of those instances when life is so perfectly ridiculous that all one can do is bow to the inevitable, so I joined Molly in her laughter.

When, at length, Molly calmed enough to speak, she pointed at the door and said, "Meet Sue, our third dog."

"Dog?" I responded. "Is it this mountain air or do I need spectacles?"

"Have a seat while I explain."

So I sat and waited until she had poured our coffee. Whether due to the outpouring of her fears or the arrival of the oversized 'dog,' at that moment I could safely say I felt closer to Mary Stark Wood than I ever had previously. I felt almost like a member of the family and not a mere outsider who had imposed himself on her hearth and home. Her coffee was delectable, her story outrageous but typically Western.

"Sue's mother fell to a mountain lion shortly after the calf was born," Molly began. "She was too young to survive on her own, so we brought her back to the house, where I could nurse her in the corral. About the same time, he came home with two puppies. To keep me company, he claimed, but I knew better. He brought them for my protection since he dislikes leaving me alone." She took a sip. "There's nothing to worry about, really. The only Indians left in this region are the Shoshonis, who have always been peaceful. And the rustlers have yet to extend their activities this far west."

Was that it? I speculated. Or were they wary of tangling with him?

"So there I was," Molly resumed. "I had this calf and two puppies on my hands, and whenever I went outside, the four of us became inseparable. The dogs would play with the calf just as if Sue was another puppy." Molly laughed at the recollection. "You would be amazed at how spry a calf can be. She frolicked all over with them, ate with them, even slept with them."

For some odd reason Molly's narrative brought to mind Emily, a wayward hen once owned by Judge Henry back in the days when the Sunk Creek hands still referred to me simply as "the tenderfoot." Had it not been for Emily's shenanigans, I might never have grown as close to the Virginian as was subsequently the case, for out of our mutual interest in her violations of nature had grown a budding friendship. But now I put my memories aside to listen.

"Well, as calves do, she grew and grew and had soon outgrown the dogs. But still she played with them and followed them wherever they went. Or tried to, because I had to put my foot down on allowing her into the house. Can you imagine the damage she would do?"

I nodded while envisioning the cow trying to make herself comfortable on the settee or reposing in front of the fireplace.

"Believe it or not, Sue tried to tag along when he

took the dogs off hunting. He had to chase her back repeatedly."

Now there was an image to cherish. I pictured the Virginian dropping a prairie chicken with a single shot, when from out of the high grass lumbered his bovine retriever to grab the dead bird in her big mouth and fetch it back to him. Coughing to stifle a rising laugh, I glanced down at my coffee and wondered if she had made it too strong.

"She has become too persistent for her own good, so now we have to keep an eye on her at all times to prevent her from wandering off into the forest with the dogs or trying to follow us when we go to check our stock." Molly's exasperation showed. "We've put her in the corral, but she kicks out the rails. We've tied her to trees, to poles, to boulders, but she always breaks loose." Her finger wagged at the door. "And I daresay if you look outside, you'll discover our hitching post in a shambles."

I rose and went to the window. Sue had shuffled off and was grazing near the shattered rail, her tail flicking from side to side. "What on earth will you do when she's full grown?" I asked.

"Eat her, I expect," declared the Southerner from the hall doorway.

I turned and saw them exchange looks that were painfully plain. For an instant the windows to their souls were open, and I peered into their innermost selves. Molly reflected hurt and something else, while he reflected a sense of baffled love. I felt terribly uncomfortable, once again the intruder instead of the guest. Grabbing the latch, I blurted, "Think I'll take a stroll. Be back for breakfast in a bit."

As I closed the door, I saw her cross the room in lithe bounds and throw herself into his muscular arms. I turned to hasten off, to give them the privacy they needed, but my path was barred by Sue. "Go fetch a bone," I grumbled, skirting her and making for the corral.

The thump of her hooves told me I had company. Halting, I regarded the pest critically. As cows went, she was rather homely. Her color was undistinguished, her head so big as to give her an ungainly appearance. But in personality she was remarkable, as she demonstrated by stepping up to me and licking me on the chin before I quite knew what she was about.

"Here. Enough of that." I wiped the saliva on my sleeve, ignored her, and walked to the creek. A buck and a doe bounded into the brush at my approach, and my fingers instinctively sought the rifle I wasn't carrying. To the east the sky was aglow with the rosy tinge of dawn. All around, the birds were greeting the new day with their ritual avian chorus. It was as if the sparrows and finches and robins and jays were nature's heralds, designated to let the world know it was time for the cycle of life to renew itself.

Sue dogged my tracks. Where I went, she went. When I stopped, she stopped. I tried unsuccessfully to shoo her away, adding a few lusty smacks to her backside to hasten her along, but I might as well have been beating on a tree stump for all the effect it had.

Presently we were joined by the dogs, Old Hickory and Lavender, and I saw for myself the truth of Molly's account. That yearling pranced and dashed in playful abandon with them for the better part of an hour. "Surely she should have outgrown this behavior by now," I mused aloud, and the next moment laughed when Old Hickory (I'd figured out how to tell the difference) got hold of her tail and she sent the dog tumbling with a tap from her hooves.

When I judged the Virginian and Molly had enjoyed sufficient time to soothe their troubled hearts, I sauntered toward the front of the house, Sue clopping along on my right, the dogs on my left. I must have presented quite a sight, for the Southerner, waiting for me at the corner of the porch, showed most of his strong, white teeth.

"If this don't beat all, seh. I reckon I should make yu' a present of one of them pipes so yu' can go around the mountains doing it proper, like that Pied Piper feller did with the younguns over to Europe."

I had a more important matter on my mind. "You're not really planning to eat her, are you?"

"Goodness gracious! Tell me yu' care."

"It wouldn't be right."

"Beeves are beeves, Professor. If they didn't make such almighty fine eatin', I suppose folks would keep a few around for fertilizin' purposes. But nowadays when people look at cows, they see steaks on the hoof."

"Sue is an exception."

"Sue is a blamed nuisance," the Virginian said, and made a show of scratching his chin. "Tell yu' what I'll do, though. Since yu've taken a shine to her, yu' can take her back to Philadelphia. Yu' have some time to work with her, so maybe yu' can box-train her like some do with their cats."

Despite myself, I grinned. But I refused to buckle. "Your attitude is perplexing. Sue is Emily all over again, and you adored Emily."

"Em'ly was the way she was from birth. That hen couldn't help being so contrary. Sue, here, learned to be different, and she can learn to be normal again."

"She wouldn't know how. She's been a dog for so long, she doesn't know the first thing about being a cow."

The Virginian thoughtfully studied the yearling. "Maybe yu' have a point. But no one has tried to show her the error of her ways. Since I'll be busy at Sunk Creek for a week, why don't yu' try your hand at it? Prove me wrong. If she's still a dog by the time I come back, I'll let her live out her days chasin' chipmunks and such."

"How do you know you can trust me?"

"You're my friend," said he simply, ending the discussion.

So, although my heart wasn't quite in it because I knew if I succeeded I was consigning Sue to the cooking pot, I spent the next seven days teaching that cow to be a cow. I started by staking her out with some of the other cows so she would see how they behaved. She'd watch them eat and drink and sleep as cows do, and in the process learn to behave like one herself. Or so I schemed. But when I removed the rope, Sue made straight for the house and the dogs. For three days this went on, and on the fourth I adopted a new strategy.

I put her in a stall in the stable directly across from another yearling and let the two of them spend the day together. Closer intimacy with her own kind than could be afforded on the range would, I reasoned, cause her bovine instincts to resurface. To make certain she wasn't distracted, I sealed off the stable so neither dog could get inside.

But that evening, when I let the two yearlings loose in the corral, Sue ignored her new companion and went instead to the rails so she could be near the two mongrels, who were whining to have her released.

Molly took sympathy on my plight, yet could offer no constructive criticisms. She had previously chalked up Sue's condition as hopeless, and she believed that no amount of training would change the cow around.

In that respect we were in agreement. But I had given the Southerner my word, and I resolved to do the best I could before the allotted time expired. So on the fifth day I resorted to a desperate tactic: I lashed Sue securely between two yearlings of comparable size and drove them a mile from the house where they could browse unmolested by the dogs.

My patience was tested to the breaking point while I let the sixth and seventh days go by without checking on her. I wanted Sue to immerse herself in the company of cows and nothing but cows. On the seventh afternoon the Virginian returned, so together we rode south to the meadow where I had left Sue and her teachers.

Only they weren't there.

A score of other cows were present, older head who went about their feeding undisturbed by our arrival.

"Where could they have gone?" I wondered.

"It's the nature o' these critters to wander," the Virginian responded. "I'm bettin' they moseyed east to the lake." He lashed Monte with the reins. "Let's hope the blamed things didn't get all tangled in that rope and drown themselves."

I hadn't thought of that eventuality. And so I deliberated their possible fate, I realized I had blundered in lashing the three yearlings together. I'd failed to take into account the danger to the cows, a failing no cattleman would ever be guilty of. I glanced at my friend, anxious lest he condemn me for my stupidity, but if he was upset, he didn't show it.

The lake was a favorite watering stop for the roving cattle. Here were dozens, among them many calves and yearlings and heifers. We made a complete circuit of the lake, checking each one, yet there was no sign of Sue.

"We might as well head on back," the Virginian said. "This is big country. They could be anywhere."

"What if something happens to them? I'd be to blame."

"Cows have been—" the Virginian began. Then he suddenly stopped and stiffened, his narrowed gaze on the damp ground at the water's edge. "Oh sugar," he declared. Swinging down, he stepped to the lake and sank to one knee, his fingers running over the ground.

I couldn't quite see what he was doing, so I asked.

"Mountain lion," was his answer. "A big one. The same cat that's been plaguin' me since I settled here." He stood and stepped into the stirrups. "The same cat that killed Sue's mother." His Winchester flashed in the sunlight as he wheeled Monte and rode slowly toward the trees, his eyes always on the tracks.

I shucked my own rifle, levered a cartridge into the chamber, and scanned the pines ahead. The prints must have been fresh, or my friend wouldn't have been following them. Was the cougar watching us at that very moment? Would it attack or flee if we pressed it? I confess the skin at the nape of my neck prickled when we rode into the woods, and I'm afraid I strained my neck to the breaking point by constantly snapping it to either side. Every shadow harbored a tawny hide. Every curved twig was a deadly claw.

The Virginian might have been riding to church. He sat relaxed in the saddle, the Winchester cocked, his forefinger touching the trigger. When rocky outcroppings barred our path, he went around them and easily picked up the spoor on the other side.

I remembered being told that mountain lions are some

of the most difficult creatures in the world to track; they tread so lightly they seldom leave impressions in the earth. This made me question how he was advancing so steadily. The answer sent a shiver down my spine.

Three sets of cow prints were visible, small hoof-prints such as yearlings might make, arranged in a row as they walked abreast of one another, so closely spaced there were only three cows on the entire planet that could have made them. My three. Sue and her friends. I mentioned this.

The Virginian nodded. "The lion was chasin' 'em."

The revelation fired me to dash to their rescue. I opened my mouth to urge him to go faster just as he came to an abrupt halt. My horse picked that moment to nicker and danced nervously to one side. I had to grip the reins firmly and use my legs to bring the animal in line. When next I looked up, I was staring at the grisly remains of one of the yearlings. Its neck had been neatly severed, its hide ripped open as if by razors. The poor animal's tongue hung loosely from its distended lips. Wrapped around its front legs was part of the rope I had used to bind the three together.

With a sharp glance at the surrounding pines, the Virginian slid off Monte, hunkered down, and dipped a fingertip into the pool of blood. "An hour ago, I'm afraid."

We advanced briskly. He didn't need to expand on his statement. I knew that in an hour's time the cat might have slain both Sue and the other yearling and dragged one or both off into the brush to eat. Soon we found another length of rope. Then another. My stomach was queasy when we emerged from the evergreens and angled up the slope of a bluff to the crest.

The Virginian reined up so unexpectedly, I nearly collided with him. Beyond Monte the bluff ended precipitously in a sheer cliff over a hundred feet high. Standing near the edge was the other yearling, her head lowered, blood matting her throat and chest. Sue was nowhere in sight.

"What could have happened?" I asked.

His Winchester tucked to his shoulder, the Virginian

eased from the saddle and stepped to the yearling. He bent over and inspected her hide, then commented, "Just scratches. This one will live." Turning, he studied the bare earth bordering the brink of the cliff. His brow knit.

"Do you think Sue got away?" I inquired hopefully.

The Virginian moved to the very edge of the drop-off and gazed somberly down at the bottom. "See for yourself, pard," he said, the drawl gone.

My feet were leaden, my legs little better, but I reached his side and bent my chin. She lay in a miserable crumpled heap among jagged boulders. Beside her was the mountain lion, its mouth twisted in a defiant snarl, several gleaming rib bones protruding from out of its ruptured skin.

"She put up quite a scrap," the Virginian said, his eyes on the tracks. "A hell of a scrap," he amended, and shook his head in amazement. "Don't this beat all!"

As we led the dazed yearling back to the herd, he made one final pertinent comment that summed up the whole affair nicely: "I reckon yu' can't judge character by the shape o' the critter."

6

The Clouds Gather

"Dear Professor:" With this salutation began the first of three letters I was to receive from Molly in the coming months. As I read those opening words, I could well imagine the mischievous twinkle in her eyes when she wrote them, since she knew how much I wished the cowboys had come up with a less Eastern-sounding handle. Still, I suppose "Professor" is infinitely preferable to "The Tenderfoot" or "The Prince of Wales."

"You've only been gone a short while, and already we look forward to your next visit with keen anticipation. Perhaps in the fall you will come for an elk hunt. He says he can almost guarantee a trophy animal if the snow doesn't come early.

"A lot has happened since your departure. He has been so busy at Sunk Creek that he has not had time to write, and so asked me if I would. Since I have so few correspondents, and since as a man of letters you might provide some insight into what men think and why he does the things he does, I eagerly accepted.

"Speaking of which, for some odd reason he decided to clean up the corner of the garden in which his collie is buried and to put fresh flowers on the grave. He hadn't done that in ages.

"The depredations of the rustlers have worsened. Sunk Creek is one of the outfits hardest hit in this area. Judge Henry estimates he has lost close to a hundred head to date, and he is at his wit's end. He refused to hire stock detectives, as Balaam and many of the other ranchers have done. (Some say these detectives are nothing more than gunmen who receive two hundred and fifty dollars for every rustler they apprehend.) In fact, the Judge has told his hands not to interfere if they spot rustling being done, but to promptly report it to him. He doesn't want any of his punchers hurt, even if it means losing more stock.

"Jessamine McLean, Mrs. Taylor, and I were paying a visit to Mrs. Henry when Balaam came by. I suspect Judge Henry was shocked to see him but never let on. When the Judge mentioned the losses he was suffering, Balaam actually laughed and told him that he was getting what he deserved for being so 'pussy-kitten.' Had I been the Judge, I would have lost my temper and had Balaam thrown off my property, but he simply reminded Balaam that trying to remedy one wrong with another only makes matters worse. Balaam then boasted that he hadn't lost a single cow since hiring his detectives, which proved the Judge's argument unsound.

"Balaam was civil enough to us four ladies, but his voice lacked any real warmth. As he was leaving, I caught him staring at my husband, who was over in the corral helping the new hand, Dapper, break a bronco. If the human gaze could kill, my husband would have died on the spot. A shiver ran down me when I saw it.

"Enough morbid news! I would imagine you're having a fine chuckle at my expense. Please write when you can, and know I remain your devoted friend. Molly."

Little did she know that instead of chuckling, I experienced my own shiver on having Balaam's hatred of my friend confirmed. The cowboys at Sunk Creek had related to me dozens of stories about Balaam's atrocities, and I realized that any man capable of gouging out the eyes of a contrary horse was easily capable of committing even more heinous acts, including murder if it suited his purpose.

I fretted for the safety of my dear friends and hoped the situation would resolve itself peacefully, although I should have known better, human nature being as it is.

Her next letter only increased my anxiety.

"Received yours, for which we thank you. He has been busier than ever, so once again the duty of writing falls on my willing shoulders.

"I wish I had good news to convey, but all is bleak here. The self-styled regulators who had been roaming the countryside at night dispensing their gruesome brand of justice have become more active than ever. In their zeal to stamp out the rustlers, these mysterious regulators have sown widespread fear among the small ranchers and homesteaders. Recently a man named Tom Waggoner, who had a little spread near Newcastle, was dragged from his home in the dead of night and hanged. I met him once at a barbecue at the Henrys' and found him polite and friendly. It's rumored that he was receiving stolen cattle, but the outfit at Sunk Creek doesn't believe he was.

"Some say these regulators are simply stock detectives out to make more money. Others say they're actually some of the big ranchers who have banded together to drive out undesirables. Either way, the finger of blame points at the Wyoming Stock Growers Association. I believe you dined at their club in Cheyenne once, so you know the Association is made up exclusively of the wealthiest ranchers in the state.

"I'm sorry to say the WSGA has compounded the problem greatly by their practices. They seem to condone the activities of the regulators. At least they haven't publicly objected to them. Jessamine, I should report, heard an unsubstantiated tale to the effect the Association is sponsoring these horrible goings-on.

"It was the WSGA that started the abominable practice of putting the names of cowboys who own cattle onto a black list, as they call it. Their reasoning is ridiculous.

They feel that any cowboy who owns stock must have rustled it. What does that make Lin and my husband in their eyes? Why, we've worked hard to increase our herd and have sacrificed many luxuries and even some necessities so our cows will prosper. It galls me to think the cattle barons might regard my husband as a common rustler!

"Since news here often escapes notice in Philadelphia, perhaps you are unaware that the WSGA also convinced the state legislature to pass a special 'maverick law.' Every unbranded calf on the open range is now legally the property of the Stock Growers Association. This is absurd! What is a small rancher supposed to do if his unbranded stock strays onto the land of one of the big ranchers? Is he expected to accept his losses graciously? Most won't.

"As you can imagine, wild rumors and gossip abound. Most of the homesteaders and the small outfits are convinced the cattle barons plan to drive them from the country. Both sides hate the other.

"It has grown so bad that now even the children are involved. Let me explain. The other day I rode over to see the old school and the new schoolmarm at Bear Creek. While we were chatting outside during the afternoon break, I witnessed a new game some of the children were playing. It's called 'Rustlers,' and it involves the children dividing themselves into two factions, with some being the rustlers and others the white caps, or cattle barons. They shoot at each other and play dead until the rustlers prevail.

"I hope you write soon. Your comforting words are needed now more than ever. Please forgive me if I haven't dwelled on personal matters, but my heart is heavy with worry. Thank the Lord the rustlers and regulators have seen fit to leave Aspen Creek and Box Elder alone!

"I could probably go on and on, but he wants to take this to Sunk Creek tomorrow and see that it gets out with the next mail bag. Take care, sweet friend. Molly."

The reading of this letter so shook me that I sat in my chair quivering for several minutes. There was no need to read between the lines, as I would have had to do with a letter of his, to ascertain how critical the situation had become. Between the stock detectives, the regulators, and the Wyoming Stock Growers Association, the homesteaders and small ranchers were under assault on several fronts. What would happen when they were pushed too far? Would they rise up against the barons?

To be honest, my sympathies were primarily with the latter. The big ranchers had settled in Wyoming first. They'd fought hostile Indians for their land, then fought the harsh elements to produce herds that eventually made them rich. Judge Henry was a case in point. He was one of the biggest ranchers and a long-standing member of the Wyoming Stock Growers Association, and yet there wasn't a kinder gentleman on the face of the planet. To hear that his ranch was particularly hard hit by the rustlers vexed me greatly.

The subsequent month was spent in anxious dread. I hoped Molly's next letter would bear glad tidings, would say that tempers had cooled, the rustling had stopped, and the regulators were no longer conducting their necktie socials, as the Virginian once informed me hangings were regarded in that part of the country.

When the correspondence arrived, I literally tore into the envelope in my haste to read the contents. Her very first words chilled me from head to toe.

"Bad tidings. The rustlers have struck at last. Five nights ago Lin McLean lost twenty-five head he had rounded up in a pasture for later shipment east. Two nights ago we were the victims. We heard a cow bawling in the morning and rode out to investigate. Three cows that had borne calves in the spring were dead, the calves gone. After a thorough check, we discovered fifteen of our best head had also been taken.

"I was furious. And puzzled. So far the rustlers have confined their thievery to the larger ranches. Why, then, were Box Elder and Aspen Creek struck? Neither of our spreads are all that big. Was it because Lin and my husband both work for Judge Henry, whom many of the homesteaders and small ranchers despise simply because he's a member of the Association?

"The situation is terribly confusing. An atmosphere of

suspicion and hatred is rampant. It seems no one can trust anyone else, and friends are turning against friends.

"The man we both love so dearly is torn both ways. As a partner with Judge Henry in Sunk Creek, he knows from experience the heavy toll the rustling has taken on the big spreads. Yet as a man who started his own ranch with a small homestead, he doesn't want to see the other homesteaders and small ranchers driven off.

"There must be a suitable compromise, if only both sides would sit down together and negotiate in good faith! But they hate each other too much for that.

"Owen, I'm scared. For the first time since this horrid business began, I'm truly, deeply scared. Not for myself, but for him. He says he's been straddling the fence too long and it's time for him to take action, but he won't confide his plans to me.

"What can he possibly hope to accomplish? Both sides in the dispute have reason to distrust him—the cattle barons because he homesteaded Aspen Creek and so in their eyes is a homesteader, the homesteaders because of his association with Judge Henry, which puts him in league with the cattle barons. As he conceded, it's a cloudy proposition.

"This is all for now. If I'm unable to write for a while, don't fret. We'll be fine. Love. Molly.

"Postscript: I can hardly write the words. Lin McLean has killed a man! Jessamine arrived as I was about to seal this letter. Lin sent her to stay with me until things calm down. Apparently he caught three strangers on his property and demanded to know what they were doing there. They claimed they worked for Balaam and they were out looking for strays. When Lin ordered them off his spread, they told him they would leave when they were good and ready. Hot words ensued. One of the three went for his gun, and Lin shot him out of the saddle, then escorted the other two off his land. This is all I know so far. As soon as I can, I will provide more details."

I put down the letter and stared through my window at the verdant garden outside, where the gorgeous flowers were in full bloom, elegant butterflies and graceful hummingbirds flitted busily about, and the merry chirping of songbirds filled the air. Yet I might as well have been surveying a bleak desert for all the effect the beautiful scene had on me. I was in an agitated daze, afraid this shooting might be the proverbial final straw, the flaming match, as it were, that would ignite Cattle Land in an orgy of unprecedented bloodletting.

A vicious man like Balaam wouldn't turn the other cheek at the death of one of his hands. He'd strike back at Lin McLean somehow. And since the Virginian was one of Lin's best friends and would side with McLean in the dispute, Balaam had the perfect pretext for openly confronting both men. Perhaps this was what Balaam had wanted all along.

I could only hope the Southerner was equal to the occasion, as he had been equal to Trampas, and that when the shooting was over and the dust settled, his wouldn't be one of the many corpses dotting the stark Wyoming landscape.

7

The Partner Has an Inspiration

The Virginian rode down from Aspen Creek to Sunk Creek not as he usually did, along the established trail, but instead by sticking to the high ground, where he commanded a hawk's-eye view of the surrounding countryside. His eyes alertly roved over the sprawling terrain, seeking any hint of telltale movement that might indicate the presence of bushwhackers. Never did his right hand stray far from his Colt, and his Winchester was always kept loose in its scabbard.

Not until Judge Henry's ranch house came into sight did the Virginian venture onto the open plain. He cast repeated glances over his broad shoulder, seeking flashes of sunlight on the ridges to his rear, but saw nothing to arouse alarm. Unmolested, he reached the ranch and reined up at the corral.

At work within stood Dapper. The black cowhand was holding his coiled rope down low, his attention glued to a bay gelding that was prancing along the high rails. Suddenly his right hand snaked up and out. The large loop sailed smoothly through the air to settle neatly on the gelding's neck. Instantly the horse surged against the restraint, but Dapper was quicker. In a flash he shifted and had the animal snubbed to the center post. Then, as if he sensed someone was watching him, he turned. "Is that how it's done, seh?" he asked, grinning.

"Keep practicin'," the Virginian quipped. "I do believe you're beginnin' to get the hang of it." He swung down, tied Monte, and walked toward the small house situated close to the bunkhouse. During his foreman days he had lived there, as later had Lin McLean. Now, since they were both married and had their own spreads, the small house had been converted into twin offices with sleeping rooms for each of them when they had to stay over at Sunk Creek. The Judge had graciously offered the Virginian space in the ranch house proper, but the Southerner had declined, citing his reluctance to impose on the Henry family, and no amount of persuasion on Judge Henry's part had prevailed on the Virginian to change his mind.

The door opened when the Virginian was still ten feet off, and out ambled Lin McLean, his normally carefree face showing new worry lines and his limp more pronounced than usual. "Howdy, Lin," the Virginian said.

"Howdy yourself."

"Been out late with the net again?"

Lin pushed his hat back on his curly hair and looked suspiciously at his friend. "I must have lost the sign somewheres. Is this a fish net we're talkin' about?"

"No, the net yu've been usin' at night when you're out chasin' moths."

"Have yu' gone loco and not told anyone?"

The Virginian was unruffled. "The Professor brought one out with him onced from back east," he said in his slow way. "Called it a butterfly net, as I recollect. Darnedest contraption you ever did see. There was this growed man traipsin' all over the countryside afteh

harmless little butterflies, wavin' that net like his arm-
pits was on fire and he was tryin' to snuff the flames.
Did the same at night, only he went afteh moths. Plumb
scared off every flyin' thing within a hundred miles by
the time he was done."

"I wish I'd seen that," Lin said wistfully, then so-
bered. "But we all know there's a wild kid inside many
a gent considered respectable. The Professor just has
more harebrained notions than most, is all, and he can't
help it on account o' he was born to high society." He
jabbed a finger at the Southerner. "But you'd never
catch *me* chasin' butterflies or moths with some silly
net."

"Yu' been losin' sleep for some reason." The Virginian finally got to the point. "Appears to me you'll need a
week o' rest to catch up."

"You're a fine one to criticize," McLean retorted.
"Taken a gander in a mirror lately?" He paused masterfully. "On second thought, don't. They're scarce enough as
is, and we don't need another one cracked."

As they talked, they had been drifting toward the
corral. Halting, they observed Dapper's skillful handling
of the gelding for a minute; then the foreman spoke
again.

"I've half a mind to go over to his spread and have
it out this very day."

"And yu' had the gall to call the Professor harebrained?" the partner rejoined. "Some deck is shy a joker,
but he ain't it. Balaam is waitin' for us to do just that so
Brazos and the rest o' those polecats o' his can fill us full
of lead."

"They'd try," Lin said indignantly. "And they'd find
out I don't fill so easy."

The Virginian draped a hand on the shoulder of his
friend. "Balaam has a half-dozen gun-sharks workin' for
him now, I hear, plus his regular hands. You'd take two or
three with yu', maybe, but they'd rub yu' out in the end."
His expression softened. "I don't want anything to happen
to yu', so promise me yu' won't do a thing without tellin'
me first."

"I don't need no nursemaid."

"If not for me, then for Jessamine."

"Yu' always was one to fight dirty."

"I know yu', Lin. You're gritty as fish eggs rolled in sand, but you're as stubborn as a long-eared chuck wagon, too. How will she take it if yu' go and waste yourself?"

"Anyone ever tell yu' that yu' have more lip than a muley cow?"

"Be patient." The Virginian refused to be derailed. "The time will come, and when it does, you're welcome to Balaam and Brazos both if you want."

A smirk curled the foreman's lips. "Shucks. I figured you'd want part of their hides. Why should I do all the work?"

They laughed, and the Virginian glanced at the ranch house just as Judge Henry appeared in the front entrance. The Judge beckoned, then returned indoors. "Appears it's time for us to earn our keep, Mr. McLean," he said, bending his footsteps toward the sprawling house.

"He's been powerful depressed lately, and I can't say as how I blame him," Lin commented. "The Bent Pine loss was the last straw, I reckon."

The Virginian glanced around sharply. "What's this?"

"Sorry. Yu' got me so nettled with that butterfly business, I forgot what I was fixin' to tell yu'." Lin took a breath. "Night before last the mangy rustlers stole those cows we put to pasture up at Bent Pine."

"All two hundred and forty head?"

"Every last critter. A gully-washer wiped out the trail."

"Damn."

Music floated on the air, coming from the piano in the drawing room at the north end of the house.

"Mrs. Henry is at it again," Lin said. "She's playin' it a lot lately."

"She does whenever she's got a heap on her mind."

The door had been left open a crack, but the Virginian paused to remove his hat and knocked tentatively. A low voice bid him enter, so he led McLean into the Judge's office, where he found that worthy gentleman slumped dejectedly in his big chair behind the mahogany desk.

"Whiskey, my friends?"

A curious light animated the Virginian's eyes when he noted the half-empty glass on the desk in front of the Judge. "No thank yu', seh. Coffin varnish has a way of addlin' the noggin."

Judge Henry stared at his partner for a few moments, then grinned shyly and shoved the glass from him. "Quite right. I don't see why these latest setbacks should have me so thoroughly at odds with myself, unless it's the thought of having all I've worked so hard to build up over the years destroyed right before my eyes. And I'm helpless to do a thing about it!" He ran a hand through his graying hair and indicated the chairs. "Please, be seated. We have much to discuss."

"Lin told me about Bent Pine," the Virginian said.

The Judge was a study in misery. "They're becoming bolder and bolder. Each raid is closer and closer to head-quarters." His hand came crashing down on the desk, causing the glass to jump and spill. "By all that's holy, I'm not a violent man by nature, but if I had them in my custody, I'd be tempted to hold a lynching bee."

"No one would blame yu'," Lin said.

"The homesteaders and small ranchers would," Judge Henry disagreed. "No matter how justified, they'd cite it as another example of cattle-baron brutality." He gazed forlornly out the window. "I can't let this go on much longer. It was bad enough when the rustlers were taking every calf they could get their hands on, but now they're taking anything with hooves."

"Those who use a runnin' iron ain't too particular about the hide they use it on," the Virginian said.

Folding his hands on the desk, the Judge gave them an appraising scrutiny. "Are you two happy with the arrangements you have at Sunk Creek?"

The two cowboys exchanged surprised looks.

"Do yu' need to ask?" Lin McLean answered first. "Yu' makin' me foreman was the biggest break I've had in my lifetime. It's meant enough money to improve Box Elder and give Jessamine some of that fancy plunder women make such a fuss over."

"And you?" the Judge asked his partner.

"I echo Lin. Although I still say forty percent of the profits is too much."

"Nonsense. Your knowledge and reliability have increased the productivity of the ranch tenfold." Judge Henry chuckled. "From my perspective, I struck quite a bargain." He started to say something else, changed his mind, and bowed his head. His next words were rasped out. "You make this hard, gentlemen. Very, very hard."

The Virginian heard the barely concealed despair in the older man's tone, and he leaned forward. "You're not thinking of cutting your losses and selling out?" he asked with flawless diction."

"I am."

"Gosh!" Lin McLean blurted.

"Pshaw," added the Virginian. "Yu' ain't the quittin' kind, Judge. Yu' fought Injuns back in the old days. Yu' survived the great blizzard. And who was it helped organize the hemp committee that went after Trampas and his bunch?"

"Trampas was small potatoes compared to these new outlaws. And I thought by stopping him I'd stop all the rustling."

"Yu' weren't the only one," the Virginian said, half to himself. "But my point is that you've never been one to give up when the going gets rough, and I'd hate to see yu' knuckle under now when there's a way to beat the rustlers at their own game."

"I won't hire stock detectives. No matter what Balaam says, hired killers aren't the answer."

"Then what is?" Lin asked, but he was staring at the Southerner.

"Montana."

Now it was McLean and Judge Henry who shared their mutual amazement. The former exclaimed, "Shucks! I was only joshin' about that loco business. There's no need to prove it on my account."

The Judge adopted a more serious attitude. "I've learned to trust your judgment as I would my own, so I'll hear you out before I express my opinion."

"Fair enough," the Virginian said. He stood, strode to the window, and admired the stirring scenery. "I never thought when I first laid eyes on Sunk Creek that it would come to mean as much to me as it has. Back in those days I was like a tumbleweed, blowin' wherever the wind took me. I'd left old Virginia when I was so young, I never had much of a home to boast of. Not until I hung my socks out to dry here."

"Madame Judge saw through you even back then," Judge Henry commented, using his pet name for his wife. "If she told me once, she told me a hundred times that I found a bona fide treasure when I hired you."

"Mrs. Henry did?" the Southerner responded, and coughed. "Well, now. She never let on." He turned to the window again. "Anyway, I expect I don't need to tell yu' how much Sunk Creek means to me now, as much as Aspen Creek does. Without Sunk Creek, there never would have been an Aspen Creek for me. Or her. And I won't let anyone destroy either."

"If the rustlers have their way, they'll bleed us both dry," Judge Henry said dolefully.

"Tell me," the Virginian said almost casually, "how much rustlin' goes on in Montana?"

"You know the answer to that as well as we do," Judge Henry answered. "None. The Eastern Montana Stock Growers Association put a permanent stop to it back in eighty-four. They hanged, shot, or burned out every rustler they could find, and those that weren't killed went to Texas. There hasn't been a single head rustled there since."

The Virginian leaned against the wall and twirled his hat in his hands. "Didn't yu' tell me onced that yu' own land right across the border in Montana?"

"True. I bought six thousand acres some years ago in case I ever decided to expand my—" The Judge stopped, his mouth falling slack in his astonishment.

"What?" Lin McLean prompted. "Why'd yu' stop, Judge?"

But Judge Henry didn't hear. He was gazing at his partner in blatant awe. "So simple!" he declared. "The answer is so simple!"

"The answer to what?" asked Lin.

"And it's been right in front of my nose the whole time," Judge Henry went on enthusiastically. "My word! Wait until Madame Judge hears! She'll want to name our next grandchild or nephew after you!"

"Why?" the exasperated Lin inquired. "What's he done?"

"Saved us!" Judge Henry cried, rising, exhilaration transforming the face that had been a mask of sorrow minutes ago into a portrait of triumph incarnate. He came around the desk, clapped the Southerner on the shoulders, then impulsively embraced him.

Lin McLean saw the Virginian's cheeks bloom scarlet and would have broke into a fit of chortling had he not been so upset by his own failure to understand why his employer was so happy. "Judge, yu' might as well hire yourself a new foreman," he said angrily. "Someone who ain't off his mental reservation like me, 'cause I'm plumb lost."

"Yu' poor tenderhoof," the Virginian declared. "Don't play dumb at our expense just because the prospect of a little hard work makes yu' break out in a sweat."

On hearing the word "tenderhoof" the Judge straightened and glanced at the top drawer of his desk.

"What hard work are yu'—" Lin began, and gasped as at last comprehension dawned. "Montana! You aim to move some of the stock to Montana!"

"Not *some,* yu' blamed newborn. Every last head on the spread, from the sucking calves to the old bulls."

"Every one?" Lin said, the magnitude of the enterprise dazing him. "Why, that'd take the better part of the summer and most of the fall!"

"Yu' got something better to do?"

All three men burst into spontaneous laughter. Judge Henry moved back around his desk and reclaimed his seat. "I'll leave all the details in your capable hands," he told them as he opened the top drawer. "Hire as many extra hands as you see fit, and requisition whatever provisions you'll require. Don't worry about the expense. If moving the herd there stops the rustling, we'll have more than made up for the cost of the drive." He examined a calendar on the wall beside him. "All I ask is that the drive be completed by the first snowfall. I'd hate to have the herd stranded on the open prairie in the middle of a blizzard. We'd risk losing them all."

"We'll get 'em there before the snow hits, seh," the Virginian promised. "I'll draw up a list of everything we'll need right away. Then some of us will take the wagon to Medicine Bow." His hat went on his head. "First off, I'd better talk to Scipio. As cook he'll be needin' a heap of victuals."

"Before you go," Judge Henry said, holding aloft an open envelope, "someone asked me to relay her best regards."

"Who?"

"My niece, Madeline."

"Don't tell me she's still bothered by that harmless prank I played on her?"

"Not at all. I know she had a bee in her bonnet once she learned the truth, but she simmered down long before she went back to New York. In fact, if you weren't a married man, she'd be writing you instead of me."

The Virginian pulled his hat brim down so low they couldn't see his eyes. "In that case, seh, be sure to tell her Molly says hello and mention how much Molly is lookin' forward to the baby comin'." He spun on his boot heels and departed.

"Mrs. Henry is right, Judge," Lin McLean remarked

in admiration as he stood. "You've got yourself a good man there."

"I did better than that. I got myself a *man*."

8

Of Lovers and Polecats

The news of the impending cattle drive electrified the Sunk Creek punchers. Where before, help-less resignation filled the soul of every hand loyal to the brand, now they thrilled to the prospect of taking action against the rustlers. Plans were laid for the special roundup and open-range branding to follow. Every horse on the spread was brought into service, and Dapper had his hands full riding the rough string, breaking those horses not used in the regular remuda but required for the drive because of the extra work anticipated.

The first order of business—after the Virginian, Lin McLean, and Scipio le Moyne spent two full days taking an inventory of the supplies on hand and estimating their needs for the long journey—was a trip to Medicine Bow.

Since there was so much work to do at the ranch in preparation for the roundup, Lin had to stay behind. In his place the Virginian took Dapper, who rode beside the squeaking wagon on his spanking zebra dun.

They were five miles out from the ranch when the black hand edged his horse a bit nearer the spinning wheel and commented, "I'm mighty obliged for yu' takin' me along, seh."

"Yu've been workin' hard," the Southerner responded with a sly wink at Scipio. "I figured yu' could use a little time off."

"That I could," said Dapper, gazing longingly into the distance.

"It gets a mite lonely on that big ranch at times," the Virginian went on conversationally. "Especially when a man has himself a sage hen caged off in town just a-waitin' and a-pinin' for him to pay her a visit."

Dapper almost irrevocably bent his neck out of shape, so quickly did his head snap around. "Exactly what are yu' drivin' at?" he asked testily.

"Sheathe your fangs, yu' longhorn. Did you really expect to keep it a secret? Some tongues were meant to wag, and those of the gossipy persuasion in Medicine Bow have been settin' new talkin' records over yu' and your sweetheart."

"I'll be damned," the hand declared. "What all have yu' heard?"

"Well, let me see. Her name is Mabel, and she's from Texas, like yu'. And she's makin' ends meet by doing washin' and mendin' and such. They say she keeps pretty much to herself, mainly because most of the white women are too uppity to have anything to do with her. Oh. And she likes to wear a red ribbon in her hair."

Dapper was properly stupefied. "I'm surprised yu' ain't heard about the scar on her elbow she got when she was twelve."

Scipio cackled and slapped his thigh. "Don't take it so hard, friend. If words was fertilizer, most towns would be neck deep."

The bronc-buster nodded. "Ain't that the Lord's truth.

But I just never figured on bein' so popular a topic with them that can't stand the shade of our skin."

"Pay them no mind. Some folks don't have the sense God gave a turnip," Scipio moralized.

"Since yu' know," Dapper said, "I might as well tell yu' both that I aim to marry Mabel and settle down hereabouts. I've been lookin' for a place like Sunk Creek for some time. It's made to order for a man in my position."

"They must have run out o' horses to stomp in Texas," Scipio said playfully.

"Not at all," was Dapper's reply. "Let's just say I had to light a shuck, and Wyoming seemed as good a spot as any to visit."

"And I'm right glad yu' came," the Virginian said. "You're cuttin' in half the time it would take us to get ready for the roundup." He lifted a hand to stroke his mustache. "Maybe later on, once we have the herd in Montana and can take the time to sit a spell, you'll see fit to bring your Mabel to Aspen Creek and have a visit with my Mary. I know she'd be delighted to have the two o' yu'."

Had Dapper been invited to dinner with the President, he would not have been more surprised. "Thank yu'," he blurted. "Mabel would like that, too, I reckon. Though I should warn yu' she's a mite on the shy side, so your Mary will have to loosen her up some first."

"Don't fret there," Scipio interjected, giving the Southerner a nudge. "This here pilgrim married a live dictionary."

"A schoolmarm?" Dapper said. "Do tell."

"She taught school onced," the Virginian confirmed. "And in about six months she'll have a little one all her own to look afteh."

"Yu' hopin' for a boy or a girl?"

"It don't make no difference, just so it's healthy," the Virginian said. "The sawbones claims Mary is comin' along right fine and that everything will go just as it should, but a man can't help worry some."

Scipio leaned back and shook his head. "And to think I recollect the days when yu' were as carefree as a lark! All this talk of wives and younguns and whatnot is downright upsettin' for an eligible bachelor like myself." He shifted his boots and examined a speck of mud on one. "When a man stands in front of a parson and says he does, what he's really sayin' is lock, stock, and barrel."

"You're nothin' but a natural-born pessimist," the Virginian retorted. "And I reckon you'll change your tune onced yu' finally tie the knot."

"Me?" Scipio declared in mock outrage. "The woman ain't been made yet who could make me step into her loop."

"Does he always brag on himself so?" the broncbuster asked the partner.

"Always," lamented the long-suffering Southerner.

"I knew me an hombre like him onced," expounded Dapper. "Down in the Staked Plain country it was. Why, every time the sun came out, he'd be so busy admirin' his shadow that he'd never get a lick o' work done."

"Yu' mean there are *two* of 'em?" asked the shocked Virginian.

"Have your fun, gents," Scipio finally got in. "But just remember which one of us can do as he blamed well pleases, including goin' drinkin' any time he's of a mind to."

"We will," the Virginian said, "if yu' remember which one o' us has holes in all his socks and has to make his own chicken soup when he's sick."

Scipio refused to be cowed. "Some ventilation in a man's footwear is a small price for him to pay for independence."

So they called that one a draw and went on to other matters. By the time, days later, Medicine Bow reared tiny and insignificant in the vast distance, Dapper had two new close friends. At the outskirts of town he glanced over and asked, "Will yu' be needin' me for loadin' right away, seh? I'd like to pay Mabel a visit."

"Go to it," the Virginian said. "I won't need yu' until

mawnin'. But be extra careful. Some of Balaam's outfit might be here, and if they see yu', they might try to prod yu' into a fight."

"I have no quarrel with them."

"Don't make no difference. Balaam has a quarrel with me, and he's not above takin' it out on Sunk Creek hands. So yu' stay cat-eyed, yu' hear?"

"I will," Dapper promised, touched by the other's concern. He wheeled the zebra dun and rode behind an uneven row of crude frame dwellings until he came to the last in the line, a weather-ravaged shack. After turning into the gap between the shack and the preceding house, he reined up at the front corner, slipped to the ground, and tied the reins to a rusted nail jutting from the wall.

In front of the shack were recently fashioned poles that supported the lines on which hung scores of fluttering garments. To the right of the open door sat a large metal tub, and in it a worn washboard.

As Dapper stood there, an attractive woman in a faded but crisp dress emerged and bent over the tub, a soiled shirt in her callused hands. She hummed "I'll Take the Wings of the Morning," one of Dapper's favorite spirituals. Grinning, he crept up behind her, waited until she straightened to brush at a drop of water that had spattered on her brow, and swiftly covered her eyes with his hands. "Yu' don't guess right and yu' can forget marryin' me."

Mabel giggled, dropped the soaked shirt into the tub, and placed her wet palms over his knuckles. "Let me see. It must be Black Jack Logan."

"That no-account!" Dapper said. "If I'd knowed yu' was partial to him, I'd never have drug yu' from Texas."

"You're not Black Jack?" Mabel teased. "Then yu' must be Elijah Wilson."

"A range bum! Oh, Lord! Shoot me, woman, and be done with it. I can't take any more." With that Dapper spun her around and they embraced warmly. "Miss me?" he asked after a while.

"Not that anyone would notice," Mabel said, but she kissed him again.

"I ain't stayin' long," Dapper informed her. "I'm here with that Virginian, the man who's partner with Judge Henry out to Sunk Creek."

"My, my. Aren't yu' keeping illustrious company these days?"

Dapper stepped back, gently took her hands in his, and beamed. "I tell yu', the future is lookin' bright, far brighter than it did when I shot Banner down in El Paso."

"Please. Yu' promised never to mention him again."

"He's why we're here, ain't he? If he hadn't put his hands on yu', I never would've had to put a bullet through his brain, and we never would've had to cut out for Wyoming."

"He had friends. What if they come after us?"

"All the way up here?" Dapper shook his head. "I changed my name, didn't I? As far as everyone around these parts is concerned, I'm just another black cowboy." He chuckled. "Once a man's north of the Red River, his past doesn't matter much." He glanced at the clotheslines. "I take it business is healthy?"

"I'm doing quite fine," Mabel agreed. "The gentlemen over to the hotel has put up a notice on his counter for me, and you'd be surprised at how many travelers want their clothes cleaned before they catch the next train out of town."

"Things keep on the way they are and you'll have that nice house I promised sooner than we figured."

"Yu' haven't been pushing too hard, have yu'? I don't want yu' working yourself to death just to please me."

"And here I figured yu' were smart. Don't yu' know I do everything I do for yu'?"

"So I gather. But I wish you'd told me yu' were having a man watch over me. Did yu' think I wouldn't notice?"

Dapper blinked and released her hands. "What's this?"

"Don't act dumb. A few days ago I caught this man peeking at me from around the corner." Mabel pointed at a nearby house. "Then, just yesterday, I saw him again. I was afraid he might be one of Banner's acquaintances, so I accidentally came up behind him while he was watching the front door." She laughed. "He about near jumped out of his boots!"

"Yu' shouldn't have done that," Dapper said gravely.

"Why? Just because yu' didn't want me to know? He told me everything."

"What did he tell yu'?"

"I asked him right out what he was doing, and he said yu' asked him to keep an eye on me, to make sure no one gave me a hard time." Mabel touched his cheek. "How sweet."

"It would've been had I done it," Dapper said. "But I didn't."

"What? Then who—?"

"I'm afraid it was me, washwoman," intruded a hard voice.

Dapper and Mabel whirled. Standing in a row to the left of the clotheslines were four men, only one of whom Dapper recognized, a man who always dressed in black from hat to boots and who sported a matched pair of ivory-handled Colts draped around his slender waist. "Brazos!"

"Know me, do yu'?" the man in black sneered. "Well, I reckon most folks hereabouts have heard of me. And they'll be hearin' a lot more before I'm through."

"Let me have him, Brazos," urged a grizzled companion. "I ain't killed me a nigger in a coon's age."

Dapper's whole body pulsed with raging resentment at the insult, and he tensed, his temper flaring. His hand hung near his six-gun, and he was ready to slap leather despite the odds. He knew Brazos was waiting for him to do just that, but he didn't care. Then Mabel stepped between them.

"What's this all about, gentlemen? My husband has done yu' no harm. Why come here and insult us?"

"Husband, is it?" Brazos responded. "Were you wed all proper and legal, or did yu' just take up with one another?"

"That's none of your damn business!" Dapper exploded. He tried to push Mabel aside, but she held her ground.

"What did yu' mean by saying it was yu' who sent that man to watch me?" she asked as politely as if she were having tea with friends instead of confronting four hard cases whose purpose was readily apparent.

"I needed to know when your *husband* came to roost, so I had a friend of mine hang around," Brazos answered, bragging a bit to show her how clever he'd been. "Now that he's here, why don't yu' be a good little runnin' mate and mosey along and do some washin'. Us men have business to take care of."

"I'm not budging," Mabel said sternly. "We've done nothing to yu'. There's no call to be doing this."

"Mabel!" Dapper cried.

"What's the matter, boy?" Brazos baited him. "Yu' let this woman do all your talkin' and fightin' for yu'? Is that how they do things where yu' come from?"

To one who was Western born and bred, certain conduct was not to be tolerated under any circumstances. Prying into a man's past was taboo. Making disparaging remarks about a man's woman friend was liable to result in hot lead. But insinuating that a man was a coward was the ultimate affront. Brazos, in the span of a minute, had done all three, and whatever restraint Dapper possessed was washed away by the flash flood of pure rage that coursed through him. Uttering an inarticulate cry, he shoved Mabel aside and took a half step forward, his body poised for the draw.

Brazos was no longer smirking. His hands hung close to his elaborately tooled holsters, and his eyes glittered with savage glee. "Make your play, black man," he goaded. "Whenever you're ready to die."

It was then, at that tension-charged instant when gunplay seemed inevitable and Mabel's heart was virtually in her throat, that a soft Southern voice interposed itself.

"Still favorin' the odds, I see, Brazos?"

The man in black whirled, his spiteful features the consistency of granite. His companions also turned, and none of them liked what they saw.

Not fifteen feet away stood the Virginian and Scipio le Moyne, both deceptively at ease, both with their hands dangling near their hardware. The Virginian took a stride, an odd sort of smile on his handsome face. "If this is a gunplay party, I hope yu' don't mind us joinin' the festivities."

"No one told me yu' were in town too," Brazos snarled.

"Figured as much." The Virginian took another step. "Scipio and me were on our way to the general store when we spotted these polecats skulkin' down an alley and figured we'd rid the town of 'em before they stink up the place." He looked to the right and left and loudly sniffed the air. "Yu' haven't happened to see any wood pussies in the neighborhood, have yu'?"

The men with Brazos all focused on him. He was their leader, and they would take their cue from whatever he did. All three expected him to respond to the Southerner's slight with blazing guns. But they didn't know their man as well as they thought they did.

Brazos adopted an easy smile and visibly relaxed, his thumbs hooking in his gunbelt. "No, I haven't seen any," he responded. "Leastways, none black *and* white."

The Virginian advanced until he was within an arm's length of his nemesis. "I wouldn't want them to come around here botherin' Dapper."

"Afraid it'd be bad for his health?" Brazos scoffed.

"Not at all," said the Virginian. "It'd be mighty bad for *their* health, though."

For several seconds their eyes clashed, and the only sound was the fluttering of the wash on the lines. At length Brazos grinned and turned lazily away. "Come on, boys," he announced. "I've got a hankerin' for a drink." He paused and fixed his wicked gaze on the Southerner. "I'm so thirsty I'd ride clear to Tombstone for a glass of red-eye." And, chuckling, he sauntered off.

Scipio walked over beside his friend. "Somebody ought to put a leash on that hombre. What the dickens did he mean by that Tombstone crack?" He stared after the departing hard cases, and when no answer was forthcoming, he glanced at the Virginian. The unbridled anguish he saw reflected on the other's face made him take a step back in shock. "What's the matter, pard? Are yu' all right?"

"He knows," the Virginian said softly.

"Who? Brazos? What's he know besides how to rile folks?"

The Virginian seemed not to hear. He slowly bowed his head and pressed a palm to his forehead. "Lord help me," he whispered to himself. "The sidewinder knows."

Scipio had never seen the Southerner so distraught. He would sorely have loved to violate their mutually held principles and pry into the reason, but the next moment Dapper stepped up to them.

"Yu' shouldn't have butted in, seh," the broncsqueezer addressed the partner. "It was my affair, not yours." Fists clenched, he watched the retreating figures as they rounded a building. "Did yu' hear what he said to me? No man has ever done that before and lived. I should go after him and show him he's not the only one handy with a shootin' iron."

"Don't you dare!" Mabel declared.

"Give me one good reason why I shouldn't."

"I've got a dandy. Banner."

Dapper scowled, then abruptly released his pent-up anger by slamming his right fist into his left hand. "Damn them all to hell!"

"We have it good here. Yu' said so yourself," Mabel stressed her point. "Why spoil things on account of some worthless white trash who's too full o' himself?"

"I don't like being talked down to," Dapper said.

"If yu' love me like yu' say, you'll let it drop."

The Virginian suddenly faced them. "We're goin' to buy the supplies we need and head back this evenin' instead o' waitin' until tomorrow."

"Shucks," Dapper grumbled. "I was lookin' forward to the stay over. Once the drive begins, I won't see Mabel again for months."

"I have a notion that might strike your fancy," the Virginian said. "Pack up all your things and we'll take Mabel back to Sunk Creek with us. Then we'll hustle her up to my spread so she can stay with Molly and Jessamine McLean until we're all back from Montana."

Mabel shook her head. "That's awful kind of yu', mister, but I couldn't impose on yu' so. I'll stay here. I have my laundry business to think of."

"Yu' have your life to think of," the Virginian corrected her. "I don't want to worry yu', but Brazos and his bunch might pay yu' another visit sometime when Dapper ain't around. Yu' see, that Brazos figures he can get at me through Dapper and at Dapper through yu'. If yu' stay, you'll likely bring more trouble down on your shoulders and his."

"What's this all about? Why does this Brazos hate yu' so? I could see it in his eyes. He wants to kill yu', make no mistake about that."

"No one knows that better than me, ma'am, but I'm not rightly sure anymore what he's about," the Virginian replied thoughtfully. "I thought I knew, but it's clear I was wide o' the mark by a mile or better." He gave a single shake of his head and his customary grin bloomed. "Now about this movin' business, it's a proposition yu' can't refuse."

"She'll come with us, seh," Dapper assured him.

"But—" Mabel tried to object.

"Or I go look up Brazos right this minute," Dapper vowed.

And so Mabel Martin came to live at Aspen Creek during the summer and fall of that year, and became a cherished confidante of her two white sisters. Which made the events that were to follow all the more tragic.

9

Horsemen of the Plains

Before the roundup came the parceling of horses. Over three hundred were driven into the main corral at the Sunk Creek Ranch in bunches of fifty at a time by Dapper, the wrangler, and several hands. Then Lin McLean called out the names of specific animals and assigned them to the punchers gathered thick as flies around the rails. In this way each cowboy acquired a personal string of eight horses, and woe to the man who failed to keep them in good condition.

All the horses were geldings. Stallions were never used in a remuda because of their tendency to fight among themselves, and mares were shunned by the punchers because they were generally regarded to be as unreliably temperamental as their human counterparts. Or, as Scipio gruffly put it one day to a new man who had signed on for the drive, "Yu' don't want no filly partial to contrary notions between your legs when Injuns come screamin' down at yu' or a rattler's about to strike. It'd be like havin' your sweetheart sittin' in your lap when her ma comes at yu' wavin' a fryin' pan."

The older hands were on pins and needles during the parceling. They knew that some of the horses had outlaw tendencies or were downright locoed, and they dreaded being required to take such animals into their string. But even if this happened, not a man complained. The custom was to accept whichever animals were allotted, and those who bellyached were held in disdain.

The day before the roundup was slated to commence, there was a last-minute flurry of activity around the bunkhouse. Clothes were washed, bedding was aired, and Honey Wiggin took on the task of cutting the hair of any man so inclined. His scissors were dull, and he handled them as a child might wield sheep shears, but the men knew it would be several months before a similar opportunity presented itself, so they splurged and took the treatment in as manly a manner as possible with the lone exception of the Toothpick Kid, who had the audacity to grouse that if he had wanted to go through life bald, he would have been born an eagle.

Came the day and the men were primed. The Virginian and Lin McLean led them out from the ranch, bearing to the south. By virtue of his knowledge of the country and of all the brands that might be found to have mixed with the Judge's stock and thus have to be culled, the Virginian was the roundup captain. To him fell the designation of duties, and he was tireless in his work.

The roundup proceeded in stages: As each district was cleaned, the men would move on to the next, and the next, and in this fashion make a complete sweep of the entire ranch. Each day the Virginian oversaw the scattering of the riders, and he always made certain that new men were paired with more experienced hands for their own benefit.

There were hardships galore. The sun baked the punchers, and there was little water to drink. Dust hung thick in the air, frequently choking the careless hand who forgot to keep his bandanna tied over his nose and mouth. Those who pulled drag duty suffered the worst and would be caked from head to toe by nightfall. Always the cows gave them trouble, whether it was calves that fell behind or contrary steers that had their bovine hearts set on going in one direction when the herd was going in another. Worst were the old bulls, who often tried to gore a rider who became too insistent on moving the brutes along.

Occasionally a cowboy took a tumble, which was to be expected in a land teeming with prairie-dog towns, gullies, and washes. One man broke his leg in three places and had to be taken back to the ranch.

Even at mealtime there was no rest for the weary. Those hands temporarily relieved would gallop up to the chuck wagon, grab their tin plates, and gobble down the red-hot food cooked by Scipio in his Dutch ovens. Then, the meal down and water hastily gulped, the punchers would swing back into the saddle and gallop off to do more work.

Scipio never had a moment to rest. His was the most important job on the drive next to that of the roundup captain, for on his culinary skill depended the happiness of every hand working for Judge Henry, and he was justly proud of always having three hot meals a day ready come rain or shine.

The fourth day of the roundup, as the Virginian sat astride Monte on a low hill surveying the progress, Lin McLean rode up.

"I'd say it's goin' right fine," the foreman commented happily. "The Judge will be pleased."

"What do yu' figure the tally will be?" asked the Southerner.

"Oh, if we keep a-goin' like we are, a little over three thousand would be my guess."

"Close enough. I'm figuring on closer to four."

"Makes yu' sort of wonder, don't it?" Lin asked.

"About the Judge?"

McLean nodded and took out the makings. "The rustlers can't have taken more than four hundred head, even countin' all the calves they've got their grubby hands on." He paused, regarding the paper. "So it don't make no kind of sense for the Judge to be talkin' about foldin' his cards over such triflin' losses."

"I don't think it was the cattle he was so concerned about," the Virginian opined.

"Then what was it?"

"Us."

"Yu' and me?"

"Our whole outfit." The Virginian leaned on his saddle horn and nodded at the rippling sea of cows and men below their vantage point. "Judge Henry is a kind sort o' man, Lin, just about the kindest I know next to the bishop o' Wyoming. He ain't quite a full-blooded Christian yet, although Mrs. Henry has been workin' hard to convert him."

"So?" replied the unimpressed foreman. "It don't hardly need mentionin' that most men make their reservations with Saint Peter in their wives' names."

"The point I'm makin' is that the Judge can't abide the thought o' any o' his people comin' to harm."

'He'd rather sell out than risk one or two of us stoppin' a bullet if we tangled with the cow thieves?" Lin responded skeptically.

"No, he'd rather sell out than risk an all-out range war."

"Range war! Do yu' know something' I don't? Exactly when did the rustlers recruit enough men to form an army? Even more important, have yu' heard if they've got their hands on any cannons?"

The Virginian mustered a weary grin. "I swear. Sometimes you're worse than Scipio, and that takes a heap o' doin'."

"Then enlighten me."

Instead of answering, the Virginian enjoyed a leisurely stretch, then remarked, "I hear there's been another raise in the price of beeves. If we was takin' this herd to sell, the Judge would get top dollar right now."

"True," Lin McLean said, waiting patiently for the revelation to come. Long ago he had learned of the Southerner's habit of taking a roundabout way of getting to the point, so he hung on every word.

"Fact is, I hear some o' the other ranchers are doin' just that."

"True again," Lin said.

"Meeker, Bower, and Grissom have all sold some head since the price took an upturn. I happened to run into Meeker in Medicine Bow. He said someone else has been doin' a lot o' sellin' o' late. Meeker took a herd to Chadron, and what should he see there waitin' to be shipped but pens and pens packed full o' beeves. A lot o' calves were also waitin'. A mighty lot o' calves."

"Folks like to eat veal too," Lin noted.

"True, but Meeker swore there were so many calves, it looked to him as if there was two for every cow and at least one for each steer besides."

Now the foreman caught the partner's drift, and he paused with his freshly made cigarette halfway to his lips. "That's a serious charge."

"True," said the Virginian with a chuckle.

"Meeker happen to say who owned all these calves?"

"Sure did."

"Well, are yu' fixin' to tell me or—" Lin said testily, but broke off when insight born of the recollection of his run-in with the three riders from the Butte Creek spread caused him nearly to drop his cigarette. "Gosh! Yu' mean Balaam!"

"None other."

"Are yu' thinkin'—?" Lin checked his statement when the other held aloft a hand.

"I don't have proof, mind. Just suspicions," the Southerner declared. "But if the repawt is true, it explains an awful lot. And yu' and me will have to be extra careful from hyeh on out. He's got more cause than we figured. Savvy, pardner?"

"I savvy," Lin said solemnly, and swallowed hard.

They sat in silence for a minute, until Lin lowered his smoke and mentioned, "We should be ready to start the brandin' in two days."

"I reckon."

"The Judge has spread the word, yu' know. There'll

be reps on hand from all the other outfits. Includin' Balaam's."

"Let the man come. So long as he behaves, he's as welcome as the rest."

"Balaam might even come himself."

"No."

"Yu' don't think so?"

"He's not the kind to work up a sweat when he can pay others to do it for him." The Virginian glanced at McLean. "We won't really have to worry until we're on the trail north."

"I was afeared you'd say that."

Just then Chalkeye rode up to announce that the district the hands had been working on all day had been thoroughly cleaned and the punchers were ready to move on to the next, effectively ending their conversation.

The roundup was completed without incident, but there was no rest for the tired cowboys, who were just getting into the full swing of the arduous toil that lay ahead. With the cattle all gathered, the next order of business was the branding.

Because of the tendency of cows to wander far and wide, stock from other spreads had strayed onto Judge Henry's ranch and had to be weeded out from the Judge's herd. Consequently, other ranches sent representatives to cut out their stock and drive the animals back to their respective ranges once the branding was concluded. These reps were always top hands, men born to the saddle and familiar with all the brands in their part of the country.

The Virginian knew five of the six reps who showed up, but the last man was new to his acquaintance, a great, burly puncher who rode for Balaam. This hand's name was Horn. From the day he arrived, he created trouble. He often insisted on double-checking the bunches of cattle brought to the holding grounds adjacent to the branding area, and out of common courtesy the Virginian was forced to hold up the operation while Horn went among the cows making a big show of inspecting each and every brand.

At other times Horn had the audacity to question the

tally, which again necessitated taking time out so the Virginian could prove to Balaam's rep that every head of Balaam stock was being properly accounted for.

An explanation is called for here. It was the job of the tally hand to keep a complete record of the cows being branded. Cattle from other ranches were taken aside and held apart from the main herd until the reps were ready to take them back. If the tally man was unscrupulous, he might "accidentally" include stock from other spreads in his count of the main herd, and it was to prevent this that the reps were sent. Such blatant thievery was rare. To ensure this, only the most widely respected and highly regarded cowboys were picked to make the tally. In this instance the Virginian himself was handling the chore.

Some of the Sunk Creek hands grumbled about Horn's repeated interference, but they were far too busy to take the man to task. During a branding operation the cowboys worked eighteen-hour days, and there was never a spare moment to relax until all the day's work had been done.

From dawn until dusk, the punchers would bring groups of cattle from the main herd to the holding spots. A half-dozen riders would then cut out the unbranded stock. Skilled ropers then took over, and it was a wonder to behold the skill with which they snaked their nooses under the rear legs of the calves and dragged their bawling charges to where the flankers waited. If grown cows needed branding, usually two cowboys worked together, one roping the legs, the other the head. Many of the newer hands openly gawked at the prowess of the seasoned punchers they hoped one day to emulate.

The flankers always worked in pairs. Their job was to grab the calves by the flanks and the forelegs, throw the frightened animals to the ground, and hold them down while the branding iron was applied.

Another hand worked as the ironman, the one who tended the fire and made sure the branding irons were kept hot enough. This was a critical chore. The iron had to be sufficiently hot to produce a scab that would peel but not so intensely scorching that it seared the hide, which not only caused the cow or calf undue pain but blurred the brand.

The brander himself had just about the easiest job of all. Once the animal was prone and held fast, he lightly applied the iron, using just enough pressure to mark the hide and no more.

Only one other man contributed to the operation. He was the marker, and it was his responsibility to cut slivers from the ears of the cows and toss the bits into a handy bucket. Later the pieces would be counted as a check against the count of the tally man. To the marker also fell the work of castrating the male calves, which he performed with a few deft strokes of a sharp knife.

To an onlooker who knew nothing of cattle and cowboys, the scene was one of total bedlam, heightened by the bawling of the cows, the excited yipping of the punchers, the constant pounding of hooves, and the cloud of dust and smoke that hovered overhead.

There was only one mishap this time around. The Judge and Mrs. Henry rode out to see how things were going. As they sat watching the branding, the Toothpick Kid took it into his nearly bald head to show off for their benefit. He was working as flanker, so to impress them he tried rolling a calf, a flashy move in which a single flanker reaches over the back of the calf and seizes hold with one hand while sticking a leg in front of the calf to bring it down with a powerful flip. Unfortunately for the Toothpick Kid, he miscalculated, and a flying hoof cracked him soundly on the temple, breaking the skin and drawing blood. To make his humiliation worse, he had to sit and let Mrs. Henry tend his wound as all around him the other punchers developed a peculiar epidemic of shaking shoulders and fits of smothered snorting.

The Virginian was pleased with their progress, though on the last day he suffered more interruptions by Horn, and that night things came to a head. The men had converged on the chuck wagon, and most had polished off their portions of the son-of-a-bitch stew Scipio had prepared, a delicious concoction consisting of calf meat, sweetbreads, kidneys, and brains thickened with flour and spiced with onions.

The Southerner and Lin McLean were seated near the tail of the chuck wagon, passing idle time with Scipio, when Horn rose and made a remark for all to hear.

"Yu' hombres call this food? Why, yu' all ought to come over to Butte Creek and taste real cookin'!"

"It's mighty strange that yu' didn't like it," said the unflappable le Moyne, his bleached-blue eyes shutting to slits, "considerin' that yu' had yu' three helpings."

General mirth greeted this observation, and Horn scowled as he carried his plate over and set it down with the rest of the dirty dishes. Perhaps to recover some of the prestige he imagined he had lost, he said, loud as before, "Have your fun, gents. I'm just glad to be shut o' this raw-hide outfit come mawnin' and to be returnin' to a real nickel-plated outfit like Balaam's."

It was Honey Wiggin who started the trouble by responding, "Too bad Balaam's horses ain't nickel plated. Maybe then he'd find it a mite harder to gouge out their eyes when they flick their tails the wrong way."

Horn turned. "Are yu' sayin' my boss is a horse beater?"

"Hell, everyone this side of the Divide knows it."

The Butte Creek rep strode over and loomed above the skinny Wiggin. "Stand, yu' bastard, and take your due."

Before Honey could answer the challenge, the Virginian was there. "That'll be enough. If yu' plan to whip every man here who doesn't like Balaam, you'd have to fight the whole outfit."

A single glance convinced Horn of the truth of the statement, but to his credit he wasn't cowed by the dozens of hostile stares directed his way. Instead, he faced the Southerner, and his thick lips curved in a scornful smile. "Well, now. I reckon I don't need to whip the entire outfit. To prove these yacks wrong, all I have to do is whip *yu'*." And with that he delivered a vicious right to the Southern-er's midsection.

The Virginian had not been expecting a physical assault. By and large, cowboys disdained using their fists in a fight; it was six-shooters or nothing. So the first blow caught him unawares and sent him staggering backward, doubled over as the air whooshed from his lungs. He tripped over someone and went down.

All around men were urgently scrambling to get out of the way while others erupted in hearty cheers of support for the Southerner.

Flat on the ground, the Virginian saw Horn walking slowly toward him and motioning for him to stand. He knew he couldn't count on help from the Sunk Creek punchers. Horn had outfoxed him, made this a personal contest rather than a dispute involving the whole outfit. And he dared not go for his gun since Horn was making no move for his, which, he reflected, must be exactly what Horn had planned all along.

Frowning at his own stupidity for falling into such a blatant trap, the Virginian pressed his right hand to the ground and shoved upright. He held his fists ready and braced his legs.

"Good!" Horn gloated confidently, as he could well afford to, since he packed nearly fifty more pounds onto his beefy physique than his wiry adversary. "I've been lookin' forward to this for days."

"Is that so? Well, I hope yu' won't be too turribly disappointed when yu' lose," the Virginian said, and had to dart aside when Horn rushed him and drove a powerful left cross at his face. Air fanned his cheek, and he stepped in close and landed two jarring blows in swift succession, both to Horn's ribs.

The big man grunted, then backpedaled and brought his ponderous arms up to protect himself. The gleam of easy victory was gone from his brutish eyes. He'd seen an example of the Southerner's quickness and felt an example of the Southerner's strength, and he realized that beating the Virginian senseless, as his employer wanted him to do, wouldn't be as simple as he had believed.

Wading in, the Virginian rained a flurry of lightning punches. Most were blocked. A few landed, and these caused Horn to retreat a bit farther. The bigger man seemed mystified by this unexplained display of skill, as might be expected, since he had no way of knowing the many hours the Virginian had spent boxing in bunkhouses from New Mexico to Montana, from Arkansas to California.

Although punchers generally refused to resort to their fists for any serious fighting, one of the most popular sports among cowboys everywhere except Texas was boxing. In Wyoming many a bunkhouse boasted two pairs of genuine boxing gloves, and frequent bouts were put on at which some punchers lost both a month's wages and their voices in the span of minutes.

So now, as the Virginian warily circled and skipped around the heavier, slower, Horn, he relied on the skill he had acquired in these matches to avoid every punch thrown his way while simultaneously connecting time and again. At one point he rocked Horn on his heels with an uppercut to the chin and followed through with a blow to the stomach that made Horn sputter and gasp.

The Sunk Creek hands were yelling at the top of their lungs and dancing like demented sprites in their enthusiasm to see Horn whipped. One of the loudest was Honey Wiggin, who so forgot himself that he tripped over a saddle and was dumped seat first into the cooking fire. Had it not been for the quick assistance of the Toothpick Kid and Chalkeye, he wouldn't have been able to sit a horse for a while.

None of this the Virginian heard or saw. He had eyes only for Horn. He jabbed with his left, and when Horn countered, slammed his right into the rep's mouth. Horn's lips split, blood spurted out. Enraged, Horn growled and flailed away wildly, seeking to hammer the Southerner into the ground. But the Virginian danced beyond Horn's reach, and when Horn stopped, winded, he dashed in and caught Horn with a rapid smash to the ear.

Blood now seeped from Horn's mouth and trickled down his neck. His face was bruised, his left eye puffy. It appeared as if he'd been caught in a stampede. Yet the wily rep wasn't about to give up. He'd noticed that every time he paused to catch his breath, the Virginian attacked.

So he used this knowledge to his advantage and pretended to exert himself by swinging several times in a row, knowing full well he would miss. Then he halted and took a deep breath. Predictably, the Virginian closed once again. Only this time Horn was ready.

Horn aimed a straight right to the body that the Virginian nimbly sidestepped, but in so doing the Southerner exposed his left shoulder for an instant, which was all the time Horn needed to strike. His knobbed knuckles rammed into the Virginian's shoulder and knocked him sideways. Then, in the heartbeat before the Virginian could recover his balance, Horn was on him, connecting with a brutal punch to the back of the head.

The Virginian crumpled. Stars exploded before his eyes. The world spun and blurred. Vaguely, he could hear someone screaming at him to stand. But his legs were mush. A fist caught him on the right cheek, splitting his flesh like a soft melon. Another drummed his forehead. He went down on his side, acute pain flaring throughout his battered body. He knew he was losing, and to those watching the slaughter, it seemed there was nothing he could do about it. But they reckoned without the nature of the man.

From deep within the wellspring of his being gushed a reserve of strength and stamina that enabled the Virginian to push to his feet once again and to turn and confront the rep. He shook his head, clearing his vision, and saw Horn draw back a malletlike fist for the final punch. As the fist streaked at his chin, he ducked, then scored with a right and a left cross to the bigger man's jaw.

Horn staggered. He got his hands up again, but his arms were oddly weak. His left forearm blocked a hook, and he parried another right cross. That lowered his guard.

This was the moment for which the Virginian had waited. A straight right to the face rocked Horn rearward. A pair of swift left jabs kept him off balance. And a devastating right crunched teeth and sent the rep toppling over like a felled tree in the forest.

For several seconds stunned silence gripped the punchers, only to be replaced by a collective chorus of whoops and yells that caused the horses in the remuda to fidget and the men riding night guard to curse under their breaths and keep a cautious eye on the cows.

The Virginian, swaying slightly, stared down at the unconscious Horn and slowly lowered his tingling arms. He felt no elation. As top man he should have averted conflict, not taken part in it. Even though he had won, he'd failed in his duty, and he would have slumped to the ground in fatigue and regret had not a wild wave of delirious cowboys engulfed him in their midst and hoisted him onto their shoulders.

Laughing and whooping, the proud and gleeful punchers bore the winner twice around the chuck wagon. They might have borne him several more times had not a pistol cracked into the crisp night air and Lin McLean strode forward to bar their path.

"That's enough, yu' blamed children! Can't yu' see the man is plumb tuckered out?"

They looked then, and carefully lowered him down next to the fire and moved sheepishly away. Not one paid the least bit of attention to the rep from Butte Creek.

Scipio brought water and a towel as Lin sat down across from the Virginian and studied his friend's troubled countenance.

"What's eatin' yu'? If I hadn't seen it with my own eyes, I'd swear yu' lost."

"Shouldn't have happened," the Southerner said wearily.

"What else could yu' have done?" Scipio demanded as he dipped the end of the towel in the pail. "That no-account curly wolf was all horns and rattles. He was askin' for it and yu' clipped his horns proper."

The Virginian sat impassively while Scipio wiped the blood and dirt from his face and neck. He flinched once when the towel brushed a knot on his head.

"Yu' won't win no beauty contests," Lin commented, "but yu' won't scare the beeves to look at 'em, neither."

"That's encouragin'," the Virginian said dryly. He suddenly realized his hands were still clenched tight. Holding them out, he had to consciously will them to open.

Blood coated two fingers, and his skin was split in several places. "I won't be playin' any cards for a spell."

"Neither will he," Scipio said, with a nod at Horn. He took the Virginian's hands in his and lowered them into the water. "Let 'em soak awhile and the sting'll go out o' 'em."

"I'm fine."

"You'll do as I say anyway. In case yu' forgot, I'm the cook of this here outfit, and that means if there's doctorin' to do on the range, I'm the one to do it." Scipio wiped his hands on his pants and stood. "Now I'd best clean up the dishes or I won't get to bed until midnight."

Lin waited until le Moyne was gone, then leaned forward and spoke softly. "Balaam will be more riled than ever over this."

"I don't rightly care," said the Virginian. "Nothin' we do will change what's goin' to happen, so it doesn't matter if we make him madder than he already is or not. He hates me and he always will. All because I had to explain myself to him onced when he was maltreatin' a hawss. That was a right smart while ago, yet he's held it against me all this time." He gazed into the crackling flames for a time and at length said sadly, "It's the past, yu' see."

"What?"

"The past has a way o' catchin' up with the future and makin' the present miserable."

"Have yu' been readin' books again?"

A shadow seemed to attach itself to the Virginian's face. "When I was younger, I was pretty headlong in what I did. I had a special pard, and we did everything together. Trouble was, he was as wild and woolly as they come, and I didn't know no better. We ended up ridin' the high-lines much of the time and pretty near wound up outlaws." He paused, the shadow deepening.

The foreman perceived that his friend was baring his soul to him, and he shifted uncomfortably, trying to think of something to say, but the Virginian went on.

"He was kin. My cousin. So I couldn't hardly ride off and leave him, not even when he got mad drunk, which he did more than he should, and made wolf meat o' some he didn't like."

At last Lin came up with a comment. "Yu' say this was a long time ago?"

"I was practically a wet-nosed kid at the time."

"Then why fret over it? We've all done loco things when we were knee-high to a heifer."

The Virginian acted as if he hadn't heard. "When they killed him, I headed north, lookin' over my shoulder the whole way. But they never came afteh me. Must've figured I wasn't worth the bother since I never prodded 'em like he did." His right hand came out of the water and touched his face. "I had to learn the hard way. Most do. And some would say it's the best way. It cert'nly shows yu' the value o' virtue."

Still at a loss as to what to say, and wondering why his friend was confiding in him, Lin simply sat and listened. This was a part of the Southerner he hadn't suspected existed, and he found the glimpse fascinating.

"Here all these years I figured I'd left my past behind me, but I didn't. Brazos knows, and I wouldn't be surprised if he'd told Balaam. If the word gets around, I won't know a moment's peace. Every gun-shark in the country will be hankerin' to see how good they really are." The Virginian shuddered. "Lord! She could never take that."

"Molly?"

The Virginian bowed his head and said no more that night, not unless addressed by one of the hands. The next day all the punchers noticed his usual cheerful disposition was gone, and speculation was rampant as to the cause. Scipio convinced some it was because of the fight. Others thought it might be because the cattle drive was starting and he wouldn't be seeing his cow bunny for several months. Lin McLean knew more now than most, but his lips were sealed and couldn't have been pried apart with dynamite.

The day after the fight, all the reps left with their stock. Horn was the first to leave, and he didn't extend a parting word to anyone. But the glances he shot in the Virginian's direction did not bode well for the Southerner.

Last-minute preparations were made. The Judge rode out from the ranch house to spend an hour consulting with his partner, bringing along provisions from the ranch for Scipio, who restocked the chuck wagon.

Dawn broke bright and cool the following morning. At a yell from Scipio, the hands threw off their tarpaulins and swiftly dressed in the chill air. The beds were rolled up and tossed into the bed-wagon, then everyone not riding herd gathered for a hasty breakfast of bacon, beans, and biscuits. As soon as each man finished, he caught the first saddle horse he would use from his string and saddled up. By the time the sun rose, the outfit was on the go.

The cattle drive had begun.

10

Blood Brothers

Trail drives differed greatly. Some were for short distances and involved relatively few cows; others were for thousands of miles and occasionally entailed moving an even larger herd than that of Judge Henry and his partner from old Virginia. So the Sunk Creek drive fell somewhere between the two extremes.

At the head of the winding column of cows rode the point men, the two who were responsible for piloting the herd in the direction the Virginian wanted. A third of the way back, on either side, were the swing riders, who had to keep the cattle moving and prevent any from straying off to the right or left. Such was also the job of the flank riders, who assumed positions two thirds of the way back from the point men.

Bringing up the rear, and wishing they were anywhere but where they were, came the drag riders, the overworked men who had to constantly goad on the many cows and calves that fell behind. Clouds of dust choked them relentlessly. The heat was so bad that the sweat poured from their bodies, but they dared not remove their shirts for fear of suffering blisters. With flicks of their ropes or waves of their slickers, they urged the slackers on. Frequently a calf or cow would break ranks and try to flee. In a flash a drag rider would be in pursuit, his rope would sail out, and the contrary critter would be dragged back none too kindly to the herd. Mile after grueling mile, hour after exhausting hour, it was the same.

That first day they drove the herd twenty-three miles. The second, twenty-one. And because the Virginian still wasn't satisfied that the herd was fully trail-broke, he had the punchers travel another twenty miles the third day. Afterward, with the cattle settled down to the daily routine, they managed an average of fifteen miles. Because the herd wasn't being taken to market, the Virginian wasn't as concerned as he normally would have been over keeping the critters well fed and watered. The object was to get them to Montana as quickly as possible; later the cows could fatten up to their bovine hearts' content on the sweet Montana grass.

Day and night the Southerner was kept busy, either roving afield in search of water and places to bed down, or moving up and down the mile-long line. Lin was often with him. Whenever they rode any distance off, they made it a point to protect each other's back. One would water his horse while the other watched, or one would stand guard while the other went into the bushes. They never let down their guard for a minute.

The days piled one on the other, becoming weeks of steady progress. The cattle behaved themselves. The weather was fine. They crossed several deep streams and a fork of the Tongue River without mishap. The drive seemed charmed.

Then came the morning when the Virginian and Lin were out seeking good noonday pasture and they came on the charred remains of a campfire. A few tendrils of smoke wafted skyward from the embers. The Virginian dismounted, sank to one knee, and touched one of the outer embers. "Still warm," he announced.

Lin was scanning the trampled grass. "Shod horses, I make it. Must be ten or more."

The Virginian rose and made a complete circuit, noting the differences between the individual tracks as surely as if they were separate signatures. "Twelve hawsses, all told," he declared, raising his head. "They went north."

"Punchers from some Montana spread, maybe," Lin speculated.

"Maybe."

Hands on their Colts, they followed the trail for five miles and reined up on a hill. The twelve riders were nowhere to be seen.

"They sure are goin' hell-for-leather," remarked Lin.

The Virginian's eyes sparkled with inner flames. "There are some hills and ravines and such about three days' ride from here. I expect they'll be waitin' there."

"I've been deceivin' myself that we wouldn't run into trouble. Should've known better."

That night trouble of a different sort threatened. The cows were bedded down, the night guard singing as they made their rounds, and the rest of the hands gathered around the fire, swapping tall tales, when the visitors came.

Scipio happened to be pouring coffee for Dollar Bill when he glanced up and saw the three rigid bronze figures at the edge of the flickering firelight. In his shock he nearly dropped the coffeepot, and blurted, "Injuns!"

There was a frantic explosion of confusion as the cowboys scrabbled to their feet and whirled, some of them drawing their revolvers and training them on the silent warriors.

"No shootin'!" The Virginian commanded sternly as he moved through the jammed hands. "We'll see what they want first."

"Be careful!" warned one of the older punchers. "Those are Sioux. From the way they Indianed up on us, they might be itchin' to give some of us an Indian haircut."

The Virginian advanced until he was halfway to the trio, at which point the tallest of the three came forward to meet him. The warrior's hands moved fluidly in a series of gestures, and although the Virginian wasn't highly versed in sign language, he knew enough to understand the Sioux's request. While he waited for the warrior to finish, he scrutinized all three, noticing the shabby shape of their leggings and moccasins and how all of them were so skinny their ribs were showing. This was a poor band, too proud to live on a reservation but unable to live off the land as they once had since all the buffalo were gone.

"What's he makin' all them contortions about?" Honey Wiggin asked.

Twisting, the Virginian glanced at a spot fifty feet away, where lay the remains of a steer Scipio had butchered for their evening meal. Only the choice meat had been used; the rest of the cow would be feasted on by wolves and coyotes and buzzards after the outfit headed out in the morning. "They want what's left," he revealed.

"Hell, that's all?" Dollar Bill said, laughing nervously. "I say give it to 'em, and I hope they choke on the hooves!"

Only a few of the men laughed, and the Virginian wasn't one of them. He faced the tall warrior and made the sign for yes, which was done by holding his right hand in front of the right side of his chest about shoulder height with all his fingers clenched except his index finger, which was extended upward, and then moving the hand a little to the left and closing his index finger over his curled thumb.

Immediately the tall warrior turned and grunted at his fellows, and all three raced into the night.

"What in tarnation are they doin'?" Scipio mused. "I thought the red devils wanted the remnants."

An answer was forthcoming a minute later when over fifteen warriors, women, and children descended on the carcass with knives and buckets. They cut off every single shred of flesh or hide, piled the internal organs in their buckets, and draped the intestines over their shoulders. There was a certain degree of desperation in their actions, as if they were so starved they could hardly wait to get the remains to their camp for a feast.

The Indians were nearly done when the Virginian

walked to the chuck wagon and said to Scipio, "Give me some sugar and flour."

"Are yu' moonstruck? We don't have all that much to spare."

"Yu' darned fool. They didn't have to ask. They could have stolen a cow and we'd never have been the wiser."

Scipio blinked at the gentle rebuke, puckered his mouth in self-reproach, and set out two small pots. Into one he poured flour to the brim, into another sugar. "I reckon sometimes my tongue gets the better o' my brain," he said as he handed them over.

"Happens to all of us," the Virginian said. The pots at his waist, he walked over to the Sioux. One of the squaws saw him and said something, and all the Indians turned. Again it was the tall warrior who came to meet him. The Sioux stared at the pots a moment, then into the Southerner's eyes. There was no need for words.

Taking the gifts, the tall warrior returned to his people and barked orders. As soundlessly and swiftly as they had materialized, they melted into the veil of darkness, leaving only the horns and hooves of the steer.

"Hell!" declared Dollar Bill once more. He had the habit of heralding practically every statement he made with the exclamation, because, as he liked to point out, he was bound there one day anyway and might as well get used to the word. "I didn't really mean that chokin' crack."

The Sunk Creek hands were a subdued lot that night as they turned in, but by morning their insuppressible, frolicsome spirits had returned. Joking and laughing, they saddled their horses and assumed their positions around the herd, ready to move out. Even those who had the sense of direction of an adobe brick knew the general route they must take, since it was one of Scipio's last duties before retiring each night to point the tongue of his chuck wagon at the North Star so the men would have a sure bearing in the morning.

Assuming a position in advance of the herd, the Virginian motioned with his right arm and bellowed, "Head 'em out." Then, as the punchers yipped and yelled and prodded the cows into motion, he spurred Monte forward and with Lin McLean at his side headed northward to check on the lay of the land ahead. They had not gone a mile when they found the spot where the Sioux had been camped as evidenced by the black rings of two dead fires and a torn discarded parfleche.

"I reckon their little ones went to bed with full bellies for the first time in days last night, thanks to yu'," the foreman remarked.

"Pshaw. It don't need mentioning."

"Confess. Didn't yu' feel a tiny bit sorry for them? I know I did."

"And how sorry do yu' feel for us?" asked the Virginian as he resumed riding.

"Us?" Lin repeated. "We're practically wallowin' in velvet. What do we have to feel sorry for? We done them a good deed, didn't we?"

"For which there's no call to brag," the Virginian said, and surveyed the waving grass on all sides. "We have a lot in common with those Injuns. One day we'll be just like they are."

"I hope to God I'm never *that* hungry," Lin said distastefully.

"It's not their hunger I'm referrin' to. It's their way o' life." The Virginian put a hand on his hip. "Once there were thousands and thousands of Injuns livin' on the prairie from down Texas way clear up to Canada. Now they're mostly confined to reservations, livin' on scraps of land and beggin' for handouts from the government and folks like us."

"I still don't make the connection."

"There was a time the Injuns had the run o' the wide-open prairie," the Virginian said with a nod at their surroundings. "Now we do. And before too long we won't have it anymore, just like they don't. We won't be put on reservations, but it'll be almost the same thing. The open range will all be fenced in, and the days when a man can ride anywhere he pleases will be gone forever."

"Shucks, it won't get that bad. I'll admit times are

a-changin', but the folks back east will always want beeves, and we'll be the ones who supply 'em. There'll always be a need for open range."

"And I tell yu' the handwritin' is there for all to see. Look at what happened after the Great Die-Up. That blizzard wiped out a turrible lot of cows, two thirds of all the cattle north o' Colorado, and the ranchers who survived, the smart ones like the Judge, did so by cuttin' back on their open-range use and concentratin' smaller herds in prime pasture. There'll be more and more o' that as time goes on." He pushed his hat back and rubbed his chin, then glanced sharply at a knoll to the northwest. "I tell yu', a man has to have his hand in more than one pie to make a go of it nowadays. Why do yu' think I picked land with coal on it? I don't want all my aiggs in one basket."

Lin McLean rode in thoughtful silence for a minute. He'd never given the matter much thought before, but now that he did, he saw the truth of his friend's prediction. And he resolved on the spot to take whatever steps were necessary to make sure his ranch was one of those still around to greet the new century. He owed it to Jessamine.

"Lin?" the Virginian said quietly.

"All right. I admit you're right. Yu' always were the deeper thinker."

"We're bein' watched."

"By who?" Lin asked, looking all around.

"Don't, yu' boxhead joker! Do yu' want them to know that we know?" the Virginian said. Keeping his gaze fixed straight in front of them, he remarked softly, "The polecat is on that knoll yondeh with a telescope. Been spyin' on us a right smart while, I figure."

As casually as he could, Lin stretched, and from behind the cover of his forearm he flicked his eyes to the northwest. Sure enough, he saw sunlight gleam off a reflective surface. "Could be a rifle," he said.

"I don't think so. The light's too steady."

"What do yu' want to do?"

"Nothin'."

"We could circle around and come up on that Daniel Boone from behind."

"And what if he slips away? No, I'd rather they keep thinkin' we don't know we have company so when the time comes they'll be mighty surprised."

"When will yu' tell the hands?"

"Tonight."

And the Virginian was as good as his word. After the chuck had been greedily devoured, he stood up near the fire and noisily cleared his throat. "I'm sorry to be disconveniencin' yu', but before yu' get around to swappin' stories about all the women yu' didn't really meet and all the wild times yu' never really had, I have a question to ask."

There were snickers and chortles from the fatigued but lighthearted cowboys. "Ask away, caporal!" one of them cried.

"I'm not goin' to mince words," the Virginian declared with rare severity. "I need to know how many of yu' are loyal to the brand and how many ain't."

Stunned silence greeted the query. To imply a puncher wasn't devoted to the outfit for which he rode was the supreme indignity. Many there could scarcely believe they'd heard the Southerner ask, and Honey Wiggin articulated the attitude of them all when he answered crustily, "What the hell is this? Yu' know damn well there ain't a one of us who ain't square."

Heads bobbed in vigorous assent.

"Hell," added Dollar Bill. "Every hand here measures a full sixteen hands high in my opinion. And I can't believe yu' don't feel the same."

Once again the heads dipped.

"Relax, yu' yacks," the Virginian said in his most pronounced drawl. "I never doubted one o' yu' for a minute. But I have to ask 'cause we're headin' for a shootin' scrape, and I don't want yu' to think yu' have to stay if yu' ain't ready to die for the big sugar."

"Is it more Injuns?" inquired the Toothpick Kid.

"No."

"Rustlers, then?" asked another hand.

"Could be, but I figure they'll try stampedin' the cattle even if they ain't."

"I get the feelin' you're holding back, which isn't like yu'," commented Dixon. "Come clean."

So the Virginian told them about the tracks Lin and he had seen, and about being spied on. He told them all he knew, but he kept his suspicions involving Balaam to himself. When he was done, silence prevailed as the cowboys shared glances.

"I ain't much on tongue oil," Chalkeye spoke at length, "but I've been ridin' for Judge Henry so long, I've plumb forgot what it's like to ride for anyone else. Sunk Creek is my home, and any cows o' his I just naturally see as bein' part mine. If a bunch of brand blotters have set their sights on our herd, I say let's give 'em hell. Maybe some of us will come down with a case o' slow and cash in, but that's life. Besides, I'd rather go out fightin' than turn tail any day."

Robust yells of agreement burst from a dozen lips.

"I'm with you," declared Honey Wiggin. "The Judge has treated us decent from who laid the chunk. He deserves the best we got to give, and if that means our lives, so be it."

The Virginian regarded his men with evident paternal affection. "I expected as much," he said, his voice husky with emotion. "I've always known this was the best outfit in Wyoming. But I don't want none o' yu' takin' chances yu' don't need to. From now on no man rides alone. When yu' ride herd, ride double. When yu' go off into the bushes, go with someone else. And never go anywhere without your artillery."

"If we ride double, boss, that means we lose some sleep," said Limber Jim.

"Would yu' rather lose sleep or your life?" the Virginian retorted, and walked off to be by himself. As partner in Sunk Creek, they were his men, too. More than that, they were his friends. He liked every last one, even the newer hands, and they had all earned his respect by their sterling behavior on the drive. His tender soul was disturbed at the prospect of losing some of them, and he racked his brain for a way to avoid the impending confrontation. But there was none.

Footsteps sounded to his rear. "Yu' hoggin' all the fresh air to yourself?" Scipio le Moyne wondered.

"I should think there'd be plenty by the fire," the Virginian answered, shifting.

"I fed 'em beans tonight, remember?" Scipio gazed at the multitude of sparkling stars that dotted the heavens. "Makes a man feel right small sometimes, doesn't it?"

"You're not fixin' to share some more o' your sagebrush philosophy again, are yu'?" the Virginian inquired with a grin.

"Just this. You're doing what yu' have to. Sometimes it's better to pull freight than hardware, but this isn't one o' them."

"I'll put that on the tombstones o' those who die."

"They're growed men. They know what they're gettin' into, and they'll take their lumps without complaint. Feel sorrier for the bastards fixin' to jump us. No one in the wrong can stand up to someone in the right when all else is equal."

"I hope so, pard. I truly hope so."

11

Nightmare

The next day was quiet in one respect, but eventful in another. Nature threw an afternoon tantrum in the form of a fierce hailstorm, with some of the hail the size of grouse eggs. There was nowhere to take shelter, nothing for the cowboys to do but bundle into their slickers, pull down their Stetsons or whatever type of hats they were wearing, and pray for the best.

The hail began slowly at first, a few small stones coming down here and there. As the herd advanced, the clouds darkened, the wind shrieked with increasingly shrill intensity, and the size of the hail likewise grew. Some of the cows bawled protests, while several of the hands had to contend with skittish mounts. The wrangler had his hands full with the remuda and barely prevented two of the horses from bolting.

Then the storm attained the peak of its elemental fury. Large hailstones crashed down thick and fast, battering beasts and men alike. The cattle and horses were pelted mercilessly. Some lost patches of hide. Dazed and blinded

112

by the deluge, the cows began to drift to the west and would have strayed farther had not the Virginian hastily gathered half of the punchers and drifted the cattle back in the right direction.

There were only three losses. Despite the wrangler's best efforts, three of the horses fled in panic at the height of the vicious downpour and were never seen again.

That night the exhausted cowboys crawled under their tarpaulins early except for the night guards, who lulled the nervous cows to sleep with their off-key but nonetheless soothing singing.

The Virginian was still bruised and sore the next morning, but no one would have guessed it from the hectic pace he set for himself. Lin never left his side for a moment now, and the pair of them ranged far afield in their search for sign of their enemies. Shortly before noon the herd reached the series of hills the Southerner had alluded to previously and wound among them.

"Where the blazes are the varmints?" Lin asked as they sat watching the cows pass below their vantage point, the top of one of the highest hills.

"Hyeh somewhere," the Virginian said. "I can feel it."

"Tonight, yu' reckon?"

"Tonight."

The herd passed through the barren hills before nightfall and were bedded down in a great circle with six men riding guard. Scipio made a fine meal of eggs and overland trout, as the punchers commonly called bacon, but even full bellies did little to relieve the crackling cloud of tension that seemed to hover ominously over the outfit. The men spoke quietly when they spoke at all. And once, when Scipio dropped a pot onto a rock, five of them leaped up with their six-shooters in their hands.

Of them all the Virginian felt the tremendous strain the most, yet showed it the least. After eating he was immediately back in the saddle, but not on Monte. His night horse was a fine sorrel someone at one time had named Chestnut.

With Lin at his heels, the Virginian made a complete

circuit of the herd, offering words of encouragement to the hands who looked as if they needed it. Often he thought of Molly, so many miles distant, and of the precious new life she carried in her womb. Would he see her again? he mused, and shuddered to think he wouldn't.

Since every cowboy worthy of the name knew how to tell exact time by the varying positions of the stars and constellations, the Virginian knew it was just minutes shy of midnight when he approached the southern perimeter of the herd. Most of the cows were down, either resting or chewing their cuds. He sang softly, one of his favorite songs:

"As I was a-walkin' one mornin' for pleasure,
I spied a young cowpuncher ridin' alone,
His hat was throwed back and his spurs was a jinglin',
As he approached me a-singin' this song.

Whoop-ee ti yi yo, git along little dogies,
It's your misfortune and none of my own,
Whoop-ee ti yi yo, git along little dogies.
 [Here the Virginian modified the traditional last line.]
For yu' know Montana will be your new home."

The Southerner spied a pair of hands approaching whom he identified as the Toothpick Kid and Dollar Bill. The Kid had his head back and was warbling his utmost:

"Oh, I'm a Texas cowboy,
Far away from home,
If I ever get back to Texas
I never more will roam—"

Lin McLean chuckled. "I swear that ranny always sings with his tail up."

The Virginian raised a slow hand in salute as he drew abreast of the two punchers. Both of them merely nodded. No one made any quick gestures or undue noise, because to a man they were dreadfully aware of how easily a herd could be spooked once it was out on the trail. A shout might do it, or the nearby yip of a coyote, or a frightened jackrabbit bounding through the grass. Even a louder than normal whinny would set them off.

Chestnut suddenly snapped his head high and sniffed, his ears pricked to catch the slightest of sounds.

"Get along, hawss," the Virginian coaxed. The wind was blowing from the northwest, so he surmised the sorrel had detected the scent of the horses in the remuda. "I don't want yu' actin' up 'cause of some mare that's caught your attention. If I have to go without, so do yu'."

"You're missin' your dulce too?" Lin asked wistfully. "I can't keep Jessamine out of my mind." He leaned toward his companion. "Don't tell no one, but sometimes when I'm lyin' in my bed at night, I swear I can feel her lyin' right beside me even though she ain't even there."

"Is that all?" the Virginian responded. "I've got it so bad, I can smell Molly's perfume when I—" He froze as a pistol cracked twice to the north. Seconds later, faint on the wind, came the universal distress cry of trail drivers everywhere, a cry that signified the very worst of emergencies.

"All hands and the cook!"

"No!" Lin exclaimed.

In a twinkling the cattle had risen to their feet, every last steer, heifer, and calf, and lurched into a full run, sweeping in a tight boiling mass to the south, toward the hills, straight at the Southerner and McLean.

"Ride, Lin!" the Virginian shouted, and heeded his own advice by roughly wheeling Chestnut and jabbing his spurs, hard, into the sorrel's flanks. Chestnut took off as if shot from a gun, yet they almost went down under the leading rows of frenzied cows. Somehow the sorrel, neighing wildly, avoided the sharp horns and gained a few yards in the initial few seconds. A second later the Virginian was in the open and racing for his life.

Rumbling in the Southerner's wake was the entire onrushing herd. To the right and the left extended the ragged line of panic-stricken brutes; he was close to the middle, without any hope of getting beyond the leading ranks to safety. The ground trembled as if from an earthquake, while the air itself vibrated to the beat of invisible drums.

Strangely enough, the cattle themselves made no noise whatsoever. When stampeding, cows are always silent, whether from fear or shock, no one knows. If not for the hammering of thousands of rock-hard hooves, it would be impossible to tell that a stampede was taking place.

The Virginian glanced to his left but saw no trace of his friend. If Lin had gone down, then he was dead, and there was nothing he could do to change what had happened. Of immediate importance was saving his own skin; a single mistake now, no matter how slight, would cost him his life. His sole hope lay in outdistancing the herd, or, failing that, to keep on fleeing until exhaustion made the cows stop.

His body hunched low over the sorrel, the Virginian rode as he had never ridden before. Vaguely, he heard shouts and gunshots. Was it his men trying to turn the herd? Or were the Sunk Creek hands being gunned down by their mysterious attackers? Such considerations would have to wait.

The Virginian saw a lone bush barring his path and skirted it on the fly to prevent Chestnut from becoming entangled and going down. Glancing back, he saw the herd had gained a few feet. For as far as he could see flowed a roiling torrent of horns and tails, a great writhing swarm that would trample to bits anything and everything in its path. His right hand pumped, lashing the sorrel, and he wasted breath by shouting, "Faster, yu' cussed hawss!" because it was impossible to be heard above the tremendous din of the stampede.

On and on the Virginian rode, nearer and nearer the upthrust hills, and the cows began to lose some ground at last. When next he looked, the sorrel was ten yards in front but still not far enough to risk veering to either side in the hope of swinging around the thundering flood.

More gunshots punctuated the unceasing clamor of the hooves. Men were shouting, cursing, screaming.

The Virginian was soon close enough to see the first

hill clearly, and he angled toward its base. Here was a shred of hope if the herd did as he expected. In a twinkling he was in the narrow space between the hills, and twisted to behold the leading rows of cows all trying to plunge into the gap at once. Instantly they were jammed up, with many of those in front unable to squeeze through and those behind, unaware of the bottleneck, surging forward. As a consequence, some of the leaders caught in the jam were plowed under, and for half a minute there was rampant confusion as the cows tried frantically to sort themselves out. Like a huge wave crashing against a sandy shore, they crested and spread out to the right and left, going partway up the adjacent hills.

By then the Virginian was fifty yards ahead and not slackening his speed a hair. He had a plan to stop the stampede, but to accomplish the deed, he would have to reach the opposite end of the hills well before the cattle did. Chestnut ran well, almost as well as Monte, and was as surefooted as a mountain goat in the dark. Which explained why the Virginian preferred the sorrel for night work.

The bedlam fell behind the Southerner, and for the first time in minutes he could hear himself think. Again he dwelled on Lin and prayed his friend was alive. A second later a turn loomed, reminding him he wasn't out of the woods yet, and he bore to the left. Reaching a straight stretch, he poured on the speed. Not until he came out onto the prairie beyond the hills did he rein up to give the sorrel a short breather.

In the distance ominous thunder seemed to rumble, although the cool night sky was crystal clear.

How much time did he have? the Virginian speculated, goading the sorrel up the closest hill on the right. A minute? Two? Time was of critical importance now, because his span on earth would be measured in seconds rather than years if his brainstorm backfired. "Yu' danged cow prod," he softly admonished himself. "This is what yu' get for chasin' cows for a livin'."

Louder grew the rumbling. Nearer drifted the thunder.

"I reckon every man has a time or two," the Virginian

continued, more to soothe his quaking nerves than anything else. "I figured my last was Trampas, but hyeh I am again."

Chestnut snorted and pranced as the ground underneath them shook.

"Calm your hide!" the Virginian said harshly. He dared not let the sorrel misbehave, not when the next few moments were so crucial. To the north rose the crackling of brush being reduced to tinder. Licking his lips, he drew the Colt and transferred the six-shooter to his left hand. "I wish—" he began, but was unable to complete his statement before the foremost line of flowing cows materialized in the night, a shorter line now that the herd was confined to the notch between the hills.

"They ain't slowed one tiny bit," the Virginian whispered, almost in awe, as he lifted the reins. His eagle eyes were on the leaders, and the moment the herd reached a point almost directly below his position, he spurred the sorrel downward at an angle, slanting his descent so that he reached the flatland at the same time the cows did, just to the right of the leading edge.

Every cowboy lived under the constant threat of stampede. Whether on cattle drives or otherwise, cows were notoriously fickle, and a puncher never knew when he might be called on by sheer circumstance to head off their headlong rush. Many a hand had died in the attempt. Over the years, though, a few tried-and-true methods had been developed to deal with stampedes, and one of them, perhaps the riskiest of all, involved the very tactic the Southerner was planning to use.

The Virginian was going to strive to turn the leaders in toward the center, which, if he succeeded, should cause the entire herd to swing in a gigantic loop, in upon itself. Once it did so, the cattle would slow and mill and be easy to bring under control.

The hard part was the turning. The Virginian must get close enough to force the cows to the left, but not so close that the sorrel was caught by a flying hoof or slashing horn and sent crashing. He had to ride by feel alone, relying totally on his legs and arms to guide

Chestnut, since he couldn't take his eyes from the cattle for a moment.

It was an eerie feeling, being all alone next to the vast herd, a solitary human caught up in an explosion of elemental animal energy, and as few experiences could, it made the Virginian realize his mortal frailty. He stood at Death's door, with one foot poised over the threshold. He must not falter.

His mouth dry, his palms slick as he edged the sorrel closer, the Virginian reduced the gap until his dangling leg was a foot from the foremost steer. This was the supreme moment of truth. He saw the animal's eye on him and knew it might lunge at any time, but he held a steady course, lowered his left arm, and banged off two swift shots inches from the steer's ear.

For all of three seconds nothing happened. Then the nearest cows started swinging to the left, forcing those on the inside to do the same. All along the line the movement was contagious, and the front ranks banked eastward.

The Virginian fired again as added incentive. More and more cows were being pressed in the direction he wanted. If he could keep them going for another fifteen or twenty seconds, they'd be unable to reverse direction. He would have stopped them before they fled on into the night and scattered to the four winds.

Suddenly a dozen or so head farther along the leading row swelled out from the main body, like a small wave breaking off from the crest of a flash flood. They were seeking to buck the flow and resume their original heading. Should they go unchecked, they might ruin everything.

So swift were the Southerner's reflexes that even as his penetrating gaze registered the danger, he was increasing his speed to cut them off. His mount came perilously close to a score of horns. Then he was even with the rebels and fired twice more into the ground in front of them. They swerved in fright, straight back into the body of the herd, and were carried along by the irresistible crush of their fellows.

But the Virginian's work was not yet done. He must

stick with the cows to ensure they turned in on themselves as he wanted, heedless of the extreme risk. At any second his horse might stumble and throw him or break a leg; at any second he might be pitched headlong into the cattle and wind up as another gory casualty in a rambunctious profession that boasted of its casualties as some men did of their sexual prowess. The easy thing to do, the safe thing to do, would have been to hold back and let the cows run unmolested. Yet doing the easy thing wasn't in his nature. No matter how hard the choice, the Southerner always did what was expected of him. Not what was expected of him by others—he always did that which he expected of himself.

Now, as the Virginian saw the cows were indeed turning inward, he finally slowed and stayed shy of the still volatile drove but close enough to thwart any malcontents that might make a break for the open range. Gradually the cattle slowed. Gradually the resonant drumming of their hooves tapered off, becoming ever lower until they were making the normal plodding and shuffling noises of herds everywhere.

The Virginian drew rein. His exhausted sorrel hung its head and wheezed. "Yu' did all right for not bein' my Monte, hawss," he said, which was the highest compliment he could give any mount, since Monte and he went back a long ways together and Monte had on several occasions saved his life. Patting Chestnut's sweaty neck, he warily watched the herd for any sign of troublemakers.

Now that the stampede was over, a few cows and calves began bawling, but by and large most were too tired to do more than stand stock-still with their horns drooping or sink in abject fatigue to the ground. They would be going nowhere until morning.

Belatedly, the Virginian realized he had not holstered his Colt. He opened the hinge, took out the five blackened, empty cartridges, and replaced them with new ones from his cartridge belt. Unconsciously, he twirled the Colt into its scabbard with a flourish born of long practice, then caught himself and stared at his right hand in reproach.

"Traitor. How many times must I remind yu' not to do that anymore? I got to quit this playactin' with guns before someone besides Brazos suspects the truth."

Just then, from out of the gap in the hills, poured a dozen excited riders. In a loose group they started across the prairie, but a yell from the man in the lead brought them all to a standstill. At a gesture from him they rode to where the Virginian sat, and had there been an artist present, the gamut of disbelief from mild surprise to outright astonishment could have been accurately sketched and recorded for posterity.

"By yourself!" Lin McLean declared. "Yu' did it all by yourself!"

"Chestnut did most of the work," the Southerner responded cheerfully, for he had good reason to be happy. His men and the herd were both safe. And Lin had survived unharmed.

There was laughter mingled with kind smiles. These were cowboys, and they knew better than to believe the Virginian's humble assertion.

"I've seen three men stop a stampede before," Honey Wiggin commented, "but never one. How in tarnation did yu' do it?"

"Well, I'll tell yu', boys," the Virginian said casually, the corner of his mouth curved like a half-moon, "yu' all know I've never been much of a prayin' man. None of us are, I reckon, since we ain't hardly what a sane man would brand a Christian outfit. But I'm hyeh to tell yu', that from the time the stampede began until these beeves figured it was time for their nap, I did more prayin' than the whole bunch o' yu' have done since the day yu' first set foot in this old world. The bishop o' Wyoming would be right proud of me."

"What are yu' sayin'?" demanded Limber Jim. "Are yu' tryin' to make out that the Almighty Himself had a hand in it?"

"Yu' got a better explanation?"

"If He did, His blessings were heaped in different-sized portions," commented Honey Wiggin sourly.

"What do yu' mean?" the Southerner asked, his elevated spirits crashing like a ten-ton boulder.

"One of us bit the dust," Lin declared solemnly. "Those damned cows put windows in his skull!"

"Who?" the Virginian asked, and bleached white when they told him. Lifting the reins, he issued rapid instructions, picking six men to remain with the herd while the rest returned to the wagons. In the morning, according to his directions, the cattle would be driven through the hills again and the journey resumed.

The casualty had been laid out under a blanket beside the bed-wagon. Gathered around were the remaining punchers, their normally straight shoulders slumped, each man speaking in hushed tones.

Dismounting, the Virginian let the reins drop and sank to one knee beside the blanket. His fingers were gripping the edge when a hand fell gently on his shoulder.

"Yu' don't want to," advised Scipio.

"I'm trail boss, ain't I?" the Southerner retorted, and his jaw muscles twitched. "I'm the partner," he added quietly, and gave the blanket a sharp yank. Despite himself, he recoiled. He—who had seen more death than most, more than anyone else in Wyoming realized, except Brazos. He'd seen bodies shot so full of lead they resembled sieves. He'd seen buckshot blast a man's chest to ribbons. He'd seen men hanged, men stabbed. But none compared to this.

The Toothpick Kid would never set a boot on Texas soil again. He had been literally crushed to a pulp. Every major bone in his body had been broken, his ribs staved in. His face had been pulverized beyond recognition, and his features transposed so that one of his eyes now hung on a shred of flesh where his mouth should be and his nose had swung around to take the place of a missing ear.

"Lord!" the Virginian breathed, flipping the blanket down. An involuntary shudder racked him, and he pressed a palm to his damp brow. "Two failures now," he whispered to himself.

But someone overheard. "Like hell. Don't be talkin'

foolishness," Scipio said. "It's not like yu' to take personal what yu' can't control."

"I should've tried to trail that varmint who was spyin' on us back to his camp, like Lin wanted."

"What would the two of yu' have done against a whole passel of badmen?" Scipio argued. "Even if yu' had scared 'em off, they would've come back. And they wouldn't've bothered stampedin' the cattle, neither. They would've swept in here with their six-shooters blazin' and given most of us lead poisonin'."

"I should have done something."

"Yu' did what yu' had to." Scipio spat into the dust. "Don't disappoint me like this. I never took yu' for one of those who admires their good judgment through a magnifying glass. I've always thought yu' were the real article."

This time it was the Virginian's turn to take the rebuke in stride. He glanced up, nodded, and stood. "I reckon I am actin' a mite pussy-kitten of late."

"The whole litter's worth," judged Scipio in disgust.

But the very next day the Virginian redeemed himself in the eyes of his friend. The cows were bunched nearby with three hands on guard; all the rest of the Sunk Creek outfit had assembled for the funeral. A shallow hole had been excavated in the hard ground, the mortal remains of the Toothpick Kid had been placed within, and dirt and rocks had been piled high on top. Then everyone stood around looking at everyone else, each waiting for the other to say a few words. They had no idea what the words should be, but they were certain *something* should be said.

"I ain't much at this buryin' business," Chalkeye said, "but I was at one once where we sung a song for the dearly departed."

"That was for a woman," someone reminded him.

"So?"

"The Kid would want it short and sweet," opined another.

"And there ain't one of us who don't sing off-key," chimed a companion.

The Virginian stepped forward then. Bending down, he picked up a handful of dirt and slowly sprinkled it on the new mound. His next words were to be recounted around campfires for years to come, whenever the story of the Sunk Creek stampede was told: "Yu' need a yardstick of gold to take the measure of some."

12

Where Fancy was Confirmed

Molly was taking her afternoon exercise, strolling leisurely along the bank of the bubbling stream with her great canine protectors in tow, when the drum of hooves rolled off across the green valley, and she spun to see the black-haired figure of her dreams galloping to intercept her. Arms out, she ran toward Monte, and could scarcely credit her senses when the Virginian vaulted down in a swirl of dust and hugged her to his broad chest. Her heart fluttered, and her lips found his.

When at length the embrace was broken, Molly gazed lovingly into his deep eyes and sighed contentedly. "I wasn't expecting you back for one or two weeks yet."

"I hurried 'em some."

"For me?"

"For me. My clothes need washing."

Molly laughed at his artful thrust and hugged him again. "Sometimes I can't stand it when you go away for long spells. You'll think this childish of me, but I'm perfectly miserable when you're not here."

"You're right," said her sweetheart, his drawl absent. "It is childish." He inhaled the scent of her hair and quivered. "But go on being childish just as long as you care to."

Something in the Virginian's posture caused Molly to draw back and scrutinize his sculpted features. "Was there trouble on the drive?"

"A heap of difficulties," the Southerner disclosed. "We had a stampede. Lost nine cows." His mouth became a mere slit. "And the Toothpick Kid."

"No!"

"Later we found the next water hole had been poisoned. Forced us to go pretty near thirty more miles with thirsty cattle on our hands. Almost had another stampede."

"What poisoned the water?" Molly asked innocently. She had, after all, been married to a cowboy long enough to know there were various natural sources that might contaminate a drinking supply. But the look in his eyes altered her a fraction before his answer.

"It was deliberate."

"Why? Who would do such a thing?"

The Virginian took her slender, pale hands in his great brawny ones and led her to a nearby log. Seating her, he stepped to one side and opened his mouth to deliver the speech he had so carefully prepared over the course of hundreds of miles, but just at that moment Old Hickory and Lavender had to take their turn at greeting him. When they were satisfied and had gone off on the trail of a rabbit, he looked at his wife again, then hesitated. His troubled mind was overwhelmed by the exquisite picture of utter beauty she presented seated there on the log, her luxurious hair shining in the sunlight, her red lips offhandedly parted, her blue dress like a shimmering pool of water against the backdrop of grass and trees.

When two people are truly in love, each is sensitive to the moods and mannerisms of the one they cherish. Molly was no exception in this regard, and she prompted, "What is it?"

"I don't know how to tell you," the Virginian confessed.

"You've always found a way before," Molly said. Her fingers dug into the log as her intuition blared that something must be frightfully, frightfully wrong.

"This is different," the Virginian said, pushing his hat back on his head. He idly slapped dust off his shirt, stalling while he organized his thoughts. The worst of it was that he had made up his mind to tell her about both the past and the present just as soon as he got back, before his nerve could fail him, and now he couldn't decide which to do first. Since the immediate danger involved her directly, he tentatively began his foray thusly: "I hate to sadden you."

"That's nice to know," Molly said evenly, exercising a masterly grip on her heartstrings. For, to tell the truth, she feared what he might say next as she had feared little in her entire plucky life. This was her golden knight, the man who had claimed her soul, and twice now he had pricked that soul with his six-shooting lance and hurt her to the depths of her being. She couldn't bear the thought of being pricked again, so she hastily constructed an emotional wall around her innermost core and girded herself to greet the worst.

"I hated to do it that time with Trampas," the Virginian went on in a rush, "but you could plainly see how I had no choice, and if I'd backed down, I would have had to leave the country because no man would have looked me in the eye after that. I had it to do."

"Eventually I understood," Molly offered when he paused.

"But did you ever accept it?" asked her knight. "I figured you did until Killebrew had to go and try to prove how bad a man he was, and all he did was learn that the only fitting place on this green earth for hombres like him is boot-hill." He removed his hat and ran a hand through his tousled shock of ink-black hair. "But then, boot-hill is full of hard cases who came down with a bad case of slow at the wrong time."

"They were human beings."

"Were they? Are we all human beings, then, those who are God-fearing and those who kill for the sheer thrill of killing? Those who try to do the right thing by marrying and raising younguns and building up, and those who go around stealing and maiming and doing as they darn well please?"

"We're all human beings," Molly insisted, and added a broadside. "Ask the bishop of Wyoming. He's a wise, honorable man, as you never tire of telling me, and he would totally agree."

"Maybe," the Virginian hedged. "At least he'd agree we're all the Lord's children. But even in the Good Book there are good and bad children, those who go about doing the Lord's will and those who'd rather pass the time slaughtering everyone in sight."

"You would remember those parts," Molly joked, and saw that she had accidentally scored again.

"I'll admit that when I was younger and listening to those preachers trying to convert me, the stories I mostly remembered were those about the battles and wars. But I'm afeared you're missing my point on purpose." The Virginian turned his pained countenance to the distant mountains. When he spoke next, his drawl was back with a vengeance. "Cert'nly you're entitled to reckon the way yu' do. Yu' say we're all human. The bishop says all men are our brothers and we're supposed to treat 'em like regular kin. Which would work out just fine if everybody lived by the same proposition. But they don't, do they? Those who live like the bishop are precious few."

"So are those who live like Trampas and Killebrew."

"True," the Virginian conceded. "But there are still *some*, and so long as there are, there ain't one of us safe walkin' down the street." Sighing, he sat down beside her but averted his gaze. "I ain't makin' excuses for what I did. All I'm tryin' to make yu' see is that sometimes yu' run up against polecats like Trampas and Killebrew and yu' have to make a stand."

Molly thought about the death of the Toothpick Kid and the poisoned water hole, and suddenly she saw through him as if he were made of clear glass. "You're trying to tell me, in your lovable, bumbling way, that it might happen again? That you might have to draw your steel on another man?"

"Yes," the Virginian exploded in anguished relief. His hand found hers and clamped tight. "But the last thing in the world I would ever want to do is sadden you again."

"So you're forewarning me this time," Molly said, and at his happy nod, pursed her lips. "You're being completely honest with me, so it's fair I be the same with you. Jessamine and I have been talking while you've been gone. She's not at all like me, you know." She laughed softly. "There I was, given a strict upbringing among those who style themselves the upper class in Vermont, and there she was catching frogs with her brother and cousins down in Kentucky. Sometimes I envy her."

"How so?"

"Jessamine is so at ease around men, more so than I can ever be except for when I'm with you." Molly shook her head in wonder, and her hair swished. "She's a perfect lady, yet she mingles with the hands as if born to the range. She can ride and rope and shoot—"

"So can yu'."

"But not as skillfully as she can, and we both know it." Molly added her free hand to the collection on the log. "No, we're very different, yet a lot alike. We both love our men, and there isn't a thing we wouldn't do for them."

The Virginian faced her at last and received a bold kiss on the lips as his reward. "Goodness gracious. I must be dreamin'. I surely didn't expect it to go this well."

"Thank Jessamine. As I was saying, we had many

conversations, the two of us, and she told me more about her upbringing. I learned about the feuds that go on in her part of the country, and how sometimes entire families, clans they call them, will be wiped out in the course of years as two clans fight back and forth."

"I know the custom," the Virginian said, and had he not developed an inordinate interest in the tip of his boot, she might have detected that he knew it very well indeed.

"So she's more accustomed to this sort of thing than I am," Molly said. "And she had a pertinent point that made me think long and hard about Trampas and the others."

Here the Virginian waited with bated breath.

"When Lin shot Balaam's man a while back, she didn't fuss and cry like I did that time in Medicine Bow. She didn't upbraid him for being a callous murderer, or tell him he was a hopeless sinner doomed to perdition. No, she held him close to her that night and told him that she loved him and always would. She reminded him that she believed in him, thoroughly, and if she didn't, she wouldn't have married him." Molly paused, her eyes on her man. "When you believe in someone, you have faith in them. That means no matter what they do, you know they did it because they thought it was right to do. And if your love is as real as you claim it is, you accept their judgment and go on with your lives together."

"So yu've accepted what I had to do?"

"Yes," Molly answered, but continued quickly. "Don't get the wrong idea, though. I still think we're all human beings and deserve the benefit of the doubt. But I promise to never, ever fall apart again if you have another"—she smirked—"cartridge affair."

Her knight jammed his hat back on his head at a rakish angle and gaped at her, bewildered. "Jessamine brought all this about, yu' say?"

"She started the train of thought, yes," Molly said. "Why do you ask?"

"Oh," the Virginian said, staring off toward the

house. "I was just wonderin' if Lin would ever want to swap wives."

A squeal of mock outrage burst from Molly's lips. Then she threw herself laughing into his arms again. The intimacies they shared over the next hour were for their eyes alone, and in due course, linked arm in arm, they headed homeward, the Southerner leading Monte.

"I don't like to spoil the day, but there's more I have to say before we get back."

Molly tilted her neck so she could see his face clearly. "I thought there might be."

"What do yu' think o' Balaam?"

The query caught Molly off guard, and she reflected a moment before replying honestly, "I don't much care for any man who makes a habit out of beating horses. He deserves to be soundly thrashed one day so he'll know how it feels."

"He's already been thrashed."

"By whom?"

"Me," the Virginian said, and detailed that fatal encounter so many months past and its subsequent outcome on the Bow Leg trail.

Molly stopped in her tracks at one point and clutched his arm tight in her anger. "You never told me this story! He deserted you? Left you for dead when he knew the Indians might have ambushed you? How perfectly typical of the man!"

"Yu' shouldn't be so hard on him," the Virginian said, but his grin was artificial. "If not for his leavin' me, yu' never would have come along later and found me bein' dragged off by the Grim Reaper. And then yu' never would have got to nurse me back to health." His fingers traced the outline of her chin. "If not for that, we might never have tied hearts. Don't yu' remember?"

"I will never, ever forget," Molly assured him. "But it still doesn't excuse Balaam's despicable behavior. Why didn't you tell someone?"

"A boy can be a crybaby when he's small, and no one will think too poorly of him 'cause he's still young, but it doesn't do for a grown man to whine or fret or complain. Not if he has any pride in himself."

"You should at least have told Judge Henry. You were on ranch business when Balaam showed his treacherous nature."

"But the doings were still between Balaam and me," the Virginian reminded her. "And there will come a time when he answers to me for what he did, and a whole lot more besides."

Insight struck Molly like a bolt of lightning out of the blue. "The Toothpick Kid!" she abruptly exclaimed. "You believe Balaam is responsible."

"Indirectly. And for the poisonin' too, and a whole lot more I can't credit to his account for lack of proof. But I know he's the one behind most of the problems we've been havin'."

"He's—" Molly started, but had to stop when her mouth went dry. She licked her lips and tried again. "This is why you brought up the gunfights? You fear matters will reach such a head with Balaam that you might have to kill him?"

"Or he'll kill me," the Virginian said carelessly, and keenly regretted his indiscretion when she trembled and her hand went cold in his grasp. "Pshaw! Don't go to puttin' the cart before the hawss. I've been tryin' mighty hard to walk the straight and narrow, and I won't prod Balaam hard unless he does the same to me first. Which ain't his way. He likes to stay in the shadows and let leather slappers smoke up the countryside for him."

"All this over the quarrel the two of you had?"

"I suspect there's a lot more to it, but I don't have the particulars yet."

"Who knows besides us?"

"I told Lin, so by now Jessamine knows, too."

"You display a lot of confidence in your friends," Molly said blithely.

"I know married men, bein' one myself," the Virginian retorted, and grew grave again. "Judge Henry knows about everything except the fight. Scipio knows a little and suspects a lot. And the Professor learned some on his last visit."

"I think you should sit down with the Judge and tell him everything you've told me. Balaam might strike again soon. The two of you need to be ready."

"We will, or as ready as we can be not knowin' where or when the polecat will cause trouble next. He must be mighty frustrated by now. Everything he's tried has been a busted cinch. First his men didn't get the Professor like he wanted, then some of 'em went up against Lin and lost, then they tried to get Dapper and had to back down. Now the stampede's failed, even if it did cost us turrible, and taintin' the water didn't work out, neither. No two ways about it. Balaam has eaten a heap of drag dust."

The buildings and corral came into view. Beside the latter stood Lin McLean, his arm draped over the shoulders of a tall woman whose broad, wholesome face reflected the stamp of a rustic background. They were watching the antics of two boys with that idyllic contentment only parents can have for their own offspring. The older of the boys, by ten years or more, was balancing on the top rail, imitating the feats of a circus high-wire performer. On the ground, cheering lustily, was a toddler who could scarce walk without wobbling as if drunk on the milk of life.

"If yu' keep on populatin' the landscape like this, Lin," observed the Virginian as he approached with the love of his life decorously walking at arm's length, "the legislature might have to divide the state in two."

"Seein' as how Billy is adopted," the unflappable McLean shot back, "I'd say we're tied, or will be in a few months."

"Uncle Jefferson!" screeched the high-wire artist. He jumped to the ground and dashed over to give the Southerner an affectionate hug. "Pa says you stopped a whole stampede all by yourself! Wish I'd seen it!"

Molly's eyebrows tried to touch her hairline. "You did?"

"I'll tell yu' later," the Virginian promised. Gripping

Billy under the arms, he whirled the boy in circles, spinning on his boot heels, going faster and faster until they both collapsed in laughter, at which point the toddler staggered over and plopped unceremoniously into the Virginian's lap.

"Children sure do think the world of you," Jessamine McLean commented. "Look at Billy and Nate. They take to you like ducks to water. Maybe you should have been the teacher instead of Molly."

"Goodness gracious, no!" the Virginian said. "I wouldn't have the patience. And the first time I turned one over my knee, I'd be set on by a mother brandishin' a pitchfork or a rollin' pin." He shook his head. "No, ma'am. If I'm goin' to tangle with someone on the warpath, I'd rather it was the real article. At least I'd still have my dignity, if not my hair."

Out the back door came Dapper and Mabel Martin. He held her traveling bag in his left hand; she was wearing her bonnet.

"What's this, then?" Molly asked. "You're not leaving us so soon? I wanted to have a special supper tonight to welcome our men back."

"That's kind of yu'. And I thank yu' for all yu've done," Mabel said, "but I really would like to move back into town and start up my laundry business again. I was makin' good money there for a while, until that Brazos affair."

The Virginian set Nate on the grass and uncoiled to his full height. "I wouldn't be in such a rush, ma'am. Brazos is still around. If yu' go into Medicine Bow, he'll find out you're back and pay yu' another visit. You're safer here at Aspen Creek."

"But it's your home, not ours," Mabel persisted. "We want one of our own someday. It might not be as grand as this, but it will be ours and no one else's." She clasped her hands and nervously rubbed her palms. "It's not like I want to leave. Molly and Jessamine are two o' the finest ladies it's been my privilege to know, and these past months have been some o' the happiest I've ever had."

She drew herself up straighter. "It's just time for me to be on my way. We have our own lives to live."

Molly went over and took Mabel's hands in hers. "If you insist, then we won't make the parting worse by arguing. But at least say you'll stay until morning. One last meal. Then we'll sit in the front room and listen to the men boast of their exploits."

Mabel glanced at Dapper, who smiled and nodded. "Very well. For you."

So they had their fine meal, and afterward the women insisted on hearing every particular of the cattle drive. When a full account had been rendered, the ladies repaired to the kitchen and the men ambled out onto the front porch and stood in the fading twilight, inhaling the crisp, rare mountain air.

The Virginian pulled his pipe from his shirt pocket, then tapped it a few times. "We are lucky men," he declared, and neither of his friends had to ask what he meant.

Lin stepped to a rocking chair, plunked his lanky frame down, and leaned back so he could stretch his legs out and rest his boots on top of the rail. "I have to get me over to Box Elder soon," he mentioned. "No one has been seein' after my spread, and I'm afeared o' what might have been done while we've been gone."

"I'll tag along," the Virginian offered.

"I don't need no nursemaid."

"Course yu' don't. But Box Elder wouldn't be deserted if yu' hadn't brought your family over to stay with Mary. So I reckon it's only fair I lend yu' a hand if yu' need it."

"Put that way, I accept."

Dapper leaned his shoulder against a post and raised to his nose a cigar the Virginian had given him. He breathed in the tangy aroma, studied the Havana wrapper. Then he gazed out over the tranquil valley bathed in the crimson glow radiating from the western horizon and sighed. "One day I hope to have me a spread like this," he said wistfully.

"What's stoppin' yu'?" Lin asked.

"The sad fact they don't grow on trees."

"Give yourself time," the Virginian said. "You're younger than us. We didn't get ours in a day. It took a mighty lot of scrapin' and plannin' before we dug in our roots."

"Ain't that the truth, pard," Lin agreed. "There were times when I figured I was plumb loco to even think I could own my own place. But I stuck with it, and now look." He wore his pride on his sleeve.

"I'm glad for both o' yu'," Dapper said, "but from what I hear, yu' both had the breaks fall your way."

"A man makes his own breaks," the Virginian stated. "Don't let anyone convince yu' different. I had to work right hard puttin' my savings together, harder than I ever did anything ever before. Yu' can do that too. Yu've already found what you're good at, which is gentlin' hawsses, and which just happens to be what yu' like to do the most. So you're better off than many men."

"I suppose," Dapper said, staring at the rippling surface of the stream. An intense longing was mirrored by his features when he stressed, "And I do so want me a ranch. To be able to walk on land that's mine. To reach down and pick up the dirt and run it through my fingers. To hear the sparrows and know they're roostin' in my trees—" Choked up, he left the sentiment unfinished.

"Every man wants to have a spot o' his own, I reckon," the Virginian drawled. "Whether it's just a run-down shack or a dugout made o' sod, a man has an urge inside o' him to own a piece o' land he can call home." He reached into a pocket for his tobacco. "The Professor told me onced that some old-time philosopher said men and women are different—"

"Bet yu' a smart man like that was from the East," Lin interrupted.

"No, he was one o' them Greeks," the Virginian said.

"Foreigner? Figures. Some folks spend too much time thinkin' about things that don't hardly need a second thought."

"Let me finish," the Virginian urged, and faced Dapper. "They say women have certain instincts men don't have, like the one that makes 'em want to have babies. And that's natural, as it should be, because if they stopped havin' babies, the human race wouldn't be around much longer." He opened the pouch. "Well, I figure men have instincts, too. Different instincts. Instincts that sort o' take up where the instincts of our womenfolk leave off. They get the urge for a baby so they can start a family, and we get the urge to provide a home for our family to live in. So it all works out even in the end."

"Sort o' makes yu' wonder if it wasn't planned that way," Lin said.

No words were spoken as the Virginian put a match to his pipe and puffed. The fragrance filled the porch, mingling with the scent of the pines and the grass.

"The two o' yu' know this country better than me," Dapper remarked. "Yu' happen to know o' land that ain't been claimed yet that's worth a look-see?"

"Yu' might check over to Willow Creek. There's a parcel there on the west side I nearly filed on myself. Only I liked Box Elder a shade better."

"I'll ride there," Dapper said, "just as soon as I get Mabel back to Medicine Bow." He began unwrapping the Havana as a botanist might unfold a delicate leaf.

"Yu' don't need to take her quite that far if yu' don't want to," Lin said.

"Don't I? Yu' heard her. When that woman gets her mind made up, she can be more cussed muley than a mule."

The Virginian winked at McLean. "It sure seems a shame to go all that way when there's a whole bunkhouse full o' grungy punchers at Sunk Creek who would pay dearly to have someone do their laundry. She'd probably make near as much as she would in town."

"Where would we live? In the stable?" Dapper responded, and shook his head. "No, I'm stuck."

"Yu' could live in the foreman's house," the Virginian proposed.

"And how would we work that miracle?"

"Easy. Lin and I move our offices in with the Judge so Mabel and yu' can have the little house all to yourselves."

Dapper chuckled. "Yu' do come up with the grandest schemes. But I doubt Judge Henry would be partial to the idea."

"He's already given his go-ahead."

"What?" Dapper said, nearly dropping the prized Havana.

"Lin and me talked to him right after we got back. Laid things out for him, and explained how we figured it's a turrible crime against nature to make a man ride so far just to see his cow bunny. So he's makin' room for our files in his office and settin' up a pair o' cots for when we sleep over. He won't be put out at all."

"Yu' didn't!" Dapper exclaimed.

"We did," Lin confirmed. "Shucks, you're the only hand in the whole outfit besides the Judge and us who has a long-haired pardner. The rest of them jokers are still in the chasin' stage, wearin' themselves out gallin' every filly who comes down the tracks." He beamed. "Tamed wolves like us have to run in our own pack and look out for one another."

The magnitude of the kindness they had rendered brought dabs of moisture to the corners of Dapper's eyes. He spun, coughed, and removed his hat, pressing his sleeve to his face as he did. "I never expected this. I reckon I'm right obliged," he said huskily.

"Don't thank us yet. Yu' still have to convince Mabel," the Virginian noted.

"She'll jump at the chance."

"She just might jump backward, clear to Medicine Bow, once she sees the mountain of laundry those boys can create in a week," Lin said. "Talk about whiffy! Why, one time we piled it all in a corner to do later, and darn if the whole kit and caboodle didn't up and walk off before we could get to it."

Dapper suddenly excused himself and hurried off the porch into the night.

"Must be the air up here," remarked Lin. "Yu' don't see people takin' sick like this down at Box Elder."

13

The Elk Hunt

The trees were resplendent in their gorgeous change of fall colors when I arrived for our elk hunt. Brilliant splashes of red and orange and yellow painted every slope. It was as if a celestial artist had taken his brush to the noble Rockies and highlighted their majestic contours with practiced strokes that transformed the landscape into an iridescent wonderland. It was one of my favorite times of the year.

I had the Virginian all to myself for a couple of weeks. After spending time both at Sunk Creek and Aspen Creek, we led our two pack animals to the west until we were in the mountains bordering Judge Henry's vast holdings. We had hunted here often and always found abundant game.

The first day was not auspicious. At my insistence the Virginian agreed to try a shortcut between two peaks, which necessitated winding down and across a lowland we had always avoided under his expert guidance. But I was full of myself, intoxicated by the delicious air and the unbounded freedom, a potent combination more heady than the strongest wine. I wanted my way.

So down into the lowland we went, and almost immediately I realized I had chosen a path through some of the worst terrain in all of Wyoming. But in my stubborn frame of mind I refused to admit as much.

In the first place, the lowland was a marsh, as bad a place as you can imagine, cold and damp and muddy from one end to the other. A chipmunk would have been hard-pressed to find a firm spot of ground to stand on. Waist-high grass clung to our legs and entangled the horses. Rotten logs repeatedly blocked our path, forcing us to make frequent detours.

Yet once the lowland was behind us, it turned out the worst still lay ahead. A steep slope was our only means of regaining the trail above, and that slope was so densely forested as to be an almost impassable barrier. Sharp limbs tore at us and scratched our faces as we climbed. Smooth rocks slid out from underfoot, causing us to stumble. The poor horses had the worst of it, as there was barely room for them to squeeze between the trees. Halfway up, my pack animal decided his intelligence was easily the equal of mine, if not of higher quality, so he tore loose from my grasp and ignored my oaths to forge his own path to the top. And damn him if he didn't get there before we did and was docilely waiting when we finally broke from the brush. If horses can laugh, that one busted a gut at my expense.

And the Virginian? His only comment came that evening as we sat sipping our strong black coffee beside the dancing campfire.

"Are yu' fixin' to act as guide again tomorrow, seh?"

I informed him that I would leave that singular honor to him from then on.

"Good," said he. "I was worried yu' might be plannin' to give up your day job to go and scout for the army."

The next day we turned southward, winding among the valleys and foothills in search of elk. To our surprise, we saw none. There was some sign but most of it old.

That night the Virginian expressed an opinion on our failure.

"It's been a right warm fall. Maybe they're way up near the peaks yet."

But the very next day we found one, a large bull. Unfortunately, someone else had gotten to it first. We were coming down off a slope into a lush meadow when gleaming white bones appeared in the grass. The antlers were lying there, too, now partially gnawed by the scavengers, and their presence mystified me. Any white hunter worthy of the name would have taken a rack of such size back to hang over his fireplace or his stable. If Indians had killed the bull, they would have taken the antlers to put them to a variety of uses. "Did a mountain lion do this?" I wondered.

"No," the Virginian said, dismounting. He examined the ground in his skilled way, his furrowed forehead showing he was also puzzled. "They were white. A man and a boy. They butchered the carcass and hauled all the meat and the hide out on an Indian-style travois." He rose and scratched his head. "They were pullin' the travois themselves when they vamoosed."

"They didn't have a horse?" I asked, amazed at this unheard-of development.

"Not unless they had it tied yondeh," the Virginian said, stepping into the stirrups. "Would yu' like to go see?"

I could tell he shared my curiosity, so I answered, "Lead the way."

"Thank yu'."

The tiny furrows made by the ends of the travois were obvious even to my inexperienced eyes. They led us across the meadow, through a patch of woodland beyond, and down a meandering valley. The whole time the man had been hauling the heavily laden travois while the boy walked beside it. We saw their tracks clearly at several spots.

"This gent must be as strong as an ox," the Southerner commented. "He's got hundreds of pounds of meat there."

"How long ago did they pass this way?" I inquired.

"Day before yesterday, I reckon."

"Where could they be going?" I mused aloud. "We're miles from any settlement or ranch."

"Nesters, maybe."

That hadn't occurred to me and I admitted as much. If they were squatters, they had certainly picked a spot far off the beaten path, perhaps deliberately. Some men valued their privacy above all else, rating it a treasure more valuable than Solomon's. I noticed the valley was taking us in the general direction of Judge Henry's boundary and mentioned this to my companion.

"We're a bit north of Sunk Creek," corrected the Virginian. "This here valley comes out above Butte Creek."

Balaam's land. Suddenly the pair of tracks acquired a whole new significance. If a nester had been foolish enough to settle on the outskirts of the Butte Creek ranch, his life and the lives of every member of his family were in dire danger. I voiced these speculations, adding, "Perhaps this fellow doesn't know."

"Then we'd best warn him."

Our path brought us ever lower, always through the open spaces where the man pulling the load would have made better time. Occasionally the boy had helped, but the father had done most of the labor himself. I envisioned someone along the order of the mythical Hercules and hoped he wouldn't be offended when he found out we had followed him.

The pair had spent the previous night by a quaint spring. We found the vestige of their fire and a tidy lean-to they had made to keep out the wind, which elicited a nod of approval from the Virginian.

"This man knows the wilds. Must be a salty pilgrim."

Below the spring the ground leveled off dramatically, and the valley widened out onto the plain Balaam called home. Off to the north was an isolated hummock, and above it curled a column of smoke.

"Our nesters," the Virginian said. Suddenly he drew rein and leaned far over, hooking an elbow on his saddle horn to keep from falling. "What's this?" he exclaimed.

"Five men on horseback cut in behind the man and his boy." Straightening, he cast a somber eye at me. "Some of Balaam's bunch ridin' the line."

"Did they see the nesters?"

"They're smack on the trail."

This ominous turn prompted us to hasten. We came over a rise and both of us stopped in alarm. Then, regaining our composure, we galloped to where the two bodies lay sprawled in attitudes of violent death.

The boy, a youth of thirteen or fourteen, had been shot once in the back of the head. His father, a great husky individual boasting the neck and shoulders of a bull, had taken a slug in the back, then apparently turned to confront his attackers and been shot eight or nine times in the chest and head. The slaughter was atrocious to behold.

We sat there the longest while saying nothing, our souls wrestling with the shock. The Virginian moved first, climbing down and closing the boy's eyes. He glanced once at the travois, which had been ignored by the assassins. A few flies had found the meat and were disporting themselves as flies are wont to do.

"What about that smoke?" I croaked.

It was another two miles to the homestead, nestled among aspens on a picturesque knob. The squatter had picked the site well. A log cabin, as neatly constructed as the lean-to, reflected the care the man had exercised. There was a small corral made of trimmed saplings, and a shed for tools and other articles.

The front door opened as we rode into the yard, and out came a beanpole of a woman in a homespun dress with a little girl in one hand and a big old Walker Colt in the other. She faced us fearlessly and announced, "Howdy, gentlemen. I'm Wilhelmina Proctor. This is my daughter, Arabella. You're welcome to water your horses and rest if you'd like."

Neither of us knew quite how to convey the horrible tidings we bore, so we hesitated.

The women noticed and misconstrued. "My husband, Robert, will be back any minute. He went off a ways with our grown son, Tim, to chop some wood."

"They went elk huntin', ma'am," the Virginian said softly, "and I sorely wish they hadn't."

Wilhelmina lowered that ponderous Colt and intently studied our faces. She was perceptive, this hardy settler. A low groan escaped her lips and she clutched the girl to her. "No! It can't be!"

"I'm afraid so," the Virginian went on in his kindly vein. He glanced meaningfully at the child. "Do yu' want to hear the particulars right this second?"

I could practically feel the emotional turmoil the poor woman was undergoing, and I bowed my head to keep from seeing her torment. I wondered why the line riders hadn't ridden on to the house and driven Wilhelmina and Arabella off, and then realized they hadn't needed to. Deprived of her husband's protection and the sustenance his seasoned hands had put on their table, she would be compelled to leave of her own accord.

"Arabella, you go in the house a minute," the mother directed. When the girl had reluctantly obeyed, the mother advanced timidly toward us, as if to her execution.

With a creak of saddle leather, the Virginian swung down. She stood rigid as he gently placed a hand on her slim shoulder and spoke softly, so softly I scarcely heard any of his words. Not that I needed to. I saw her features cloud over, saw the trembling of her lips and the fluttering of her eyelids, and I winced when the deluge came. She broke down utterly, collapsing against the Southerner and sobbing until the front of his shirt was soaked.

A movement at a window drew my gaze. There was the girl, watching her mother flounder in the pit of human misery. What was the child thinking? I asked myself. Did she fully appreciate the gravity of the calamity that had befallen them? Being so young, and endowed with the eternal optimism of children everywhere, she might make a swifter recovery than her mother. If, I reflected, anyone ever truly got over the death of a parent at so young an age. I knew a man back east who had lost his father at the age of eight and never, ever rebounded from the loss.

Presently the woman collected herself, dried her eyes, and went into the house.

"Come," the Virginian said, remounting. "We have work to do."

I followed him back to the bodies. We removed the elk meat from the travois and piled it in the grass for the wolves and coyotes to devour later. Then we carried the man to the travois, straining every muscle in our bodies in the act; he must have weighed three hundred pounds if he weighed an ounce. Finally we placed him on his back and aligned the boy beside him.

The Virginian took his rope from his saddle and lashed to his horse the poles jutting from the narrow end of the portable platform. This was new to the knowledge-able cow horse, who twisted his neck to regard the alien apparatus quizzically. Lesser animals would have fought or kicked. Monte accepted his lot without complaint, with a trust born of his total devotion to his master. I often thought that Monte was the most knowledgeable cow horse I ever encountered. If he'd made the attempt, I'm sure he could have learned English.

Awaiting us in the yard was a ghostly specter of a hu-man being wrapped in a blue shawl. What she had done with the child, I had no idea. In our absence she had tapped into whatever reservoir of the human spirit enables us to deal with sorrows of the first magnitude, and re-mained composed as she escorted us around the cabin to a brown plot of earth under a stark tree that had already lost most of its leaves.

The Virginian went to the shed and came back bear-ing two dirt-encrusted shovels. We had to pound and pry and poke to excavate the hard earth, yet eventually our dil-igent efforts were rewarded with adequate graves.

Stepping back and mopping his brow, the Southerner said, "Ma'am, yu' might want to go through their pockets and get their personal effects."

"Would one of you be so kind as to do it for me?" Wilhelmina requested. "I—I don't think I could."

I will never know what possessed me to kneel. The bodies were stiff, cold, and pale, and my skin crawled as I eased a hand into one of the husband's pockets. I discov-ered less than a dollar in coin and a small pocketknife. In another pocket was a broken watch. That was all. The boy's pockets were empty.

The Virginian and I laid the bodies side by side, then filled in the dirt. I soon noticed that every time a spray of fine earth rained down on the deceased, Wilhelmina would blink and shudder. In regular cadence she did this; blink, shudder, blink, shudder, as if she were some sort of mechanical contrivance operating without conscious thought. It was eerie, unnerving, and I avoided looking at her until the ghastly job was finished.

"I don't mean to be rude," the Virginian said, "but what will yu' and the little one do now, ma'am?"

Wilhelmina blinked a few times and focused on the Southerner with conspicuous effort. "Do?"

"Yes, ma'am. Yu' can't hardly stay here by yourself. If yu' want, my friend and I will see yu' safe to Medicine Bow. Or we can take yu' to Aspen Creek, where I live. There are a couple of ladies there like yourself, and it might be nice to have someone yu' can talk to."

"I don't know what you mean. I intend to stay."

"By yourself?" the Virginian emphasized. "How will you make ends meet?"

"I won't leave," Wilhelmina vowed. "My Robert cleared this land all by himself. He built our house from the ground up with his own two hands. He intended for this to be our home, and it will be."

"But—" the Virginian began.

"Don't fret yourself," Wilhelmina said with a sickly smile. "I can manage. Really I can. Robert taught me how to shoot, and there are plenty of deer and squirrels about. In the spring I'll plant a garden with the seeds we've hoarded, so by the middle of next summer we'll have more vegetables than we can eat. I'll probably sell the excess in Medicine Bow and use the money to buy our necessities. We'll do quite fine, I assure you."

Her words had a false ring to them, and the manner in which she clipped them added to the impression of insincerity. I thought I detected an odd gleam in the depths of her eyes, but how could I be sure under such trying circumstances? To my subsequent sorrow, I offered no objections to her ridiculous reasoning. Thank God the Virginian did. We weren't entirely to blame.

"Ma'am, if yu' won't mind my sayin' so, I don't think yu've thought this all the way through," said he. "You'd raise your little girl way out here all alone? Why, in the winter the snow gets as deep as your cabin roof. There's bears and such to keep in mind. And"—he paused—"the men who did this to your husband and son are the kind of no-account trash who would do the same to a woman. Do yu' savvy?"

Wilhelmina drew the shawl tight around her. "I'm not leaving, sir, and that's final. We put every cent we had into our new home. Can I lightly abandon it?"

"There's nothin' light about murder, ma'am."

"No. Thank you. Good day." Wilhelmina spun, and moved toward the house with measured, unnatural strides.

"I plumb want to shoot someone," the Virginian muttered.

To prove I wasn't completely bereft of ideas, I offered, "She doesn't feel comfortable talking to us, but she might to her own kind. Would Molly and Jessamine be willing to come back here and console her?"

The Virginian was a sunrise unto himself. "Yu' are a wizard, Professor! I reckon they would, and that would solve that." Taking my shovel, he hurried to the shed while I walked to our horses. As I did, I spied a lone swayback mare tethered to a post on the east side of the house. The animal had been in the shadows until just then. This calmed me somewhat. If they wanted to leave before we returned, they could.

"It's no wonder the settlers hate us so," the Virginian said bitterly as he joined me and took the lead in heading southward. "Much more of this and they might declare open war."

I suspected he was exaggerating but held my peace.

"Yu' can tell a heap about a man by the pride he takes in his property," my friend observed, "and if I'm any kind o' judge, that Robert Proctor would have made something o' his place in a few years. He would have done his family proud."

"No doubt."

"How many more would yu' say there are like him out there?" the Virginian asked, encompassing all of Wyoming with a single sweep of his arm. "Hundreds? Thousands? Each one wantin' to carve out his own little piece o' the whole pie. And how can I blame 'em? How, even though the pieces they're carvin' are out o' pies belongin' to the big ranchers, men like Judge Henry?"

I would have told him that in my estimation the right to carve up any pie was vested in the one who owned it, who had baked it in the first place, as it were, but I never uttered a syllable. For at that very instant there was a muffled blast within the log cabin.

"No!" the Virginian cried, and wheeled Monte on the head of a pin. He streaked toward the house like a madman.

My obstinate nature prevented me from admitting the inescapable, even when I heard his string of violent curses as I was dashing through the entrance. On seeing the mother, I stopped short.

Wilhelmina Proctor was on her left side, her head framed by a spreading crimson pool, the big Walker Colt lying next to the curved fingers of her right hand. Her eyes were locked wide, the wild gleam gone forever.

A few yards away, slumped over the small kitchen table, was Arabella. I took in her story in a glance. The terror of it caused me to lean against the wall and gasp. Her mother had placed a plate of cake in front of her, and while the young girl was engrossed in eating, had plunged a large kitchen knife into her back, piercing the innocent heart with a single thrust. "How could she?" I blurted.

The Virginian checked the girl to see if there might be a flicker of life, but the extermination of the Proctor family had been complete. He went past me without saying anything, and shortly I could hear the shovel being wielded. Rather than stay in that house of death, I staggered outside and over to the shed. The shovel felt strange in my grip. When I tried to dig, my movements were awkward, those of a bumbling simpleton. I was lucky if I dug out a spoonful of dirt.

By sunset the four graves were arranged in an even row with separate markers to identify them. Lengthening shadows fanned across them as we rode off, leading the mare along with our packhorses, and when last I looked back, the entire house was plunged in darkness, blotted out as if it had never been.

14

A Living Parable

When next I saw the Virginian, it was in Philadelphia, of all places, and it came about in the following fashion.

By December of that year Molly was feeling more homesick than she had ever been before, a state brought on by the combination of her delicate condition and the fact that her mother was in a poor way. She longed to visit Bennington, to see with her own eyes how her mother was faring and to spend time with her beloved great-aunt. To this end she sat her husband down in the front room, took his rough hands in her smooth ones, gazed lovingly into his eyes, and made formal petition. What man, being human, could refuse?

On the fourteenth day of the month the pair sat on a train rumbling eastward. Since the cowboy and the mother-in-law had not yet come to terms, he was not quite as anxious as Molly to make the trip. This she knew, and cherishing his happiness as she did her own, she proposed that he spend but a few days in Bennington and then fulfill a desire he had long held: to visit me in Pennsylvania.

I had no inkling of his coming. The first I knew he was anywhere within a thousand miles of my doorstep came when I answered a polite knock in the middle of a sunny but frigid afternoon, and on opening the door beheld a distinguished gentleman in a fine straw hat and a Scotch homespun suit of an expensive make. "Yes?" I said blankly.

"Goodness gracious, seh! Has all this soot in the air blinded you?"

I must have done a marvelous imitation of a fish stranded on land, because he threw back his head and laughed, fully revealing his chiseled features for the first time. "You!" I exclaimed. "Here!"

"If I'm not, I don't know where I am."

My daze passed and I grabbed his hand and literally yanked him inside. "What the devil are you doing here? Does Molly know? When did you arrive? Why didn't you write me first so I could prepare?" I asked, and would have gone on had I not run out of breath.

The Virginian fixed me with an amused eye. "If this is what high society does to a man, I don't want no part of it." His drawl was virtually gone.

Throwing my arms around him, I patted his back and roared with joy. "I don't care what brought you here! I'm simply glad you came. How long can you stay?"

"Three or four days," the Virginian answered, lowering his bag to the floor. He proceeded to explain about his beloved and extolled her generosity in allowing him to visit, concluding with, "I don't rightly know if it's a sad state of affairs when a man's wife rations his pleasures or a step forward for the marriage institution."

I must admit I positively bubbled over at this unforeseen fortune. Ordinarily my holidays were drab affairs consisting of visits with relatives and a visit or three to my favorite club. Excitement? Not unless you count playing the piano for hours on end and singing Christmas carols until my throat was raw. With the arrival of my cherished

Southerner, I felt certain things would be different. Little did I know.

To start off, I took him on a grand tour of the house, which ended in the plush chamber that would be his during the course of his stay. I noticed he gave the room a strange look and me an even stranger one, so I asked him why.

"I thought Wyoming was big, but this place of yours . . ."

The comment sparked inane laughter on my part since I totally missed its true significance. He set me straight the next moment.

"You live in this big old house all by yourself?"

"You know I do. Why?"

"I don't see how you do it. I'd be so lonely I'd commence howlin' at the walls." He rested a hand on my arm. "You really ought to give some thought to ropin' yourself a filly and settling down, pard. A man your age shouldn't have to keep himself company all the time."

"My age?" I blustered, although his words were similar to those I had often harbored in my own mind.

"What I mean," the Virginian elaborated, "is that a man should set his priorities straight. First win the regard of a good woman, then all else will follow."

"All else?" I repeated skeptically.

"Happiness will. And what else counts?"

He had me there. I covered my embarrassment by taking him to the sitting room and pouring him a little something to warm his insides after the chill of being outdoors. Which, I should say, hadn't affected him in the least. He took a seat and raised his glass.

"To us."

"To us." I swallowed happily, but too swiftly, and had a coughing spell.

"It's a good thing Scipio ain't here," the Virginian drawled, forgetting himself. "He'd take away your drinkin' privileges till yu' can handle your liquor."

"How is that rascal? And everyone else?"

"Fine, just fine. Lin and Jessamine are back at Box Elder. Most of the hands have scattered for the winter, but

Dapper and Mabel stayed on at Sunk Creek at the Judge's request."

"And Balaam?"

"Quiet. Too quiet. I figure he'll show his hand in the spring."

I saw his features crystallize, and to lighten the mood, I declared, "Well, what would you like to do while you're here? Philadelphia has a lot to offer. We can take in the tourist sights such as Independence Hall and the house Betsy Ross lived in. We can visit my club. We can go to the opera. Oh, there are just a hundred and one things we can do."

"Opera?" said the Virginian, as one might say "tooth extraction."

I shrugged. "Not if you don't care to. You tell me. I'm at your disposal."

The Southerner pondered a minute. "I did sort of want to see that bell with the crack in it."

"The Liberty Bell. It's housed at Independence Hall. Anything else?"

"I reckon I'll leave it up to you. You've long been sayin' that I should come here and let you play the host, so play away."

"Fair enough," I said, raising my drink. And as the glass touched my lips, my eyes happened to alight on a Western painting by Remington adorning the nearby wall. Inspiration gave me a chance to redeem myself. "You might enjoy seeing a herd of Pennsylvania buffalo while you're here."

"Pshaw! There ain't no such animal. Everyone knows that you Pennsylvanians have killed off all your game bigger than a tadpole, and you'll likely get around to wipin' *them* out once the word gets around how fierce they are."

His comment reminded me of the train incident with Trampas, the second time I ever saw my Southern friend, and I laughed. "Don't be so hard on us civilized sorts. There are still plenty of deer and bear left." I set my glass down. "As for the buffalo, would you be willing to place a wager on that?"

This gave the Southerner pause, and he regarded me

suspiciously. "You never bet unless it's on a sure thing. What's your secret?"

"Grab your coat and I'll show you."

"Whatever for? Is it fixin' to turn cold?"

I bundled in mine and off we went. The air was crisp, the day ideal for a walk. On the way to Fairmont Park I pointed out prominent landmarks and provided a historical sketch of the City of Brotherly Love. He took it all in amused stride. We were still some distance from our destination when he tilted his head back and sniffed loudly.

"What is that awful stink?"

"I don't smell anything," I responded, straining my nose to its utmost.

"If buzzards were still livin' hereabouts, I'd expect to see a heap of 'em."

A few seconds later I detected the same rank odors. Ordinarily they weren't so strong, and I commented that the wind must be blowing just right.

"If this is right, I'd hate to smell wrong."

Presently we arrived at the entrance where a lot of people were gathered in conversation or coming and going, many of them small children being treated by their parents. "This is it," I announced.

"The Philadelphia Zoo," the Virginian read from the large sign attached to the fence, and his face brightened just like those of the youngsters around us. "Son of a gun! I've always wanted to visit one o' these critter farms."

I suspected he had made that comment for my benefit, and didn't disappoint him. The remainder of our afternoon was spent strolling from cage to cage admiring the various creatures on display. I said little, preferring to enjoy his reactions to the many exotic animals he had never beheld before. It amazed me that someone who had seen so much of the country, who at times exhibited a maturity and insight belying his years, and who was rightfully feared by the foulest criminal element in Wyoming, could be so like a child on occasion. He marveled at the elephants ("Imagine havin' to reach for everything with your nose!") and the hippopotamus ("There's enough meat to feed the whole outfit!"), laughed at the monkeys ("They remind me of my kin back in old Virginia."), and gawked at the giraffes ("I wouldn't want to be one of them and stand in a draft!").

Toward the end of the day I detected a certain melancholy had settled upon him, which became most pronounced when we stopped in front of the lion cage and he watched one of the maned males pacing back and forth. "Is something the matter?" I inquired.

"The cages they keep these animals in don't leave much room for gettin' exercise. Sort o' reminds me o' bein' in jail."

"I didn't know you had ever been in jail," I joked, and was surprised by the slightly haunted aspect that crept into his eyes. It called to mind the several times he had intimated at a less than sterling past, and I wondered again about his experiences during those unknown years of his youth when he traveled extensively. As I'd learned previously, at one time or another he'd been to Arkansas, Texas, New Mexico, Arizona, California, Oregon, Idaho, Montana, and finally Wyoming. On first hearing of his widespread travels, I'd chalked them up to youthful wanderlust. But of late I was no longer so certain.

"I could use a bite to eat," the Virginian abruptly declared.

"My club offers a fine selection of food, and the wine there is excellent," I suggested.

"Lead the way, seh."

I didn't much care for such formality between us, but given his troubled frame of mind, I let it pass and led him toward the front gate. The sun, or what could be seen of it through the sooty air and the low slate-gray clouds, had dipped partway below the western horizon, and already the shadows were quite long. Most of the visitors had departed. We saw few souls as we wound among the noisy beasts until we entered a narrow path between the bears and the seals. Here, when we were in the deepest shadows, our path was unexpectedly barred by two burly men in well-worn clothing.

"Good evening, sir," declared a smirking specimen.

"Have pity on a fellow without work and give him enough to buy his supper, would you?"

The effrontery of the man quite galled me, and I would have given him a severe tongue-lashing had I not noticed how each of them kept one hand in a pocket, which brought to mind recent newspaper articles dealing with bold robberies at the zoo and other popular sites. Footpads had become quite a nuisance in the past year or so, and the mayor and police were at a loss as to how to deal with the rampant problem. Since I desired no trouble, I reached into my jacket.

"If yu' need money, gents, yu' should work for it," the Virginian told this pair. "A little honest sweat has never drowned anyone."

The two of them looked at one another, and the smirker chuckled. "Is that so? What have we here? Where are you from, mister?"

"Wyoming."

"Never heard of it," said the other footpad.

"It's west of here. Nothing there but cows and rattle-snakes," the smirker declared.

"Most of the United States is west of here," the Virginian said pleasantly. "And not all the sidewinders are out west."

"So you know your geography. Do you also know what this is?" demanded the spokesman, and his right hand came out holding a large knife.

I don't know what I expected to happen next; I admit to being too taken aback to think clearly. The blade glinted dully in the growing darkness as the man started to extend his arm, when suddenly the Virginian took a swift stride and something else glinted as it streaked from his waist and slammed into the footpad's chin. The man's knees buckled. Moaning, he began to sink to the ground in a graceful pirouette and was struck twice more before he slumped in an inert pile. About then the other robber snapped out of his astonishment and tried to bring his own knife to bear. But the Virginian merely shifted and touched the tip of his revolver barrel to the man's nose. The click of the hammer being cocked made the man start.

"Do yu' really want to?"

Words tried to issue from the man's throat, but all he did was croak and shake his head.

"Enough of this foolery. I'd be obliged if yu' would pick up your friend and vamoose before I forget where I am and give the two of yu' lead pills for what's ailin' yu'."

The expression the footpad wore as he hoisted his companion up and hurried off was priceless.

I saw the Virginian's hand move, and his six-shooter twirled neatly under his jacket. He looked down at his hand as if mad at it, then chortled.

"You sure can find first-rate entertainment, Professor. This has the opera beat all hollow."

We were on the sidewalk, en route to my club, when I thought it prudent to mention, "You do know that carrying concealed firearms is forbidden in the city limits? The fine can be quite stiff."

"Are you planning to turn me in?" the Virginian responded in flawless English.

"Don't be absurd!" I snapped, not spying his grin until too late. "But if you were to display that pistol of yours in public again, you might be arrested. And I wouldn't want to be the one to contact Molly so she could come down and bail you out."

"You wouldn't bail me out yourself?"

"No. It would serve you right."

The Virginian patted his side. "I suppose it was silly to bring it, but it's been part of me for so long I feel plumb naked without it." He sighed. "She doesn't know. On the train east she told me how proud she was that I'd left it behind, and I couldn't bring myself to tell her differently."

"I've never known you to be deliberately deceitful," I remarked.

"You should have known me when I was—" the Virginian said, and cut his statement off. "Well, yu' have me there, seh. I'll have to own up to her when I get to Bennington and hope she finds it in her heart to forgive me."

"She would forgive you of anything and you know it, my friend."

"Yes," the Virginian said, and somehow he unconsciously managed to convey the depth and breadth of his life in that single word. "I know I'm a lucky man. Any man is who finds a woman willin' to overlook his flaws. Combine that with a gentle disposition, and you have the perfect wife."

"I know Molly, so I won't dispute you."

"One day you'll find yours," the Virginian assured me. "Every man has the right woman waitin' for him somewhere. Some just have to look harder than others to find her. I pretty near scoured half the country."

"Was that why you traveled so much when you were younger?" I impudently asked, hoping to elicit new revelations.

"No," said he, and allowed the matter to drop.

That evening I introduced him to my closest friends, all of whom had heard so much about him over the months from me. And do you know what? Had they not been told that he was Western through and through, they would not have known. He was the model of Eastern civility, his drawl barely noticeable. His charm and wit were as keen as ever, and I admit to being disconcerted that he was my equal in my own element. But, as I'd noted previously, while he was but one of thousands who were wresting a new life from the raw frontier, he was one in a thousand in stature.

A light snow was falling as we headed home. The light white mantle gave Philadelphia a virgin purity the city seldom possessed. Many shoppers were out, getting an early start on the holiday season by taking advantage of the shops that were open late, and the sight of so many people in such fine spirits made me nostalgic for the Christmases of my childhood. But I was deluding myself. It's impossible to recapture such wonderful lost innocence once the virus of adult cynicism infects us; the best we can hope for is a few precious, fleeting moments of thinking in similar channels and reliving those times that made our childhood memorable.

We had passed a number of gaily lit stores when the Virginian gave my arm a nudge. .

"Do you mind if we do some shoppin'? I'd like to find a special gift for Mary before I go."

"I can direct you to the right store if you'll tell me the kind of gift you have in mind. Is it jewelry? Clothes? Perfume?"

"Perfume? Oh sugar! You do have a lot to learn about women. Once they've been married a spell, they take to thinkin' in more practical terms. I once gave Molly the choice between flowers and a new saddle, and she picked the saddle." He grinned. "A man can always tell when his wife starts thinkin' o' their marriage as a serious proposition and not some paperbacked romance."

"So Molly will want something practical. Can you be more specific?"

"No. But I'll know it when I see it."

I took him to Market Street, where the shops were most plentiful, and we spent an idyllic half hour going from one to the other. Nothing caught his fancy, however, until we strayed into a pet store just as the owner was about to put up his Closed sign.

"What will it be, gentlemen?" he inquired impatiently.

"I'm lookin' for something for my wife," the Virginian disclosed.

Instantly the proprietor attached himself to the cowboy. "Your wife, you say, young man? Well, then, what you need is a dog. Every woman has a soft spot for a nice, sweet, cuddly puppy to keep her warm on those nights you have to work late."

"We already have two dogs eatin' every rabbit, squirrel, and chipmunk they can catch. If we get another one, they're liable to start in on the cows."

The proprietor never missed a beat. "A kitten, then? A cute, soft bundle of joy guaranteed to make your loved one laugh until she cries with its wild antics."

"I don't think so. Mrs. Taylor's boy brought over a mountain-lion cub once, and Mary didn't seem all that happy about pettin' it."

"A mountain—?" the proprietor blurted, and coughed. "Oh, I see. You live *far* out in the country. Why didn't you say so in the first place? What you want is something more quaint, and I have just the thing. It's the latest novelty for those with discriminating taste."

"And what might this marvel be?"

I knew the Virginian had been merely curious about the animals he would find in the store, so I was surprised when he submitted to being pulled over to a glass container in which rested several small lizards.

"Here you are, sir. A unique pet I'll warrant your wife has never seen before, one that will make her the envy of all her friends and the talk of your community."

"One of these puny things will do all that?"

"Yes, sir," the man vowed with due gravity. "These charming little animals are"—and he paused to heighten the suspense—"chameleons."

"What makes 'em so special?"

The proprietor drew himself up to his full height of five feet two. "You couldn't ask for a more perfect animal to give as a gift. They have clean habits. They're quiet as mice. They rid your house of insects. And best of all, chameleons can change their color at will."

"Pshaw!"

"I'm serious, young man." Opening the container, the owner reached in and gently picked up one of the green reptiles in his palm. He raised it out and carefully deposited in on a piece of tree limb positioned beside the container apparently for that very purpose. "They change their hue to match their surroundings. Just you watch," he said.

Before the Southerner's incredulous gaze, the ungainly-looking creature with the bulging eyes, flat body, and spiral tail gradually altered its hue from green to brown. "Oh, my gracious! I'm blamed if I've ever seen the like." He reached out tentatively and touched the chameleon's back.

"It won't break, son," the proprietor said with a smile. "They're hardy for their size. No problem to keep at all. Just remember to keep yours warm. They don't last long in the cold."

The Virginian glanced up at me, his face aglow. "Did you see? What do you think?"

"There might be a more appropriate Christmas gift somewhere in Philadelphia," I answered tactfully. "I can't help but wonder what Molly would do with such an outlandish creature." Another thought occurred to me. "Some people have a natural aversion to reptiles of all kinds, you know. Have you ever asked Molly how she feels about them? Does she, for instance, like snakes?"

"Not a tiny bit," the Virginian admitted, his glow fading fast.

"Then we should keep searching. There's always tomorrow if we don't find what you want tonight."

The proprietor, seeing his sale threatened by my logic, fixed me with a fleeting glare, then stepped forward and clapped a hand on the Virginian's broad back. "Who are you going to listen to, my young friend? Him or your heart? This beauty is the ideal present. Take my word for it."

I expected to see the Southerner bristle at such blatant false familiarity, but he surprised me by simply nodding his head in agreement. A second later he surprised me even more.

"You've done made a sale, mister. I'll take one of these here lizards."

"Chameleons, son. They're as far above the run-of-the-mill lizard as a thoroughbred above a plow horse."

Completely mystified, I remained by the door while the Virginian paid and was handed a small container in which reposed his purchase. He held it as he might delicate china on his way over to me.

"Would you do me a favor and carry Jeffrey? I don't have a coat on, and I don't want him to catch his death."

This was too much. "You've had it less than one minute and already you've named it? And how do you know it deserves a masculine handle? Perhaps 'Martha' would be more appropriate."

"Please."

Grumbling under my breath, I cradled the creature in my hand and stuck both under my coat. He opened the door for me. Outside the snow was falling in a steady shower; the walk and the street were both covered. Ordinarily I would have admired the scene, but not now. I was confused. And, I confess, profoundly disappointed. I had never seen him commit a legitimately foolish act until this very moment, and I flatly told him as much.

"So yu' figure I'm actin' childish, do yu'?" he replied, his drawl returning with his high spirits.

"What else would you call it? A grown man purchasing such a frivolous thing! If Molly likes it, I don't know her at all."

"I'm buyin' her something else. This chameleon is for me."

"For you?" I exclaimed testily. "Why didn't you purchase something sensible, like a new knife or a watch? Why waste your money on something fit for a kid?"

"I like it."

"That's all?"

"Do yu' remember Em'ly?"

The question made me break my stride. Of course I remembered that errant hen.

It had been during my first visit to the Sunk Creek ranch. Eager to be of service, I had taken charge of the farmyard and set myself the task of building a bigger chicken coop. My carpentry skills being comparable to those of a ten-year-old, I had inadvertently given the punchers more cause to chuckle than they'd had in years.

When not trying to impress the chickens, I strayed off into the brush after game. Since my hunting skills were comparable to my carpentry skills, Judge Henry deemed it prudent to assign a nursemaid to watch over me and keep my blunders from proving fatal. The Virginian was given the job, and at first, despite my heartiest efforts, he remained distant. I couldn't blame him. To be torn from the company of his carefree fellows and required to attend my every need was humiliating, yet he'd borne the indignity graciously.

Then along came Emily to cement our friendship. We both took an interest in her quirky ways, for Emily, you see, was addlebrained. Unable through some fault of nature to lay eggs of her own, she had tried to hatch anything and everything even remotely resembling the real article—potatoes, onions, balls of soap, green peaches, and more. When this failed, she tried to steal the young of other fowl to raise as her own, including young turkeys that wanted nothing to do with her, but always was she frustrated. Eventually, after a series of misfortunes, the Virginian took pity on her and gave her an egg belonging to another hen. When the egg hatched shortly thereafter, well before the normal incubation period, Emily seemed to go crazy. She flew into a tree and squawked for hours, stopping only when, of a sudden, she keeled over dead. The Virginian and I buried her.

No, I would never forget Emily, and I now informed him as much, adding, "Why do you mention her?"

"Em'ly and Jeffrey have a lot in common. They're both what you might call livin' parables."

I could understand how the hen qualified, but the unassuming, single-talent chameleon symbolized no deeper meaning that I could discern. Not caring to appear ignorant, I held my peace and mulled over the possible inferences all the way home. As we neared my front door, the Virginian dashed over to a nearby tree and picked up a broken branch that he snapped in half over his knee. Once inside, the branch was set on the table near the fireplace.

Preparing drinks and a bite to eat kept me busy in the kitchen. When I brought them to my guest, he had the chameleon perched on the branch and was watching it change once again from green to brown. Beside the branch was one of my folded towels. To induce the reptile to change back to green, he shortly placed it in the center of the towel and leaned down to observe the transformation. He couldn't seem to get enough of the oddity. Over the next hour I watched him shift the chameleon from branch to towel and towel to branch a dozen times, and he was still doing it when I yawned and explained that I must awaken early the next morning.

"If yu' don't mind, I'll sit up awhile with Jeffrey," the Virginian said.

"Feel free. My home is yours for the duration of your stay. Tomorrow, if you're willing, we'll visit Independence Hall and other attractions."

"I'm game," the Virginian said, and bent to his prize again. "Oh. I plumb forgot. Do yu' have a cellar?"

"No, but my neighbor does. What do you need with one?"

"Jeffrey needs bugs and such to eat. It's too cold out to catch flies, but I figure there might be some spiders hidin' out in cellars hereabouts."

"I'm sure Mr. Tyler has a few spiders he can spare. I'll talk to him in the morning."

"Thank yu'."

I went to my bed, my last sight of him that of his muscular form curved over the chameleon in smiling expectation. The smile, however, was gone from his face when I awoke early the next morning and shuffled into the room to kindle the embers. There he was, seated in a chair and staring absently out the window at the dawn. He had on the same clothes he'd worn the night before. "Good morning," I said sleepily. "I didn't think you would be up this soon."

"I haven't been to bed yet."

"Don't tell me you stayed up all night playing with your toy?"

"My toy, as yu' call him, kicked the bucket about midnight."

I glanced at the table and saw the chameleon on its side on my towel, its color now a sickly, ashen tone, its tail relaxed in death, its tongue distended. "I'm sorry," I said, although for the life of me I couldn't feel a smidgen of remorse. "What happened? Did we fail to feed it in time?"

"I figure I wore the poor thing to a frazzle."

"You what?"

"I had it change color so many times, it did like Em'ly and just dropped dead."

What does one say under such circumstances? "I see.

Do you want to go back to that shop today and buy another?"

"No. One was enough."

"Enough how?" I asked, but he fell silent, and I didn't presume to broach the subject again during the remainder of his stay. I wondered, though. A lot.

15

Reconciliation

From Philadelphia the Virginian traveled to Bennington, Vermont. Since none of his in-laws knew when he would return, there was no one to greet him at the train station. He strolled around the quaint town for over an hour, ostensibly admiring the sights but in reality mustering his courage for the final leg of his journey. At length his desire to be reunited with the woman he loved prevailed over his trepidation about confronting her mother again, so off to the Wood home he went.

Molly was delighted to have her lover back and welcomed him with hugs and coos. Mrs. Wood observed their coziness with a reserve bordering on icy disdain, and at supper that evening she didn't so much as ask a single question about her son-in-law's experiences in Pennsylvania. Nor, for that matter, had she asked him anything about Wyoming, nor about the status of his partnership with Judge Henry nor about Aspen Creek. To her they were part of an alien, distasteful world, alien in their strange barbarity and distasteful because her daughter had chosen to live there rather than in Bennington where she belonged.

Mrs. Wood, you will gather, had never entirely accepted her daughter's marriage to "that quixotic cowboy," as she habitually referred to the Virginian except when Molly was in the same state. She regarded their union not as a triumph of love over adversity, but as a shameful disgrace, a blight on the Wood family tree that must be expunged from the family records so that future generations of the Wood line would not know of the depths to which her own flesh and blood had sunk.

What particularly galled Mrs. Wood was Molly's ingratitude. Mrs. Wood had labored devotedly in her daughter's best interests to smooth the way for Molly to wed Sam Bannett, of the extremely rich Bannetts of Hoosic Falls. Sam Bannett, the social catch of any season, the man who could have given Molly anything her heart desired, had been left sulking in the wings while Molly took up with her frontier gadabout.

This sore had festered in Mrs. Wood's soul to where she could scarcely tolerate thinking about the affair, and now that she was ailing, it festered all the more, an emotional canker demanding relief. She sorely longed to give her son-in-law a piece of her embittered mind, and to date she had refrained only because of the sincere affection she harbored for Molly. That, and the fact that if Molly found out, she might well never see her daughter again.

But this night, as Mrs. Wood sat watching her offspring and the quixotic cowboy rubbing elbows and laughing merrily, she resolved to approach him on the morrow and air her grievances. She gave no thought to the consequences. Her own interests, as always, were all that mattered.

So intently was Mrs. Wood brooding that she didn't realize Molly had addressed her until she heard her name repeated several times. "Yes? What is it, dear?"

"What do you say to a drive tomorrow? I'd like to see how much the old haunts have changed."

"The doctor says I'm not to overexert myself, dear,"

Mrs. Wood answered, unwilling to countenance being cooped up in a wagon for several hours with *him*.

"Nonsense, Mother. Dr. Philbin told me that you need to take fresh air daily. It's essential to your vitality, he said."

"He's a sweet man, but he can make such a fuss at times. I'd really rather not tax my strength."

Molly straightened and demonstrated why she was her mother's daughter. "I refuse to take no for an answer. This is my first visit home in how long? And you can't see fit to indulge in a peaceful ride through the countryside? Honestly, sometimes I'm at a loss to understand you."

Mrs. Wood bristled, as she invariably did when her authority was challenged on even the most trivial of matters. An argument loomed.

At this juncture the Virginian politely cleared his throat. "Excuse me for venturing an opinion, Mary, but I have to agree with your mother. If she doesn't feel fit enough for a drive, she shouldn't have to come."

Now this seconding of her position was as unexpected to Mrs. Wood as it was unwelcome. She had already set herself at odds with this man in her own mind; consequently, she was unconsciously prepared to disagree with him on any and every subject. If he had commented that the flowers in the vase across the room were blue, she would have told him they were greenish blue. Had he remarked that the sky was mostly cloudy, she would have retorted that it was partly sunny. This was her disposition when he came to her defense, and before she quite knew what she was doing, she had blurted out, "Oh, if it means that much to my daughter, why of course I'll go along."

Mrs. Wood was trapped. The next day, shortly after noon, she donned her wrap and walked with Molly out to the street where a fine six-passenger canopy-top phaeton awaited. "My goodness. What is this?"

Molly nodded proudly at her husband. "It was his idea. He felt you should travel in comfort, so he rented it for the day."

"Really?" Mrs. Wood said, pleased in spite of herself. She permitted her son-in-law to give her a hand into the vehicle and took a seat with her back to the driver, a young man who worked at the stables. And then, as she sat there being envied by Mrs. Flynt and Mrs. Howard, who were passing by, an odd thing happened. For the very first time Mrs. Wood noticed the tender solicitude with which the cowboy treated her daughter, and how his every gesture bespoke of the affection he bore Molly as he helped her up. This startled her, and she blinked and shook her head in annoyance at her own weakness.

The Virginian had the opposite seat all to himself. At a word from him the driver clucked the horses into motion and the phaeton rattled off. "Are the seats comfortable enough for you, ma'am?" he inquired.

"Quite comfortable, thank you," Mrs. Wood replied, and stared up at the green canopy. If her memory served her, this particular wagon was the most expensive one old man Bentley had to rent. How was it, then, her son-in-law could afford it? Her cousin, who knew practically all there was to know and never tired of broadcasting this expertise, had led her to believe cowboys received positively paltry wages. Putting a smile on her face, she commented, "I do trust you didn't spend your entire savings for my benefit!"

"Mother!"

"No, ma'am," said the Virginian. "I suppose Mary hasn't found the time to tell you how well we're doing with our ranch. We have close to three hundred cows now grazing on pretty near two thousand of the greenest acres in the whole territory."

"Did you say two *thousand*?"

"Yes, ma'am. Course, I'm bragging a bit. It's a middling ranch as ranches go. And I shouldn't hardly count the mountain we own, since it's not good for anything except the coal."

"You own your own mountain?" Mrs. Wood said in amazement, quite overwhelmed by this staggering series of revelations. So overwhelmed, in fact, that it took several seconds for his last few words to register. "And you have *coal*?"

"A heap of coal, ma'am. One day soon I'll be selling

it to the railroads, and then I'll own seven of these fancy rigs, one for every day of the week."

Molly snickered. "You will not. We'll spend our money wisely and invest for the future. I want to have all our debts paid in full before we're ready to retire to our rocking chairs on the front porch."

These latter statements Mrs. Wood hardly heard. Her senses were literally spinning as she conjured a mental image of the extent of her son-in-law's holdings and what those holdings meant in terms of social standing in Bennington. Why, not even the Bannetts owned two thousand acres! And his own coal mine! Mercy! Vaguely she realized he was speaking again.

"I know you've had some worries about Mary's welfare, so I'm letting you know here and now that I'll do all I can to give her all the things she deserves. She'll never go hungry or lack for clothes on her back if I can help it." The Virginian fixed his eyes on his mother-in-law. "I love her, ma'am."

This was the first time Mrs. Wood had heard him utter those passionate words, and they had an unforeseen effect, causing a faint stirring in the depths of her matronly heart as she recalled the early days of her romance with Mr. Wood. She looked at her daughter's cowboy, *really* looked at him for the first time in their acquaintance, and was startled by the ruggedly self-possessed man she beheld. "Yes," she said softly. "I can see my daughter has picked wisely."

The Virginian was pleased by the compliment; his wife was absolutely stunned. Molly knew her mother as she knew herself. She'd long been aware that her mother disapproved of her marriage, and had resigned herself to enduring the bitter barbs of her mother's wounded pride for years to come. Mrs. Wood, as everyone in the family conceded, made an excellent martyr. So to hear this sincere statement being tendered was such a shock that Molly forgot herself and gaped.

Mrs. Wood noticed. "Are you all right, child? We're not about to add to the family, are we?"

"Heavens, no," Molly said, forcing a laugh. "I have another month to go, as you well know."

"You took a big risk traveling so far in your condition," Mrs. Wood remarked. "What if you deliver early? You might be on the train when it happens. Just imagine! All those strangers."

The Virginian saw the corners of his wife's mouth tighten, so he casually observed, "I agree with you, ma'am. I wanted her to wait until after the baby came, but she wouldn't listen. All she could think of was you ailing. She said you were more important than a little discomfort."

"She did?" Mrs. Wood declared, and felt herself growing hot in the cheeks. To disguise her sentiments, she removed her bonnet and placed it in her lap. Too much was happening too fast, she reflected. What had started out as a simple ride in the country was turning into an emotional whirlwind, and she wasn't sure if she liked the changes she was undergoing.

The normally picturesque Vermont landscape was at its most stark. Every tree had long since lost its leaves. The fields were all brown. Snow had fallen several days ago, and although much of it had melted, leaving muddy puddles here and there, occasional white patches accented the shadows.

Following Molly's directions, their youthful driver took them to the Hoosic Bridge, once one of Molly's favorite spots in all the state. On a previous visit she had still been struck by its placid beauty. This time she merely stated, "The river would be so much prettier if it had rapids like those in Wyoming."

Leaving the bridge, the phaeton rattled up the Little Hoosic valley. The woods, ordinarily green and sparkling in the sunlight, resembled somber ranks of decimated soldiers, their barren limbs askew, which led Molly to comment, "Vermont could do with a few more evergreens so the forests wouldn't look so drab in the winter. Wyoming has them in abundance, and the mountain slopes are lovely all year round."

At Mount Anthony, Molly had the driver stop so she

could alight and admire the view. But as she stood there with the narrow valley sweeping into the hazy distance, she stated, "Some mountains seem so much higher when one is a girl."

"You never complained before," Mrs. Wood noted. She had remained in the vehicle, the better to study surreptitiously her son-in-law as he paced in a small circle to take in the sights.

"This sort of reminds me of Virginia," the Southerner said.

"That's right," Mrs. Wood responded. "You did say you're from there. Do you ever feel homesick?"

"I get a twinge once in a while, mainly when I think about my brothers and sisters. We were right close when we were sprouts, but I had to go off and see the world with my cousin. Now I'll never go back there to live."

"You never mentioned your cousin before. What is his name?"

Providence, claim those who believe, watches over children and other pure souls. If so, that might account for what transpired next. Just as the Virginian turned to answer Mrs. Wood, the phaeton gave a sudden lurch, almost unseating her, and the horses took off down the road at a gallop.

The young driver was to blame. He had heard the clack-clack-clack of a stone lodged in the front hoof of one of the lead horses as they climbed Mount Anthony, and conscious of his employer's instruction to remove such stones always at the first opportunity, he had climbed down, opened his folding knife, and lifted the offending leg. Prying the stone out took but a minute. He tossed it aside and turned just as Mrs. Wood posed her question to the Virginian, but he neglected to close his knife first. His swinging arm jabbed the blade into the horse's sweaty flank. Instantly the horse bolted. The whole team, taking their cue from their panicked fellow, did likewise. "No!" the youth cried.

"Mother!" Molly shrieked, aghast.

Of them all, only the Virginian did more than waste his breath. The moment he saw the phaeton lurch, he took a swift stride, and as it started rolling down the road, he took another. Arms outstretched, he leaped. His steely fingers caught hold of the top of the backseat just as the vehicle attained its top speed. He saw Mrs. Wood, frozen in abject terror, clinging to the side rail. The horses were in full flight, the reins loosely looped around the rail on the driver's seat.

Abruptly, the road curved. Unable to get his feet on the brace in time, the Virginian swayed outward as the phaeton took the turn at twice the safe speed. His left hand began to slip. Gritting his teeth, he clung tenaciously to his precarious perch and swung his legs inward. His shins banged against the brace, sending sharp pangs shooting up his thighs.

Mrs. Wood found her voice and screamed.

A second later the Virginian slammed into the back of the vehicle as it hit the straightaway. His boots dangled inches from the surface. If they should catch, he'd be torn loose. Bunching his shoulder muscles and surging upward, he succeeded in planting his soles on the brace and held still for a second, gathering his strength. Then, in a fluid motion, he catapulted up and over the back of the seat, and came to rest on the floor at Mrs. Wood's feet. Her eyelids were fluttering; she was about to swoon.

"Hang on, ma'am!" the Virginian yelled. He gave her arm a squeeze and pulled himself up. A bump in the road jolted the whole vehicle, knocking him against her. Wailing, she started to go over the rail. His hand closed on her wrist, arresting her plunge, and she clung to him in desperation.

"I have to stop this wagon!" the Virginian told her while urgently prying her fingers loose. Ahead had appeared another curve, and this time the horses were going much too fast to negotiate it without spilling the whole vehicle. He freed his arm, gripped the top of her seat, and vaulted upward. What he saw sent a chill down his spine.

Gradually the reins had slackened more and more, so that as the Virginian hurtled onto the driver's seat, they came off the rail and fell toward the team. Once they were out of reach, there would be no stopping the horses before they raced into the curve. Frantically the Virginian lunged. His outflung right hand clutched the ends of the reins at the very last moment. But in doing so he lost his grip on the seat and now hung upside down, his right knee the only part of his body still retaining a purchase. Another bump would pitch him into eternity.

Exerting all his might, the Virginian pushed up into the seat and grasped the reins in both hands. They were so close to the curve that the heads of the horses blocked it from sight. With an almost savage wrench he hauled on the reins, throwing his full weight into the effort. For several anxious heartbeats it appeared the team wouldn't respond. Then they did and the phaeton slewed to the right, tilting on two wheels for a few harrowing seconds before righting itself and coming to a gradual stop. The horses were panting and wheezing and caked with lather.

Letting out the breath he didn't know he'd been holding, the Virginian turned to see how his mother-in-law had fared. A pair of skinny arms encircled his neck, and a moist cheek was pressed to his neck.

"Thank you! Thank you!"

This was one of those rare times when the Virginian didn't know what to say. He sat still while she cried herself dry, an arm around her quaking shoulders. Neither of them moved until the pounding of footsteps heralded the arrival of their winded driver.

"Are you people all right?" the youth asked anxiously, and went on before they could answer. "My goodness, mister! That was the bravest thing I've ever seen. How did you do that?"

"Take these," the Virginian said gruffly, and shoved the reins at the youth. He climbed over the seat and sat beside Mrs. Wood, comforting her while the vehicle executed a turn and returned to the top of the mountain for his wife.

Molly had started in pursuit but had been unable to run far in her state. Her heart had been in her throat when she saw the phaeton careening down the road, and when it nearly flipped over, she had bit down so hard on her knuckles she had drawn blood. Now, as it coasted to a halt beside her, she anxiously hauled herself up before the Virginian could lend a hand and sat down on the other side of her mother. In the anxiety of the moment all their petty squabbles were forgotten. The many clashes of personality that had so alienated them from each other over the years counted as nothing. All that mattered to Molly was her mother's distress. They embraced wordlessly and clung to one another.

"Where to now, folks?" their driver asked. He nearly recoiled in fright when the tall, bronzed man with the mustache turned and gave him a stare the likes of which no one had ever given him before. The short hairs at the nape of his neck prickled. He had an instinctive urge to jump down and flee, only he was too scared to budge.

"Home," the man growled. "And the next time yu' take this hyeh rig out, be mighty careful how you wave that neck-blister of yours."

The youth nodded vigorously, amazed at the man's sudden accent. He had never heard a knife referred to as a neck-blister before, and under more peaceful circumstances he might have laughed at the term. But there was no laughing at this man. Even he sensed that.

By nightfall the story had spread like wildfire through Bennington and into the surrounding communities. The youth told no one; he was too embarrassed at being the cause. Neither Molly nor the Virginian mentioned it to a soul. No, it was Mrs. Wood who told all and sundry of her miraculous deliverance by her brave son-in-law. That afternoon, for the first time since she had learned Molly and the Virginian were coming for a visit, she took a stroll to get her exercise, and in the course of a mile walk she relayed the news to over a dozen of Bennington's leading gossips.

From Bennington the couple traveled to Dunbarton to visit Molly's dear old great-aunt. As always, they met with a warm, loving reception, the high point of which came when they were ushered into the plush nursery being readied for their next visit. The three spent many hours reminiscing, and it was with reluctance that the Virginian and Molly bid the kindly great-aunt good-bye.

Snow fell again the morning they boarded the puffing

train for the first leg of their westward trip. Molly was excited about returning home and couldn't wait to see Jessamine, Mabel, Mrs. Henry, and all her other friends. The Virginian was more reserved. On the one hand he looked forward to getting Molly safely back to their house, where she could have the baby undisturbed, but on the other he could not help thinking about Brazos and Balaam and the fate they had in store for him if he let down his guard. He was cheered somewhat by his conviction that little would happen before spring, allowing him to enjoy a quiet, restful winter with his family.

At that very moment, however, unknown to the Virginian, Judge Henry was innocently writing a letter that would shatter this hope.

16

The Judge Cultivates
Particulars

The joyous day finally arrived. Not only was the doctor on hand, but the Virginian had prevailed on Jessamine and Mrs. Taylor to be there, "just in case." He spent the two hours Molly was in labor pacing the front room and working the brim of his hat into a limp ruin. Lin McLean, true friend that he was, sat there the whole time offering tidbits of seasoned fatherly wisdom.

"Yu' have to learn to relax when this happens," the foreman advised the partner at one point. "Just look at it like yu' would the birth of a calf or the hatchin' of an aigg."

Pausing in his effort to wear a rut in the hardwood floor, the Virginian looked at Lin until the latter coughed self-consciously and developed an interest in something out the window. "I swear. Yu' ought to be playin with a string of spools. Babies ain't aiggs. And anyone who says different is full growed in body only."

"Shucks. I never claimed they were, and if yu' weren't as techy as a teased snake, you'd know that." Lin sat back and stretched his gangly frame. "All I'm sayin' is yu' can't let yourself get tensed up like a strand of barbed wire. Go for a walk outside. Take deep breaths. Singin' even helps."

"I don't feel much like airin' my lungs."

"Bet yu' yu' could if yu' tried," Lin urged, and to demonstrate his point he threw back his head and commenced warbling one of his favorite songs:

> " 'Twas a nasty baby anyhow,
>   And it only died to spite us;
>   'Twas afflicted with the cerebrow
>   Spinal meningitus!"

The Virginian stiffened, spun on his heel, and marched over to McLean's chair. Lin, about to launch into the second verse, choked off the words as a finger tapped the end of his nose. "Why don't yu' sing a mite louder?" the Virginian asked. "Maybe then *she'd* hear yu'!"

"What'd I do?" Lin blurted in surprise.

"Yu' tell me what toy shop yu' escaped from, and I'll tell yu' what yu' did right before I wind yu' up and send yu' back."

Lin blinked a few times, then abruptly realized why the Southerner was upset. "Oh. I reckon I should've picked another." And he promptly raised his voice to the rafters again:

> "Once in the saddle I used to go dashing,
>   Once in the saddle I used to go gay;
>   First took to drinking, and then to card-playing;
>   Got shot in the body, and now here I lay."

"Give it up," the Virginian said. "Yu' are plumb hopeless."

So they bided their time in silence except for the clomp-clomp of the Virginian's boots until from overhead wafted the delicate wail of newborn life. In several bounds he was in the hall, waiting breathlessly for someone to appear, but he did not have to bear the suspense for long.

Jessamine hurried toward him, her beaming face assurance that all was well. "It's a boy," she disclosed. "A healthy, cuddly little boy."

"Have yu' given thought to the name?" Lin asked at the Southerner's elbow.

"We decided a while ago to call our first son John."

"After your pa or your grandpa?" Lin guessed.

"After my cousin," the Virginian said softly. "Of course, most folks called him Johnny when he was little." He took a tentative step. "How soon can I see them?"

"Doc says you can go up right this minute if you want," Jessamine answered. "If you hurry, you might be the first one Johnny sees when he opens his eyes."

"He ain't opened them yet? Why not? Are they stuck shut?"

"Mercy, no. Sometimes babies do that."

Shoving his hat on his head, the Virginian took the stairs three at a stride and bounded to the bedroom door. There he stopped, seized by an inexplicable nervousness. Then, lightly, he knocked.

"What are you waiting for?" Mrs. Taylor called out. "It's your house."

Molly was propped on the fluffy pillows, her hair slick and in disarray, her brow dotted with perspiration, her features limp with fatigue. Cradled in her slim arms was the quiet bundle that meant so much to them.

The Virginian moved past the grinning sawbones and sat down on the edge of the bed. Tenderly, he reached out and stroked his wife's cheek. Then he leaned forward and gazed fondly down at the tiny face framed by the swaddling clothes. Small brown eyes regarded him serenely. "Goodness gracious! Ain't he lovely!"

"Handsome, you mean," Molly corrected him.

"Johnny," the Virginian said reverently, and touched a finger to his son's temple. He saw a clenched fist at the edge of the blanket and touched that, too, and when he did, the boy grabbed hold of his fingertip and held fast.

"What a grip he's got," he boasted proudly. "He'll be a strong one when he's done growin'."

"Just like his father," Molly said.

Their eyes met, and the Virginian swore he had never seen his wife looking so lovely as she did at that frozen instant in time. He thought of all she had gone through, the bloating of her body during the pregnancy and the hours of strenuous exertion preceding the birth, and love for her gushed out of his devoted soul, making him tremble with the intensity of his feelings.

"Do you have a chill?"

"I never felt better," the Virginian said quietly, taking her hand in his. And his heart swelled with happiness.

One month later the Virginian sat in his office at Sunk Creek working on the books when Judge Henry entered and stepped over to a chair.

"Am I interrupting?"

"No, seh," the Virginian replied, setting his pen next to the inkwell. "I've been at this hyeh arithmetic so long I'm startin' to see double."

The Judge made himself comfortable and took out his pipe. "I don't believe I've gotten around to properly expressing my gratitude. Do you realize that we haven't lost a single head since you took the herd to Montana?"

"Yu' should thank the Eastern Montana Stock Growers Association, not me. They're the ones who gave the rustlers such a scare the polecats went back to bein' virtuous."

"Nevertheless, we would have lost countless more cattle if not for your brainstorm. You saved us thousands of dollars."

The Virginian shrugged. "We're pardners. I was just lookin' out for our interests."

"No one could do a finer job," Judge Henry complimented him. "And since you mentioned our partnership, I'd like to say I think it's high time we had a talk about the additional steps we need to take to ensure Sunk Creek remains profitable for the foreseeable future."

"What do yu' have in mind?"

The Judge idly tapped his pipe against his palm. "With all our cattle up north, the home range is empty. That's a terrible waste of space."

"Don't tell me you're thinkin' o' bringin' in more beeves? We'd be right back where we were before we moved the herd."

"I'm not crazy," Judge Henry said with a grin. "I have been giving a lot of thought to the matter, though. At first I considered selling off some of the land, such as that acreage we rarely use over by Twin Forks, but I've worked too hard at making this ranch a success to ever part with a single acre." He glanced at a map of Sunk Creek hanging on the west wall. "Owning land is like owning gold in that respect. It gets into your blood and won't let go."

"Every man wants to have a plot o' dirt he can call his own," the Virginian commented.

"Except for men like this Brazos I've been hearing so much about lately. All his kind care about is owning a fast horse and a nickel-plated pistol. But then, they're fools."

"They are a bit shallow," was all the further the Virginian would commit himself.

"A mature man knows when to dig in his roots and make something of himself," the Judge went on. "I did it. You've done it. This Brazos never will. The only plot of dirt that he'll claim will be in boot-hill."

"He seems to be a lot on your mind today."

"With good reason. Or haven't you heard the latest news from Medicine Bow?"

"I've been too busy with diapers and such to go grazin' for gossip."

"You have?" Judge Henry said, much surprised. "Somehow I thought you'd be exempt."

"Is any man?"

Judge Henry smiled, then turned sober. "Well, then, allow me to fill you in. There's been another shooting in town. Five days ago Jim Meeker and his two sons went in to buy supplies. They stopped at a saloon to wash the dust down, and while they were there, this Brazos and some of the other quick-draw artists who work for Balaam came up and offered to buy them a drink. Meeker and his boys accepted, then went to leave."

The knuckles on the Virginian's hands, which were clasped on top of the desk, had gone white.

"Brazos wanted them to have another whiskey, but Jim Meeker declined. This made Brazos mad, and he claimed he was being insulted." The Judge stopped. "You know Meeker. He doesn't back down for any man, so he up and told Brazos that he didn't care how Brazos took it. Brazos started calling Jim every dirty name there is, trying to prod Jim into drawing, but Jim kept on walking. He's been around awhile, like me, and we're too smart to be goaded into resorting to gunplay over mere words."

The Virginian divined the outcome and remarked, "One of Jim's boys went and bucked Brazos?"

"Young Phil. He never gave Jim any warning or Jim would have stopped him. Just went for his gun and was dead before he could clear his holster." Melancholy lined Judge Henry's features. "There was nothing Jim could do. It would have been the same as committing suicide if he had gone for his own gun. And there were plenty of witnesses to say Phil drew first, so trying to bring the law in would have been pointless."

"I'm right sorry to hear this," the Virginian said. "Someone will have to do something about this Brazos character before too long."

"It can't be soon enough to suit me," Judge Henry said. "But I didn't come here to discuss cat-eyed bastards like him. I want to present an idea I have and see if you like it."

"Present away, seh."

"All right." The Judge stuck his unlit pipe back in his pocket and leaned forward. "All I ask is that you hear me out before you render judgment. If you agree, we'll start first thing tomorrow."

"What's your hurry?"

"We have a chance at a good deal, and I'll need to

write a letter to confirm our interest," Judge Henry replied. "But I'm getting ahead of myself." He rubbed his hands together. "Since I won't sell the land, we should put it to good use. And since our cattle will stay north of the border until this rustling business is over, it has to be something other than cows."

"Were yu' thinkin' o' raisin' frogs?"

Judge Henry straightened, his eyes widening until he remembered. Then he laughed and slapped his thigh. "No, thank you. From the story I heard, those frog ranches you sold Trampas on went out of business. Something about pelicans in the spring pasture?"

"There was more to it than that," the Virginian coyly admitted.

"Frogs are out, in any event," said the Judge. "No, what I have in mind is raising horses. And not just any old broncos or cutting horses, either, but top breeds we can earn top dollar for by selling them to interested parties back east." His expression became animated. "We can start small. I'd like to buy a few palominos and Morgans, since both are recommended so highly, then see which we like the best. With all the prime grassland we have at our disposal, we can double our investment in no time."

The Virginian scratched his chin, pondering. "The notion is mighty appealing," he conceded. "The rustlers are only interested in cows. They wouldn't touch our hawsses anyway, not when hawss-thievin' is a sure-fire hangin' offense."

"My way of thinking exactly," Judge Henry said with vigor.

"I don't know much about Morgans, but those buttermilk hawsses are supposed to be some o' the best."

"So they say," Judge Henry agreed heartily.

"We'd have to be extra careful about epizootic and such."

The Judge's head bobbed. "Of course. That goes without saying. We wouldn't want to lose a valuable thoroughbred to something so common as distemper."

"We couldn't treat 'em like we do bunch grassers, either. They'd have to be looked after day and night, them and their stud bunches."

"They're an important investment, after all."

A slow smile curled the Virginian's lips, and he nodded. "Yu' can rest easy, Judge. Yu've sold me on the proposition. I reckon before too long Sunk Creek will be sellin' more Morgans and buttermilk hawsses than cows."

Judge Henry's elation showed. "I was hoping you'd agree. I've done a lot of checking around, contacted knowledgeable friends back east and so forth, and this new enterprise of ours can bring big rewards if we do it right."

"So what's the first step? Sendin' off the letter yu' mentioned?"

"Yes. I've been in touch with a man named Finley who owns a Morgan. He bought it from someone in Rochelle, Texas, with the intention of breeding his own stock, but the Morgan hasn't taken to the climate as he would have liked. So Finley wants to sell."

The Southerner chuckled. "What are yu' waitin' for? I can tell how much yu' want this animal."

"But I know little about judging quality horseflesh. You, on the other hand, know a lot."

"About mustangs and cow hawsses, maybe. Not Morgans and palominos."

"You're still the man for the job."

"Is this job what I think it is?"

"Visiting Finley. If you decide his Morgan is everything he claims, then make him an offer on behalf of both of us. If not, don't. It's that simple." Judge Henry paused. "It was through a mutual acquaintance that I learned Finley had begun looking for a buyer, which was what gave me this idea in the first place. I took the liberty of writing Finley and explaining I might be interested. At the time, you were back in Vermont with Molly, so I couldn't commit myself beyond that."

"Did he answer yu'?"

"Yes. He told me that his Morgan would be available after the first of the year, and if I was still interested then, to write and let him know. Three weeks ago I did just that, and I received his reply today." Judge Henry pulled an envelope from his coat. "Finley has been waiting to hear from me. He says the Morgan is mine if I want it."

"Then I reckon I'd better get home and pack," the Virginian said. "It's a darn shame Mary can't go with me. She'd be mighty pleased to see her kin again, but it wouldn't be healthy for the baby to go traipsin' halfway across the country in the dead of winter."

"Oh," Judge Henry said. "Did I give you the impression you would be heading east? Well, don't worry. Molly won't be upset on that score, because you're taking the train south."

"Where to?"

The Judge smiled, thinking how delighted his partner would be. "To one of the healthiest climates in the world, or so they say." He paused for effect. "Arizona. Tombstone, Arizona."

A tremor seemed to rack the Virginian's powerful frame, and an odd, distant look came into his eyes. He took a breath, then held it. His fingers curled into claws on the desk in front of him.

"Is something the matter?" Judge Henry asked, quite bewildered by the reaction.

"Maybe," the Virginian said, the word seeming to lodge in his throat, "maybe someone else should go. Lin has a heap of hawss savvy. He can do as good a job as I could."

In all the years Judge Henry had been acquainted with the Southerner, this was the first time he had balked at doing a job, and it so flabbergasted him that he said nothing for many seconds.

"Besides," the Virginian went on hastily, "it might be best, what with the baby and all. I really shouldn't be leavin' Mary for weeks at a time just yet." He averted his gaze. "Yu' know how it is when yu' have a new addition to the family."

Judge Henry found his voice. "No, I'm sorry to say. I don't." His features drooped. "We can't ever have any. I had—" And here he paused, displaying the innate uncertainty most men do when on the verge of revealing deeply personal information. "I had an accident shortly after we were married. A horse I was trying to tame kicked me."

The Virginian looked up then and plainly saw the courage it had taken for the Judge to share the secret. He realized fully the depth of his partner's affection, the degree of his friend's trust, and sour guilt washed through him, filling him with bitterness directed at himself. He was letting the Judge down, wounding the man who had time and again demonstrated more confidence in him than any other, who had elevated him to foreman and given him a chance at a future he had once thought out of his reach.

"My wife, bless her, has never complained," Judge Henry went on slowly. "Sometimes I think she has the compassion of an angel. She's far too good for me."

"I reckon every man feels the same way about his cow bunny," the Virginian said. "My grandpa used to say that a man should always marry a woman who's better than he is so some of it will rub off on him before the last roundup. That way he just might make it to the misty beyond."

"I see you took his advice," Judge Henry said with a weak grin.

The Virginian nodded, then calmly folded his hands and announced formally, "I've changed my mind, seh. You're right about Tombstone havin' a right healthy climate, especially since they stopped most of that lead slingin'. I'll go see about this hyeh Morgan hawss for yu'."

Judge Henry's brow creased. "Are you sure? If you'd rather stay, I have no real objections to sending Lin."

"Knowin' that joker, he's likely to get lost and wind up in San Francisco by mistake. He did that once, yu' know. Headed for Boston, and when he stepped off the blamed train, he was in Idaho. The man has got the sense o' direction of an addled goose. No, it'd be a mighty disconvenience to send him. I'm the one should go."

"If you insist," Judge Henry said, brightening.

"Yu' get me all the particulars I need, and I'll go tell Mary," the Virginian said, rising. He walked out quickly into the cool, invigorating air and inhaled deeply to steady his nerves. Extending his arm, he held his fingers out and watched them to see if they were shaking. When he saw his hand was as steady as ever, he chuckled and said to himself, "I ain't got buck fever yet, but if I ain't careful, I'm liable to booger myself to death."

A hail drew the Virginian around to find McLean ambling toward him. "Just the hombre I was comin' to see," the Southerner said.

"What for?"

The Virginian nodded at the corral, and as they walked, he told about the plan to buy the Morgan and his impending trip to Tombstone.

"They say Arizona is no place for amateurs," Lin commented. "But yu' must know all about it. Yu' was there once, if I recollect correctly."

"Twice."

"Did yu' ever get to Tombstone?"

"Now and then."

"Then yu' must know some folks down thataway. This trip'll give yu' a chance to look up old friends."

"From what I hear, most o' those I knew have gone over the range."

"Lead poisoned?"

"Mostly."

Lin McLean glanced at his companion out of the corner of his eye. "I remember hearin' there was a heap o' gunmen down there at one time. Were you there when they had that big to-do at the O.K. Corral?"

"Seems to me I was."

"Did yu' ever meet that Wyatt Earp they're always writin' about in the paperbacks?"

"Seems to me I did."

"They say he's a hellion with a pistol. About the best there ever was, outside o' Hickok."

"There was one better than both o' them."

"Who?" Lin innocently asked.

The Virginian abruptly stopped. "Anyone ever tell yu' that sometimes yu' cackle like a biddy hen?" he snapped. Then, tugging his hat brim low, he wheeled on his heels and stalked off.

Lin McLean scratched his head and happened to notice a coyote dun in the corral that was regarding him quizzically. "Yu' and me both," he told the horse, and stared at the retreating back of Judge Henry's partner.

17

Into the Past

Arizona had not changed much in ten years. The Virginian gazed out the train window at the same naked hills and the same arid flats he remembered so well. Their monotony was broken now and again by the ragged peaks of barren mountains or the stark outlines of lonely buttes. It was a harsh, hostile land, a land he knew well, from the Mongollon Rim in the south to the Grand Canyon in the north. This had been the main stomping ground of his youth during those years he'd ridden with his fiery cousin, and many were the intense memories stirred by beholding these familiar sights.

The train left him in Tucson. From there the Virginian caught a stage. Since he was on official Sunk Creek business, he wore his best suit of clothes and a new hat he had purchased in Medicine Bow just for the trip. He wanted to present the best possible picture when he arrived at the ranch of Walter Finley. His range clothes, though, were packed in his bag.

Sharing the stage with the Virginian were three men, two beefy specimens in greasy clothes who sat across from him and a refined elderly gentleman who sat at his side. The wheels had hardly started to roll when one of the heavyset men leaned forward and cracked his mouth in an oily smile.

"Greetings, gentlemen. Allow me to introduce myself. Thaddeus Wells is the name, selling goods is my trade. Perhaps I can interest either of you in something?"

The Virginian shifted his gaze from the window to the drummers and shook his head.

"Don't be so impetuous, friend," said the second one. "You haven't seen what we have to offer yet." He opened a case on his lap. "We don't specialize in just one or two items. We can get you anything your little heart desires."

"No, thank yu'."

"Ahh. Is that a Southern accent I hear?" asked the first drummer. "Why, every Southerner I know is a ladies' man. You smooth-talking devils have a natural knack for loosening a woman's defenses." He cackled ruthlessly at his own ribald humor.

"Which is why," took up his partner without missing a beat, "you owe it to them and yourself to have on hand a few trinkets designed to melt the hardest heart. We have some jewelry—"

"No," the Virginian said.

"Then how about a pair of ladies' bloomers?" insisted drummer number one. "Women are always—"

"I'm married."

The drummers exchanged knowing looks, and the second one tapped his case. "Why, sir, we have dozens of articles a wife can't do without. Does she need new pots or pans? We can get them. New blankets? We can have them sent to anywhere in these here United States. Or—"

"We have all we need," the Virginian said, his voice noticeably hardening.

"No man ever has all he needs," countered drummer

number one, heedless of the warning sign. "Take ailments, for instance. Are you prone to headaches? Or stomach troubles? Have warts or corns? Ever get bit by mosquitoes? We have the perfect cure. It's called Dr. Herman's Miracle Elixir, and it's guaranteed to—"

The Virginian's arm casually brushed the flap of his coat aside as he moved his hand from the window to his knee. In doing so, he exposed the butt of the Colt jammed under his waistband. "If I think of anything I need, gents, I'll let yu' know."

Both drummers promptly turned to study the bleak countryside.

Adjusting his coat, the Virginian leaned back and heard a soft chuckle beside him.

"If you don't mind my saying so, young man, you bring back memories of the old days," the elderly passenger remarked, his smile the genuine article.

"They *were* wild and woolly, weren't they?"

"Most people don't know the half of it," the gentleman responded. He offered his hand and, as they shook, said, "My name is Ben Kinslow. I've lived in these parts for the better part of forty years, so I imagine no one is better acquainted with the goings-on around here than I am." He cocked his head to study the Southerner better. "You're not a local, but I have the strangest feeling I've seen you before. Have I?"

"Folks like to say that anything is possible."

"Well, it doesn't really matter." Kinslow placed the end of the cane he carried on the floor and used the ivory knob as a rest for his forearms. "Men come and go all the time. Even more so back in the old days. Half of them were whipping a tired pony out of Texas, and the other half were on the dodge from points elsewhere." He sighed and turned his pale-blue eyes to his window. "They were snuffy times, sure, but I was glad to be part of them. The Earps, Holliday, the Clantons, the McLaurys, I knew them all. Not on a first-name basis, mind you, but I shared a saloon with all of them at one time or another. And despite what gets printed in the likes of the *Police Gazette* and

Harper's Monthly, they were men just like you and me. No
better, no worse."

The Virginian knew he had a talker of another type
on his hands, but he said nothing that would silence the
older man. Instead, he responded by asking, "Whatever
happened to those gun-sharks you mentioned? The Earps
and Holliday?"

"Oh, Doc drifted up to Colorado for his health. He
was tubercular, you see. Died in Glenwood in bed with his
boots off, the story goes, which is a hell of a note, considering he did more to fertilize Tombstone's reputation for
being the deadliest town in the West than almost all the
other gunmen combined." Kinslow laughed at a memory.
"No one could stand up to that scrappy little son of a
bitch, unless it was that wildcat from Missouri or Texas or
wherever the hell he was—"

"What about the Earps?"

"Them? Let me see. Morgan was shot down while
playing billiards about five months after the O.K. Corral.
Virgil, last I heard, was out in California. Wyatt too, although he gets back this way a couple of weeks each year
to visit old friends."

"He does?"

"Yes, indeed. Matter of fact, he's back here now.
Spends most of his time out at the Hooker Ranch south of
Tombstone."

"What about Buckskin Frank?"

Kinslow faced around. "Frank Leslie? Now there's
another mean one. He used to practice his marksmanship
by having his lady friends stand in front of a wall so he
could shoot out their silhouettes. That animal is in prison,
thank the Lord. About three years ago he shot his
girlfriend to death after they quarreled. Blond Mollie Wil-
liams was her name, and she used to work at the Bird
Cage. I saw her a few times. Fine figure of a woman, but
a poor calico queen who couldn't go the day without her
quart of tornado juice."

"Is it true Leslie once killed a man named Billy
Claiborne?"

"That he did. Claiborne thought Leslie had killed a

friend of his, that Missouri wildcat I was fixing to tell you about, so Claiborne went gunning for him, but Billy made the mistake of being drunk when he braced Buckskin Frank."

"And what about Johnny Behind the Deuce?" the Virginian casually asked.

"That blowhard? He met his Maker in the Sulphur Springs Valley. Pony Deal tracked him down and shot him in revenge for—" Kinslow stopped and regarded the Southerner with renewed interest. "Strange you should be asking about those two. Both Buckskin Frank and Johnny Behind the Deuce were suspected of bushwhacking the same man." He scrutinized the Virginian's face for the longest time, then said softly, "I'll be damned."

"It's been a while, Ben."

"That is has, son. Didn't recognize you with that mustache and those fancy clothes. Plus you've grown some."

"I'd appreciate it if yu' keep my visit to yourself."

Kinslow nodded. "I'm a firm believer in minding my own business. Always have been." His gaze shifted to the drummers, who were doing a poor job of pretending they weren't interested in the conversation. "I'm not like some who jabber just to hear themselves talk."

The Virginian posed one last question. "Curly Bill still around?"

"Hell, no. He was the only one with a shred of horse sense. No one has seen him since Billy Breakenridge shot him in the face. He wised up then and lit out. Wyatt went around telling everyone he blew out Curly's lamp, but I know for a fact Curly drifted west and is probably still alive." Kinslow fell silent for a while, then cleared his throat. "You're not here to settle accounts after all this time, are you?"

"Goodness gracious, no. What gives yu' that notion?"

"It must gall you not knowing who killed your cousin. Was it Buckskin Frank, as Claiborne claimed? Was it Johnny Behind the Deuce, like Pony Deal claimed? Or was it somebody else?" Kinslow added,

"There are some who say Wyatt did it, but that's more hot air. Wyatt was never shy about adding to his reputation, and he wasn't too particular about sticking to the facts when he did."

"Anyone else claim credit for the murder?"

"Oh, there were whispers that Holliday was the one. He was a prime candidate, seeing as how Johnny braced him right there in broad daylight in the middle of Tombstone." Kinslow laughed softly. "There wasn't another man alive who would have done that. No, sir. Your cousin was as gritty as fish eggs rolled in sand, maybe the grittiest son of a bitch who ever wore britches."

"And look at what it got him," the Virginian responded thoughtfully. "He was hell on wheels, but that didn't stop him from being dry gulched."

"Let me ask you," Kinslow said. "Who do *you* figure did it?"

"I've been a-thinkin' about that for an awful lot o' years now, and I'm no closer to knowin' than I was the day they found Johnny sittin' in that oak tree, shot and scalped both."

Many minutes went by before either of them spoke again, and it was Kinslow who ventured wistfully, "Knowing him was a real joy. He was the only man I've ever met who could recite Shakespeare and read from those Roman and Greek books he always toted around in his saddlebags. A rare man."

"He taught me practically all I know," the Virginian confessed, at which point the shadow under his hat brim seemed to deepen.

"I'm surprised you've managed to keep yourself out of trouble," Kinslow mentioned, "since you were as good at gunslinging as he was."

"After a while every boy grows up."

"The smart ones do. And, come to think of it, you always did impress me as being smarter than the rest of those crazy cowboys. The Clanton outfit and the McLaurys were too carefree for their own good. It takes a lot of experience to sweat the fat off a brain, and those boys just weren't experienced enough to know when they were up against a stacked deck."

"They learned their lesson the hard way," the Virginian said.

"Don't we all?"

The remainder of the ride was spent in idle small talk. The Virginian danced around the subject of his cousin whenever it threatened to come up again. Neither of the drummers uttered a word until the stage rumbled down Allen Street.

Here the Virginian leaned back to scan the buildings better. Many he recognized: the McAlisher House, the Nevada Boot and Shoot Store, the two general-merchandise emporiums, and others. Bittersweet memories washed over him, and instead of the quiet street containing a few afternoon strollers, he saw in his mind's eye Allen Street as it had once been on a typical summer evening, crammed with raucous cowboys, miners, and gamblers, and everywhere the painted ladies for which Tombstone had been notorious during its silver heyday. Then Kinslow spoke, and the vision shattered under the oppressive weight of reality.

"Where will you be staying while you're in town?"

"Arrangements have been made for me at the Palace Hotel."

"I'll look you up in a day or two and we'll go out and drink to old times."

"To old times," the Virginian said rather sadly.

Exactly how much Tombstone had changed was not clear to the Virginian until half an hour later when he took a walk to stretch his legs. Entire blocks had been abandoned to the elements. Formerly grand hotels, plush saloons, and many stores now stood empty, their windows broken or cracked, their doors boarded over. Dozens had been scarred by fires or reduced to ashes. He walked among the desolation, contrasting it to the splendor of former days, and his sadness expanded. "A man should never go back again, I reckon," he said to himself, a habit he shared with countless punchers who spent endless hours in the saddle, alone except for their horse. "Nothin' is ever the same."

"Ain't that the truth, youngster."

The Virginian turned to find a grizzled prospector scrutinizing him from the recessed doorway of a nearby building. "Didn't know I had an audience, or I wouldn't have aired my thoughts."

"Don't mind me," the old-timer declared. His grin revealed three of his top teeth were missing. "Amos Secomb is as harmless as a newborn babe."

"What happened?" the Virginian asked, nodding at one of the burnt-out ruins.

"Lots of things. The silver played out, so most folks left. Dropped from eight thousand citizens to less than six hundred in just a few years." Secomb squinted at a blackened beam. "Then we damn near burnt to ashes twice. With all the trees gone for miles around, there was no more wood to rebuild and no one willin' to haul what we needed from Tucson or wherever." He made a resigned gesture. "So folks just let it be. One day, I expect, Tombstone will wither away to nothin' and blow away with the dust."

A little farther on the Virginian found an inhabited section of town. Thereafter he stuck to the streets where there were people. The landlady at the Palace Hotel had generously given him a free meal ticket good at the Cancan Oyster Parlor, considered the finest eating establishment left in Tombstone. He went in, half expecting to be greeted by lively music and willing women in tight dresses, but instead took a seat at a modest table in a drab room and was waited on by a mild man in a nondescript suit.

"We have roast beef with pork and beans and peach pie for dessert," intoned this meek worthy, never once meeting the Southerner's eye. "Will you take soup?"

From the Cancan the Virginian's steps took him to the Parlor Saloon. Here he downed a single drink, his limit since he had to be on his way to the Finley ranch at first light. Afterward he sat in with four locals and played stud poker until past ten. Then, fatigue gnawing at his limbs, he excused himself and strolled out the batwing doors.

"Have a word with yu', mister?"

So quickly did the Virginian turn that the man who had addressed him took an inadvertent step backward. The Virginian's right hand, which had been dangling at his side, was now at his waist, his thumb hooked under his belt. "Didn't your pa teach yu' better than to go sneakin' up on someone in the dark?"

"My apologies," the sturdy stranger said. He was in his thirties, well groomed, and wore a tin star on his vest that glittered in the lamp light. "Jim Adams, deputy sheriff. There's no need to tell me who you are. Everyone in town knows."

The Virginian thought of the drummers and wanted to curse.

"I'm here on behalf o' certain members of our community who are worried yu' might cause trouble," Adams said, and when the Southerner's eyes narrowed, he went on hastily, "Now I'm not sayin' yu' will, and I'm not sayin' yu' won't. And since I have no cause to ask yu' to leave, I'm simply payin' yu' the courtesy of explaining how things stand and to let yu' know that if yu' do stir up a fuss, the law won't stand for it. Savvy?"

A tree would have displayed more emotion than the Virginian did.

"Things have been real quiet in Tombstone for years, and we'd like to keep it that way," Adams continued, his tone neither friendly nor hostile. He was a messenger for the vested interests, nothing more, and he wasn't about to provoke a gunfight that might get him killed. "Most of the gun fanners are cavortin' in hell. All those of the old crowd who are left have agreed to let sleepin' dogs lie. Can you do the same?"

"I'm here on business," the Virginian finally said. "When I'm done, yu' won't see me again."

Adams pursed his lips. "I'll pass on the information." He pivoted on his boot heel, took a stride, then halted and looked back. "Are you open to some advice, mister?"

"Depends on what it is."

"From one Southerner to another. Keep your back to the wall and don't stand under any lamps. There are a few people who are mighty riled about yu' comin' back after all this time. I don't know why they're so upset and it's not my place to ask. Whatever the reason, they all own guns. Savvy?"

"I savvy. And I'm obliged," the Virginian said. He watched the deputy walk off, then hugged the front of the saloon until he came to an alley. A full moon shone on high, and far to the north he could see the Dragoon Mountain Range outlined in black against the paler sky. He went on, past McCullough's New York Coffee House, a tin shop, an assay office, and a furniture store. A vacant lot loomed on his left. Ahead, across an open space, was the New Orleans Saloon, from which piano music tinkled gaily. He reached under his coat, touched the butt of his Colt, then moved boldly along dusty Fourth Street. His skin prickled, but nothing happened.

The Virginian was feeling foolish by the time he stepped into the lobby of the Palace Hotel. He was surprised to see the landlady still up, seated in a chair reading, and he nodded to her as he passed.

"Pleasant dreams," she said. Then, as an afterthought, "Oh. Did that gentleman find you?"

"Ma'am?"

"There was a man in here to see you earlier. Asked an awful lot of questions. Wanted to know how long you were staying and what you were doing in Tombstone. I told him I had no idea, and he seemed quite disturbed."

"It wasn't Deputy Adams by any chance?"

"Certainly not. I know Jim well. This man didn't bother to introduce himself. He was a fine-looking fellow, if I do say so myself. Wore one of those black frock coats and a cute string tie. Reminded me of our church deacon, he did. Do you know him?"

"Yes, ma'am. I believe I do." The Virginian thanked her for the information and strode on. As he slipped the key in, he shifted his body to one side in case an assassin should be waiting for him. The door, however, creaked open on an empty room. He pulled the shade and propped the chair against the latch to deter unwanted visitors; then he lit the lamp, dimming the flame until it was nearly out. From his bag he took another revolver, a spare he used when the need dictated—as it had that day in Medicine Bow when he confronted Trampas—and with a pistol in each tanned hand he reclined on his back, his head propped on the fluffy pillow.

The walls of the hotel were paper-thin, enabling the Virginian to hear low laughter, loud coughing, and once a muffled moan. Try as he might, he couldn't fall asleep. His mind raced of its own accord, reviewing the events of the day. Several times he reflected that he couldn't wait to complete Judge Henry's errand and return to his wife and son; yet each time the image of his cousin's handsome, smiling face would shimmer in the air before him and a knot would form in his throat. At length slumber claimed him.

Sunlight streaming through a crack in the shade awakened the Virginian shortly after dawn. Rising, he washed in the basin, stuck the pistols under his coat, one on each hip with the barrel wedged loosely under his belt, and checked the picture he presented in the small mirror. There were no telltale bulges. To a casual observer, he would appear unarmed.

Forgoing breakfast, the Virginian went directly from the hotel to the O.K. Corral Stable located on Allen Street. A pudgy man in grimy overalls sat in the office munching on a cold biscuit and reading a newspaper. He never looked up when the Virginian's muscular frame filled the doorway.

"I'd like to rent a horse for the day," announced the Southerner.

"How well do you ride?" the man absently asked, still intent on the *Epitaph*. "If you need a gentle horse, I've got a sweet little mare that a child could handle." His head lifted ponderously and he gazed at his customer.

Then his whole attitude miraculously changed. He cast aside the paper and came off his stool in a rush. "Yes, sir. One horse, coming right up." He grinned as he shuffled past the Virginian. "And I reckon you can ride just about anything, so I'll save that mare for the next old lady who comes in."

A large black gelding was brought from a stall for the Virginian to inspect. He liked it and said as much.

"Thank you, sir," said the proprietor. "This is my best animal." He paused. "Will you be needing a saddle, or did you bring your own?"

Five minutes later the Virginian was riding briskly eastward. He was glad to be shy of Tombstone, out in the open spaces he loved so much. The gelding responded superbly to the least bit of pressure, and it was evident from the way the horse strained at the bit that it had been cooped up for quite a while and was eager for the exercise.

The desolate landscape fanned more recollections. Most vividly, the Virginian recalled the talk he'd had with his cousin before Johnny went off on that final, fatal binge. They had just eaten at Dial's, over in the south pass of the Dragoons, and had stepped outside for some fresh air. He remembered the odd look his cousin had given him, and the even odder statement that was voiced: "There comes a time when even the best of pards have to take separate trails."

"Are yu' talkin' about us?" the Virginian had asked.

"I'm thinkin' o' going to Galeyville tomorrow, and it's best if I go alone."

"Got yourself a painted cat staked out?"

His cousin had turned to survey the mountains. "No. I just need some time to myself. We all do, now and then."

There had been a hint of tension in his cousin's tone, and the Virginian had moved around to where he could see the older man's face. "Yu' in trouble?"

"No more than usual," the most feared gunman in

the whole territory had replied, and then he'd laughed. "Wyatt and Holliday are afteh me, but I can stay one step ahead o' those jokers without workin' up a sweat." He had sighed. "I need to do some serious thinkin', *compadre*. This ridin' the high-lines is wearin' thin. There has to be somethin' else we can do. Has to be."

"We could go into ranchin' like I've been sayin' we should do since we crossed the Pecos."

"Honest ranchin' yu' mean," his cousin had responded with a grin. "It's a proposition worth considerin'."

"Yu' sure yu' ain't just in one o' your moods?" the Virginian had remarked. "Didn't yu' get another letter from her a few days ago?"

"Keep her out o' this."

"I'm plumb sorry, John, but I hate it when yu' let yourself go to pieces like yu' do, and yu' a growed man. How long are yu' goin' to keep pinin' for her? It's been *years*."

The Southerner's cousin had drawn himself up to his full height, eyes blazing, and declared, "When yu've been in love, youngster, then I'll listen. And I'm not talkin' about the silly sort o' love yu' feel for a willin' filly at a dance hall or a dove in a saloon. I'm talkin' about real love, the kind a mature man feels for a mature woman, the true sort o' love that reaches deep down into the depths o' your soul and won't let go no matter what. The kind that cuts yu' to the core if yu' lose the one yu' care for." He had paused. "When yu've known that type o' love, then tell me about what it's like being a grown man."

A nicker from the black stallion brought the Virginian back to the present. He shook his head, dispelling the memories, and scanned the eastern horizon. Finley's ranch lay ten miles east of Tombstone; he should arrive there about midmorning.

As the Virginian's head swiveled farther and his gaze roved over the Dragoon Mountains, he suddenly tensed. On top of a nearby hill bordering the mountains, something flashed. He saw it again a few seconds later, and all his old instincts returned with a vengeance—the animal instincts he had honed during those hard years he rode the owlhoot trail with his cousin and acquired, firsthand, the wide knowledge of evil that later enabled him to appreciate more fully the supreme value of good. He tried convincing himself the flash had been a fluke of nature, perhaps sunlight reflecting off quartz or something else, but he knew better. Those outlaw instincts that had often meant the difference between life and death during his early years now told him that someone was up there watching him, spying on him either with a telescope or field glasses.

The Virginian was minded to cut toward the hill and try to reach the top before whoever was up there could ride off, but the distance was too great and there was no cover between the trail he followed and the hill. So he rode on, frustrated, pretending he hadn't noticed, and wondering if the mysterious watcher was none other than the gentleman in the frock coat. He doubted it. No one who knew them had ever accused *that* clan of cowardice. Their way was to march right up to someone they didn't like and air their grievances man to man. But if not the ex-lawman, he mused, then who? The Virginian was stumped, and he didn't like being in the dark when his ignorance could prove fatal.

When at last the Finley ranch house materialized in the haze, the Virginian had developed a kink in his neck from repeatedly checking his back trail for sign of pursuit. He saw a large corral filled with horses adjacent to the house and a number of punchers engaged in various activities. Moments later a pair of mounted cowboys galloped to intercept him. He smoothed his jacket, adjusted his hat, and plastered a friendly smile on his face.

They were typical of the breed: lanky frames, features burnt brown by constant exposure to the sun, and possessed of devil-may-care twinkles in their eyes.

"Howdy, mister," declared the oldest of the pair. "The

name is Latimore. I'm foreman hyeh at the Bar F. What can I do for yu'?"

The Virginian introduced himself and apologized for arriving a day earlier than the Judge's last letter had indicated he would. Once the cowboys learned who he was, they treated him as if he were visiting royalty.

Walter Finley turned out to be a soft-spoken man in his early sixties who knew more about horses than any other man the Virginian had ever met. They struck it off immediately and spent several hours swapping tales of the early days in the territory and their various adventures back in Texas, which was from where Finley hailed.

Shortly before supper Finley took the Southerner out to the barn to see the Morgan. The moment the Virginian laid eyes on the animal, he tingled all over. Here was a horse as God had meant horses to be, perfect in build and poise, with a delicate head, tapering neck, and resplendent coat. As he admired it, he thought of the line it could sire, and he knew that in the matter of inspirations, the Judge's had equaled his.

As outstanding as the supper was, served up by a matronly Spanish woman who took great pride in her tacos, enchiladas, and frijoles, the Virginian hardly noticed. All he could think of was the Morgan. After the meal Finley invited him into the sitting room, where the two of them talked and smoked their pipes until after seven, at which time the Virginian made his apologies and headed back for town. Finley tried to persuade him to stay the night, but the Virginian pleaded the arrangements he had to make for the transfer of the funds involved in the purchase and for the shipment of the Morgan. He didn't reveal he had an ulterior motive for not staying.

The Virginian hoped he could lure whoever was shadowing him out of hiding by making the rounds of various saloons. If he kept his eyes skinned, sooner or later he might notice a face that cropped up at each establishment. That would be his man.

Engrossed in thought, the Virginian paid scant attention to his surroundings until he was more than halfway to Tombstone. Then, as he rounded a bend, he heard a sound off to the right that made him tingle in an entirely different manner.

It was the metallic rasp of a rifle lever being worked.

18

Ghosts of Yesteryear

A lifetime spent on the raw frontier had honed the Virginian's reflexes to a razor's edge. His was a lightning-quick coordination few men possessed, which he exhibited now by launching himself from the saddle at the selfsame instant he heard the click of the rifle. In the very next heartbeat the night reverberated to the blast of the bushwhacker's gun, and a slug whizzed through the space his body had just occupied.

The Virginian landed on his left shoulder and rolled into the brush on the other side of the trail. When he came to rest in a crouch behind an isolated saguaro, he held both pistols. The rifle thundered twice more in rapid succession, but the assassin was firing wildly and missed. Then all was still save for the receding clatter of the stallion's hooves as it fled westward.

Fingers flying, the Virginian stripped off his spurs and set them down. The musty scent of the earth filled his nostrils as he glided silently to the right, always keeping vegetation between himself and the trail. Ten yards from the saguaro he halted and strained his ears, hoping to detect the rifleman on the move, but all he heard was the soft sigh of the wind. He stayed put, relying on his dark clothes and hat to blend into the background and shield him from probing eyes. The temptation to call out a certain name was almost irresistible, but he held his tongue because of his conviction that his old enemy would have come right out in the open when the time came and not try to shoot him from ambush.

Minutes weighted with anchors dragged past. The Virginian shifted his weight from foot to foot but otherwise might have been sculpted from marble. Then, when he was beginning to think the assassin had left, an inky shadow flitted east across to the road. His pistols barked in unison and were answered by the rifle, but the shot went wide. He dived, thumbing the hammers as he did, and sent two bullets into a patch of darkness he hoped was the killer. Once again the rifle responded, the slug throwing dirt into his face.

Rolling to the right, the Virginian nearly collided with a jumping cholla. At the last instant he realized what it was and jerked aside. Had he not, its stinging spines would have torn into his flesh. He didn't hear the footsteps until he stopped, and when he did, he leaped erect and raced in pursuit of the fleeing bushwhacker. Across the trail and into the brush beyond he went, limbs snatching at his clothes and scratching his boots. He didn't care. All he wanted was the man who had tried to kill him. Fate dictated otherwise. He was approaching a low knoll when the drumming of hooves showed the assassin to be in full flight, heading for Tombstone.

The Virginian pounded to the top of the knoll anyway and tried to catch a glimpse of the rider in the ashen moonlight. All he could distinguish was the man's outline, which gave him no clue at all as to the killer's identity. Simmering at being thwarted, he shoved the pistols under his belt and walked to the trail. It took him a while to find his spurs; then, squaring his shoulders, he hiked toward town.

A long trek afoot was the scourge of all cowboys, but

this time the Virginian didn't mind. He had much to ponder, and he speculated again and again on the identity of his attacker. Only one thing was certain: It must have been the same man who spied on him that morning, and who had waited patiently all day long for him to make the return trip. Had it not been for the ambusher's carelessness in not injecting a round into the chamber of his rifle sooner, the Southerner would have given up the ghost without knowing who killed him or why.

The moon had climbed high into the sky by the time the Virginian reached the deserted outskirts of Tombstone. His feet throbbed, his legs ached. Cowboy boots, he ruefully reflected, simply weren't made with hiking in mind, yet another reason why punchers everywhere dreaded being stranded without a horse.

Tired as the Virginian was, he didn't go directly to his hotel. Instead, he ambled down Fremont Street and stopped at a vacant lot situated between the office of the county recorder and a building that was once C.S. Fly's Lodging House. He couldn't say what had drawn him to the spot, unless it was the many ghosts that had haunted him since his arrival. This was where the climax of the bitter feud had taken place, and had he not been with his cousin that distant day, off in the mountains, he might have shared a plot of dirt alongside Tom and Frank McLaury and Billy Clanton in boot-hill.

"Ringold."

The whisper brought the Virginian around in a blur, his six-shooters out and cocked and leveling on the dark form standing at the corner of the recorder's office. He would have fired, too, had he not been able to tell that the man's arms were extended from his sides and neither hand held a revolver.

"I'm not heeled. I want to talk, not fight."

"Quit skulkin' in the shadows, then."

Into the moonlight stepped a long-legged, mustachioed man wearing a black frock coat and string tie. His stride was purposeful, his movements deliberate. He had the air of someone whose confidence in his own ability knew no bounds, tinged by a certain vanity evident in his haughty stare and the arrogant tilt of his chin. "I saw you come into town and figured now would be as good a time as any." He paused. "You seem a mite jumpy."

The Virginian deliberately gave the Colts a twirl before tucking them under his belt within easy reach. "Yu' would be too if some mangy polecat tried to bushwhack yu'."

"It wasn't me."

"If I thought it was," the Virginian said with a dour expression, "you'd be filled with lead, Wyatt."

The other man's lips compressed. He shifted to gaze at the empty lot and commented, "I've often regretted that you and your braggart cousin weren't here that day. There would have been five for the undertaker to plant, not just three."

"No, there would have been four," the Virginian corrected him. "And as for John bein' a braggart, I seem to recollect yu' backed down when he called yu' out on Allen Street."

"I was running for sheriff. I couldn't afford to take part in a gunfight."

"Yu' always were good at makin' excuses."

Tension crackled between them. They glared at one another until the man in the frock coat casually folded his arms across his chest and declared, "You still have more guts than you could hang on a fence, I see."

"Spare me the flattery. What do yu' want?"

"Fair enough. Straight tongue, Jeff. Did you come here to kill me in revenge for your cousin's murder?"

"Now you're flatterin' yourself."

"Am I? Clear out of the blue, you show up at the same time I'm here on a personal visit. Sure, it's been a decade, but what else am I supposed to believe? Your family was always tight-knit, as close as my own. Harm one and the rest were on you like a pack of wolves."

"Those were the days," the Virginian said fondly.

"To be honest, I was surprised when you didn't look me up right after they found John's body. Doc and me both figured you'd be on the peck, but then we heard you'd gone north." Wyatt studied the Southerner a bit. "I finally decided Big Nose Kate was right about you all along."

"Doc's woman?"

Wyatt nodded. "That whore could read men a far sight better than she could a book. She took a shine to you, remember? Always had a nice word to say to you when you were in town." He tilted his hat back. "She claimed you weren't like the rest of those loudmouthed cowboys. Tried to convince Doc and me that one day you'd make something of yourself."

The Virginian remembered the kindly woman with the hooked nose and sad eyes, and frowned. "She deserved better than Holliday."

"Easy to say when Doc is feeding the worms."

"Yu' don't think I wouldn't have told him to his face if there had been cause?"

"Oh, you would have, all right. That was what riled me the most about you and your cousin. The two of you weren't afraid of anyone or anything." Wyatt shook his head in amazement. "John challenging me like he did right there in front of half the town. And then trying to provoke Doc into a handkerchief duel." He locked his eyes on the Southerner. "In a way you were lucky he always looked out for you and kept you from getting mixed up in Clanton's dealings. He wasn't all bad."

"I never thought I'd live to hear yu' give *him* a compliment."

"He was my enemy, but I respected him. Is that so hard to understand? Hasn't there ever been someone you ran up against you liked just a little?"

The Virginian made no answer.

"Well, enough of this. I didn't look you up for old time's sake. We weren't friends then, and we'll never be friends. But if you say you're not out for revenge, I'll take your word." Wyatt extended his right hand. "Shake on it, and I won't trouble you again."

Ever so slowly, his body tensed in case this was a trick, the Southerner clasped the ex-lawman's hand. He felt Earp's fingers clamp tighter than was called for and knew right away that his strength was being tested, that

Wyatt wouldn't be satisfied unless he demonstrated that he was the better man. That's the way it had always been. Wyatt Earp couldn't abide being second-best at anything, which was the real reason Earp had so hated the Virginian's cousin. When it came to gunplay, there had never lived a deadlier soul than the man most knew as Johnny Ringo.

Wyatt grinned now, a sly, superior sort of grin that rankled the Virginian and transformed the corded muscles of his right arm into bands of iron. The Virginian was accustomed to hard living, to riding the range and working with cattle, to using his hands constantly. Earp, however, was accustomed to the easy life, to running a saloon, to gambling, and seldom worked up a sweat. For a long minute the pair stood as immobile as twin statues, their hard features betraying their innermost feelings, and then the Virginian could feel Wyatt's fingers beginning to yield under his greater pressure. Fleeting surprise etched Earp's face. Suddenly Wyatt broke the handhold and stepped back.

"I'm satisfied if you are," Wyatt said, then turned on his heel. He went only a few yards, though, before he glanced back. "If you don't mind my asking, I've got to know. What the hell *are* you doing in Tombstone?"

The Virginian told him, in as few words as possible.

"Well, I'll be damned," Wyatt said. Slapping his thigh, he threw back his head and roared.

"What has yu' so tickled?" the Virginian wanted to know.

"Do you have any idea what I do for a living these days?"

"Don't much care."

"I raise thoroughbreds."

The Virginian stood and watched until the frock coat vanished in the night. Then he headed for his hotel along streets mostly deserted. The landlady had already retired, and there was no one in the lobby or in the halls as he made his weary way to his room.

Uppermost in the Virginian's mind was his encounter with the man the paperbacks had made into a living legend, the very same magazines and books that always portrayed his cousin as a bloodthirsty murderer. Where was the justice in that? he reflected. Wyatt Earp didn't have a halo. If the truth was known, Earp had done more than his share of shady deeds over the years, far more than most men. Earp was a recognized card cheat, a claim jumper, and a swindler, yet he was revered by an adoring public from coast to coast. Johnny Ringo had done none of those things and was reviled. History had been rewritten by the journalists to their satisfaction, and now posterity would never know the real story.

Shaking his head at the inequities of life, the Virginian inserted his key and was about to turn it when the hall echoed to the blast of two gunshots. Slugs slammed into the wood panel near his head, sending stinging slivers into his cheek. The Virginian instinctively dropped into a crouch and drew his pistols. At the far end of the corridor a shadow slipped around the corner. The Virginian gave chase, stopping shy of the turn to peek out. Instantly a revolver spat lead, and something tugged at the flap of his coat. He answered, saw the shadow dart around the next bend, and followed. Throughout the hotel shouts erupted. Doors were opening, men demanding to know what was happening.

The Virginian heard a resounding crash and the splintering of wood. There was an angry yell. At the corner he paused. In the hall ahead were several irate men in various stages of undress clustered around a shattered side door. The Virginian ran toward the doorway, paying the men no mind. "What the hell!" one exclaimed. They all glanced at his Colts, then permitted him to pass without interference.

The cool night air struck the Virginian at the same time as the bullet. He had taken but a single step and was looking both ways along the alley when to his right a six-shooter cracked and his new hat was snatched from his head. He threw himself forward to his knees, replying with two shots that sent the assassin scurrying for cover around the hotel.

Up and down the street shouting had broken out, and lights were coming on in several buildings when the Virginian pounded from the alley and flattened against a wall. To the east a stocky figure sprinted into the darkness. Without delay the Virginian launched in pursuit, his arms and legs pumping, his Colts glittering in the intermittent glow from the few street lamps.

"Hold on there!" someone bellowed to his rear.

The Virginian wasn't about to stop. Forty yards was all that separated him from the answers he wanted, so he poured on the speed. His quarry ducked into an alley, and he glimpsed a pale face fixed in his direction just before the man disappeared.

"Stop, damn it!"

Hoofbeats sounded as the Virginian reached the alley mouth and stopped. He cocked both Colts, then swept around the corner, but he was too late. The assassin, mounted on a bay, was at the opposite end, turning onto the next street. He raised his right Colt and took hasty aim, but an instant later both horse and rider were gone. He stood no chance of catching them.

Resentment at the constant game of cat and mouse coursed through the Virginian, making him tremble with suppressed rage. Now the assassin would try again later, he realized, unless he left Tombstone before his work on behalf of Sunk Creek was completed, which he would never do. He let the Colts droop to his side and cursed.

"This is yours, I believe?"

So wound up was the Virginian that he spun at the first syllable. Standing at the corner was Deputy Sheriff Jim Adams holding his new hat.

"I heard all the ruckus in the hotel and was coming on the run when I saw yu' in the alley," the lawman stated. "Who was that yu' were after?"

"Yu saw him?"

"Just a glimpse. I gather he doesn't think much of yu'."

"Enough to want to fill me with lead," the Virginian replied. He shoved the Colts out of sight under his coat and reclaimed his hat. "I'm obliged to yu' again."

Adams stared at the Southerner's midsection a moment. "You're lucky the town marshal and the sheriff are escorting an escaped prisoner back to Tucson. They're real sticklers about the ordinance that prohibits anyone from wearin' firearms in the town limits."

"And you're not?"

"Let's just say I'm not going to ask for your hoglegs if yu' don't let anyone but me see them."

"Why are yu' bein' so charitable?"

"I know Wyatt Earp," Adams said, and turned to confront an angry crowd of citizens rapidly gathering from all directions. Over his shoulder he added, "And I don't like that pompous ass one bit. When he asks me to do something, I know he's up to no good."

The Virginian wanted to question the deputy further, but the hubbub of approaching voices reminded him of the drone of riled hornets. Donning his hat, he ran down the alley and turned to the left. Reaching the hotel undetected was easy, since most of Tombstone was badgering Jim Adams for answers about the gunfire. He thought he would reach his room unmolested, but he reckoned without his landlady, who was waiting for him in front of his door.

"Do you have an explanation for what just took place?" she demanded brusquely, jabbing her thumb at the bullet holes in the top panel.

A lie would have cleared the Virginian. He could have told her that he'd just returned and had no idea what had happened. Or he could have fibbed and claimed a drunk had done the shooting. But he did neither. "Someone is tryin' to kill me, Mrs. Miller," he confessed.

The landlady's owl eyes widened, and she primly folded her wrinkled hands at her stout waist. "Mercy me," she said softly. "Does Jim Adams know?"

"He does. But there's nothin' he can do since we don't have the faintest notion who it is."

"I don't know quite what to say, Mr. Ringold. I can't have someone going around shooting up my establishment. There are the other guests to think of, you know."

"I understand, ma'am," the Virginian said. "I'll check out in the mawnin'."

"You'll do no such thing. I'm not about to throw out a paying customer." Mrs. Miller's eyes twinkled. "We'll simply move you to another room and not tell a soul. I won't even enter it in the register. That way, this killer won't know where to find you." She giggled girlishly. "How does that sound?"

"More than fair, ma'am. I don't know how to thank yu'."

"I do. Come down and have cookies and tea with me before you leave. Something tells me you've lived a rather interesting life, and I'd like to hear some about it, if you don't mind."

"Not at all."

And so within half an hour the Virginian and his belongings were in a back room and he was sound asleep, a Colt in each hand. He tossed and turned and muttered, caught up in a disturbing dream about a mysterious figure who haunted his every move and ultimately shot him in the back. The sensation of pain was so realistic that the Virginian sat bolt upright in bed and almost snapped off several shots at the blank wall. Caked with sweat, he moved to the window, opened it, and knelt by the sill to suck in mouthfuls of cool, fresh air.

Somewhere a dog was yapping. The Virginian rested his brow against the sash and reminisced about the glory days in Tombstone, in particular a conversation he'd had with his cousin that warm August night less than a week before old man Clanton and his men ambushed a pack train of Mexican smugglers in the Peloncillo Mountains.

"Why can't I go?" the Virginian had groused. "I can handle a six-gun and a rifle as good as any o' Clanton's men."

"Better," John had said.

"Then why don't yu' want me to?"

"Because I don't want that shifty-eyed son of a bitch to get his hooks into yu'. Help him once and you'll be helpin' him for life."

"You're goin'."

"I have to. Ike did me a favor once, and I gave him my word I'd help out his family whenever they needed it." John had placed a hand on the Virginian's shoulder. "And when a man gives his word, he has to keep it. Never forget that. There's nothing more important in life."

"It's not givin' your word that counts so much as who yu' give your word *to*."

His cousin had smiled. "You'll change your tune once yu've added a few hairs to that pansy-blossom mustache o' yours."

"Bet me."

Johnny had ridden off with the Clanton outfit and returned over a week later a changed, bitter man. That very evening the two of them had gone drinking at the Alhambra Saloon, and as they stood at a corner of the bar sipping their whiskeys, his cousin had leaned closer and spoken softly so no one else would overhear: "I should've listened to yu', pard. It wasn't no fight. It was a slaughter. All we did was hide out on the canyon rim and keep pumpin' shots into 'em until there wasn't a one left. They didn't stand a prayer." He'd taken a gulp from his glass. "I'll be hearin' their screams until the day I die. Yu' were right. A man has to be true to himself above all else."

Now the Virginian straightened and repeated those words to himself. How fitting they'd been, especially in light of the obituary printed by the *Tombstone Weekly Epitaph* after his cousin's body had been found. He still remembered one particular paragraph: *"Friends and foes are unanimous in the opinion that he was a strictly honorable man in all his dealings and that his word was as good as his bond."* "A strictly honorable man," the Virginian said aloud. Then he returned to bed and lay down with a sigh of relief. He knew what he had to do.

Come the morning, the Virginian was up before daylight, dressed in his range clothes, and at the stable to see if the black stallion had returned of its own accord. It had, and although the proprietor balked at renting it out to him again, he was on the road out of town just as the golden crest of the rising sun rimmed the eastern horizon with brilliant streaks of red and yellow.

Walter Finley would have to wait. The Morgan would have to wait. The Virginian was going to settle affairs once and for all. He made straight for the Chiricahua

Mountains over the old trails he knew so well, the same secluded byways he had taken countless times during his outlaw years.

That night the Virginian made camp under the stars. As he sat next to his fire, drinking coffee, he spied a flickering pinpoint of light far along his back trail, and he smiled and declared, "Got yu'."

The next day was like the first. The Virginian stopped several times, but only long enough to rest and water the stallion. He had a specific destination in mind, and he wanted to reach it as swiftly as possible. Any and all ranches and isolated homesteads he scrupulously avoided since he desired no contact with anyone except the man dogging his trail.

Another grim smile was the Virginian's reaction when the Chiricahuas finally reared into sight. Once among them he urged the stallion to a gallop and sustained the gait until he neared Turkey Creek. He hadn't been to the area in more years than he cared to recollect, although he'd been tempted to pay a visit after the murder of his cousin. And murder it had been, despite the official verdict to the effect John Ringo had committed suicide.

The Virginian laughed bitterly. That had always bothered him. John was supposed to have put his pistol to his temple and blown his brains out. And there had been some who claimed they'd heard him express such a death wish during his frequent bouts of melancholy. But no one had known John better than the Virginian, and the Virginian had never heard his cousin say any such thing.

Then there was the matter of the bullet wound itself. If, as the law had claimed, Johnny Ringo shot himself with his revolver held close to or touching his brow, why had there been no powder burns? The Virginian had talked to several of the men who helped in the burying, and they'd all agreed that there hadn't been so much as a smudge.

The most glaring discrepancy of all had been the scalping business. The Virginian and nearly everyone else in Cochise County had scoffed at the notion John had scalped himself before taking his own life, but since no one had any solid evidence to the contrary, the official judgment had stood on the books for the past ten years.

Across Turkey Creek the Virginian now rode, and close to the mouth of Morse Canyon. Finding the tree was ridiculously easy. It was an oak, or more precisely a cluster of oaks springing from the same stem, each arching skyward at a different angle. Between them was an open space, and here someone had long ago placed a large flat stone. On that stone his cousin's body had been found.

The Virginian sat staring at the spot, overwhelmed by a surge of emotions. Mentally he leaped back in time to that last talk he'd had with his cousin, right after John had lectured him on the nature of true love.

"I may not be long for this world," Johnny had said while thoughtfully surveying the Dragoons. "I might have two days left to me. I might have two years. Whatever, I want yu' to give me your solemn promise that you'll head for parts unknown and start your life over again the day I die."

"What are yu' goin' on about?" the Virginian had responded.

"Yu', yu' boxhead joker. You're still young. Yu' can still do yourself proud. Find a sweetheart, settle down, have kids, do all the things proper folks do. *Make* something of yourself, damn it."

The Virginian still vividly remembered the passion in his cousin's voice when those words were spoken. How had his cousin known? *What* had his cousin known? He shook himself, shattering the grip of the past so he could concentrate on the present. He had work to do.

Hours later, toward evening, a stocky rider appeared on the same trail the Virginian had used. He reined up sharply on spying the figure in the dark suit seated on the rock in the middle of the cluster of oaks, and his dark eyes flicked to the right and left to make certain there were no other riders anywhere in sight. Then, his thin mouth curled in a sadistic smirk, he shucked a new Winchester from his saddle scabbard and pressed the stock to his shoulder. "Easy as pie," he said to himself, cocking the hammer.

At the blast, the figure pitched forward and sprawled on the ground in front of the makeshift pedestal. The rider chuckled, then gouged his spurs into his mount. In a flurry of hooves he pounded up to the oak and jumped down before his horse had stopped moving. Wicked glee lit his brutal features as he stepped up to the prone figure and nudged it with the Winchester barrel. It took a moment for his brain to register what his eyes were seeing, and when he did, he uttered an oath, leaped backward, and went to level the rifle.

"Don't!"

Ignoring the command, the rider started to work the lever, but a shot rang out and he spun half-around, letting go of the Winchester to clutch at his right shoulder. He sank to his knees with a grunt, then turned malevolent eyes on the man who had risen from behind the tree.

"Thank yu' for not disconveniencin' me," the Virginian commented, his smoking Colt steady at his side. "I figured yu' would be along before dark."

"Go to hell!" the rider growled through clenched teeth.

"Yu' first," the Virginian said amiably. By then he was standing over the man. Without warning he lashed out with his Colt, pounding the hard case across the temple. The rider toppled, then sluggishly put his other hand to the welt left by the gun. "Yu' and me are goin' to have a little talk, hombre," the Virginian announced. "And if yu' don't come down with a bad case o' diarrhea o' the jawbone, what I'm goin' to do to yu' don't need mentionin'."

"I won't tell you a damn thing!" the rider snapped. He arrogantly started to push himself up on his palms.

There was hardly any movement on the Virginian's part, but suddenly the man was flying through the air to crash down beside the clever likeness of the Virginian, constructed of a black suit and a number of broken limbs. "Yu' will tell me," he said matter-of-factly. "Either straight out or after yu' scream some, but one way or the other I'll learn all I need to know."

The man rose slowly onto his elbows. His head swayed as if he were drunk, and his eyes were vacant. "Quantrill brat," he mumbled before slumping down into unconsciousness with a gasp.

"What was that?" the Virginian demanded, towering over the limp form. He leaned down and plucked the man's six-shooter from its holster, then expertly ran his hands over the man's clothes seeking a hideout gun. Satisfied there was none, he straightened and stepped back. Something about the weather-seamed face below him seemed oddly familiar, although he couldn't quite place it, and he spent the next several minutes racking his memory for a match, in vain.

In due course the rider stirred again, then sat up. Hatred contorted his features. His left hand was clenched into a knobby fist that he wagged at the Virginian while declaring, "I knew I should have bedded you down years ago! I told him, but he wouldn't listen."

"Told who?"

The man smiled and answered, "Expect me to tell? Jackass! You can beat me all night and all day and you won't get a peep out of me."

"I don't aim to waste the energy when there's an easier way," the Virginian said, and shot the rider in the left leg. The man vented a screech of commingled rage and agony and doubled over, clasping his shin tight, his fingers oozing blood. As composed as could be, the Virginian swiveled the Colt, training it on the other leg. "If yu' want me to chip away at yu' piece by piece until we're down to the bone, go right ahead. But I'm a-thinkin' it might be a heap smarter to fess up while you still can." So saying, he cocked the revolver.

The man's head jerked up at the loud click and his mouth gaped wide. *"No!"* he screamed. "For God's sake, not again!"

"That depends on yu'," the Virginian said. "Give me your handle."

Eyes glued to the Colt, the man barely hesitated. "Yoast. Skinner Yoast."

Again the Virginian experienced the feeling that he should know the cold-blooded killer, but for the life of him he couldn't remember from where. He was going to pose more questions when Yoast went on.

"Now that you know, you're probably wondering why I made wolf meat of John and tried to do the same to you, since neither of you ever done me any wrong either here or down in the Skillet."

The reference to the Texas panhandle made the Virginian stiffen. He felt an odd sensation, as if the inside of his head were tearing wide open, and suddenly he remembered. "Yu' were a mule skinner workin' for old Pete Jenkins. Came from Illinois, as I recollect. We drank with yu' and your friends a few times."

Yoast nodded. "Later on I drifted to Tombstone. With so much ore being shipped out, I figured I'd find a job easy. I did, but not hauling silver. I landed me a job hauling wood for Sorgum Smith."

"We hardly knew yu'," the Virginian said softly. Discovering that the killer of his cousin had been no more than a casual acquaintance was a profound shock. Of all the suspects, he'd been inclined toward believing Johnny Behind the Deuce had been responsible.

Yoast misunderstood and so forgot himself as to smirk. "Knew me well enough. Your stupid cousin didn't even lift a finger when I went up to him to ask what was wrong." He glanced at the stone wedged in the oak tree. "I was hauling a load of wood out of the mountains when I saw him sitting there, his head down low, as if he was sick. So I stopped the wagon and walked on over. He must've heard me, 'cause he said, 'Jeff, is that you?' Then he looked up, and even drunk as he was, he knew me. Said, 'Howdy, Skinner.'"

"And yu' up and shot him?" the Virginian asked, his features acquiring the cast of tempered steel.

Skinner Yoast didn't notice. He was trying to staunch the flow of blood from his leg, which was far worse than the wound in his shoulder. "Not right away," he responded. "I was too damn scared at first. I knew about the bounty on his head, but I was afraid to so much as touch my gun. You should know why. There wasn't a man faster than Johnny Ringo in the whole Southwest." Yoast winced, pressed a palm over the bullet hole, and continued. "He asked me to go get you. Said he was fixing to leave this country and take you with him so the two of you could start over. Imagine! John Ringo a rancher!"

Had the mule skinner looked up, he would have seen the face of death incarnate blazing down on him. "Go on."

"He told me his horse had wandered off, and he'd started to walk, but his boots hurt so much he'd thrown them away and wrapped his feet in strips he'd tore off his undershirt—"

"Tell me how yu' killed him," the Virginian broke in.

"Oh, that was simple. He went and passed out." Yoast finally lifted his head. His breath suddenly caught in his throat and he blanched. His left hand, which had been side by side with his right on his shin, drifted lower. "Now you hold on!" he declared. "I'm telling you everything, ain't I?"

"Why'd yu' scalp him?"

"I didn't," Yoast said, and when the Southerner took a short step forward, he cried out, "That's the gospel! I tried to scalp him, to take that black hair of his back as proof of what I'd done so I'd collect the bounty with no problem, but I didn't have the stomach for it so I stopped after slicing off a small part. That's all! Honest." His left hand was perched above his boot.

"Who was payin' this hyeh bounty?"

"You don't know?" Yoast cackled long and hard. As he did, he slipped several fingers inside his boot. "Hell, the joke's on me, I reckon. The hombre told me you did. Claimed you knew everything. Claimed you'd come back to kill both of us. That's why he paid me to bushwhack you." Yoast nodded at his rifle, lying in the grass nearby. "Even bought me that, so I could do the job right."

The Virginian glanced at the Winchester, and out of the corner of his eye he saw Yoast's hand leap out of the boot clutching a derringer that gleamed in the sunlight, a gleam as bright as the gleam of triumph infusing Yoast's face. His Colt cracked once.

A red hole materialized squarely in the center of Skinner Yoast's forehead, and his head snapped back. In slow motion he sank back onto the earth, his arms going limp, the derringer falling from his slack fingers. There was a muted popping sound inside his pants, and moments later a vile stench filled the air.

The Virginian commenced replacing the spent cartridges, his every action deliberate and controlled. When he was done, he gave the Colt a spin on his finger and slid the six-shooter into his holster with a flourish. Then, seizing Yoast by the shoulders, he dragged the killer around the oak tree and into the thick brush beyond, to where the stallion waited, to where he had scooped out a shallow grave hours earlier.

Only one other incident of note occurred during the Virginian's last-ever visit to his old haunts. The very next night the doors to the Parlor Saloon crashed open, and in stalked a dust-caked avenger who strode up to a table where four men had been engrossed in poker moments before, and halted beside a long-legged player in a frock coat. "On your feet."

"I'm busy. Come back later."

"*Now!*" the Virginian exploded. Before anyone could intervene, he had grabbed Wyatt Earp by the front of his shirt and hurled the ex-lawman clear across the narrow room into the wall. The other patrons all came to their feet and prudently backed away. Behind the counter, the bartender bent down as if to grasp something. "Yu' do and you'll regret it," the Virginian warned, causing the man to straighten empty-handed.

Earp's cards had fluttered to the floor. He stood with

his back against the wall, his eyes glittering. "I could have you arrested for this," he stated.

"Go right ahead. Jim Adams would be mighty interested in what I have to say."

"You have no proof."

"I don't need proof. Yu' weren't man enough to do it yourself, so yu' let it be known you'd pay the man who did it for yu'."

"A court needs proof," Earp reiterated smugly.

"I pack my own court," the Virginian snapped, his right hand slapping his Colt.

Earp flinched and flattened against the wall, bracing for his doom. But he saw the Southerner had only smacked the pistol, not drawn it, and he relaxed, making a show of smoothing his clothes for the benefit of those watching. "I'm trying to be patient with you, but I've really had enough of your nonsense. Go away and bother someone else."

"Draw," the Virginian said.

"I wouldn't waste my time."

"*Draw*, damn you!"

"I'm not heeled," Earp said. To prove it, he carefully opened his coat and made a complete turn. He was sneering when he faced the Virginian again. "So what now? Do you prove I was right all along? That all you cowboys were worthless trash? Do you gun down an unarmed man? Do you spend the rest of your life on the dodge or in prison?"

The Virginian's future hung in precarious balance for the next thirty seconds. His whole frame shook as his right hand lowered to within a fraction of an inch of his six-shooter. Elemental fury contorted his ordinarily handsome face, and had Earp made one more insulting remark, the outcome would have been drastically different from what it was. For into the Virginian's mind an instant later drifted the images of a beautiful, vibrant woman full of love for him, and an innocent infant whose life lay in their caring hands.

Gradually the Virginian's fury subsided. His body uncoiled. A great breath escaped him, and his volcanic expression gave way to a perfect mimicry of Earp's haughty grin as he hooked his thumbs in his gunbelt. "One of us is trash, that's for sure," he said loud enough to be heard at the back of the saloon. With that he spun on a boot heel and jingled out into the night.

19

The Ladies Speak Their Piece

While the Virginian was confronting and conquering his past in Arizona, other events were taking place in Medicine Bow that were to have a marked impact on the eventual bloodbath. On a sunny Friday afternoon, into town rumbled a wagon containing the former Molly Stark Wood and her baby; Jessamine McLean with her brood; and Mabel Martin. Trailing them were Mr. McLean, Dapper, and Scipio le Moyne, the last venting his spleen at the foreman's expense and mincing no words in the bargain.

"This is the most harebrained notion yu've ever had, yu' darned fool. Sometimes I wonder if you'd know honey from a buffalo chip. What if Balaam's outfit is hyeh? Yu' know that they're painted for war, every last one of them. And there's just the three of us."

"Yu' didn't have to come," Lin noted with uncommon diplomacy.

"No one twisted your arm," added Dapper defensively, since his own woman had been a party to the decision, making him equally guilty.

"And who twisted yours?" Scipio shot back.

"They did," Lin said, bobbing his chin at the wagon. "If yu' wasn't so ignorant about married life, you'd know that once a wife takes it into her head to go shoppin', the best a husband can do is hang on tight to his britches and hope his pockets ain't all plumb empty by the time she's done."

"Amen," Dapper intoned.

Scipio clucked like an irate hen and remarked, "It's downright distressin' to see growed men changed into puppies right before a man's eyes. Makes me more leash shy than ever."

"You'll step into a loop soon enough," Lin shot back in good spirit. "Sooner or later some cookie pusher will come along who cooks better than yu', and that will be the end o' your airs."

"Airs?" Scipio practically spat. "Common sense is more like it. You're both just jealous 'cause I've got more brains than to let a female put her choke strap on me." He drew himself up in the saddle. "I've courted my share, sure. But every time I get to thinkin' serious about lettin' a filly darn my socks, I recollect what my pa used to say."

"Which was?" Lin prompted.

"Never trust a woman when courtin' her. If she believes yu', it shows she's too gullible for her own good. If she don't believe yu', she's a candidate for a halo."

Dapper glanced at the wagon, then lowered his voice conspiratorially. "My pappy used to have a sayin' o' his own." He paused. "There's two kinds o' women in this old world, those who are married and those who still have blood in their veins."

All three punchers roared.

Jessamine McLean, who was handling the reins of the team, glanced over her slender shoulder and called out, "You behave yourself, Lin McLean. We're among civilized people again."

"Yes, dear," the foreman answered.

"Oh, Lordy," Scipio le Moyne said, and had a fit of mirth right there in the saddle.

Medicine Bow lay tranquil under the cloudless azure sky. Few citizens were abroad. Horses dozed at hitching posts, and dogs were curled up in convenient quiet corners. These were the serene hours before twilight, when the town would come to rowdy life again.

Perched on the seat beside Jessamine, Molly adjusted her hat and smoothed the front of her dress as the wagon rolled to a stop in front of the general store. She picked up tiny Johnny and cradled him tenderly in her arms, about to climb down, when Scipio materialized at her side, arms outstretched.

"Allow me, ma'am. With your husband down to Tombstone, I reckon I should be the one to look afteh yu', since him and me are such good friends."

"Everyone should have a good friend," Molly agreed as she transferred her baby to the cowboy's arms. "But rest assured I can look out for myself. A woman doesn't fall to pieces just because she's left to fend for herself for a while."

"I cert'nly didn't mean to imply that, ma'am," Scipio said sheepishly, stepping back as she lowered herself to the ground. "All I meant was that I'm hyeh to do whatever manly things need doin' if yu' want me to do 'em."

Molly's left eyebrow arched. "Manly things?"

"Well, yu' know. Things *he'd* usually do," Scipio responded, abruptly averting his gaze and turning a pretty shade of scarlet from his collar to his hat.

"Oh, fiddlesticks. *Those* things," Molly said, unflappable as ever. "Rest assured that if I need any grizzlies wrestled or buffalo heaved, you will be the first person I think of."

"Thank yu', ma'am," Scipio said, eagerly handing back the baby. Doffing his hat, he strategically retreated, and bumped into Lin McLean as he rounded the rear wheel. Lin playfully jabbed him in the ribs, and the pair took to whispering. Then Lin faced the women and announced, "Yu' ladies go have your fun. And take your time. We want to make the rounds and find out what the latest news is."

"Just be sure you can still sit a horse when you're done," Jessamine told him.

"That's mighty unfair," Lin said. "When have yu' ever seen me drunk in broad daylight?" Hitching at his gunbelt, he whirled and led his companions toward the nearest saloon.

"Men," Jessamine said, and somehow she managed to define the entire gender in that single word. "Half of them are still boys at heart, and the other half are wolves."

Mabel nodded. "If I knew how to write, I'd write me a book about them and be rollin' in money."

"Who would read it?" Molly wondered. "Men aren't interested in learning about themselves, and women already know all there is worthwhile."

Now the three ladies took a turn laughing. Then Molly stepped into the stillness of the general store. Immediately young Billy and his shadow, Nate, scooted past her to the grocery side, there to gaze in the rapture of untainted childhood at the hard candy glistening in the various jars.

"Children, you behave yourselves," Jessamine warned. "Remember, look but don't touch."

"Yes, Ma," Billy said dutifully.

"Two minutes from now he'll forget and be into something he shouldn't be," Jessamine said to her friends. "Sometimes I think someone should invent branding irons for kids. Then we'd only have to remind them once. After that, they could just lift their shirts and read their stomachs."

Mabel chortled, but Molly was aghast and said, "Where *do* you come up with your ideas? I can hardly stand to see calves branded, let alone think about doing it to children."

"Slapping a hot iron to a squalling calf is like anything else in life," Jessamine said as she rummaged through a stack of quilts on the dry-goods side. "It just takes some getting used to."

"That's the secret of living out here, isn't it?" Molly said while looking out the window at a buggy. "To have the courage to realize there are some things that have to be done no matter what, and to go out and do them."

"I'd say you've hit the old nail on the head," Jessamine responded. "And come spring you'll be able to put your understanding to the test."

"You agree with him, then? That's when Balaam will strike?"

"Lin and your man are both inclined to that opinion, and I trust their judgment. Especially that black-haired devil of yours. There's a man who is as gun-wise as they come."

"So I've learned."

"Don't tell me you're still pouting over that? I thought you had cleared the air."

"We have," Molly said. She made a survey of the store to verify no one could eavesdrop. "But I'm scared, Jessamine. Sometimes I lie awake at night dreading the first thaw. I imagine how horrible it would be if he's killed, and how lonely and miserable it would make me."

"Talk about fretting over spilt milk before it's even spilt," Jessamine said. "Keep this up and you'll work yourself into a dither. It'll be three or four months yet before anything serious happens."

Molly was far from reconciled to the inevitability of it all. Sighing in frustration, she turned and saw Mabel wistfully examining a bolt of cloth. She went over. "Lovely, isn't it?"

"Never seen lovelier," Mabel replied. "One o' these days I'll be able to buy me some and make a dress fit for a queen."

"I can lend you—" Molly began.

"No, thank yu'," Mabel said quickly. "I'd rather scrimp and save. It'll mean more to me that way."

Johnny started cooing, and Molly bent her head to

smile and indulge in baby talk. She tenderly stroked his chin and touched the comma of dark hair that fell over his brow. Suddenly she sensed the store had grown unnaturally dead, and straightening, she was shocked to see both Mabel and Jessamine staring at the entrance as if they were seeing a ghost. She pivoted, then felt her stomach tighten.

Framed in the doorway, blocking out the sunlight, was the massive form of Ira Balaam. His great bullet head swiveled on his thick conical neck as he surveyed the interior of the store, and when his dark eyes landed on Molly, his face acquired an amused smirk. "Well, well, well," he said drolly in that booming voice of his. "I reckon it's ladies' day in Medicine Bow and no one told me." He stalked into the room like a grizzly on the prowl, touching his hat as he passed Molly and Jessamine. Whether by intent or accident, he gave no indication that he had seen Mabel.

The owner of the store cleared his throat as Balaam neared the counter. "Howdy, Ira. Wasn't expecting you in for your supplies for another week yet."

"Came in early," Balaam said. He grinned at Billy and Nate, then raised his voice. "Heard tell some stray dogs have been giving the fine folks hereabouts a hard time, so I figured I'd have my boys wipe out the whole pack."

"Stray dogs?" the owner said. "This is the first I've heard of them, and I'm usually kept well informed by my customers. I doubt there are any."

"You'll know them when they're stretched out in a pine box."

"Who ever heard of burying dogs in coffins?" the owner asked, and cackled.

Molly looked at Jessamine, who was gesturing at the entrance, signaling they should leave. Mabel had already started for the door. Biting her lower lip, Molly hesitated. She gazed at the wide shoulders of the rancher and the bulge under his coat where his big six-shooter hung, and came to a hasty decision. Holding Johnny close, she walked over, saying sweetly, "Mr. Balaam?"

If Ira Balaam was surprised, he had his emotions under control by the time he completed his turn. "Why, Mrs. Ringold. How nice to see you again. And the baby!" He leaned forward, his moon face hovering over the gaping infant. "I'd heard about the new addition to your family. Congratulations."

"Thank you," Molly said.

"Always wanted children myself. But Mrs. Balaam . . ." Balaam left the thought unfinished.

"Perhaps one day you will remarry," Molly said.

"I doubt it, ma'am. Once was enough for me."

The determination that had prompted Molly to approach him began to evaporate under the blistering intensity of Balaam's level gaze. There was a unique quality about him, Molly reflected, an almost physical force the man radiated that in an odd way brought to mind her beloved Southerner. She gave her head a toss and said quickly, "I'm sorry to be bothering you this way, but there is an important matter we must discuss."

"There is?"

"I'm referring specifically to the grievance you seem to have against my husband."

Now the silence in the store was total. The owner glanced from Molly to Balaam and back again as if he couldn't believe what his ears had just heard. The other customers all had their backs to the counter, but their postures betrayed their interest.

Balaam's eyelids narrowed. "Did he send you to talk to me?"

"Considering how the grapevine telegraph never misses anything of importance, I'm sure you know that he's down in Arizona buying a Morgan for Sunk Creek."

"I do recollect hearing something to that effect."

"Then you also know I'm doing this of my own accord," Molly said. "You must forgive me if I'm being forward. I wasn't reared in Wyoming, like you were, so I don't always do things the way ladies here would. At heart I'm still an Eastern girl, and I'm afraid Vermont women have always been a bit bolder than decorum allows."

"Is that a fact?" Balaam responded, his amused smirk firmly in place.

Although Molly was galled by his patronizing attitude, she never once let her true feelings show. "Yes. And I'd very much like to know if there is any truth to the rumor that you hate my husband as much as people say, and whether you intend to cause him trouble once the warm weather returns."

"Idle tongues have been busy, haven't they?" Balaam said, resting his huge hands on the countertop. "I don't usually discuss my affairs in public, but since you're being so up front with me, I can do no less." He tapped a forefinger a few times, then said, "Your husband and I haven't seen eye to eye for some time, and it's no secret we'd each like nothing better than to bust the other's skull. As for this business about causing him trouble, why would I? I don't care what he does so long as he keeps his nose out of my concerns."

"But—" Molly began.

Balaam held up a hand. "I'm not finished. To be honest, I don't much appreciate having someone accuse me of things I haven't even done. If you were a man, you'd be picking your teeth out of your throat right about now." He motioned toward the street. "Run along now. I'll forgive you this time. Like you said, you're Eastern bred, and that makes a heap of difference in the way people behave."

The rebuke stung Molly. So cleverly had Balaam used her own words against her, she was too flustered to argue. She became aware of being stared at by the other customers and the owner, and goaded by feelings of humiliation, she rotated and hurried out.

Her friends were waiting.

"Goodness, what yu' did!" Mabel exclaimed in reproach.

"What in creation did you think you were doing in there?" Jessamine tore into her. "Are you so naive you thought he'd tell you his plans?"

"Why are the two of you so upset?" Molly rejoined. "I've helped our cause, not hindered it. Once the word spreads, everyone in Medicine Bow, in the whole territory, will know that Balaam was planning some sort of move against our husbands. Now he won't dare carry through with whatever it is because the finger of blame will point straight at him."

"Oh, mercy!" Jessamine said. She boosted her boys into the wagon, told them to stay put, and swung around. "Do you think Ira Balaam *cares*?" she asked in a low voice. "He's used to having his own way no matter what. Public opinion doesn't faze him in the least. And as for blame, unless there is evidence that will hold up in a court of law, he can do as he damn well pleases and get away with it."

"I don't think—"

"No, you don't," Jessamine snapped, and pressed a hand to her temple as if she suffered from a headache. "Don't you see, Molly? Balaam is the kind of man who does things out of spite. The only time he's happy is when he's making others miserable. If someone he doesn't like wants him to do something, he does the exact opposite." She closed her eyes for a moment. "He'll provoke Lin and your man for certain now, just to spite you for what you did today."

Molly's thoughts were all jumbled and her soul heavy with sorrow. She thought she had been doing the right thing, and to learn she might have aggravated the situation depressed her immensely. "I'm sorry," she mumbled.

In that moment of quiet, when none of them were speaking and a shroud of lethargy hung over Medicine Bow, the air cracked to the retort of two shots coming from one of the saloons, the very saloon Lin, Dapper, and Scipio had entered a short while ago.

"No!" Jessamine cried. She darted to the wagon and took her handbag from under the seat. "Stay there!" she ordered her boys, and, hiking her skirts, she sprinted toward the establishment.

"Wait!" Molly cried, but there was no stopping her friend. So holding Johnny tight, she sped on Jessamine's heels, Mabel at her side. They pounded up behind Jessa-

mine, who had a batwing door ajar and was staring at the
tableau within. Molly peered over her shoulder.

Wisps of gunsmoke hung in the air. Standing with
their backs to the bar were Lin, Scipio, and Dapper, while
confronting them were seven men, one of whom had his
pistol out. This tall, burly cowboy had the air of a vicious
wolf and a face to match. He was taunting them, or rather,
one of them: "When I want a man to dance for me, he
dances whether he cottons to the notion or not. Folks are
always sayin' how good yu' darkies are, so prove it, black
man. Dance!"

"I'll see yu' in hell before I do!" Dapper responded,
his right arm hovering close to his six-gun.

The burly man took a menacing stride. "Dally your
tongue, boy, or we'll fix yu' proper right this instant."

"Who are yu' tryin' to fool, Horn?" Scipio said. "Yu'
don't aim to let us off anyhow."

Horn and the men with him exchanged looks, and
some of them laughed or snickered. Another gunman drew
his iron and trained it on Lin and company.

"Who knows?" Horn said sarcastically. "If yu' behave real nice, we might send yu' home with just a spanking."

Molly was in a quandary. Her first impulse was to go
in and denounce the men to their faces, but the squirming
baby in her arms made her fearful of the consequences
should gunfire erupt. She glanced at Jessamine, who was
scarlet with fury, and then at Mabel just as Mabel dashed
past her and over to a spot midway between Dapper and
the uncouth character named Horn.

"Yu' leave my man alone! He's done nothing to
yu'!"

"Well, lookee here!" Horn said, and chuckled. "This
black man has someone to fight his fights for him!" He
peered over Mabel's shoulder at Dapper. "Yu' like hiding
behind her skirts, boy?"

Dapper took a step to the side, giving him a clear
shot at his hulking tormentor. He virtually radiated outrage. His whole body seemed to quiver, and his hand
was tensed for the deadly plunge. There was no doubt he

would have drawn the next instant had not Lin McLean placed a restraining hand on his forearm and moved in front of him.

"Holster your lead chucker, and we'll do this man to man," McLean addressed their enemy. He stood calmly, even casually, a thumb hooked in his gunbelt, an insolent grin adding insult to his challenge.

"This is mine to do," Dapper said before Horn could reply. "Yu' have no right."

"I'm foreman, ain't I?" Lin retorted.

"But this is personal," protested the bronc-buster.

"Not hardly." Lin shifted so he could keep an eye on both Horn and the other gunman who held a revolver. "This has been buildin' for a right smart while. It's between Balaam's outfit and Sunk Creek, which makes it ranch business to my way of thinkin'. And since I'm foreman of the ranch, I have a right to dabble in gore first."

"It don't make no never mind to me which one of yu' two fools wants to die before the other," Horn said. "Reach for your hardware, either of yu', and come supper time folks will be talkin' about how yu' bucked out in smoke."

Lin had his eyes on Horn's six-shooter. "Yu' like your decks stacked, I see."

"My ma didn't raise no tinhorns."

"Yu' looked in a mirror lately?"

Horn bristled at the insult and raised his pistol several inches so that the barrel was pointed directly at McLean's stomach. His intent was obvious, his compunction none. The rest of Balaam's men were equally aglow with blood lust, and the specter of impending death hung as heavy in the air as the damp before a thunderstorm. Everyone there braced for the flash of gunfire, and the bartender started to ease himself down below the bar. But the blast, when it came, came not from Balaam's bunch. Nor did it come from the three punchers at the bar. The shot thundered at the very entrance to the saloon, and simultaneously Horn's arm jerked, his pistol flew, and blood sprayed onto the floor. With one accord, all eyes in the establishment swiveled to the doorway.

A thin tendril of gray smoke curled lazily upward from the small, bright pistol clutched in the steady right hand of Jessamine McLean. She swung the revolver to cover the other armed gunny and said ever so sweetly, "I'd be grateful if you would see fit to lower that six-shooter of yours to the floor. As you just saw, my husband has taught me to shoot the heads off of chickens at twenty-five paces. Can you imagine how easy it would be for me to do the same to you?"

Astonishment drained whatever resistance the hired killer might have offered. It was one thing to face another man in a gun duel; quite another to confront a woman.

"I'm sorry to spoil your fun," Jessamine went on as if lecturing her two boys. "But where I was raised, men don't take unfair advantage unless they're cowards, or worse. And you, Mr. Horn," she stated with a jab of her pistol at the chief offender, "make a sidewinder seem dignified by comparison."

Horn, a hand pressed to his bleeding forearm, declared gruffly. "Yu' had no call to step in, lady. You're the one who's takin' advantage."

Jessamine uttered an unladylike snort. "I gave you the same chance you were about to give my husband. At least you're still alive, which is more than he would have been."

At that particular moment there was a commotion at the rear of the saloon. Customers were parting to permit a huge figure passage through their ranks. Ira Balaam strode to the open space between his men and the tables and calmly appraised the situation. His baleful eyes lingered on Horn; then he removed a fat cigar from his mouth and said, "Will someone kindly explain to me just what is going on here?"

"I reckon yu' already know," Lin McLean answered. "But it hasn't turned out the way yu' hoped. Your rooster had his feathers plucked by a feisty hen."

Balaam glanced from Horn to Jessamine and seemed to notice the pistol in her steady hand for the first time. "*You* shot him?"

"That I did, Mr. Balaam," the lady said defiantly. "And if he ever gives me or mine cause again, I'll shoot him a few more times and not be so fussy about my aim." She took a step, her glare that of a she-cat defending her own. "There's something you need to understand. Something important. You think this is strictly between you men, between your hands and our husbands. But you've miscalculated. It's not just our menfolks you're threatening, it's us, too. It's our families and our homes. And we won't stand for it. Do you hear? When the time comes, we'll be there right beside our own, and your men will have to work twice as hard to earn their pay."

"Feeling contrary today, are we?"

"Make light all you want to. Just remember that a wife has as much stake in her family's happiness and in the land her family calls home as the husband does. And we're not about to stand back while you wipe us out. We'll fight too. And women can be just as dangerous as men when they have to be."

Balaam deliberately took a studied puff on his cigar and watched the smoke spiral toward the ceiling before he commented. "There's no need to convince me how tough women can be. I was married, if you'll recall. I saw my wife bear up under a horrible illness for months on end. She was stronger than I had ever believed, stronger than I might have been if the circumstances had been reversed." He lowered the cigar. "You have my range word that I'll never make the mistake of underestimating you or your friends there."

Lin McLean had listened impatiently to the exchange. Now he moved toward Balaam, his right hand drifting to his hip above his Colt. He paused when Balaam faced him, and the two locked wills. After a while Balaam licked his lips. Lin glanced at his wife and her companions, then at the baby in Molly's arms. That cherubic face decided the issue for him. He slowly backed toward the entrance, nodding at Scipio and Dapper to follow suit. And only when everyone else had departed did Lin speak his own mind, saying simply, "It ain't finished yet."

Balaam nodded. "Not by a long shot."

20

The Van Man

The Virginian heard all about this incident, of course, upon his return from Arizona. He complimented Lin for having the good sense not to provoke a gunfight with the women present, and soothed Dapper's hurt feelings over Lin's unwanted intervention by pointing out that Lin had only been doing what he thought best and that Dapper was bound to have another chance to show his mettle. He said absolutely nothing at all to the women. Not, that is, until the third evening, when Molly came out as he was enjoying the view from their front porch.

"Johnny is asleep," she informed him. "We actually have some time to ourselves."

"A few more years and we'll have so many little ones runnin' around hyeh we won't have a moment's peace," the Virginian quipped as he draped a muscular arm around her shoulders.

"A few more years," Molly repeated softly, unable to keep from wondering if they would have that long together. She cocked her head to study him and asked, "Was I wrong?"

"About what?"

"It's not like you to pretend. You know what."

"Any man who goes around tellin' women they're not in the right is just as likely to go around standin' too close to the backside of mules. I'd rather be branded sensible."

"Don't hedge with me. I need to know. Jessamine upbraided me severely, and I fear she might have had a point."

"Yu' did what yu' had to."

"But did I stir things up by doing so? Did I make the situation worse than it already is? Will Balaam be even more determined than ever?"

"Is that what's worryin' yu' the most?" the Virginian asked. When she nodded, he kissed her cheek and said, "Then yu' can stop your frettin'. Balaam has been a poor example of manhood since he quit attendin' Sunday school, and he ain't improved none with age. I'd wager our entire savings that he forgot what yu' told him the minute yu' were out o' his sight."

"I'd like to think that," Molly confessed.

"Even if he didn't, he's playin' for bigger stakes than most realize. Your words were no more bother than a sliver under the skin."

"What are the stakes? How much do you know that you're not telling me?"

"I don't savvy all the particulars yet, but I expect to have a repawt right soon that will shed some light."

"From whom?"

"The Tinkerer is due in a week."

"Is it that time already? I have a pair of scissors and a kitchen knife you can take down."

"Yu' trust me not to cut myself?" the Virginian responded, and smothered her grin with his lips.

Five days later the Southerner was in his office at Sunk Creek when through the window he had cracked to admit fresh air wafted faint sounds, unusual sounds, as if dozens of tiny bells were being rung at once. Pushing the

ledger back, he turned and gazed out over the fenced
meadow leading up to the ranch house. Paralleling that
fence was a wagon as unique as the man handling the
reins of the team.

Cyrus Hackett was his name, but he was known far
and wide among the cow fraternity as simply "the Tinkerer." His handle stemmed from his trade, which involved fixing anything and everything that needed
repairing. Did a homesteader have a clock that wouldn't
work? He gave it to the Tinkerer to fix. Was there a
rancher who needed a wagon wheel repaired? He gave
the Tinkerer the job. And when knives or saws or scissors needed sharpening, the man to take care of the
chore was the Tinkerer. He also sold a variety of items,
everything from files to hairpins. No one knew exactly
how old Cyrus Hackett was, although there were cow-
men with gray hair who remembered the visits he had
made when their hair was still black or brown. He had
been around forever.

So had the Tinkerer's wagon. Brought with him from
somewhere back east, it was an early-model van, one of
the first of its kind, sporting a hardwood top and sides that
folded out on hinges so the wares inside could be displayed. There wasn't another wagon like it in all of Wyoming, perhaps even in all the West.

Lin McLean was coming from the barn as the Virginian stepped from the house, and together they waited for
the clanking rattletrap.

"Too bad he's early," the foreman mentioned. "Mrs.
Henry sets store by their chats, and the Judge and her
won't be back for two days yet."

"I reckon we can persuade him to stay over," the Virginian said.

The bearded jack-of-all-trades saw them and waved.
With a flick of the short whip he carried, he cut the wagon
in close to the corral and then executed a tight loop, the
wheels coming to a rest directly in front of the two
cowpunches. "How-do, gents! How-do!" the Tinkerer gave
his customary greeting. He tied the reins to the brake,
hooked a skinny leg over the side, and dropped as lightly

as a feather to the earth. "How have you been treating life?"

"Don't yu' have that backward?" Lin asked.

"Depends on which way you're facing."

Lin leaned over to whisper in the Southerner's ear, "The poor geezer is still as crazy as a coot."

"You'd think so," the Virginian responded, and offered his hand to their visitor. "We've got a heap o' business for yu' this time around. Hope yu' won't mind stayin' a few days."

"If you fill the bottom half of the hourglass at one place, you have to empty it elsewhere," the Tinkerer said, showing by his shake that the years had not diminished his strength.

"I'll take that as a yes," the Virginian said. He mentioned at the pump. "Care to wash up or have a bite before yu' get down to work?"

"How long have you known me now, son? It's always business first, pleasure later. A man who wastes daylight has committed a cardinal sin against Father Time."

"Oh, Lord," Lin muttered. "Don't get him started."

"Just show me the pile and stand back so you're not caught in the draft," the Tinkerer went on, heading for a shed near the barn without being bidden. Stretching, he inhaled and commented, "Always did like the scents around here. In the summer Mrs. Henry has all those flowers. And in the winter—" He paused. "What is that I'm smelling today?"

"Manure," Lin said.

The Tinkerer bestowed a look on the foreman that spoke eloquently of fire and brimstone. "If you don't restrain that ornery nature of yours, young McLean, it will be the death of you."

"I don't know what the dickens you're talkin' about," Lin retorted. "I haven't lifted a finger against yu'."

"Does a stallion apologize for being a stallion?"

"Yu' done set a new record," Lin said peevishly. "Yu' haven't been here two minutes and already you're spoutin' craziness."

"To those who know, no words are necessary. To those who don't, no words will help."

Lin stopped and shook his head in amazement. "How yu' manage to think and walk at the same time, I'll never know. Me, I've got work to do. Adios." So saying, he wheeled on a boot heel and tramped off.

"Shallow waters run swiftest," the Tinkerer said to the Southerner.

"Yu' misjudge him if that's your opinion."

"Do I? Or does friendship speak louder than reason?"

The Virginian didn't answer. He was mulling over his strategy on how best to proceed, knowing from long experience that the direct approach did not always work with the craftsman. At the shed he stood back while the Tinkerer rummaged through the assortment of broken and dulled items, muttering all the while. Two saws and a handful of knives were selected out of the bunch, and they headed back to the wagon.

"I'll start out easy and work up to the hard stuff," the Tinkerer declared. "Always save the difficult jobs for last."

"Yu' like to savor your challenges," observed the Virginian.

"It's true what they say," the Tinkerer replied with a smirk. "Still waters do run deep." A chuckle was added commentary. "At my age challenges are luxuries, son, so of course I save 'em for last."

"Come on many this trip?"

"Not enough," the Tinkerer sighed. "Boredom has about done me in."

"Not even in Medicine Bow? I should think yu' would there. It's the biggest town in this hyeh district."

"Size don't make the challenge any more certain. Why, this time around all they had for me was tools and knives to sharpen. Nary a clock or a music box in the whole bunch."

"What about Fort Washakie?"

"Oh, please. Since when can anyone on an army payroll afford anything of interest? As for the Injuns—the government keeps them so poor they have to sharpen their own knives."

"Separ, then?"

"Haven't you heard? About ready to blow away with the next chinook. That railroad never can make up its mind."

At last the Virginian got to the point of his questioning. "I'll get yu' this time. How about Drybone?"

Now Drybone, as everyone in Wyoming knew, was the wildest, toughest town north of Texas. Once an army post, but subsequently deserted when the Indians were considered tamed, it boasted a rowdy population of riff-raff such as had not been seen together in one spot since the heydays of Abilene and Dodge City. Gamblers, gunmen, fallen doves, footpads, killers of every stripe, men and women wanted elsewhere by the law, they all called Drybone their temporary home. Why temporary? Because as soon as the federal government got around to handing the former post over to the state government, every last one of Drybone's inhabitants would head for parts where they were unknown. As things stood, the federal government had jurisdiction, but there was no one there to administer it, and the state's authority stopped at the town limits. Ridiculous, yes. But bureaucracy has ever been as fickle as the wind and as devoid of logic as a horse afflicted by locoweed.

At the mention of this den of iniquity, the Tinkerer cocked his head at the Virginian and snorted. "Seems to me you're growing a mite feeble before your time. Eating enough greens, are you?"

They arrived at the wagon. The Virginian let a suitable interval pass, and when Cyrus was hard at work on a saw, he remarked, "All those thieves, and they ain't stole anything worth your while? Not very decent of 'em, if yu' ask me."

"It's plain you don't know much about outlaws," the Tinkerer responded, his eyes glued to the chore in front of him or he might have wondered at the Southerner's expression. "Thieves like money most. They like to feel their pockets bulge with the illusion of riches." He laughed. "When was the last time you ever heard of an outlaw stealing a grandfather clock?"

"Can't recollect as I ever have."

"No, the only thing I saw of interest in Drybone was that man doing all the recruiting."

"For the army?"

The Tinkerer broke his concentration long enough to look up. "You're worrying me, son. You truly are."

"I'm plumb sorry."

A minute went by, with the only sound that of the saw blade being sharpened. Then the Tinkerer elaborated. "The recruiter I'm talking about is the one who was hiring all the gun-sharks he could find. You should've seen 'em lined up to sign on."

"I think yu''ve jogged my mem'ry some. A while back I heard there was something like that goin' on over there, but not steady-like."

"You heard correctly. The man comes in every couple of months and offers top dollar to any hard case who can show he's not all bluster when it comes to putting a bullet through a playing card at twenty paces."

"Tests 'em, does he?"

"I should say so. One morning they were at it for hours. Course, they were doing a lot of drinking and socializing with the ladies, but some of them still managed to hit the targets."

The Virginian rubbed his chin. "That's right strange. Why would someone be hirin' those who pack their guns loose?"

"I didn't ask," the Tinkerer answered. "You don't live to the ripe old age I have by meddling in where you're liable to provoke a storm of lead."

"Yu' must have some idea, though," the Virginian prompted. "Yu' must have heard a few things."

"A few." The Tinkerer suddenly stopped working and straightened. "Is it me, or are you a bit more curious about the affairs of the world this time around than I've ever known you to be?"

"A man can always stand to broaden his horizons."

"What's your interest? You fearing trouble?"

"Could be."

"Damn. So that's what this is all about." The Tinkerer surveyed their vicinity to verify they were alone. "All right. Since it's you. But if word ever got around—"

"Yu' know better."

"The name of the gent doing all the hiring is Brazos. There's talk he's wanted down to Texas and Arizona for withdrawing funds from banks where he didn't have accounts."

"Do tell."

"They also say he's filled a half-dozen graves. To look at him, I'd believe it. If ever there was a natural-born sidewinder, there's your man. Fancies wearing black, from reading too much cheap literature, I figure. And he's an honest-to-goodness two-gun terror. With my own eyes I saw him draw both pistols at once and blow the hell out of two bottles tossed thirty feet into the air. Quick, he is. Lightning quick."

"Vultures like to flock together. He have any friends?"

"Four or five. I only caught the name of one. Santee, I think it was."

"Do yu' happen to know who Brazos and Santee work for?"

The Tinkerer shook his head.

"Ira Balaam."

A long, low, meaningful whistle wavered from the Tinkerer's lips and he leaned back. "I'm not one of them Gypsies who go gazing into crystal balls, but I know enough about weather to recognize a storm when I see it coming. Has the Judge been filled in?"

"About Brazos and Santee, yes. About Drybone, no. I ain't told him yet." The Virginian pushed his hat back and ran a hand over his brow. "I was sorely hopin' the repawts would turn out to be fiction. Now it's goin' to get right serious, right fast."

"I heard about the sprout."

"So yu' can see the fix I'm in."

Melancholy did not fit the Tinkerer's weathered face

well. "I'm afraid so, old friend. I'd like to help out, but there isn't much I can do except keep my eyes skinned and give you a holler if I hear anything I think you'd be interested in."

"That's all I ask," the Virginian said, offering his hand. After they shook, he strode to the corral where Lin and Dapper were involved in examining the leg of a mare that was doing a dandy job of displaying her independent nature. He climbed to the top rail and took a seat. Presently Dapper removed a stone from the offending hoof, turned, and did a double take.

"Didn't see yu' there, seh."

Lin also turned, a quizzical cast creeping into his face. "What are yu' doing? Gatherin' dust, or pickin' up pointers on how to handle contrary fillies?"

"I'd say the hawss was doin' all the handlin' until she got wore out," the Virginian said. "As for what I'm doin', I figured I should let yu' know I'll be gone for a few days in case Judge Henry starts askin' about me."

"And where might yu' be goin'?" Lin asked as he sauntered over, Dapper at his side.

"A place that ain't fit for greeners like yu'."

"Insult me with class or don't waste your breath," Lin countered amiably. "A ranny like me can handle anything yu' can."

"Can yu' handle Drybone?"

McLean hardly broke verbal stride. "Shucks. It won't cramp my style any."

"Brazos is there."

"Whoop-dee-do."

"Santee and the rest, too."

"Doesn't put a spoke in my wheel."

"I'm not goin' there to pass out daisies."

"Gosh, no."

"Jessamine might object."

"And I suppose Molly will send yu' off with hugs and kisses?"

The Virginian coughed. "I wasn't fixin' to tell her."

"What's good for the big sugar is good for the top screw."

"Now hold on. Don't go blamin' me if this proposition goes sour. I don't want Jessamine out for my scalp."

"I'll claim I was booze blind. She'll leave some hide on me then."

The Virginian and Lin laughed, and the Southerner twisted to jump off the fence when the bronc-buster, who had been fidgeting anxiously during the conversation, interjected his pent-up feelings.

"Am I invisible or just no-account?"

Shaking his head, the Virginian responded, "One of us has to stay. Just in case."

"It won't be me," Dapper declared. "I stood by and did nothin' when yu' interfered at Mabel's, and I didn't raise a fuss when Lin hyeh stopped me from killin' that four-flusher Horn. But I won't take no more babyin' off of anyone, not even yu', seh. Either take me or give me my time."

"Since yu' put it that way," the Virginian said sadly, and reached into his pocket. When the hand emerged, it held a spent cartridge. "Now where did this come from?" he wondered, winking at Lin. Finally he faced the black man. "Be ready to leave in three days."

Dapper was joy personified. "I will be. And don't yu' worry. I won't breathe a word to Mabel."

The Virginian and McLean were halfway to the office when the foreman grabbed the former's arm.

"Hold up a minute. I just had a thought."

"You're treadin' on dangerous territory."

"Yu' brought up this visit to Drybone because yu' wanted me to tell Judge Henry yu' would be gone for a spell."

"So?"

"So we ain't headin' to Drybone for three days, and the Judge gets back in two. Yu' can tell him yourself."

"Yu' don't say."

"One o' these days somebody will shoot yu' and put the rest of us out o' your misery," Lin joked.

"Just so it ain't Brazos," the Virginian declared, suddenly as sober as a judge. "I aim to make damn sure that polecat goes first." He didn't add that before the week was out, he might have the opportunity to put those bold words to the test.

21

Public Opinion

The three stern riders reined up in a swirl of dust atop the single hill overlooking the dilapidated town of Drybone. On all sides were dozens of unmarked graves of vagrant souls who went to meet their Maker unexpectedly and unsung. Scattered among the forgotten and the forlorn were the plots of soldiers slain defending United States property and the lives of its citizens from rebellious Indians, and here and there were graves of pilgrims laid low on their way to the Promised Land in Oregon.

"Mrs. Johnson," Lin McLean read, "found scalped on Willow Ridge." Shifting, he recited, "Sacred to the memory of Private Clark, found mutilated on the Lower Cottonwood, March third, 1876."

"Boot-hills give me the same feelin' a hell wind does," Dapper commented, and gave a little shiver. "Why'd we stop, anyhow?"

It was the Virginian who answered. "Yu' wouldn't go

walkin' into a cave that reeked of grizzly without first having a look-see, would yu'?"

"Listen to that music," Lin said. "It's the shank o' the afternoon and already they're kickin' up their heels."

The tinny sound of a piano being poorly played wafted by on the cool breeze. Raucous laughter sounded now and then. There was a horse race being conducted on the former parade ground, with much yelling and whooping from those on the sidelines who had wagers riding on the outcome. Other men lounged in front of the various buildings that had once been part of the military post, and scattered among them were a few women.

From a distance it all appeared so innocent, but the Virginian knew better. He loosened the Colt in its holster, then slid a hand under his shirt to check the six-shooter concealed there. "Remember," he admonished his friends, "we're not hyeh lookin' to dabble in gore. We want answers, that's all."

"Yu' must be totin' all that iron for bluff or balance, which?" Lin responded impishly.

"Don't fret none over me," Dapper said. "My pappy taught me long ago that a cowboy buckin' gamblers soon enough comes up against a stacked deck. I aim to behave unless prodded."

"All I ask is that yu' pull in your horns if yu' can," the Virginian clarified. "Now let's go see if the atmosphere hereabouts is as bad for the lungs as they claim." Clucking Monte into motion, he angled down the slope to the edge of Drybone, where he slowed and swung wide of the buildings so he could command a clear view of both sides. His eyes roved over every face in sight, every window and doorway.

Lin came alongside. "I'm a mite gut shrunk from all this ridin'. I figure to find me some grub first. Care to join me, pard?"

"If we split up, we might learn more faster," the Virginian said. He glanced around at Dapper. "We'll all meet in the saloon in about an hour."

The saloon had once been the captain's quarters. Adjacent to it, in the former adjutant's office, poker games were in progress twenty-four hours of the day. The barracks were where the majority of Drybone's shady inhabitants hung their hats, except for one that was reserved for the gilded ladies and their trade. And the commissary, the biggest building of them all, now did double duty as a combination hotel and dance hall.

Sitting loosely in the saddle, the Virginian made for the saloon. Most of the hard cases ignored him; to them he was just another cowpuncher in town for a good time. A few quizzical looks were thrown his way, and of these he took note, as he did of the sole hostile stare he received, from a bearded beanpole who promptly turned and vanished into the adjutant's office.

The hitching post was nearly full. Prudently, the Virginian tied Monte at the end nearest the doorway in case he should have to light a shuck. Hooking both thumbs in his gunbelt, he ambled inside, blinking at the sudden onslaught of acrid smoke. The rank smell of sweaty bodies tingled his nostrils as he pushed through the crowd to the bar and called on the bartender for a whiskey.

With his back to the room, seemingly uninterested in the goings-on around him, the Virginian surreptitiously took in everything in the big mirror decorating the wall above the liquor shelves. Every table was full, the floor packed. Loud voices, curses, the piano, and off-key singing by a plump woman on a small stage at the rear of the establishment created quite a noisome racket.

The bustling scene revived more memories that the Virginian had long kept buried, recollections of the countless saloons in which he had idled his time away during his travels with his cousin. Once he had reveled in such a life, in wandering wherever the wind had taken him, in being footloose and fancy-free, as the saying went. Garish lights, willing women, the clink of glasses and the clatter of chips, they had all caused his veins to pulse with excitement.

And now look at me, he mused. Settled, respectable, and responsible for more lives than just my own. The Southerner had changed so drastically that those he had called friends during his roving years—those few still alive—would hardly know him. And he didn't mind the change one bit.

Deep in his reflection, the Virginian didn't realize someone had sauntered near until an arm draped over his shoulder and a warm palm touched his neck.

"You look lonely, cowboy."

The Virginian smiled into the powdered face of a blonde who had seen her prime a decade ago. A few too many whiskey mills, a few too many friendly gentlemen, had all left their mark in the form of premature wrinkles and the angular look of someone too fond of firewater for her own good. "Not tonight, ma'am," he said softly.

"I *do* so love black hair." The woman ignored him, lifting her hand to brush her fingers against the back of his head. "And you've got about the blackest I ever did see." Her green eyes alighted on his. "But not the blackest heart."

"Ma'am?"

"A gent who is overly polite usually has some mighty unpolite thoughts on his mind, but not in your case," the woman declared. "Trust me, cowboy. I've known enough men to populate a country. I know what I'm talking about."

A strong whiff of alcohol inclined the Virginian to the opinion she was loaded on dynamite. Gently prying off her arm, he said earnestly, "Yu' would be better off findin' yourself another puncher."

"You don't like me?" the woman asked, sounding hurt.

"You're right pretty," the Virginian allowed. "But the fact is, I'm married."

The blonde laughed. "So? Most of the men I've known have had a wife hidden away somewhere. It didn't make no difference to them."

There was a spark of fire in the Virginian's expression and tone when he responded, "It does to me. Now be a polite little filly and mosey along."

"Oh," the woman said, straightening. "Oh," she repeated softly. About to leave, she glanced at his glass, licked her overly red lips, and asked, "Before I do, how about treating?"

"Didn't yu' hear me?"

"Yes, I most certainly did. And I'm not about to throw myself at you." She leaned closer to plead in his ear. "I just want a few minutes of peace, without some damn drunk pawing all over me. Five minutes, cowboy. That's all I ask." She glanced around the saloon. "This way, if my boss spots me, he won't think I'm not earning my keep and lay a hand on me later."

"Barkeep," the Virginian declared loud enough to be heard above the general din, "another whiskey for my friend, if yu' please."

"My goodness, you sure do have fine manners," the woman said, genuine joy transforming her haggard features into the lovely woman she must have been before her life of dissipation caught up with her. "Where are you from, anyway?"

"Virginia."

"Well, Virginia, my name is Melody Vickers. Course, Melody isn't my real name, but it's the one I've been using for so long I've plumb forgot what my ma and pa named me." Melody laughed and gave his arm a slap. "Imagine that! Who ever heard of anyone forgetting their own name?"

"There're a right smart number of long riders around who have done just that," the Virginian mentioned. "Makes it mighty convenient for 'em when they run into someone wearin' a tin star."

"Ain't that the truth," Melody said. Her drink came, and she scooped it off the bar so fast she spilled some. Cradling the glass in both hands, she took a slow slip, closed her eyes, and sighed. "The nectar of the gods."

"I used to think so myself."

"What changed your mind?"

"I grew a brain."

Melody studied him, trying to determine if she had been insulted. Mirth burst from her, and she clapped him on the shoulder. "Damn! If you ain't bone seasoned, I never met a man who was! Where'd you get all your experience, Virginia?"

"Life."

"I'll drink to that," Melody said somberly, and she did so, nearly polishing off the contents. Frowning, she regarded the remainder and said, half to herself, "Ain't it a cryin' shame the way life is sometimes. I hate getting old."

"Don't be. The alternative is a lot worse."

"It is?" Melody said, her brow knitting. Comprehension brought more laughter. "I declare! You're a case, Virginia, and that's a fact." Her shoulder brushed his. "Listen. I feel sort of guilty taking your whiskey this way. Are you sure there isn't something I can do for you?"

The Virginian was on the verge of reprimanding her for violating her promise when he changed his mind and put his cheek close to hers. "How are yu' fixed for information?"

"Depends. What kind are you interested in?"

"I'm lookin' for an hombre who goes by the handle o' Brazos."

At the mention of the name, Melody stiffened and slapped her glass down. She twisted to look at their neighbors on either side, ensuring no one was paying attention. "Hell, Virginia!" she whispered. "What do you want with him?"

"It's personal."

"Take my advice, handsome. Don't go throwing that name around unless you're looking to take up residence on boot-hill. Brazos has a lot of friends in Drybone, and there ain't a one who wouldn't dry gulch his own mother if the price was right."

"Is he in town?"

"He was yesterday morning, because I seen him with my own eyes. Him and that wild bunch of his."

"How many?" the Virginian inquired.

"Eight or nine, I reckon. All as cat-eyed as riled bobcats." Melody polished off the last of her drink. "Nights they spend drinking and dancing. This time of day they're likely to be playing cards."

"I'm obliged," said the Virginian, pulling his hat down. He turned to go, but at that instant, at a nearby table, an unshaven scarecrow in tattered buckskins suddenly hurled a glass to the floor, sending razor shards flying, and leaped to his feet, his right hand shaped into a claw poised to grab his six-gun.

"Draw your steel, bastard!"

Without thinking, the Virginian spun, seized Melody by the arms, and sank to the floor, dragging her down beside him. He had witnessed enough shoot-outs to know that innocent bystanders were often hit in the cross fire, and he had no desire to be one of them. Others were doing the same. Thunder erupted, eliciting screams and oaths. Slugs thudded into the bar above, raining splinters down on his head. The shooting lasted only a few seconds. Then there was a loud thump, and the crash of a table overturning. Then drawn-out silence.

"It's all clear, folks!" the bartender finally called out.

"Yu' can get up now, ma'am," the Virginian said softly, and tugged on Melody's wrist. She had fallen on top of him, her head between his chest and his arm, preventing him from seeing her face. "Did yu' hear me?" he asked. "Come on, now. The fuss is over." He transferred his hand from her wrist to her chin and gently started to raise her head when a moist drop splattered onto his fingers. The contact froze him long enough for more drops to fall. Around him there were exclamations and cries, and two men came over and took her off him. Only then could he see the neat hole above her right eye, and the crimson stain soaking her blond hair.

Angry shouts attended the discovery. Men converged from all four corners. The bartender clambered over the counter to help lay out Melody Vickers on top of the bar.

Amidst the hubbub, the Virginian slowly stood. He stared at the blood smearing his skin, the blood of a woman he had hardly known but who had been alive and laughing but moments before, and he felt sick to his core at the senselessness of her death. Over at the upturned table a number of men had pounced on the man in buckskins and wrestled his pistol away. Under the table sprawled the object of the man's wrath, two bullet holes in his chest.

"—ought to know better than to burn powder in a crowded place like this!" someone was shouting.

"The damned fool! Let him be the guest of honor at a string party to teach him a lesson!" someone chimed in, the words as slurred as the speaker was unsteady on his feet.

Instantly the hue and cry was taken up by dozens of throats. "A hanging! A hanging!" they shouted gleefully, as might children playing a game at school. Seconds later a general swell of totally and partially sodden humanity rippled across the floor and out the door, carrying the screeching guest on their crest. So swiftly did the mob depart that the Virginian and a half-dozen others were left standing dazed in their wake, unable to intervene even had they been so inclined.

"For the love of God! *Noooooooo!*"

The piercing wail of desperation galvanized the Virginian into running outside. To his horror he found the vultures who frequented Drybone's dives flocking thick and fast from every direction, some bringing their own bottles, quite a few laughing and joking, all eager for the festivities. To the center of the parade ground they flew, gathering without being bidden into a great circle around the old flagpole, showing by their smooth precision that this was something they had done before, perhaps many times.

"Where the hell is the Judge?" warbled a dandy in a bowler hat.

"Find Judge Slaghammer!" went up the shout among the throng, and in groups and singly they hastened after the only government official of any sort tolerated in their lawless community.

Judge Henry Slaghammer actually lived in nearby Albany County, where he served as county coroner. Part of his duties, however, on behalf of the state, consisted in making regular trips to Drybone to keep a tally of the fatalities suffered there, for which he was paid ample fees and mileage. Although originally Slaghammer had balked when the idea was posed, lo and behold his whole attitude changed drastically once he saw how liberal the state was with the taxpayers' money. Within no time at all he had taken to making monthly trips to Drybone, then weekly ventures, and now, complained the good citizens of Albany County, their coroner was never around when *they* needed him. Slaghammer refused to be intimidated and continued to divide his time as he saw fit. And was it his fault that his wife owned the Drybone dance hall, compelling him to be there more often than he would have liked?

The Virginian, on hearing the Judge's name and realizing the next step the aroused inhabitants would take, was busy trying to force his way through the crowd, but those nearest the center and the flagpole had no intention of giving up their vantage points; they craved the equivalent of the best seats in the house for the show that was shortly to follow.

Near the flagpole stood the hapless scarecrow in buckskins. His wrists had been bound and there was a nasty welt on his forehead. For the moment he was being left alone except for a pair of burly guards, so to one and sundry he protested his innocence and pleaded to be freed. His listeners, for the most part, jeered or cackled or otherwise displayed their disdain.

One grizzled sot, after tipping his red-eye, summed up the feelings of most of those present when he bellowed, "Hell! Quit your whinin', Cain. You're guilty as sin and we all know it, so quit flappin' your gums and take your medicine like a man! It'll all be over before you know it."

Public opinion applauded his outburst.

Encouraged by the acclaim, the spokesman walked up to Cain and jabbed a finger into his chest. "And 'nother thing," he declared, somehow contriving to slur each and every syllable, "I warned you a dozen times about that damn temper of yours. So did most everybody else. You've always been too ready to get your back up for no cause at all."

"Now listen, Jim—" Cain tried to protest.

"Don't try to haze the talk. I ain't done yet," Jim snapped. He took another swallow of red-eye to fortify his outrage, then said, "Do you know what your real problem has been? I'll tell you." A sneer accented his insight. "You've so soured on life you don't have the faintest notion how to drain all that acid out of your veins."

"And you do?" the indignant Cain retorted.

Jim gave his bottle an affectionate pat. "You don't see me goin' around shootin' folks, do you?"

Just then a commotion broke out at the east edge of the crowd. The Virginian saw a half-dozen hard cases propelling a hefty individual in a soiled suit toward the flagpole. He recognized Judge Slaghammer from one of his previous visits, and redoubling his efforts, he pushed and shoved in an attempt to break through to the condemned.

The party bearing the Judge halted and gave Drybone's sole claim to political dignity a rude shove that sent him stumbling forward into Cain. Recovering his balance, Judge Slaghammer blinked his owl eyes as he looked all around him, his thick tongue running around and around his thick lips. "What is the meaning of this?" he asked at last. "Why was I roused from my bed at this ungodly hour?"

"Bed, hell!" someone responded. "We found you lyin' under a card table at the back of your wife's place, huggin' a flask like it was her."

This tidbit tickled the fancy of public opinion, and the majority roared.

"Now see here!" Judge Slaghammer upbraided the culprit. "I'll brook no ungentlemanly remarks about my dearly beloved. No, sir, I won't!"

"Calm down, Judge," another chimed in. "And get to the business at hand."

"What might that happen to be?" Judge Slaghammer inquired, glancing at the bound figure in front of him. "I assume it has something to do with Cain here being trussed up like a pig for the slaughter."

"He's killed two people, Judge."

"Since when is that a crime in Drybone?" the county coroner pointed out. "We average about eight or nine a month, and that's when things have been slow."

"One of 'em was a bystander," mentioned a portly

citizen in city clothes whose tie bore food stains from his last few meals. "Poor gal never knew what sent her on to those pearly gates."

Judge Slaghammer shrugged. "Hell, we lose an innocent bystander every now and then. It's nothing unusual. Keeps the rest of us on our toes when shooting breaks out."

"Are you saying we can't hang this bastard?" snapped one of the civic-minded.

"I'm saying it would be a bad precedent," Judge Slaghammer replied in his most authoritative tone. "Accidents are a natural part of life. If we took to punishing everyone who makes a mistake, there wouldn't be a one of us left before too long."

"This is a special case," an irate individual said.

"How so?"

"It was poor Melody Vickers the fool done shot."

"No!" Judge Slaghammer exclaimed, aghast. He cast a dire eye at the accused. "Sweet little Melody? How could you, sir? She was the friend of us all. An ear to listen, a shoulder to cry on, she was always willing. Why, just the other day she and I—" The Judge caught himself, coughed, and tried to distract those with inquisitive minds by flicking a piece of lint from his lapel.

"So can we string him up?" pressed one of the restless.

Judge Slaghammer encompassed them all with a friendly look. "Now, boys, you know damn well I can't authorize a hanging. This is out of my bailiwick. I tally the dead. I don't consign them to boot-hill."

"We want this to be official," an anonymous voice cried.

"Since when has legality been a deciding factor in public behavior here?" Judge Slaghammer stood by his guns. "No, ladies and gentlemen. I cannot condone this action. I will not be a party to it. If you want to hang Cain, then do so. But the authority must be derived from consensus, not my say-so."

There was grumbling among the multitude. A woman in a blue dress waved a lace handkerchief and called out,

"What the hell do those big words mean, Judge? Can we or can't we?"

"Yu' can't!"

All eyes swiveled to regard the speaker with a mixture of curiosity and contempt. Those who knew him, or rather *of* him, suddenly decided their drinks were getting warm or their horses needed feeding and began drifting off.

"Yu' can't," the Virginian repeated, striding to the ring of open space at the base of the flagpole and halting beside the Judge and Cain. "This man deserves a trial."

A ripple of laughter greeted the appeal to justice, and from out of their midst, where bravery was easier to exercise, came a mocking cry. "Tarnation, where do you think you are, mister? Denver?" More laughter ensued.

"No one wants to see this hombre pay more than I do," the Virginian declared. "I was standin' next to Melody when it happened. But if he's to be strung up, it should be done proper."

"I agree," interjected a new, gruff voice, and from out of the throng strolled five hard men, the stamp of viciousness on each of their somber faces. In the lead walked an arrogant figure who was partial to dressing all in black and who sported a matched pair of gleaming pistols around his slender waist.

"Hello, Brazos," the Virginian said.

"Ain't this a surprise?" Balaam's top gun responded, sounding genuinely pleased. "Here I was, about to ride out with the boys a while ago, when a friend tells me that you're in town. I thought he'd had a few too many. Yet here yu' are, big as life."

"I was a-hopin' we'd meet."

"Were yu', now?" Brazos halted, wedged his thumbs in his gunbelt, and grinned that crooked grin of his. "Well, I expect yu' won't be so tickled about it by the time I'm done."

"Have plans, do yu'?" the Virginian asked, swiveling so he could keep an eye on them all as the four with Brazos fanned out.

"If yu' only knew," Brazos said. Smirking, he came

a few steps nearer and addressed civil authority. "Did I hear yu' rightly? You're saying we can't string up a guilty man when we need to?"

Judge Slaghammer seemed to be trying the miraculous feat of shrinking into his clothes so as to disappear. "No, sir," he bleated. "I never said any such thing. I just made it clear I can't authorize a hanging." He worried a button on his coat and added meekly, "Everyone knows there is no legal authority in Drybone."

"You're wrong there, Judge," Brazos said. With a grand wave of an arm he gestured at the crowd. "The good folks o' this town are their own legal authority. If someone is a menace to the community, then they have the right to protect themselves from him, don't they?"

"I suppose," Judge Slaghammer offered tentatively.

Brazos nodded and raised his voice for all to hear. "I can't see why you're all bein' so fussy all of a sudden. If yu' have the guilty man, get on with what has to be done."

Scattered cheers and whoops broke out, but some there were who had not forgotten about the Southerner, and one of them ventured to shout, "What about that black-headed guy? He says we can't."

"Does he, now?" Brazos said, his words as venomous as a rattler's bite. "And you're going to let him tell yu' what to do? He's only one man."

At this there was general ferment, with much muttering and whispering and spiteful glares cast in the Virginian's direction. The innermost ring edged a bit closer to the center. One man, a puncher by his dress, held a rope, which he gave a few twirls while staring meaningfully at the top of the flagpole.

Legs spread wide, the Virginian stood his ground. His right hand dangled close to his Colt, and his expression sufficed to intimidate the timid. Still, others stalked nearer, and violence loomed when two newcomers pushed through the mob and took their places, one on either side of their friend.

"Sorry about the delay, pard," Lin McLean said. "I didn't want to leave my meal half-finished."

Dapper's teeth were a sharp contrast to the hue of his

skin. "Is this how yu' pull in your horns? If so, I'd hate to see yu' when you're on the peck."

The Virginian hadn't taken his eyes off the leader of the opposition. Brazos, strangely enough, was composed and grinning, which disturbed the Virginian greatly. He knew how men like Brazos thought, so he knew the man in black would not be acting so self-collected unless he believed he held the high card. But he had no idea what it could be.

"Yu' brought some company?" Brazos was saying. "That's good. A man should always have pardners around to comfort him when he makes a fool o' himself."

"Lucky for yu' that yu' have a right smart of 'em hangin' around yu' all the time," the Virginian said with silken sarcasm. He put a hand—his left hand—on Cain's arm. "Now unless yu' have an objection yu' want to make, we're takin' this joker and vamoosing."

"Me? Object?" Brazos said. "I won't lift a finger to stop yu'." His sinister smile broadened. "But those gunwise gents behind yu' might like a say in the matter."

The Virginian froze on hearing the metallic rasp of a rifle lever being worked. Keeping his arms still, he twisted his head and discovered Santee and two other men holding Winchesters trained on himself and his two friends.

"Howdy." The grizzled puncher beamed. "Haven't seen yu' since Medicine Bow. How have yu' been keepin' yourself?" Suddenly his eyes darted to McLean. "I wouldn't be so eager to push up buffalo grass if I was yu', friend."

Lin had partially turned, and with his right arm screened by his body he was inching his hand toward his holster. He stopped at the warning, his posture showing he might change his mind at any instant.

"Don't yu', Lin," the Virginian said.

"There's only the three o' them."

"And what'll I tell Jessamine?"

Santee tilted his head toward Brazos and said, "What do yu' want done with 'em? Say the word and we'll bed 'em down so they can't meddle now or later on."

"You'd spoil my fun?" Brazos responded. "I'd be

plumb disappointed if they weren't around for the frolic. No, I have me a better notion." He pointed at one of his men, then indicated the covered trio. "Preston, I want yu' to go on around behind them and gather up their hardware."

Before the gun-shark could move, Lin took a half step toward Brazos and growled, "No one takes my six-shooter away from me. Ever."

"It's your pistol or your life," Brazos said, and shook his head in amusement. "Yu' have more lip than a muley cow, McLean, but yu' don't have the sense of a rabid wolf. Rake your spurs at us and you'll be one dead saddle warmer." He gestured sharply at Preston. "Now do as I told yu', *pronto*."

Resistance would have proved useless. The Virginian realized as much when he noticed that a goodly number of men in the crowd had drawn their hoglegs and were prepared to throw in with Brazos if a shooting scrape started. He had hoped to be able to bluster them into letting him take Cain; the unexpected interference by Brazos and company had ruined his plan. Worse, he was being made to back down publicly, a galling treatment he resented with every atom of his being.

Preston reluctantly did his work quickly, almost dropping Dapper's revolver in his nervousness. "What now?" he asked when he had all three pistols in his grasp.

"Empty the cylinders and put 'em back where yu' got 'em," Brazos directed.

"That's all?"

"Yu' can hit yourself over the head with 'em first if yu' want."

Coarse laughter from some of the onlookers turned Preston crimson. His embarrassment wasn't enough to provoke him into making any slurs about the man who had caused it. He wisely did exactly as he had been told, then moved back.

The Virginian glanced at Cain, whose face was beaded with perspiration and who seemed almost in a state of shock. He still had his spare Colt under his shirt. If he waited for the right moment, he might be able to blast his

way out of the fix he was in and take Cain with him. Yet
if he touched his pistol, Santee and the others would cut
loose, and their kind wouldn't be any too particular about
who got caught in the cross fire. An instant later the decision was taken out of his hands when cold steel touched
the back of his neck.

"Just in case yu' get any wild ideas," the grizzled
killer cackled.

Shifting, the Virginian saw the other riflemen had
done likewise with Lin and Dapper. The bronc-buster
seemed resigned to the inevitable, but lightning played
across the foreman's face.

Brazos lowered his hands and strode right up to the
flagpole. He made sure he was the exclusive focus of attention of all those present; then, savoring his victory, he
raised his arms and shouted, "I leave it to all o' yu', the
fine people o' Drybone, one last time. What should we
do? Do yu' want Cain to go free? Or do yu' want him to
make good for the life o' poor Melody the only way he
can? The way the Good Book says? An eye for an eye!
Which will it be?"

A chorus of coarse yells erupted. "Hang the son of a
bitch," "String the jackass up," "Measure his neck with
some hemp," and variations on the theme served as the
verdict of public opinion.

Cain let out a pathetic wail as several brawny citizens
grabbed hold and hauled him closer to the pole. At the
same time the man with the rope started shimmying upward. And from out of the packed throng came two men
leading a bay.

"This ain't right," Dapper said softly to himself.
"This just ain't right."

"Yu' can say that again," Lin rasped.

But the Virginian said nothing. Outwardly he was as
calm as a cool slab of polished marble; inwardly he simmered, choking back his building fury. He saw Cain
hoisted onto the bay, saw the man atop the flagpole lashing the rope securely. Footsteps brought his gaze lower.

"I don't want my generosity wasted, so I just had to

ask," Brazos said. "Yu' know why I'm sparing your pards and yu', don't yu'?"

The Virginian gave a curt nod.

Brazos chuckled. "Knew I could count on yu'. Maybe next time yu' reckon on bluffing someone at cards, you'll think twice."

"Cards?"

"It'll come to yu' soon enough." Brazos glanced over the Southerner's shoulder and said, "Keep 'em covered until it's done. Then join me and the rest where we have the hawsses."

"Will do, boss," Santee responded.

Touching his hat brim, Brazos sauntered off into the milling mob he had handled so masterfully and was soon lost in the excited sea of hats and waving arms.

"He sure is somethin', ain't he?" Santee said proudly. "Best I ever rode with, bar none."

"I've known only one like him," the Virginian answered.

A cry of delight went up from the populace. The rope had been tied, and now a worthy citizen who had climbed up on the bay behind Cain was fitting a noose over the condemned man's head. Cain tried to throw himself from the saddle but was restrained by a dozen willing hands. He blubbered, begging for mercy, but they only laughed at him. He offered to leave the country and never return, but they paid no heed. He tried to bribe them, claiming he had a sister who would pay handsomely for his release, and was slapped across the mouth.

Public opinion had made up its collective mind, and it was not to be denied. They knew what was best; it was what they wanted. Dissenters, and to be fair there were a few, were shoved or ridiculed into silence. No one took them seriously. After all, they had to be wrong, since so many were right.

Public opinion cheered when the noose was eventually tightened and Cain sat alone on the bay. A few of his friends drank to their friendship. One man laid vocal claim to his boots, another to his shirt.

Then came a remarkable change. Public opinion fell

totally silent as an expectant hush fell over the former parade grounds. The same citizen who had fastened the noose now drew his Colt, stepped up behind the bay, and paused. He waved those nearest the flagpole away, waited until an ample space had been cleared, and pointed his six-gun at the ground. The residents of Drybone practically crackled with expectancy, their faces aglow with primitive passion. Everyone was watching the gun, and when it spat lead and smoke, nearly half of them flinched as if struck. One dove fainted.

At the retort the horse lurched into motion, the abrupt motion nearly toppling Cain off. He squawked in abject fright and clamped his legs on the animal's sides, trying to stay on the hurricane deck for as long as he could, clinging to his last moments of life as tenaciously as he had squandered it until this fateful day.

The bay plunged into the throng, scattering spectators right and left, and within moments came to the end of the rope. With a brutal wrench Cain was torn from the saddle, the whites of his eyes like miniature moons as he started to swing back toward the pole. His legs pumped wildly, seeking support that wasn't there. He screamed, or tried to, but the cry was strangled off by the constricting noose. Twisting and thrashing, he struggled mightily, his arms surging against his bonds. Yet all he succeeded in doing was hastening his own end. A crimson flush crept over his features and his mouth worked, but no more sounds came out. He swung in a wide loop, circling the pole as he performed his ghastly aerial acrobatics. Round and round he went, kicking and jerking all the while, the heads of those below swiveling to follow his flight, as if he were performing a grotesque ballet and they were his attentive admirers. Many even smiled in satisfaction when his movements weakened, his tongue lolled out, and his eyes bulged. And when, at length, Cain went completely limp, there were widespread sighs of contentment.

The body kept on swinging in an ever narrowing circle, closer and closer to the flagpole around which the rope was wrapping itself with each revolution, until finally the body hit the pole with a loud thud and was still.

No one spoke for a full minute. They simply stood and stared, appreciating their handiwork. The spell was broken when someone belched and the man named Jim stepped up to the pole and peered intently into the discolored, distorted features above him. "Yep. He's dead." He made it official.

"Game to the last, Cain was," commented another. "Put up quite a fight."

"Oh, I don't know," carped a critic. "I've seen better."

In groups, pairs, and singly the assembly gradually dispersed, taking up their lives where they had been when they were interrupted by the call to civic duty. Presently there were only three left standing on the parade ground, the three cowboys from Sunk Creek, who took it upon themselves to cut down the corpse and cart it off to boot-hill, where they gave Cain a solemn burial just as the setting sun faded behind the western mountains.

Below, in the lairs and dens of Drybone, the denizens were having a grand old time. Tinny music wafted on the cool westerly wind, a songstress mutilated a popular ballad, and rowdy laughter sounded every so often. Poker chips clattered onto tables, glasses tinkled, chairs scraped across floors. Life went on as usual as night enveloped the town in its inky grasp and patches of glowing light glared through scores of windows, like the unblinking orbs of enormous beasts lying in wait for unwary travelers.

22

The Leaden Lull

The Virginian took his defeat hard. Upon his return to Sunk Creek a marked change came over him. Gone was the carefree cowboy who joked so freely with the punchers. Now he never smiled, and he rarely spoke unless spoken to first. When the subject of Balaam came up, as it inevitably did on occasion, thunder hung heavy on his brow but he seldom made a comment. Brazos, by unspoken common consent, was never mentioned. At least not in his hearing.

But the man in black was certainly the talk of the countryside. Cowboys and gamblers brought the news to Medicine Bow, Fort Washakie, Lander, Cheyenne, and other points in Wyoming, and from there it spread like a prairie fire. Within a month of the hanging, the tale was being related around every campfire and in every saloon and bawdy house from the Rockies to the Mississippi.

In the process of being told and retold, the story changed, expanded, taking on a life of its own. Because

Brazos worked for Ira Balaam, it became linked to the ongoing dispute between the cattle barons and the nesters and rustling element. Had there been someone curious enough to check, they would have found that the sources of this new version were men in Balaam's employ, or friends or casual acquaintances of his—anyone, in short, who had contact with Balaam.

Brazos was portrayed as a man who had simply been doing his job as foreman at Butte Creek. He had been passing through Drybone when he happened to spot a horse stolen from his employer. The unfortunate Cain suffered a further indignity: He graduated from a rash fool with a shady past to a full-fledged badman who, rumor had it, operated a thriving rustling ring. Caught on the stolen animal, Cain had paid the traditional price for his folly.

In this new account the Virginian was made out to be the second villain of the piece. He had brazenly interfered and tried to prevent Brazos from doing his duty. A firm reason was never given, but it was hinted that the Virginian himself might have links to the rustling trade. As proof of the allegation, his old friendship with Steve, a known rustler, was brought up. When listeners objected, as they often did by noting that the Virginian had been part of the necktie social that had disposed of Steve, it was claimed the Southerner had acted merely to cover his own tracks. No one who knew him believed this lie for a minute, but the many who didn't know him or had heard only of his gunslinging exploits against Trampas and Killebrew, accepted the story as gospel. Ill will against the Virginian became widespread.

If the Virginian knew, he gave no indication. As the weeks rolled slowly by and the days lengthened degree by degree, he attended to his work at Sunk Creek and his responsibilities at Aspen Creek. Every Sunday his family got together with the McLean clan and Dapper and Mabel, and once or twice a month the Judge and Mrs. Henry would join them.

Winter retreated under the warming influence of approaching spring. The jagged peaks in the mountains were still cloaked thick with glistening mantles of snow, but the lower slopes changed from white to brown to green. The rich grass thrived. Brightly colored flowers bloomed.

Another sign of the change was the renewed activity of the abundant wildlife. Herds of elk left the lowlands for high-country meadows. Bears were seen in increasing numbers, and lone riders had to be wary again of roving grizzlies. Squirrels flew through the trees or chattered fiercely at intruders, both human and bestial, while over hill and dale scampered hordes of playful chipmunks. Ravens and jays were seen in increased numbers. Eagles and hawks were more in evidence, too, as they circled high in the sky seeking prey.

Ordinarily spring was one of the Virginian's favorite times of the year. A spirit of renewal was abroad, a sense of the cycles not only of the seasons but of all life, a spirit he usually found invigorating. In past years he had often ridden to a special spot high on a mountain bordering Aspen Creek and from his perch admired the spectacle of the earth transformed. Not this spring, though. He kept close to home except when work required him to be elsewhere.

There was something else different about the Southerner, something obvious, something commented on by everyone: The Virginian now packed two pistols openly. From out of a dusty trunk stashed in a seldom-used closet he had taken an old gunbelt, and after cleaning it and applying a light coat of oil to the inside of the holster, he had strapped it onto his left side. Thereafter, every day he practiced, without fail, rain or shine. When he was at Aspen Creek, he went off by himself into a secluded grove north of the stream; when at Sunk Creek he preferred to go behind the barn where the hands often gathered to plunk tin cans.

Lin McLean was the first to witness one of these practice sessions. He was approaching the ranch house after a visit with Jessamine and his boys when he heard the crisp crack of gunfire, six shots spaced so close together they were like the staccato beating of a drum. Curious, he rode to the corner of the stable in time to see the Virginian blow six more cans into the air. And although he had seen his friend draw twice before, although he had been privileged to be on hand when both Trampas and Killebrew met their Maker, neither incident had prepared him for the sheer grace and precision he now saw displayed.

The Virginian was a blur when he drew, his hands empty one moment, filled with glittering hardware the next. When he cut loose, he didn't fan the hammer as some men liked to do, though doing so caused the gun to jerk and spoiled accuracy. No, the Virginian stood straight and firm and blasted away from the hip, his six-shooters pointed instinctively at the targets. He never had to aim consciously. Like others who had made a name for themselves as shootists, he had a natural knack, an inherent aptitude few men could hope to match.

Dapper was the next to learn of the Virginian's new pastime. Then came Judge Henry. Eventually, as more and more returning punchers signed on for the new year, the news became common knowledge. And since cowboys were only human and had the grapevine telegraph to feed, word spread throughout the immediate territory. The cattlemen discussed what it might mean, often in the same sentence in which Brazos was mentioned. In Medicine Bow conversation loosened enough tongues to make it a regular topic. Whether it was talked about at Butte Creek or not wasn't common knowledge, but it would have been preposterous to think Balaam and company didn't know.

A few weeks after the sessions had begun, Molly was in the kitchen fixing their supper when she heard the crack-crack-crack of pistols shatter the tranquil solitude of their remote valley. She set down the flour she had been about to pour into a bowl and moved to the window to listen. More shots echoed off the mountains. Her brow puckered in thought, she hurried upstairs and made certain the baby was fast asleep in its crib. Donning a yellow shawl, she hastened outside, across the creek, to the grove.

Molly stopped on seeing her man. He was facing a row of sticks jabbed into the hard ground, his hands loose at his sides. Suddenly the Colts leaped clear and boomed once for each stick, and when the booming stopped, only shattered stubs were left. She saw the pistols spin, saw him slide them smoothly into his holsters, and then he turned and saw her.

The Virginian's surprise showed. He recovered, smiled, and advanced to give her a hug and a kiss. "Come out for some more lessons?" he asked.

"I want to talk," Molly informed him.

"It must be turrible important if yu' couldn't wait until I was done."

"It is. I know how much you despise prying, but as your wife I think I have the prerogative to be an exception."

"Bein' a woman makes yu' exception enough."

"I'm serious, dearest," Molly said gravely. She nodded at the shattered sticks. "You do this every day now. And at night you don't sleep well. I know, because I've lost count of the number of times you've awakened me with your tossing and turning."

"Goodness gracious. Then there is somethin' to be said for separate bedrooms," the Virginian tried joking with her. "I'll start tonight."

"You'll do no such thing." Molly took his big hands in hers and gazed lovingly up into his eyes. "Can't you see how worried I am? This isn't like you, not at all. And if you keep going the way you are, you won't be in any shape to meet the trouble you've been expecting when it finally comes."

The Colts received a few pats. "I'll be in fine shape."

"I wonder. No one can carry the weight of the world on his shoulders without wearing down sooner or later. You need to take more time off, to lie back and relax now and then." Molly glanced at the house, wondering if a noise she had just heard was the crying of their offspring or a distant bird. Bothered by maternal guilt over having left Johnny alone, she began leading her husband homeward. "Another reason I've brought this up is the way you've been acting since you returned from Drybone—"

"I'd rather not talk about it," said the Virginian.

"Well *I* would. Do you realize you haven't laughed in ages? You're not the same adorable man I married, and it bothers me greatly. I want him back."

The Virginian, as if to prove her wrong, laughed now. "I've been called a heap o' things, but 'adorable' is a new one on me. Shucks. If Lin ever heard yu' say that, I wouldn't ever hear the end o' his joshin'."

"He's worried about you too. He told me so. So did Judge Henry and Dapper."

"Seems to me there's been a heap o' jabberin' goin' on when I wasn't around. Must be an epidemic o' leaky mouth hereabouts. Sure hope I don't catch it."

"Can you blame those who care for you the most for being concerned about your welfare? You do have friends, you know. There is no need for you to bear the burden alone." Molly held up a hand when he went to speak. "Hear me out." She stopped and studied him pensively. "Not opening up to your friends is one thing. What upsets me the most is that you won't open up to me. I'm your wife, in case you've forgotten. The two of us were made one. Heart to heart, soul to soul, we're linked. That means I'm entitled to share your innermost feelings." She surveyed their picturesque valley and its protective ring of stately mountains. "And another thing. This land is mine as much as it is yours. I love it no less than you do. When someone threatens all we hold dear, when they threaten our happiness together, they threaten me as well. I have every right to do my share to help defend our home from those who would destroy it."

"I never said yu' didn't," the Virginian threw in when she finally took a breath.

"True enough. But the way you treat me makes me feel as if I don't really count, as if you'd rather do everything all by yourself. I get the impression you'd rather have me tend to the housework and our son and not bother you over the truly important matters." Molly sadly bowed her head. "It's as if I'm second-rate, fit to do chores but not competent enough to think for myself or to stand on my own two feet. And it hurts me, Jeff. It hurts me so much sometimes I want to curl into a ball and cry myself dry."

The Virginian halted and stared at her in shock. "I had no idea," he said softly. Enfolding her in his strong arms, he kissed her forehead, then rested his chin on top of her hair. "I wish you would've told me this sooner, Mary. It's a poor excuse for a husband who treats his running mate as if she's a child." The next moment a warm tear touched his neck. He flinched and went on quickly, his drawl totally absent. "It's not like I do it on purpose. I'd never hurt you deliberately, as I hope you know. But all my life I've been accustomed to holding things inside of me, to dealing with every problem that came up without looking to anyone else for help." He forced a chuckle. "My ma used to tell me how I had this saying I tossed at her a lot when I was a kid and she'd be trying tell me how to do things. 'Me do it meself,' I'd always say, and I reckon that sort of stuck with me over the years to where I'd seldom rely on anyone else except maybe my cousin those years we were riding together." A heavy sigh escaped him. "I know I shouldn't, but some habits are a lot like wrinkles. Once they set in, they're with you for life."

Molly's response was to nuzzle him under the chin and lightly touch her lips to his skin.

"No one knows you're a grown woman better than me," the Virginian continued. "I apologize for treating you different, and from here on out I'll do my best to open up to you the way you want." He pulled back to stare into her moist eyes. "Just don't expect miracles. Changing the way we think isn't as easy as changing clothes. It might take me a while."

"I can wait," Molly said. "Because I know that you will change, eventually. When you set a goal in your mind, nothing stands in your way."

The Southerner was an imp in a cowboy hat when he

remarked, "I set my sights on yu' onced, didn't I? And look at what happened."

"Momentary insanity made me say yes."

"Pshaw! Was it that, or was it this?" the Virginian asked, pressing his mouth to hers.

The shadows had lengthened considerably when the pair resumed their stroll homeward. Arm in arm, they passed the barn and the corral, and here the Virginian stopped.

"That's mighty strange."

"What is, my love?"

"Have yu' seen the dogs lately?"

"No," Molly answered. "They're probably off after another rabbit or a deer."

"Could be," the Virginian conceded. "Although they never stray so far that they don't come pester us the minute we step foot outside." He gazed the length and breadth of their verdant domain. "Now that I think of it, they never showed when I came out for my target practice. Usually they do."

"They'll be whining at the door as soon as their bellies are empty," Molly predicted. "I learned long ago not to worry about them. They can hold their own against anything except maybe a mountain lion or a grizzly, and we haven't seen sign of either since that cat died trying to kill poor Sue."

"Tell yu' what," the Virginian said slowly, his carefree smile back again. "Why don't yu' go in out o' the chill while I take a look around?"

"If you want." Molly laughed and gave his arm a squeeze. "But if you ask me, you're turning into a worrywart." She took several steps, then shot a glance over her shoulder, uneasiness replacing her levity. "Is there something you're not telling me?"

The Virginian was about to tell her everything was fine, to claim there was no cause at all for alarm. But he had given her his word he would try to mend his ways, so he answered truthfully instead and felt foolish for doing so, not because he was confiding in her but because he was probably making a fool of himself. "Just a feelin' I have. Nothin' I'd wager a month's salary on."

"Surely it's too soon?" •

"The weather is warm enough now. I saw a wood pussy by the lake the other day, so I reckon all the polecats in this neck o' the country are out catchin' up on their huntin'."

"You be careful."

"Always," the Virginian assured her. An unusual stillness gripped the surrounding forest as he made a circuit around the ranch house, reloading his pistols along the way. He was relieved to hear sparrows twitter in a thicket near the southeast corner and a raven give voice to a series of caws from the top of a pine, since animals were keenly sensitive to any and all intrusions into their territory and always stayed silent when danger was abroad.

Once back where he started, the Virginian cupped his hands to his mouth and called the names of both dogs several times. Old Hickory and Lavender did not respond with their rumbling bays, nor did they crash out of the brush to paw and lick him. After waiting several minutes, the Virginian shrugged and went inside.

Molly was just entering the kitchen, Johnny bundled in her arms. "Anything?" she inquired.

"No. I reckon I'm about ready for my rockin' chair and cats."

"I beg your pardon?"

"I knew this old lady onced. She lived all by herself except for a passel of uppity cats who had her so trained, all one of 'em had to do was meow and there'd be a new bowlful of grub on the floor."

"Where's the similarity? Is it because cats are independent and contrary, just like you are?" Molly asked sweetly as she handed him the baby and stepped to the counter.

"The similarity ain't in the cats, it's in the old lady. Every time she heard a noise, she'd go leapin' up out o' that rocker to take a peek out o' her window. Worst case o' nerves I ever did see."

"She probably kept her worries bottled up inside her all the time. It's not good for the health."

"My, my," the Virginian said, taking his seat at the table. "When yu' sink your teeth into a morsel, yu' plumb worry it to death."

"Haven't you heard?" Molly countered matter-of-factly. "Chewing aids the digestion and promotes health and vigor. It's a scientific fact that men who wolf their food are more prone to have moody dispositions."

"Is this the same science that claims we all came from a bunch o' apes?"

"Evolution, my worldly cowboy, is accepted by all the best minds in Europe and America. Don't tell me you disagree."

"I never argue with schoolmarms and folks who get calluses from pattin' themselves on the back because they think their minds are so much better than the common herd," the Virginian responded. "But I do wonder."

Molly was working with her flour again. "About what?" she asked idly.

"Last year the Professor told me about an article he'd read. Seems this scientist was sayin' that before we were apes, we were frogs."

"You're twisting the case. He didn't say we *were* frogs, just that our ancestors *came* from frogs. His argument was very logically presented."

"And yu' believe that? Yu' really think you're great-great-grandpa was a-hoppin' around from lily pad to lily pad in some old pond?"

"Now I know you're trying to get a rise out of me. If the Professor told you about the theory, I'm sure he mentioned that the evolution from frogs to humans took millions and millions of years."

"Must be the result of all them fairy tales," the Virginian muttered to his offspring.

"What are you telling him?"

"I bet yu' were partial to fairy tales when yu' were a girl."

"My mother and father read them to me at bedtime, yes. What bearing does this have on anything?"

"Did yu' hear the one about the turtle and that jack-rabbit?"

"The tortoise and the hare, yes."

"And the one about that snow filly and her seven midgets?"

" 'Snow White and the Seven Dwarfs,' if you please."

"Did yu' like 'em?"

"Every child does. They fire the imagination."

"Did yu' believe they were true stories?"

"Oh, come now. Not even a child is so gullible."

"What about that one where the princess kisses a frog and it turns into a handsome prince? Did yu' hear that one?"

Molly looked up, her expression showing she was miles and years away. "I'll say I did. It was one of my favorites. Always has been."

"Did yu' believe it?"

"And you say I worry a point to death! Who in their right mind would believe such an outrageous fable?"

"So you're sayin' that a kiss changin' a man into a frog is downright ridiculous, but a million years doin' the same thing is logical?"

Whatever reply Molly might have made was forestalled by sudden loud whinnies from the corral. The Virginian rose and gave Johnny back to her, commenting, "That's Monte. I'd better see what has him so upset." He was almost to the door when a low-pitched whine came from the other side.

"The dogs!" Molly exclaimed cheerfully.

"About time," the Virginian said. Working the latch, he yanked the door wide. The smile of greeting that was curling his mouth turned into a frown of outrage when he saw the bloody body of Old Hickory sprawled at his very feet. "What the—?" he blurted, leaning down, and in doing so he inadvertently saved his own life.

There was a whizzing sound, and from out of the twilight streaked a spinning shaft identical to the two arrows the Virginian suddenly saw embedded in Old Hickory. It clipped the top of his hat, sending it flying. Without thinking, he threw himself to the left just as the crisp mountain air exploded with the blast of gunfire. Slugs ripped into both jambs and the floor. Slivers flew like swarms of bees. "Get down!" he bellowed.

Molly complied, dropping close to the floor. Above and on both sides the counter and the cupboards were being blistered by rifle and pistol fire. Wood splintered and showered on top of her as she huddled over tiny Johnny, screening the baby with her own body. Glasses and dishes were shattered where they stood. A china shard struck her temple, stinging terribly, and she cried out. Then a gun thundered almost in her very ear, and she looked up to find her husband had shot out the lamp.

With a flick of his other arm the Virginian slammed the door shut, bounded to her side, and hauled her upright. He propelled her into the hall so fast she was there before she realized it. "Stay close," he advised, and made for the front room.

"Are they Indians?" Molly cried.

"With pale hides," the Virginian responded angrily. He reached the corner and peered out. Across the room the front door slammed inward to reveal a dusky figure looming tall on the porch. The figure took a step, spotted the Southerner, and froze. A rifle cracked, spitting flame and lead, which the Virginian's pistol answered in kind. Staggering backward, the figure worked the lever of his Winchester, then raised it high to aim. Again the pistol spoke, and this time the figure twisted to the right, stumbled into the railing, and pitched from sight.

Guns opened around the house from all directions. Shots poured into the sturdy structure, breaking every window on the ground floor and pockmarking every wall. The Virginian and Molly crouched by the baseboards, their arms over the baby, waiting for the deadly hail to cease.

A shout outside was the signal. There were a few scattered retorts to the north and the south, followed by silence.

Molly put her mouth to her husband's ear. "Will they

leave now?" she asked breathlessly while struggling to control the fluttering of her heart that was making her half-dizzy.

Before her husband could say a word, the same gruff voice in front bawled, "If they ain't dead, they're close to it! Rush the house and make sure!"

23

No Man's Land

It had been Molly's dubious fortune to enjoy the benefit of a sheltered childhood. Her parents had done all in their power to spare their precious child from life's harsher realities in the mistaken belief that by doing so they spared her tender soul from possible harm. Never once did it occur to them that out of hardship often came strength; out of adversity grew character. They did so fine a job that the only calamities of note Mary experienced was a broken finger when she was six and measles at the age of ten. During both disasters they fluttered over her like frenzied hummingbirds, darting off to fulfill her every whim. Miraculously, she recovered.

Because of this treatment, Mary spent her early years convinced life was all sweetness and light. Bad things happened only to bad people, her parents repeatedly told her, and since she was a good little girl, nothing bad would ever happen to her. She went around with her dainty feet treading terra firma and her mind drifting off with the clouds.

Everything changed midway through Mary's twelfth year when her father died. She came crashing to earth like a blazing meteor, her emotions shattered by the impact. Gradually she came to see that her earlier attitude had been wrong, that bad things did indeed happen to good people and sometimes there was nothing anyone could do to prevent it. She accepted this fact as readily as children do all truth, and she learned to make the best of what life had to offer without useless whining or complaining. The only scar was deep-seated resentment that her parents had so misled her, but she never let on to her mother.

In later years Mary dealt with the financial setbacks her family suffered with as cool a head as ever graced the shoulders of any of her illustrious ancestors. She made ends meet without relying on anyone else. Then came the invitation to teach in Wyoming, and she surprised her relatives and herself by accepting. Into the raw frontier she ventured, there to meet and vanquish the uncertainties of living among those her prim and proper brethren deemed simpleminded barbarians. In so doing, her heart was in turn vanquished by one of those whom the East so disdained.

Never, however, was her life in peril. At no time was she in any real danger, other than those induced by romantic fancy. The closest she came was when she found her cowboy lover sprawled by a spring, near death from an Indian ambush. Even then the Indians had been long gone, and her anxiety had been more for him than for herself.

So Molly had never, ever known what it was like to feel true fear. She had never had her life threatened, never had to deal with personal violence or to face the grim prospect of her own death. Now she did. At the shout from outside the house, Molly blanched and gulped, her body trembling uncontrollably. Terror surged through her, setting her temples to pounding and her lungs to working like the bellows of a forge. She was completely, helplessly afraid, so afraid she was virtually paralyzed. At that moment she wanted nothing more than to grab her baby and flee into the night, to find sanctuary in the dark forest where no one could find them, but her limbs refused to respond to her mental commands. For a few moments she was twelve again, helpless in the grip of forces she could neither comprehend nor accept, and she almost threw her head back and screamed in abject mortal terror.

Then Molly felt a warm hand on her arm. It jolted her out of herself, and she saw the pistol her husband was offering and heard his grave words.

"Here. I can't cover both sides at once. Yu' have to watch the back door."

Molly mechanically took the revolver. She offered no protest when the Virginian lowered their child to the floor, and she let herself be pulled upright.

"Whatever yu' do, don't let these polecats get inside. Onced they do, we're pretty near finished."

The calmly uttered words had a soothing effect on Molly's frayed nerves. She glanced around and saw him outlined against the opposite doorway, feverishly feeding cartridges into his Colt, cartridges that would be used to kill other human beings. Just as he expected her to do with the cartridges in her gun. But could she? Was he expecting too much of her?

Molly was jarred into movement by a tremendous crash from the rear door. Without thinking she stepped close to the kitchen and peered within. Two men were in her house, standing near the counter as they looked all around seeking the man she loved so they could slay him.

The next moment Molly gave a faint gasp. One of the intruders was striding toward the hallway. She glimpsed the glint of metal in his right hand, and suddenly she realized he wanted to kill them all—her husband, their innocent little Johnny, and her too—and he'd do so without hesitation the second he laid eyes on them. He'd been sent to murder her loved ones and destroy her home, to put an end to everything she held near and dear.

How dare he! Molly fumed, clenching her Colt tighter. What gave him the right to ruin her life? What made Balaam and his kind think they could do whatever they pleased whenever they wished, and the devil take the consequences? *This was her house! Her family!* Cold fury steeled her resolve and her arm. She lifted the Colt higher, training it on the killer's chest, then opened her mouth to shout a warning.

Thunder roared in the hall and was echoed by booming in the front room. A man screamed. Another cursed.

Molly saw the figures in the kitchen dash toward the hall. The nearest was only a yard away when her Colt added to the din, the recoil kicking her arm upward. Stunned that she had actually squeezed the trigger, Molly watched the man pitch forward, his own gun sending a slug into the floor. Beyond him the second gunman opened fire, fanning from the hip. Bullets smacked into the jamb within inches of her face. More from instinct than design, she returned fire. Once, twice, three times her Colt bucked, and on the third shot the assassin stumbled backward into the counter, clutched at his chest, and fell.

Out in the front room glass shattered. There was a lot of yelling, followed by the heavy clomp of boot heels on the wooden floor, then on the porch. In the distance a horse whinnied. Gradually the racket ceased, to be replaced by total silence.

Slowly Molly lowered the Colt. She could hear ringing in her ears. She smelled the acrid gunsmoke. Her mouth was dry, her palms slick with sweat, which impressed her as odd; it should be the other way around. One of the men on the kitchen floor groaned, and she was about to go to him when her baby gurgled, reminding her of her first priority. She spun and darted to Johnny's side and knelt. "Are you hurt, my love?" she asked, her voice trembling as badly as her whole body had earlier. Anxiously she plucked him up and examined his smiling face and squirming form. He was unhurt. She pressed her brow to his and uttered a heartfelt, "Thank you, Lord."

"I reckon they won't try that trick on us again."

The Virginian towered above her, looming grim and terrible in the darkness, his smoking Colt in his right hand. He took the other six-shooter from her and reloaded both.

"I shot two of them," Molly said softly. "One of them is still alive, I think."

"I'll tend to him."

"You wouldn't—" Molly blurted as he stalked off,

but she checked her objection. Rising, she leaned on the wall for support and waited for the blast she was certain would come. None did.

"They're both candidates for kingdom come," the Virginian announced when he rejoined her. Pausing, he dropped his left six-gun into its holster, then tenderly touched her cheek. "You did fine, Mary. Real fine. I never could have held them off without you."

"I killed two men," Molly said blankly, and when she did, the magnitude of the deed she had done hit her with the force of a hammer blow. Her knees went weak, her stomach felt queasy. *Thou shalt not kill!* echoed over and over in her mind. She remembered those words chalked in pale white on the Sunday-school blackboard; she recalled snatches of Sunday sermons on the wickedness of those who lived by the sword; and fresh as yesterday came recollections of the countless times her parents had stressed how wrong it was to harm another living being. "I killed two men," she said again, softly this time, every syllable pregnant with horror.

"You did the right thing," the Virginian responded solemnly. "It was them or us."

"But that doesn't make it *right*."

"If it doesn't, then no killing ever is." The other Colt was wagged toward the kitchen. "There's a difference between cold-blooded murder and self-defense. You need never feel ashamed about protecting yourself."

"Then why do I?" Molly stared at the ceiling. "Why do I feel as if a bolt of lightning is going to strike me at any minute?"

"Guilt," the Virginian said simply.

"But you just said there's no need to feel any," Molly said with a tinge of desperation.

"I said you shouldn't. I didn't say you wouldn't." He grew so sober he was almost severe when he continued. "Takin' a life is a mighty serious proposition, so serious most folks shy away from just the thought. No one ever wants to do it, yet there are times when it has to be done. Lawmen have to shoot outlaws. Soldiers have to kill in times of war. And when a few buck society too far, sometimes a jury has to set them straight at the end of a rope. It's all the same in the end."

"No," Molly disagreed. "That's all legal and proper. This was different. This was—" And she stopped, vainly seeking the precise word.

"Personal," the Virginian finished for her.

"Yes. Terribly personal." Molly sagged, her head bowed over the dozing infant. "And now my soul must bear the burden for the rest of my life."

"You can handle it."

"How can you be so certain?"

"Because I know you. I know you have true grit. Tomorrow or the next day, whenever you sit down and think about what happened without your emotions interfering, you'll see that you had no other choice. Unless, of course, you *wanted* to die."

"It can't be so simple."

"I'm afraid it is." The Virginian abruptly stiffened, his right hand falling to his waist. "Shhh, now," he cautioned. "I thought I heard something." Pulling his hardware, he moved cautiously to the front room.

Molly was unwilling to be left alone with her turmoil. She followed him, fearing the band of cutthroats had come back, and felt Johnny shift in her arms. Clutching him closer, she happened to glance down and see a limp arm in time to avoid tripping over it. A gunman lay sprawled on her floor, his features distorted in a grimace of death. Gingerly lifting her legs she took only a few more steps when she found another. A third was braced against the inner front wall, a new eye where the top of his nose had been.

A tug of war ensued between Molly's conscience and her heart. So much slaughter was appalling, almost too gruesome to endure. But once again she reminded herself that these men had come to Aspen Creek for one purpose and one purpose only. Did they deserve her pity, then? Never! Should she be upset over the fate they had brought on themselves? No! As her beloved great-aunt in Dunbarton had once told her, "If you live long enough, dearie, you'll find out that most people are about as happy as they make up their minds to be, and ninety percent of the time they get out of life exactly what they ask for. So always remember to put happiness in your bonnet and never settle for less than the best. That's my philosophy." And what a grand outlook it was, Molly reflected. She became more composed merely thinking about it.

A fourth body blocked Molly's path on the porch. This time she hardly paid any attention. She was staring at her husband's back, impressed by the thought that if he had not been there, she might now be dead. What was he thinking about? she wondered, envying his calm, his self-control.

Had Molly been able to see into the man whose self-possession she so admired, she would have discovered that the outer surface in no way accurately reflected the inner truth. For the Southerner was in the grip of a rage so intense it bordered on the volcanic. His body was literally hot, almost burning up, yet not from the heat of battle. Rather was the Virginian furious that his enemies had seen fit to invade his home and imperil his family. He had often fretted they might. His knowledge of the ways of evil had taught him that no atrocity was beyond men who lacked scruples. But he had persisted in hoping his reputation would work in his favor for once and they wouldn't risk his wrath. He should have known better! he smoldered. His foolishness had nearly cost him those he cared for the most.

Gun leveled, the Virginian stopped at the edge of the porch and listened to the receding hoofbeats of a single horse. A straggler, perhaps a wounded badman, was trying to catch up with the rest of his fleeing *compadres*. He longed to saddle Monte, chase the man down, and get certain questions answered if he had to beat them out of the gunman, but he had a wife and son to attend to first. "Pack a bag," he said over his shoulder. "I'm takin' yu' to Lin's."

Nodding, Molly hastened indoors.

In her absence the Virginian examined each of the dead men. There wasn't a single one he recognized, none he could say for sure worked for Ira Balaam. Moving rapidly, mindful of streaking the floor with blood, he dragged those inside outdoors and arranged them in a row at the bottom of the porch. As he finished, his wife appeared.

"Ready."

"Stick close in case there are skulkers," the Virginian advised. He folded her slender hand in his and hurried around the north side of the house. A twig snapped as they neared the far corner. Motioning for her to stay still, he advanced to scour the corral and the stable. Monte and Molly's mare were at the rail nearest the house. Otherwise there was no sign of life.

Taking a breath, the Virginian sprinted to the corral and crouched low next to the horses. No shouts or shots greeted his maneuver, and partially satisfied, he risked opening the gate and saddling both animals. Molly was at the corner when he brought them over. It was the work of a few seconds to boost her up, give her the baby, and step into the stirrups. He lifted the reins to leave when an oversight occurred to him. "Oh, sugar!" he muttered.

"What is it?"

"Be right back," the Virginian said, goading Monte to the back door, which still hung open. Although he disliked leaving Molly and Johnny alone, he slid down and raced inside to the gun cabinet. A pair of Winchesters and two boxes of ammunition were cradled under his arms when he emerged. "It wouldn't do to be caught short," he explained, sliding one of the rifles into the scabbard. The ammo went into his saddlebags. The spare rifle he held as he swung aboard once again and applied his spurs. "Step along now, yu' pie-biter. We have us a heap o' ridin' to do."

And ride they did. The Southerner stuck to the highlines all the way to Box Elder, stopping to rest only twice and then only briefly. After the first hour he swapped the spare Winchester for the baby, since the mare was giving Molly a difficult time.

The pink flush of imminent dawn painted the eastern sky when the Virginian rode out of a gully and saw the McLean ranch house a quarter of a mile off. Smoke curled lazily from the chimney, while in the yard chickens were moving about.

"Thank God!" Molly exclaimed. She pulled alongside him and placed a hand on his elbow. "What will you do now?"

"Yu' know what I'm fixin' to do."

"Must you?"

"I do if yu' don't want it to happen again. They failed to bed us down last night, so now they'll wait a spell and give it another try unless I persuade them different."

"Why not go to Sunk Creek and inform the Judge? There isn't a puncher there who wouldn't go along if you asked. You shouldn't do it alone."

"It was our spread they struck, not Sunk Creek."

"Take Lin with you, at least."

"I'll make better time alone," the Virginian said, and tapped his heels against Monte. The drumming of their mounts brought the McLeans outside, both with rifles in hand. "I'd be obliged if yu' would let Mary stay awhile," he stated without preliminaries. "I'll be back for her just as soon as I can."

Lin and Jessamine glanced at one another, and Jessamine came quickly over to take Johnny.

"What happened, pard?" Lin asked.

Molly answered him, giving the bare essentials, concluding with, "Jeff is going after them all by himself. But it's too dangerous. Go with him, Lin. Please!"

"Why, sure I will—"

"No," the Virginian said, his voice a whiplash. "This is mine to do, not yours. Don't make it any harder than it is." He wheeled his horse, then paused, and when next he spoke, his tone was softer. "A man has to go through with his responsibilities or he can't lay claim to the title. Yu' can't have lived with me all this while and not understand."

"I do," Molly said in a whisper.

"Keep the Arbuckles warm," the Virginian said, and was off in a puff of dust, his hat pulled down low on his brow, his body hunched forward as he galloped across the flat and on into the mountains. Presently he located an old

Indian trail that shaved miles off his previous route. He was not making for home, but for a valley situated midway between Aspen Creek and Butte Creek, a valley anyone passing between the two must cross to reach either destination. Straight to where the established trail curved out of the foothills he went, and there in the bare earth he found the tracks he sought, evidence of a large body of riders headed toward Aspen Creek within the past twenty-four hours. Oddly, there was no sign the outfit had returned.

The Virginian sat down on a rock and studied the hoofprints for a while, tapping his finger on his chin the whole time. At length he rose, forked leather, and turned eastward along the hills to a secondary trail seldom used by honest men. Here were fresher tracks, though only four, all put down since midnight. "So yu' stayed in small bunches," he said to himself. "Probably figured it'd be easier to lose me, but yu' figured wrong."

For two hours the Virginian wound steadily on into the depths of uninhabited country known locally as No Man's Land, the same stretch of country the Southerner had crossed once before on that fateful day long since when he had been forced by circumstance to escort Ira Balaam and two horses borrowed from Judge Henry to Sunk Creek. They never had made it. Indians had seen to that. But if not for those marauding warriors, the Virginian would never have won his lady's heart. His convalescence under her loving care had been the final straw that broke the rigid back of her proper Eastern upbringing.

Now the Virginian sat alertly in the saddle, his Winchester across his thighs. The grim sun was well on toward the midday position, casting a harsh glare on the dull sagebrush. In the distance pale peaks stood like somber sentries.

The gunmen had chosen their route wisely. Tracks were hard to read in packed, dry earth, but a seasoned tracker, a man like the Virginian, who had been weaned to the hunt at the tender age of six in the verdant hills of old Virginia, was not easily deterred. Tenaciously he clung to the trail, which, it soon became apparent, would take the quartet to the crossing at Little Muddy, an oasis in the wasteland, as it were, boasting a solitary tree and a thicket or two. Beyond the crossing, no more than a six-hour ride, lay Butte Creek—Balaam's home range.

"Will they stop or keep goin'?" the Virginian asked Monte. "That's the question. It depends, I reckon, on how safe they're feelin'."

A little farther on the Virginian patted his horse and commented, "I hope he's with 'em. It'll make everything so much easier." He gnawed his lower lip for several seconds. "But why wasn't that his voice I heard? He'd be in charge, since Balaam wouldn't be loco enough to go himself."

Then again, when they were less than a mile from Little Muddy, "I've been a-doin' some thinkin', hawss. And it strikes me there's a right peculiar fact about livin' in this day and age. Do yu' know that it's easier for a man to be bad than it is for him to be good? Or, as the parson would have it, it's easier to be evil than virtuous. Now why do yu' suppose that should be? Seems to me it ought to be the other way around. But it ain't." He saw a coiled rattlesnake in his path and skirted it. "Back in the old days, when I strutted around dressed to kill, if there was an hombre who'd taken a dislike to me, it was no trouble at all to walk right up to him and settle accounts. He'd draw his steel if he was so inclined, I'd draw mine, and that would be the end of it." A heavy sigh was vented. "But things are a heap different now. I'm on the side of the angels, or so she tells me, so I can't go around shootin' folks just 'cause they hate my guts. Everything has to be fair and square. But it's mighty tryin', hawss. It surely is." He pushed his hat back. "It'd be so damn simple to go find Balaam, slap him a few times to get his dander up, then give him a few lead pills for that sour disposition o' his when he goes for his hogleg. So damn simple."

The top of the lone tree at the crossing blossomed ahead, a dot of green in an expanse of brown, so the Virginian slowed to a walk. He worked the Winchester lever, feeding a cartridge into the chamber. Angling to the west, he bent low, his chest touching the saddle horn, and rode in a loop that brought him up on the tree from the rear. A hundred yards out he dismounted, ground-hitched Monte, and removed his spurs.

Since the wind was blowing toward the Little Muddy, the Virginian stalked forward on cat's feet, stopping often to tilt his head and listen. The shadow of a thicket enveloped him before he heard voices. Instantly he crouched, pinpointed the exact location of the speakers, and slanted in their direction. Coarse laughter drowned out the crunch of his boot heel on loose soil. Easing onto his stomach, he crawled to an opening in the dry vegetation.

All four were seated around a small fire, drinking coffee. The fire was positioned under the tree so the limbs overhead dispersed the smoke. Only one of them the Virginian recognized, the hard case called Santee.

A pudgy man in a Stetson was talking. "—the sweetest filly this side o' the Divide. Kept me goin' for two straight days, she did, and plumb wore me out."

"Two minutes is more like it, Larn," Santee said, eliciting more mirth. He tipped his tin cup, then glanced at a lean man with a sallow complexion. "What the hell is the matter with yu', Beckwirth? Yu' haven't cracked a smile since Eve ate the apple."

"Do yu' want the truth or do yu' want it sugarcoated?" the man responded testily.

"Straight tongue will do."

"We made a mistake back there. We never should've rode off with the job unfinished."

"We got out alive. Nothin' else matters."

"Like hell it doesn't." Beckwirth sat up and jabbed a bony finger at each of them in turn. "Yu' all know what I'm talkin' about. Yu've all heard the tales. He won't rest until he hunts down each and every one of us."

"He's just one man," Santee said.

"Jeff Ringo ain't no ordinary man. Haven't yu' listened to what Brazos has been tellin' us? He's entitled to more notches than all of us put together, and me, I don't cotton to the notion o' havin' to look over my shoulder for the rest o' my life."

"Ah, yu' worry too much," Santee growled. "So we

lost seven men! There are still over forty in the outfit, and that's more than enough to get the job done."

"If'n yu' ask me," spoke up the fourth man, "yu' don't worry enough, Santee. And I ain't talkin' about that Virginia feller, either. Yu' should be worried about Brazos."

The Virginian had been about to work his way around the thicket, but he paused to listen.

"He don't scare me," Santee responded.

"Then you're a darned fool," said the fourth man. "Brazos is hell on two legs, and when he hears what we did, he'll be fit to be tied."

"The boss will set him straight."

"You hope. But since when has Brazos taken to bein' told how to behave? He's made it plain he wants the Virginia feller for himself. He's flat-out told each and every one of us that he's goin' to be the gunny who makes wolf meat o' the son of a bitch. Hell. Didn't he say onced that if any man tried to cheat him o' his due, he'd put them under so fast they'd think they was struck by lightning?"

Santee fidgeted, then swirled his brew. "It ain't my fault I was asked to lead. Brazos was off in Medicine Bow when the boss got the notion into his head."

"Did yu' ever stop to think that maybe that's *why* the boss decided to move when he did?" Beckwirth interjected. "He doesn't like the cat and mouse Brazos is playin'. He wants the Virginian out o' the way now so the bastard won't be a thorn in his side later, when the real fightin' starts."

"If'n yu' ask me," the fourth man opined, "yu' should have said no when the boss gave yu' them orders."

"Why, yu' dumb punk. Buckin' him is just as bad as buckin' Brazos. Say no and you're liable to be put to bed with a pick and shovel."

"Suit yourself," Beckwirth said. "For your sake, though, I hope Brazos is in a forgivin' frame o' mind when he hears about it."

A gloomy air of depression settled on the four, and while they sat and mulled over their mistakes, the Virginian snaked to the north end of the thicket, rose slowly, and taking measured sideways strides, stepped into the open. None of them noticed him at first. Then Larn, as he leaned out to grab the coffeepot, happened to look up, and his face became the color of a bed sheet.

"Oh, God!"

"What's got yu'—" Santee began, swiveling. His eyes widened into saucers, and his cup fell from his fingers as his hand started to swoop to the butt of his gun. He caught himself in time and froze, except for his mouth, which twitched uncontrollably in feral hatred.

Larn, Beckwirth, and the fourth man were rigid in attitudes of shock and fear.

"Howdy, boys," the Virginian said amiably. He moved farther from the thicket, closer to the Little Muddy, giving him a clear line of fire if they made a play for their irons. "That coffee sure smells invitin'."

They were too flabbergasted to respond.

"I see your hawsses are plumb tuckered out, and I can't say as I blame them afteh the hard ridin' yu've been doin'," the Virginian said, distracting them with talk until he reached a spot directly between their fire and the crossing. "How did yu' like the country up Aspen Creek way?"

Santee was the first to regain control of his vocal cords. "Quit baitin' us. We know what you're here for. Why rub it in like a damn fool kid?"

"You're right. I should shoot yu'. I want to. Almost more than I've ever wanted to shoot anyone. But I won't. Not because I've gone all pussy-kitten. No, yu' have my wife to thank for still bein' alive."

"Your wife?" Larn croaked.

"Yep. She's a big believer in justice and decency. In law and order." The Virginian's mouth creased in a devilishly delicious grin. "In badges and rope."

"Rope?" Santee blanched.

"I'm takin' yu' to Sunk Creek where Judge Henry can set up a hemp committee all legal and proper-like. Should draw in people from all over. They might even send out invitations, like they do in some parts, and invite everyone to a picnic afteh." The Virginian watched their hands, his own steady on the rifle. "Why, I reckon you'll be famous. Four at once is a real treat. Even better than that double affair they had down Colorado way. Drew in ten thousand, if I recollect correctly."

"I won't end my days gurglin' on a rope," Santee said.

"That's your choice," the Virginian replied harshly. "It doesn't make any difference to me which way yu' pick. Yu' can die with throat trouble, or yu' can slap leather. Just don't take all day makin' up your minds."

The gauntlet had been thrown down. Now the Virginian waited, his body rigid from shoulder to belly as if he had been carved from marble. He looked at all of them and yet at none of them, primed to explode into action at the first inkling of movement. Which came with a suddenness that afforded no time to so much as blink. He saw Santee's revolver leap clear and he fired. The slug tore into Santee's throat and spun the killer around, and even as Santee spun, the Virginian was levering another round and shifting to train the barrel on Larn, who had gone for his six-gun next but was fumbling as he drew. The Virginian's trigger finger tightened, but the rifle had not yet thundered when Larn reacted as if kicked in the head by a Missouri mule. A fraction of a second later there was the sound of a rifle shot, only from far off, from the north. Both Beckwirth and the fourth man, neither of whom had tried for their pistols, began to rotate, to face this new threat, but they were not quite halfway around when they both staggered and two more shots cracked.

The Virginian whirled and raised his Winchester. At the limits of its range was a rider in the act of turning his horse. The Virginian took a hasty bead as the man broke into a gallop. He had often shot antelope at such a distance, and they were harder to hit. For over ten seconds his sights lingered on the rider's back; then, with an oath, he jerked the rifle down and stared at the four corpses ringing the fire. "They weren't foolin'," he said quietly.

"The varmint really does want me all to himself." Twisting, the Southerner watched the receding figure of the rider, the figure of a man dressed all in black, as it dwindled into the haze of No Man's Land and was soon lost to view.

24

A Mysterious Request

I arrived at Sunk Creek months earlier than I had
planned, because my writing commitments were now
taking up so much of my time that I feared I wouldn't
be able to come out during the summer. Judge Henry and
his gracious wife received me courteously and then proceeded to fill me in on all the events of importance since
my last visit. Naturally I was appalled to learn about the
escalating violence and to hear the Judge's dire prediction
that "the worst is yet to come."

The Virginian and Molly, I was told, were back at Aspen Creek, only now they weren't alone. Out of fear for
their lives, and for the McLean family as well, the Judge
had called in his partner and his foreman and persuaded
them to allow a pair of Sunk Creek punchers to bunk
at their respective spreads until "the situation resolved itself."

Both the Southerner and McLean had balked at first,
their independent natures resisting the idea they needed
any help protecting their families. Judge Henry, though,

proved his wisdom by stressing that should anything befall either of their wives or their children while they were at Sunk Creek, he would blame himself for keeping them away from their homesteads when they were needed the most. His worry was genuine, his guilt valid, so, reluctantly, they gave in to his wishes.

The morning after my arrival I was made privy to interesting news: Judge Henry had received an invitation from several friends of his in the Wyoming Stock Growers Association to attend a formal function at their pleasure resort and place of amusement, the Cheyenne Club, in the state capital. The dinner was to take place about the same time I had planned to head east, so the Judge invited me to go along with him and be his guest for an evening of fine food and friendly discussion. I gladly accepted.

Little did I realize that a whim of Fate was to dictate a drastic change, which in turn enabled me to understand better the widespread bloodshed so soon to erupt across northern Wyoming. It happened in this fashion:

Three days before our intended departure for Medicine Bow and the train station, Judge Henry took me out to the stable to see his fine new Morgan. As ignorant as I was about what constituted superior horseflesh, I knew enough to know a sterling animal when I saw one. I complimented him on his purchase as he led me back toward the ranch house. We were passing the corral, when suddenly he stopped and said, "Here. You'll find this interesting."

The object of his attention was Dapper, who had a rope in hand and was stalking a bay gelding that kept a wary eye on him as it moved at a trot around the perimeter.

A dozen or so hands, including the Virginian, were perched on the rails watching the battle of wits. He slid aside to make room for us, saying to me, "I saw yu' practicin' your ropin' out behind the house yesterday. A few more visits, seh, and I reckon yu' can have Dapper's job."

"Not unless you're more fond of walking then I

imagined," I bantered back. "Give me his job and the outfit will be short of broken horses within a month."

"Pshaw. Yu' underestimate yourself," the Virginian countered. "Most of the hawsses will keel over with laughter as soon as yu' get your loop all tangled around your head like yu' done when I was watchin'. It should be right easy to catch 'em then."

His charming grin disarmed my budding irritation at being reminded of my incompetence. "I'll be ninety before I get the hang of using a rope," I admitted.

"Yu' could get your start as a ketch hand at the next roundup," the Virginian suggested. "Most punchers earn their ropin' savvy thataway."

"I appreciate the offer," I said, "but I'll spare the poor calves the indignity."

Dapper, meanwhile, had been following the gelding with his eyes, his body as motionless as a post. Now, as the horse came in front of him again, he tossed his rope instead of throwing it. By that I mean he didn't swing the rope over his head before letting go. He simply had the loop spread out at his side, and when the time was right, his arm snaked up and out, so did the loop, and the deed was done so neatly that the gelding was snared before it realized the rope had left his hand. Once it awoke to the fact, it tried to break into a gallop and started to jerk its head, but by then Dapper had the rope snubbed, and all the horse succeeded in doing was choking itself.

The bronc-buster's next step was to apply the bridle. Surprisingly, the gelding didn't object a bit to this operation. It also stood meekly while Dapper hobbled it with a short piece of grass rope. A tenderfoot might have jumped to the conclusion the gelding was as tame as could be, but I knew better, having seen how horses brought in from the open range behaved once they laid eyes on the blanket and saddle. This bay was no exception.

As soon as Dapper made for it with the blanket in hand, the gelding went into a frenzy, trying to break free. Unable to move much because of the hobble and the rope, it nonetheless put up quite a fight before it was willing to let the blanket be draped over its back. Puffing and snorting, nostrils flaring, it stood timidly once again as Dapper brought over the saddle.

If horses could curse, I have always thought that one would have put even the cowpunchers to shame when that saddle found its proper resting place. Glaring balefully at Dapper, the gelding waited until after the stirrup had been hooked over the saddle horn, and the cinch had been tightened, to explode in a fury.

Dapper skipped backward, away from those heavy hooves, and held on to the rope until the bay quieted once again. When, presently, the horse was too winded to continue, Dapper warily approached. He swiftly lowered the stirrup, removed the hobbles, and slid off the loop. Holding the reins in his right hand, he put his foot in the stirrup, then suddenly reached out and gave the gelding's ear a sharp twist.

Its attention diverted by the pain, the horse didn't realize Dapper was on board until the bronc-buster let go of its ear. For a few moments the bay stood rigid, its eyes wide. Then it practically erupted, shooting straight up and coming down with all four legs extended so that Dapper received the full force of the jolt.

Whoops and cheers went up from those who rode for the brand as the bay made Dapper earn his pay. Bucking, twisting, whirling, kicking, the horse used every trick it knew in a mad effort to send the impudent cowboy flying. Dapper hung on regardless.

All went well until the gelding hit on a ploy that showed it had a truly nasty streak. When the bucking and spinning bore no result, the horse suddenly angled straight at the corral, ramming into the rails with all of its might, trying to crush Dapper, who lifted his leg out of the way barely in time. A puncher on the outside squawked and leaped off, eliciting hoots and laughter for his prudence.

Again the bay attempted to pound its tormentor into a pulp, but this time tragedy resulted. The horse had turned from the corral as if giving up the idea and had sped across to our side. Too late I divined its intent. I heard the Virginian's yell of warning and felt his steely fingers on my arm. The next second I went flying. Behind

me there was a tremendous crash followed by shouts and
oaths. I landed on my shoulder, dazed, and heard a swirl
of voices.

"Is he hurt bad?"

"Out o' the way, damn it!"

"Somebody fetch Scipio! He knows some doctorin'!"

"Scipio, hell! Fetch Mrs. Henry!"

Rising on an elbow, I saw all the hands gathered
around someone on the ground. The bay was also down,
lying amidst the shattered rails, its front leg broken, the
bone protruding from the ruptured skin. But the punchers,
in their anxiety over the injured man, were paying no attention to the outlaw.

Hands seized hold of me from behind and boosted me
upright. I turned, expecting to find the Virginian, and
found Lin McLean. "I took a tumble," I blurted self-
consciously.

"No yu' didn't," Lin responded. "Jeff chucked yu'
out o' the path o' that crazy high roller."

"Where is he?"

Lin pointed into the middle of the cow crowd.

"Oh!" I exclaimed, fearing the worst. Thinking the
Virginian had been hurt helping me, I tried to push my
way into the steadily growing crowd. Men were coming
from all directions. Among them was Scipio le Moyne,
who cleared a path for himself courtesy of language so
blue it was unprintable. I was despairing of being able to
catch so much as a glimpse of the stricken Southerner
when a miraculous calm came over the whole lot. Every
mouth closed. Not a single oath was uttered. And they all
moved to make more space.

The name of the miracle was Mrs. Henry. Anxious
yet composed, she had her hem hiked as she ran from the
house, Chalkeye at her side.

At last I was able to see the man who lay grimacing
in pain. My apprehension changed to sheer horror when I
recognized Judge Henry himself, his arm bent at an unnatural angle. The Virginian was there, too, but he had the
Judge's head in his lap and was holding the Judge's other
hand.

I was temporarily forgotten. Under Mrs. Henry's guidance, six of the punchers carefully lifted the Judge and bore him into the house. I began to follow but stopped since I could be of little assistance and might only get in the way. So it was that I saw the fate of the gelding.

Lin McLean had gone over to the animal, which was quivering and whinnying pitiably. Others had clustered near and were muttering among themselves.

"Serves this bronco right," Nebrasky said.

"That leg ain't never goin' to set proper," Baldy commented.

"Someone has to put it out of its misery," said Limber Jim.

I saw Lin step closer, but he was checked by Dapper, who, head bowed, drew his Colt and stood over the ailing animal. I wanted to turn away, but I couldn't. I watched Dapper crouch and touch the tip of the barrel to a spot behind the ear, and I tensed when there was a crisp click.

"It's mine to do," Dapper said sadly. He squeezed the trigger.

The bay's head arced up off the ground. Mouth agape, it uttered a drawn-out, fluttering neigh that seemed to go on and on and on, its three good legs kicking feebly all the while. Then it sort of sighed, its lips trembled, and its head thudded to the earth.

Blood was oozing from the bullet hole. It was more than I could stomach, so I hastened indoors, seeking a stiff whiskey to fortify my stomach. I nearly blundered into one of the hands, who was bringing an armful of blankets into the front room. Judge Henry had been placed on the big table there, and his wife, the Virginian, and Scipio were examining his shattered arm. Outside, hoofbeats rumbled from the stable into the distance.

"Let's hope the doc is over at the Taylors' like we was told," someone said.

"Stringbean can ride like the wind on that sorrel of his. He'll have the sawbones here inside of two hours," remarked another.

Someone had produced a knife, and the Virginian was engaged in cutting away the Judge's coat and shirtsleeve.

He worked gingerly, mindful of his friend's every twitch and groan. Mrs. Henry crouched over her man, whispering in his ear and stroking his perspiring brow.

"Is there anything I can do?" I couldn't resist asking.

"We need hot water, Owen," the Virginian said.

Have you ever noticed how those who are generally incompetent to perform the greater chores of life are inordinately grateful for the simpler tasks? I leaped at the chance to be of some good and dashed off to the kitchen, where I soon had a pot on the stove and was impatiently waiting for the water to heat.

While I waited, I reflected, and my musing took a dark turn. All the stories I had ever heard about those who had died from being thrown or trampled or just plain kicked by a contrary mount came back to haunt me. The trouble with living on the frontier, you see, is that adequate medical services are so few and far between that even common injuries and sickness frequently prove fatal because the afflicted aren't able to reach a doctor in time. I personally know of one puncher whose horse had gone down in a prairie-dog town, breaking the man's leg. Infection set in while the cook was rushing the hand in from the range. When the doctor finally arrived, the patient was six feet under.

Bubbling water brought me out of my morbid reverie, and mindlessly I snatched at the metal handle. My yelp was probably heard out at the stable. Grabbing a towel, I wrapped it around my palms and quickly carried the pot to the front room.

Judge Henry was sickly pale, his lips as thin as paper. They had exposed his arm, revealing the break was about two inches below the elbow. Thankfully, the bone had not broken the skin.

"Thank yu'," Scipio said, taking the pot from me and depositing it at the head of the table. "Have yu' ever helped set a broken bone?"

"Me?" I responded.

"No, your sister," Scipio declared. He gazed at me as one might a complete lunatic. "We need someone to hold his shoulder down."

"I'll do what I can," I offered, trying to ignore the flip-flops my insides were doing.

"Go ahead, then." This from the Virginian. "We can't wait for the doc. Something has to be done now."

Scipio nodded. "Even if we only get it partly right, the Judge won't be in so much pain."

Mrs. Henry gave me a smile of encouragement as I took my assigned place and lightly placed both hands on top of her husband's shoulder.

"Do it harder," Scipio instructed me. "Once we get to pullin', yu' can't let it move at all."

There are times in our lives when we fervently wish we could be anywhere but where we are, and this was one of those for me. I slid a hand under the Judge's shoulder, then clamped hold with all of my strength. Because I had to face him to do it, I couldn't avoid seeing what transpired next. And I nearly fainted.

Scipio put his hands next to the break. The Virginian clasped the Judge's wrist. They looked at one another, Scipio nodded, and suddenly the Virginian gave a sharp yank on the arm while at the same time Scipio applied pressure on the broken bone, wrenching it back into place with a horrid *Snap!*

Somehow I held tight. For several moments my vision spun, but I held tight. My stomach tried to heave, but I held tight. I saw Mrs. Henry cringe in sympathy and heard the Judge cry out, but I held on tighter than I have ever held on to anything.

"Yu' can let go now," the Virginian said softly. "We're done."

The arm did appear much straighter. Eyelids fluttering, Judge Henry licked his lips and mumbled a few words. Blankets were thrown over him and a pillow was brought. One by one his loyal hands filed out, most offering words of encouragement.

I lingered, trying to think of something appropriate to console Mrs. Henry, when there was a tug on my arm and I was beckoned by the Virginian. Morosely trailing him outdoors, I squinted in the bright sunlight and studiously avoided looking at the gelding. My trip, as far as I was concerned, had ended in unmitigated disaster. Should Judge Henry die, I would lose one of my best friends, perhaps second only to the Southerner himself.

"That's awful kind o' yu', but I expect the Judge will pull through. He didn't get to be top man in these hyeh parts by bein' a quitter. He's tough and he's orn'ry, and my guess is he'll be ridin' his Morgan hawss in no time."

My blank stare amused him. Belatedly I realized he hadn't read my mind; I'd mumbled my thoughts aloud. "I wish I had your natural optimism about things," I replied. "In the east we're bred to think negative all the time. From childhood we're taught we can't do this or we can't do that. Our parents start in when we're barely out of the crib, then our schoolteachers take up the refrain, and by the time we're pretending to be adults, the politicians are the ones telling us how we're allowed to live and what is inappropriate behavior. No wonder we always carp on the bad in our lives."

The Virginian seemed surprised by my outburst. "Well," he said slowly, "I wouldn't rightly say my outlook is so natural. It's taken a heap o' life to make me see that always lookin' at the dark side o' things makes a man's disposition as dreary as a rainy day." He chuckled. "Course, the moon helped my outlook considerable too."

"The moon?"

"There's two sides, ain't there? And which side is the one those star gazers say is always facin' away from us? Seems to me that should be a clue o' sorts."

I surprised myself by laughing at the novelty of his observation, the surprise stemming from my being able to find humor in anything so soon after the ordeal in the house.

The next two hours were spent in restless anticipation. Most of the Sunk Creek punchers were gathered near the corral, and if I had been given a dollar for every worried look cast in the direction of the Taylor place, I could have bought my own Morgan. At last dust appeared on the horizon, and shortly the silhouette of a buggy being driven at reckless speed was seen.

There was a general press toward the house as the sawbones, with Stringbean in tow, thundered into the yard. The doctor was out of his seat and inside before anyone could say so much as "Howdy!"

I was still in the company of the Virginian, and I couldn't help but remark on the somber air of the hands, adding, "How great do you think the risk of infection is?"

"Not much at all. It's havin' his innards stomped I'm afeared of."

As incredible as it might seem, until that moment I hadn't even considered whether the Judge had suffered internal damage or bleeding. My apprehension quadrupled. And when, eventually, the doctor emerged, I was in the forefront of those who rushed to hear the news.

"Judge Henry will be all right," was the physician's prognosis. "He'll be laid up for a while, and it'll take six months or better for him to get full use of that busted wing of his, but he'll be good as new by Christmas."

Cheers, whoops, and Comanche yips went up from a dozen throats. In no time the ranch was back to its settled routine and I was left to my own devices until late the next morning when Mrs. Henry came into the study where I sat reading a deluxe bound edition of Tennyson and informed me the Judge wanted to see me.

A shaft of sunshine from the east window bathed the pale figure under the frilly canopy when I entered. He mustered a smile, then flicked a finger at a chair near the bed. "Mrs. Henry tells me I must make this short," the Judge explained. "And she fusses terribly if I don't follow her instructions." He tried to twist to see me better and winced in pain.

"I can always come back later," I volunteered.

"Nonsense. This will only take a minute." Judge Henry fixed me with a probing stare. "I'm afraid our jaunt to Cheyenne is off."

"Think nothing of it. I've long wanted to visit the famous Cheyenne Club, but there will always be next year."

"Not for you."

"Pardon?"

"I've prevailed on my partner to go in my stead, and I would be grateful if you would accompany him."

My imagination boggled at the mental image of the Virginian mingling with the very wealthiest men in all of Wyoming. I knew he was adaptable, yet it was bound to be a reach, even for him. "I would be delighted to go."

"There's more. Hear me out before you agree." Judge Henry hesitated, seeemingly reluctant to reveal the rest.

Mistaking his attitude, I blithely said, "Don't worry. I'll look out for Mr. Quick-on-the-Trigger."

"It's not him that concerns me. It's them."

"I don't understand."

The Judge frowned. "Circumstances prevent me from being as specific as I would like to be. Suffice it to say there are elements involved here of which you know nothing, and it would be better for you if you learn little more."

"This is most perplexing," I declared. I was mystified as to why the Judge saw fit even to bring up the subject if it was best I remain ignorant.

"As well it should be. But this much I can disclose," Judge Henry said, gazing rather forlornly at the window. "A note was included with my invitation, a note from a lifelong friend of mine, a fellow member of the WSGA. He revealed certain things that have disturbed me greatly. I don't know all the details myself, as yet, which is why they invited me to Cheyenne. I suspect they want to present their full proposal and demand my answer."

"Demand?"

"Some of them, that damned Wolcott for one, can be a bit dictatorial at times."

I don't know which startled me more. The Judge's rare use of profanity or his condemning of Major Frank Wolcott, one of the leading lights in the Wyoming Stock Growers Association.

"All I ask is that you keep your eyes and ears open,"

Judge Henry had continued. "If you should become aware of anything you feel I should know, feel free to write me the particulars. As for him, you should know better. He can hold his own anywhere."

"I'll do what I can," I promised, not having the vaguest idea what benefit I could be.

"Excellent." Judge Henry smiled at me again, closed his eyes, and was immediately asleep.

25

The State of the Nation— Act the First

Cheyenne, Wyoming, owed its prosperity to two main factors: the progressive march of the rails and basic human greed. First to influence its growth was the Union Pacific Railroad, which made it a division point early on. Second was the discovery of gold in the Black Hills of the Dakota Territory. Thousands flocked there, and Cheyenne became their final stopping place before they ventured illegally into sacred Sioux land after riches most of them would never acquire.

In its youth Cheyenne was typified by its bawdy Golden Gate District, where women sold their favors at bargain prices and gamblers fleeced the gullible of everything but the clothes they wore. Shootings and knifings were not at all uncommon, and famous members of the shootist fraternity added to their stature at the expense of those whose reflexes were not up to snuff. Wild Bill Hickok himself, who had become a legend in his own lifetime, spent a full year in Cheyenne. And the infamous Tom Horn, whom the locals fondly called the "exterminator," had a special liking for the town.

In recent years the capital had quieted considerably, in part due to the influence of the politicians who didn't care to have their careers suffer because of rowdy riffraff. Cheyenne *must* be a sterling example for the entire state, and so local law enforcement was more efficient there than anywhere else.

Another contributing factor was the Wyoming Stock Growers Association. Composed exclusively of cattle barons, the WSGA had made Cheyenne its headquarters some twenty years earlier. Their no-nonsense attitude toward illegal activities, an attitude enforced by the bullet and the rope, helped shape Cheyenne into a prosperous, peace-loving community.

All these historic facts I reviewed mentally as the carriage carrying us to the Cheyenne Club clattered along the well-lit streets. While not on a par with Philadelphia, Cheyenne was nonetheless a cradle of civilization in the heartland of the wild frontier, and I liked the bustling, orderly atmosphere immensely.

My companion had been exceptionally quiet since Medicine Bow. He wore his very best suit, hat, and boots. Although I saw no evidence of hardware, the incident at the Philadelphia Zoo reminded me that you never see a wolf's fangs until it bares its teeth. "How are you feeling?" I now asked, curious whether he was the least bit nervous.

"Hungry enough to eat two beeves," was the response. "The Judge told me we'll be eatin' grand hyeh, so I've saved up my appetite."

That wasn't what I meant, but I didn't press the point. "Maybe you'll belong to the Club one day," I mentioned. "Once Aspen Creek prospers, you'll be able to afford the very best."

"Money don't buy respectability."

"True. But there are some who maintain it can buy a lot of happiness."

The Virginian snorted. "Genu-wine happiness comes

from deep inside. It's all a matter o' how yu' take life in stride, not how wide your stride is."

Judge Henry had told me most of the Club's members would be on hand this night, but I was unprepared for the large number of stately, expensive carriages lining the street, all much more luxurious than the common model we had hired at the station. At the entrance we were greeted by a doorman, who opened for us with a flowery sweep of his arm and a plaster smile that must have left permanent wrinkles.

To describe the interior as opulent does not do it justice. When the extremely wealthy spare no expense, they can create tasteful elegance of the first order. Only those in political office who see the public treasury as their private mint can match such largess, and often the result can in no wise be dignified with the term "tasteful."

My own club, the Boone and Crockett, paled in comparison to the lavish trappings and rich decor. Trying to keep my tongue in my mouth, I walked beside the Virginian as we were conducted into a spacious room packed with members enjoying a before-dinner drink. The first person we encountered was none other than Ira Balaam.

I saw him at the instant he saw me, but he quickly shifted his attention to the Southerner, and a scarlet tinge crept up his great bull neck. He jerked a Cuban cigar from between his thick lips, then spoke loud enough to draw the interest of many nearby.

"What are *you* doing here? Where's your employer?"

The curt tone was highly insulting, but the Virginian never batted an eyelash. His calm reply came in perfect English, as silken as a spiderweb. "Hello to you, Mr. Balaam. What a surprise to see you here when everyone has been saying how busy you've been at Butte Creek adding to your herd." I thought Balaam was about to jam the cigar in my friend's face. "About the Judge, I shouldn't think I would have to remind you that he and I are *partners* in Sunk Creek. So, since he couldn't make it tonight, he sent me as his rep, in a manner of speaking. Of course, I won't cause near as much trouble as some reps I've met."

Two blows had been delivered in a span of seconds.

Had Balaam been intelligent instead of merely devious, had he possessed character instead of bluster, he would have taken the remarks in stride. But he showed his true nature by stuffing the cigar back into his mouth, grunting like a hog in a wallow, and stalking off through the crowd.

One of their number promptly took his place, a congenial gentleman who was going bald on top but sported a mustache resembling a huge hairy caterpillar. "Ben O'Folliard," he said as he shook. "I was the one who sent the invitation to the Judge, and I can't tell you how disappointed I am he couldn't make it tonight."

This man, the Judge had claimed, was a friend. I smiled broadly to show we were allies. The Virginian, however, maintained a certain reserve.

"Judge Henry sends his regards, sir. He had an accident the other day, and he'll be laid up for quite a spell."

"What kind of accident?" O'Folliard inquired with real concern.

The Virginian supplied an account of the mishap, which drew a score of listeners. The Judge was well liked and highly respected. Many members had known him for years and were quite close to him. Consequently, we were asked to relay all their condolences. Afterward O'Folliard escorted us over to the bar and ordered our drinks. "On my account," he told the bartender; then, when the glasses were brought, he coughed to clear his throat and asked, "Did the Judge happen to tell you what to expect tonight?"

"Fine food," the Virginian said.

"He gave some inkling," I hastily chimed in, hoping that if O'Folliard thought we knew a little, he might be inclined to tell us a lot.

The mustache bobbed up and down. "Just remember no one can force you to contribute if you don't want to," O'Folliard addressed the Southerner. "Many of us won't on general principles. Some think it's merely bad politics. Others say it's insane."

My curiosity as to what "it" could be was bubbling over. I was set to inquire when O'Folliard suddenly whispered, "Shhhh." A moment later a shadow fell over us followed by the source.

"What the devil is this about the Judge not showing? We made it perfectly clear how important this is."

The words were gruffly spoken, each one punctuated with a distinct snap. Since the way in which we speak often reflects our innermost character, I turned expecting to find someone along the order of a two-legged mastiff, nor was I disappointed. The gentleman glaring at us was almost as squarely built as Ira Balaam but lacking Balaam's bulk. He wore a perpetual scowl, and his surliness was further accented by the manner in which his head was held permanently slanted to one side.

"Ah, Major," O'Folliard said pleasantly. "Judge Henry suffered a terrible accident." Briefly he explained, and then he introduced us.

Major Frank Wolcott was the mastiff's name. I recalled hearing that he was one of the more prominent cattlemen, and that he ruled his vast dominion in Cattle Land with an iron fist. Once he had been an army officer in Kentucky, which was reflected in his military bearing. As for the neck, a cowboy had once had the temerity to disagree with him, and when Wolcott had slapped the puncher for his impertinence, the cowboy had left Wolcott's neck permanently crooked.

"I must say," Wolcott declared. "This is an inconvenience of the first order. A lot of us are counting on his backing—" He caught himself, glanced at me, then said, "—on his influence being brought to bear in our behalf in a certain important matter. Oh well." He shrugged expansively. "We must make do with what comes along, no?" His dark eyes alighted on the Virginian. "Perhaps you can give us some insight into how the Judge will react?"

"I'll be glad to help out however I can, Major."

"Hmmmmph. See you at dinner, then. And don't forget the special meeting afterward."

I waited until Wolcott was out of earshot before asking, "What meeting is this he mentioned?"

O'Folliard took a long swallow. "All the principals are getting together with those who are uncommitted later this evening. They're hoping to sway more to their way of thinking." He swirled his drink. "Not that it matters much.

They're going through with it whether everyone joins in or not."

The approach of other Club members prevented me from questioning him as I would have liked. Presently the call to dinner was sounded and everyone filed out to the dining room. O'Folliard, the Virginian, and I were seated at a table with one Herbert Teschemacher of Boston and one Fred Hesse, who hailed from England and now managed one of the largest ranches in the state.

Little talk was carried on during the meal, and I must confess to being so busy stuffing delicacies down my throat that I failed to notice a certain aloofness toward us until much later. Here was dining such as I hadn't tasted since Philadelphia, starting with real French hors d'oeuvres followed by plates laden high with thick steaks heaped round with buttery potatoes. For those with a Continental taste, there were pickled eels and other unique fare. To wash all this down there was ample red wine and champagne.

I almost regretted the end of the meal. O'Folliard lit a cigar and led us to another plush chamber where men were standing around in close-knit groups speaking in low tones. The meal had made me drowsy, but not so drowsy I didn't realize I must keep my wits about me if I hoped to uncover the mysterious secret of the Cheyenne Club. I thought we might be reunited with Teschemacher and Hesse so I could delve into the matter at length. Imagine my shock when I saw that O'Folliard was leading us to a corner where Ira Balaam stood with two strangers.

Balaam looked around as we neared him and whispered something to the others that caused them to smirk. Then, aloud for our benefit, he remarked, "Those who are weak-kneed will always be weak-kneed. Trying to draw gumption out of the gutless is the same as trying to draw water from a dry well. It can't be done." His twinkling gaze was bestowed on us. "Wouldn't you agree, gentlemen?"

"I wouldn't equate caution with cowardice," O'Folliard answered testily.

"What about you?" Balaam challenged the Virginian. "Do you think I'm right?"

"There was a time I might have said yes. But not since I saw that sparrow."

"Sparrow?" Balaam repeated. "What the hell does a bird have to do with my question?"

"Well, it's like this." The Virginian wedged his thumbs in his belt, as he often did when launching into one of his tales. "A few years back there were these two little sparrows that took to roosting in the Judge's stable. Came regular as clockwork every year to build their nest and have their babies."

"How delightful," Balaam said, his voice dripping sarcasm.

Once again the Virginian ignored him. "All went along smooth as could be until the year Mrs. Henry got herself a cat. Before she knew it, customers for her bird troughs were downright scarce. There wasn't a songbird brave enough to come near the house. So the cat wandered over to the stable and set its big green eyes on those sparrows way up in the rafters. Before long it figured out how to get up there, and one day, when the male bird was off hunting for worms and such, the cat snuck on in and commenced to climbing."

No one, I noticed, was mocking him now.

"So there sat that lady sparrow, all alone." The Virginian gave his audience a sweeping glance. "I'm sure you'd all agree, gentlemen," he said in imitation of Balaam, "that a sparrow is just about the most timid creature on this here planet. Try walking toward one sometime and you'll see what I mean. All you have to do is look crosswise at a sparrow and it heads for the blue yonder with its wings beating in a frenzy. And should one see a cat—goodness gracious! It about drops dead then and there."

"Sparrows ain't hawks," Balaam snapped, forgetting his Eastern grammar in his irritation. "Any blamed fool knows that."

"True," the Virginian said thoughtfully. "So you can understand why I was so surprised at how that lady sparrow behaved. No sooner did that cat climb onto the same beam as the nest than she was on the attack, flitting around and around its head, shrieking like one of them banshees."

"My goodness," said one of the listeners.

"Yep. That lady sparrow tore into that cat with no regard at all for her own safety. Don't think that old cat just stood there, either. It came close to taking her head off more than a few times, but somehow it always missed. But it kept edging closer and closer to her nest. The closer it got, the more determined that little sparrow got. She began diving at its eyes, which made it fit to be tied."

"What happened then?" O'Folliard asked.

"Why, just when things looked mighty grim, along came the male sparrow and he tore into that uppity cat too. Between the two of them they about drove the thing crazy. It was swinging and hissing and turning every which way trying to kill them." The Virginian's next pause was masterly.

"And?" prompted the other stranger.

"Danged if that cat didn't slip and fall! It missed on one of its swings and went right over the side. Would have died, too, falling from that high up, if it hadn't landed smack in the hay. Missed the pitchfork by a hair. And from that day on, the cat left those little sparrows alone."

"Where's my handkerchief?" Balaam asked, plucking at his pockets. "I know I have it here somewhere."

"So what's your point?" asked one of the unknowns.

"That you can't measure grit from the outside," the Virginian answered. "Most folks, even the most timid, draw the line somewhere. They all have something they'll fight for, even if they wouldn't lift a finger where most would fly into a rage."

"People aren't sparrows," Balaam carped, expanding his theme.

"Most parsons would disagree," the Virginian countered.

"Oh, Lord," Balaam said. "Keep religion out of it. If

we wanted to be bored with that version, we would have invited the bishop of Wyoming."

"You could do worse. He's as straight as a wagon tongue."

None of them were willing to dispute this, so O'Folliard availed himself of the opportunity to make more introductions. Mr. Laberteaux and Mr. Whitcomb were a study in contrasts, with the clean-shaven Laberteaux dressed in a suit so new the creases were razor sharp, while Whitcomb, a distinguished white-haired oldster, looked as if he slept in his clothes.

It was the latter who remarked, "We heard about the Judge. Please give him our regards."

"I will, sir," the Virginian said.

"Did he happen to tell you why he was invited here tonight?" Laberteaux inquired.

"He told me some."

"Did he indeed?" Balaam interjected suspiciously. "I might not be his best friend, but I credit him with more intelligence than to go spreading the information around willy-nilly."

"As partners we pretty much share anything that has to do with the ranch," the Virginian said, and for an instant his armor cracked, revealing a fleeting fire in the depths of his eyes. "Neither of us makes an important decision without talking it over with the other first."

"How democratic of you," was Balaam's retort.

"I expect the Judge would be the first to admit he's a firm believer in democracy," I spoke up for the first time. "He likes to say that America gets her greatness from the excellence of her ordinary citizens."

"Only Judge Henry," Balaam responded, then laughed.

"What about Abraham Lincoln? Does he count? They say he shared the same sentiments," I noted.

"Lincoln was a scheming meddler, nothing more. He should have left the South to handle slavery the way it saw fit. But all the Northern munitions interests prodded him into interfering."

"Your outlook on history is novel, to say the least."

"Prove me wrong," Balaam snorted. "As for the excellence of ordinary citizens, Judge Henry must be thinking of those in the WSGA. He certainly can't mean the stinking nesters and rustlers who have made our lives so miserable in the past few years. There's nothing excellent about *them*!"

Whitcomb and Laberteaux murmured assent, but I refused to concede. "I will grant you that the mental state of many Americans is best described as a howling wilderness, but by and large they show more wisdom than they're given credit for. They voted Lincoln into office, and Teddy Roosevelt, too. So they're not total wastes of organic matter."

"Oh, please," Laberteaux said. "Half of them vote for a particular candidate because they like the way he looks, a fourth vote for him because they like the way he talks even if they don't understand a word he says, and the rest vote for him because they have the deluded notion he can somehow make government better."

"Government!" Whitcomb said bitterly. "Thank God it's not really accountable to the common man."

"Who is it accountable to, then?" I wanted to know.

"Who else?" Laberteaux rejoined. "Who else has the right other than those who have the most to lose? The rich control affairs of state, and don't let anyone tell you otherwise. Those with money have always influenced the course of government. They always will, too."

Whitcomb nodded. "Look at Wyoming. The politicians like to play at running the state, but we're the ones who run the politicians. Without our money they wouldn't survive in office."

"So you think the Wyoming Stock Growers Association controls all of Wyoming?" I asked, unable to avoid a snicker.

"We *know* it does," Laberteaux said.

"And not just Wyoming," Whitcomb bragged. "We have friends in the very highest of circles, even in the nation's capital."

Laberteaux gleefully rubbed his hands together.

"Money is power, my friend. If you have enough of it, you can do any damn thing you please."

"Money and land," Balaam corrected him. "Own an acre and go before a government official with a special request, and you might get what you want if the official is in a good mood. Own fifty thousand acres and go before a government official, and he'll gladly do whatever you want and lick your boots clean while he's doing it."

"Crudely put, but true nonetheless," Laberteaux said. "Still, if you have a million dollars and no land at all, you'll be a power to be reckoned with regardless."

"Only if the government is as completely corrupt as you make it out to be," I remarked.

"And you think it's not?" Whitcomb responded.

"Some of us still have faith in American institutions," I stated. "Yes, there are politicians whose only reason for entering government service is to get rich. But there are equally as many who are inspired by the urge to serve their fellow man."

Laughter met this observation.

"Aren't writers supposed to have keen insights into the state of the world?" Laberteaux asked. "How, then, can it be that you are so naive? It's every man for himself and the devil take the hindmost."

"Don't be so hard on him," Whitcomb said in my defense. "Writers are idealists by nature. At least the best ones are. Our friend here believes in the quaint notion that our government has the best interests of the country at heart. He doesn't see that government serves only one interest, and that is perpetuating more government." He pursed his lips a moment. "Our government and the country are really two separate things. You might think of the government as a buzzard and the country as the carcass on which it's feeding."

"How pathetic," I snapped. "Where does that leave you? What does that say of the rich, whom you claim control the government?"

"We do what we can," Laberteaux said lamely.

"When it serves your own interests," I ventured.

"Do ordinary citizens do any differently?" Balaam

shot at me. "They're just as selfish. Even more so, some-times. Just look at what the nesters have done!"

The Virginian had been strangely quiet for a while. Now he suddenly straightened and said, "Yes, let's take a look at them."

And the battle was joined in earnest.

26

The State of the Nation—
Act the Second

"Don't get me started on those vermin," Balaam spat. "Every member of this club is convinced they're a blight on the land, a plague of locusts eating away at our livelihood. And there's only one thing to do with locusts—exterminate them!"

"Not every member sees it that way," O'Folliard said cautiously.

"The Judge doesn't think so," the Virginian threw in. "Most of them are decent enough folks just trying to make a new start in life. Do you hold it against them that they want a parcel of land all their own and a home for themselves?"

"I wouldn't, except for the fact a lot of them are taking their parcels from ranches belonging to *us*," Balaam said. "Take a good look at the men in this room. They've worked damn hard to get where they are today, and now they're supposed to stand back and do nothing while shiftless squatters move in and take some of their prime property. How outrageous!"

"That's not all," Laberteaux declared. "A lot of them aren't satisfied with just taking our land. Most of them are rustling our stock as well."

"There are some who would say the rustlers and the nesters are two different breeds," the Virginian said. "But I'll get back to that in a moment." He faced Balaam. "You say the homesteaders should all be wiped out. Then I reckon you'd agree with what happened to the Proctor family?"

"The who?" Balaam said. "Never heard of them."

"That's right peculiar," the Virginian responded, "seeing as how they settled mighty close to Butte Creek."

The consistency of Ira Balaam's face was granite when he huffed, "Do you think I bother to learn the names of every no-account nester who moves in close to me? What about them?"

"They were trying real hard to make something of themselves. Had a lot of hope they could do real well. Then the father and his boy made the mistake of going off elk hunting, and while they were off by themselves with no witnesses around, some riders came along and shot them to pieces. It so upset the mother she went and killed her daughter and herself, both."

O'Folliard put his hand to his chest. "How awful! Were the culprits ever caught?"

"They got plumb away," the Virginian said, his flinty gaze never drifting from Balaam. "And there have been others who met the same fate. Between all the killing and the rustling, it's almost as if someone is going around our part of the country trying to stir things up."

"Not necessarily," Whitcomb said. "Conditions are pretty much the same all over. Why, Johnson County is even worse. Five or six people have died there in the last week alone."

"And what was their crime?" the Virginian asked. "Was it being so poor they couldn't afford to go to the politicians for help? Was it not having enough land to count? Which?"

A tense silence gripped our little group. I saw Balaam's eyes narrow and his hands clench and unclench before he made his counterthrust.

"To listen to you, one would think you were a saint! But everyone here has heard about the men you've put under. If you're looking for guilt, go look in the mirror. Your hands are no whiter than ours."

The riposte was a telling blow, to judge by the hardening of the Southerner's features. "If all you're talking about is the taking of life, then you're right. But I'm talking about the reasons life is taken, and in that category there are some in this room who are setting themselves up as the Almighty and deciding who has a right to live and who doesn't. Compared to them I'm small potatoes."

"At last we agree on something," was Balaam's remark.

"Now hold on, young man," Whitcomb said. "You're making a rather harsh judgment about a state of affairs in which you have little stake." His arm swept the room with a gesture. "These men are the ones who have the most to lose if conditions don't soon change. As Ira pointed out, the members of the Association have invested a lot of time and energy in their spreads. Collectively they have millions of dollars at risk."

Laberteaux took to the new line as a bloodhound to the scent. "And there is no way you can justify comparing the likes of the Cheyenne Club membership to common squatters. We've all proved ourselves, demonstrated the quality of our character and our leadership time and again. What have the squatters demonstrated but an utter contempt for their betters?"

"I know I must be awful thick-headed at times," the Virginian said with disarming grace, "but I could have sworn you just claimed that being rich as you are makes you sort of superior to those who don't have much more than the clothes on their backs."

"Doesn't it?" Laberteaux said. "Face facts, friend. Quality will always prove itself." Shifting, he pointed at a man across the room. "Take him, for example. Frederic O. de Bilier, who comes from one of the finest families in all of New York State. A true blueblood." His finger jabbed at a second worthy. "Or that gentleman. William Irvine. He came out here with nothing more than the backing of a syndicate of Omaha millionaires and now can boast of managing one of the biggest outfits anywhere."

"I'm not denying they've all done themselves proud," the Virginian conceded. "I'm just saying it doesn't make them better than anyone else."

"By whose standards?" Laberteaux asked. "The rabble who pour into Wyoming every day and so overrun the land that there isn't enough room for our cattle to graze? Surely you can tell the difference between mere quantity and quality?"

Whitcomb nodded. "You should have been here last week when we had a most interesting discussion. One of the members brought up a question that held our attention for hours." He idly toyed with the gold chain of his watch. "What percentage of the people in this country would you say are a detriment to the general welfare?"

I could not even guess at the Virginian's reaction, since he was being inscrutable, but I was flabbergasted, and after an uncomfortable pause I inquired, "Detrimental in what respect?"

"Useless. Good for nothing. Having no redeeming virtues whatsoever," Whitcomb elaborated.

"Or, to put it simply," Laberteaux clarified, "what proportion ought to be done away with for the common good of mankind?"

"You can't be serious!" I exclaimed.

Whitcomb and Laberteaux exchanged amused glances, then the latter said smugly, "Come now. Why are you so shocked? Do you forget you're in Cattle Land? Ranchers have to deal all the time with culling stock. They have to decide how many head should be kept on pasture, and how many are fat enough for market, and which ones are too old or sickly or outright worthless and should be destroyed. This is no different."

"There's a big difference. People aren't cattle."

"You're taking this in the wrong vein," Whitcomb assured me. "The question is purely hypothetical." He stroked his white beard. "So how much would you say?"

"None. Absolutely none."

"Ridiculous," Whitcomb said. "What about the criminal element? What about the hopelessly insane? Surely they can be culled without any loss to humanity."

"Not a single soul," I maintained. "All life is too precious to be taken away on the whim of those who see themselves as superior to everyone else."

"The question isn't meant to be applied to us personally," Laberteaux said indignantly. "It's a general issue." His hand went into his pocket and came out holding his polished pipe. "And I'll have you know that few of us could come to any agreement. I, for one, held to about forty percent. Others thought sixty percent of humanity qualified as rubbish fit for the trash heap. And there was one"—he looked around as if in search of this paragon of compassion—"who thought eighty percent was a more realistic figure."

"Amazing," was all I could say.

The Virginian had been listening attentively, as his next query demonstrated. "Where do the homesteaders fit into the scheme of things? Would they be part of the eighty percent?"

"Most definitely," Laberteaux said.

"Deserving all to be tucked into shallow graves?"

"We're not suggesting they be lined up and shot like diseased cattle," Whitcomb said in defense of their stance. "We're only saying the world would be better off without them."

"I'm impressed, gentlemen," the Virginian said with a nod. "I truly am. It beats me how you can find time to come up with so simple a way of solving all the problems of the world when you're so busy with your fox hunting and harness racing and tennis and such."

Balaam rolled his eyes. "I knew it. I knew we would be wasting our time the minute he showed up tonight." His chest rumbled in imitation of the growl of an irate grizzly. "And Judge Henry will be the same way. Pussy-kitten, the two of them."

"We owe it to the Judge not to make assumptions," Whitcomb said. "He has Sunk Creek to think of, after all."

Although I had not yet gleaned the underlying motive behind the conversation, I was disturbed by the general drift. In order to learn more, I prompted, "Is there any message you would like relayed to the Judge? We'll be more than happy to pass on whatever you wish."

"Excuse us a minute," Balaam said quickly, perhaps too quickly, and with a commanding glare at Laberteaux and Whitcomb, he stalked off. The two of them trailed obediently.

O'Folliard moved closer. "I'm sorry about all this. Had I known how you would be treated, I would have urged you to leave after dinner."

"Was it your notion to hook us up with Ira Balaam?" the Virginian asked.

"No. Originally Tisdale was going to speak with you, but he bowed out after Balaam had a talk with him. Frankly, I don't know what Balaam is up to. But it's safe to say he's not very fond of either of you."

"Can't imagine why," the Virginian said with a straight face.

For my part, I was scanning the room taking note of the small clusters of men scattered about, and suddenly it occurred to me why there were so many. I remembered the comment made earlier in the evening about those who were "uncommitted" to whatever enterprise the other Association members were scheming up, and I realized that in each of the many groups must be at least one uncommitted member who was being pressured by his peers to agree to their views. But why? Obviously it must have something to do with the nesters, but what? Surely they didn't— I left the thought unfinished, certain my imagination was getting carried away with itself.

"I'll be so glad when this dreadful night is over," O'Folliard was saying, "so I can go home, bolt my doors, and not come out until the fall."

"You'll run short of provisions by then," I joked.

"Better provisions than my self-respect. Thank God

my ranch is near the Nebraska line. I won't be anywhere near when the fuse is lit."

"What fuse?" I asked. Unfortunately, the bull of Butte Creek and his friends chose that moment to return, causing O'Folliard to clamp his mouth shut and keep it shut.

"Very well," Laberteaux began the next volley, addressing the Virginian, "we've decided to be as candid as we can in the hope you will be the same."

"I'll do what I can to oblige. But you have to admit you haven't given me much to go on."

"Deliberately, my friend. We're not about to reveal our plans to someone who can't appreciate the wisdom of our operation."

Balaam had lit a fresh cigar during their absence. He now removed it and said, "Tell us the truth. If you had a choice to make between Sunk Creek and the nesters, which would you choose?"

"Choose how?" the Virginian said.

"Let me put it this way," Laberteaux said. "If you knew for a fact that a bunch of squatters had started building on part of Sunk Creek, would you do whatever was necessary to drive them off? Would you kill them if you had to?"

"The Judge would likely ride out to have a talk with them and see if he couldn't convince them to move elsewhere."

"And if they wouldn't?"

"Then we'd have to sit down and figure out what to do next."

"Pussy-kitten," Balaam said.

Whitcomb sighed. "Let me try one last time." His hand seemed to be glued to his watch chain. "What if some of the other ranchers had had enough of nesters and rustlers alike and decided to take matters into their own hands? What if they wanted to drive the undesirables from the country? Would you support such a move?"

"How would you go about choosing who was desirable and who wasn't?"

"Simple. Anyone who wasn't our neighbor before

this whole business started has no right to be our neighbor once we're done culling the herd."

"That's mighty harsh. And what you're proposing would take a heap of doing. Those you brand nesters aren't about to sit still while you ride roughshod over them."

"We've taken that into account. What good is all our money if we don't use it to preserve our rights and our land?"

"I see," the Virginian said. "You're fixing to do like Balaam here and import all the quick-draw artists you can find."

Balaam, Whitcomb, and Laberteaux all visibly stiffened.

"We never claimed we'd do that," Laberteaux said. "But suppose for the sake of argument we did. Would you object to our fighting for survival the only way we know how? Bear in mind we're losing thousands of head a year to the rustlers and there's only so much good land to go around, nowhere near enough to satisfy all the nesters and still meet our needs. How would you feel?"

"Relying on a gun to settle a dispute makes more problems than it solves."

"Fine talk coming from you," Balaam sniffed.

The Virginian hesitated before answering, his head bowed as he pondered. I wasn't the only one on pins and needles until he gave us all a steady eye and said, "Since you're being so honest with me, I'll be honest with you. There was a time I might have agreed with you, back when I thought lynching a few rustlers would rid the country of the rest. But I learned better. Killing one badman doesn't always cure the rest of their bad habits."

"What if you were to kill them all in one fell swoop?" Laberteaux interrupted.

"It can't be done. There are too blamed many," the Virginian said. "But that's not the real reason I'm against your proposition. There's a principle involved here. The basic right of folks to live where they please and as they please so long as they don't hurt others in the doing of it. You say the nesters are taking up the whole country. I'd have to agree they've taken up a sizable chunk, but there's still plenty left. There's still enough for all to share."

"Share?" Balaam scoffed. "Don't tell me you've gone Christian all of a sudden."

"Most men don't get around to deciding whether religion is worth the bother until they're knocking at the pearly gates, and I'll likely be no different," the Virginian answered. "No, I was talking about there being a lot of unclaimed land that hasn't been squatted on yet. If the homesteaders could be convinced to settle on those parcels and not the big ranches, then everyone could live together peaceably."

Ira Balaam hooted. "You are a caution! Maybe you should give up ranching and go into vaudeville. I read in the *Herald* the other day that the Gaiety Museum in Boston is looking to hire new talent."

Everyone there knew that Balaam subscribed to the prestigious New York newspaper, because he constantly reminded everyone of the fact. He was forever mentioning it in passing as if it constituted a badge of cultural superiority over the lowly inhabitants of the frontier. "What do you have against the idea of a peaceful settlement of differences?" I asked him. "Wouldn't that be better than rampant bloodshed?"

"It depends on whose blood is being shed," Balaam parried.

O'Folliard found his courage. "I, for one, would rather see peace and prosperity for all than ruin for some."

"That's just the issue," Laberteaux said. "Prosperity is like intelligence. Everyone has a little, but only the special few have a lot. It's theirs by right."

"So you're against making peace with the homesteaders?" I pressed.

"Have you ever played poker?" Balaam rejoined.

"Occasionally," I said, then blundered by adding, "but whist is my favorite."

"To those with Eastern tastes, even the tame must seem wild," Balaam said, ever so politely, which only compounded the slight. "Poker is a man's game, though. It tests the mettle of each and every player, weeding out the strong from the weak—"

"And here I figured it was all a matter of the luck of the draw," I couldn't help interrupting.

"That helps. But as you well know, a good bluff can beat a good hand any day." Balaam puffed on his cigar and blew a great cloud toward the ceiling. "Back to my point. If a man has a good hand and the pot is high enough, he's not about to fold come hell or high water. Well, the pot at stake here is our ranches, which we're not going to give up without a fight." He stared at me triumphantly. "And we won't have to because we hold all the high cards."

"How convenient, if true."

"How soon some forget. Money is power, remember? And in this room are the men who own nine tenths of the wealth of the entire state. How much power do you think that gives us?"

"A lot," I reluctantly granted.

"You don't know the half of it," Laberteaux said smugly. "Both senators are in our pocket, the governor in the palm of our hand. And thanks to our contacts, we have the ear of the President himself. We are the single most powerful organization in existence in Wyoming, and we know how to flex our muscles when the occasion demands."

"How will you flex them in this case?"

It was Balaam who replied, and he did so with such a peculiar expression and using so unusual a tone that all of us showed how puzzled we were. "Each of us will do what he has to do, each in his own way."

"Meaning what specifically?" I asked.

"Wait and see."

The Virginian planted his feet wide and hooked his thumbs at his waist. "Whatever you're cooking up, gentlemen, just remember there are those of us who won't stand for seeing the settlers treated like sheepherders. If you resort to gunplay, be prepared to be met with gunplay."

Whitcomb appeared shocked. "You would actually draw your irons on a fellow cowman?"

"If he was fixing to gun down a helpless nester, I would," the Virginian stated.

"What if it was a rustler?"

"I'd need proof he was a brand artist before I'd sit still for seeing him put under."

"Proof!" Balaam said. "Do you think a rustler is going to walk up to a cattleman, hand over his running iron, and confess to his trade? Never! When dealing with their kind, suspicion is as good as conviction in my book."

"And what if you're wrong?" I asked. "What if you string up or shoot an innocent man by mistake?"

"For every innocent we'll get twenty who are guilty, and that's all that counts."

Again a strained silence claimed us. All that was going to be said had been said, although it wasn't all that needed saying. I, for one, had been hoping the Club members would reveal more of their strategy for dealing with the rustlers and the squatters, but in this I was doomed to disappointment.

Laberteaux stared at his companions and shrugged. "Well, we tried."

"I told you," Balaam said. "I told all of you." Wedging his cigar into his mouth, he glowered at the Virginian, bobbed his thick chin at me, curled a lip at O'Folliard, and departed.

"Nice meeting you," Whitcomb told me. "The next time you're in Cheyenne, look me up and we'll do the town properly." Laberteaux at his elbow, they moved off whispering to one another.

"That's that, I reckon," the Virginian declared to no one in particular, lapsing into his familiar drawl. "A right smart o' words, meanin' nothin'."

O'Folliard had not shaken his doleful outlook. "I apologize again for this evening." He gazed sadly around the room at the illustrious members of the Cheyenne Club. "They're going to go through with it no matter what." His gaze lingered on us. "Do yourselves a favor, gentlemen. Forget every word you heard here tonight. Go back to your homes and turn a deaf ear when the trouble starts. Believe me, you'll be happier." Shaking his head, he left.

"What now?" I mused.

"Yu' go back to Philadelphia and I go to Sunk Creek," the Virginian said.

I sighed wearily. "Do you mind telling me what we've accomplished by coming here tonight? What do we tell Judge Henry?"

"We repawt the truth," was the response. "We tell him Cattle Land is fixin' to run red with blood."

27

The Bloodbath Begins

Lin McLean stepped from his chicken coop, a full
basket of eggs tucked under an arm, and happened
to glance to the east. His smooth forehead creased
at the sight of a thin column of black smoke curling skyward miles distant. "Now what do yu' suppose that is all
about?" he mused aloud. He made some mental calcula-
tions as he slowly ambled toward his house. "Must be the
Hardesty place, those new homesteaders."

Halfway to the porch Lin suddenly drew up short and
spun. For from less than a mile off had come the sharp
crack of gunshots, three in all, and as he listened intently,
there was another flurry, a half dozen more, one right on
the heels of another. Then only the soughing of the wind.

A loud slam heralded the opening of the front door,
and out rushed Honey Wiggin, his left boot on, his right
dangling from his right hand. "Did I hear what I think I
just heard?" he called out.

"Yu' did," Lin confirmed, pointing. "Thataway."

"Limber Jim rode off to the east meadow before first

light to check on how many critters had strayed over there," Honey mentioned. "Yu' don't figure—?"

"Oh, Lordy," Lin breathed. He sprinted like a madman across the yard and gained the house just as Jessamine emerged wiping her fingers on her apron. "Here!" he exclaimed, shoving the eggs in her face. Startled, she took the basket and gaped as he headed for the stable under a full head of steam.

"Wait! What's wrong? Where are you going?"

"Stay with Honey," Lin yelled. "I've got to check on Limber Jim." He tried telling himself there must be a perfectly logical explanation for all the shooting. Maybe, he reasoned, Limber Jim had shot a lion or a bear. Maybe Jim had just been target shooting. Maybe Jim had shot off his guns for the hell of it. Maybe. Maybe. Maybe. But he knew better.

It took but a few minutes for Lin to throw a saddle onto the cow horse he most liked; then he was out the gate and angling at a gallop back to the house for the crucial item he had overlooked. "My rifle!" he bawled. "Someone fetch it!"

Young Billy had the Winchester outside in no time. Lin leaned over to scoop it up. As he straightened, his eyes met his wife's. "I'll be back pronto," he promised.

"You'd better," Jessamine said, strangling the apron in her grip.

"Maybe I should tag along," Honey offered.

"No," Lin disagreed, thinking of the consequences if the worst came to pass and there was no one at all to protect his family. "Limber Jim is helpin' me out. He's my responsibility." Jabbing his spurs into his mount, he raced eastward. "Come on, yu' danged puddin' foot!" he chastised the animal. "Show me yu' ain't wind-broken."

To reach the meadow, Lin had to pass through a quarter-mile stretch of trees, mostly pines with some cottonwoods thrown in for variety. He tugged his hat low to keep from losing it and surveyed the woods on all sides. "Please let it be nothin'," he said under his breath, over and over again.

Out of nowhere appeared a horse, running as if someone had wrapped a burning rag around its tail. Lin had seen the same animal a lot in recent weeks, ever since Judge Henry had sent Honey Wiggin and Limber Jim over to help defend his spread should the same outfit that had struck Aspen Creek hit Box Elder. It was Limber Jim's mount.

Lin slowed, cut to the left, and intercepted the horse as handily as if it had been a spooked steer. Lunging, he got a grip on the bridle so he could slowly bring the panicked animal to a stop. "Where's your lunkhead owner?" Lin asked. He started to turn the horse to take it with him when he spied drops of fresh blood on the saddle.

An old scar on Lin's temple lit up scarlet. At a trot he pressed on, leading Limber Jim's mount by its reins, the Winchester across his saddle. Coming within sight of the meadow, he slowed to a walk. A little farther on he saw a pair of feet.

Jutting from out of the high grass at the base of a cottonwood were two brown boots, one with a tiny hole in the sole. Nearby lay a hat the same color as the missing cowboy's.

"No," Lin said softly. He drew rein ten feet away, ground-hitched both horses, and advanced with all the caution of a coyote approaching a baited trap. The Winchester made a loud click when he worked the lever. Holding the stock to his shoulder, his eyes never still for a moment, he neared the sprawled figure.

Limber Jim had been hit five times, twice in the chest, once in the leg, and twice low in the back as evidenced by the nasty exit wounds where his stomach had been. His six-shooter was clutched in his limp fingers. Both eyes had locked wide at the moment of death, and he now stared blankly at the canopy of green, his face framing an unknown question.

"The sons of bitches!" Lin growled. "I'll blow out the lamp of each and every one o' them."

"Will yu', now?"

Lin whirled at the whiplash taunt and recoiled a stride on seeing figure after figure materialize from behind trees and logs. He was surrounded by a score or more. Nearest the horses stood the deadly man in black, both of his pistol butts gleaming white in the sunlight. "I knew it," Lin said.

"Then you're a fool for comin', and comin' alone," Brazos said, his hands poised on his thighs. "Or did yu' think we didn't know about the Judge sendin' wet nurses here and to Aspen Creek?"

"It ain't possible," Lin said.

"What ain't?"

"Yu' knowin' how to think."

Brazos actually laughed. "Yu' always did have more gumption than brains. But I'll say this. You'd do to ride the river with."

"I wouldn't ride a swamp with yu'," Lin responded, easing the rifle down in front of him. His nimble mind pondered the odds and he accepted the inevitable. The Winchester would be of little use; it took longer to work a rifle lever than the trigger of a six-shooter.

"Ain't yu' the least bit curious why?" Brazos asked.

"The why is one word. Balaam."

"Partly true. At least for yu'. Your Southern friend is a different matter."

"Wish I could be here to see that. He'll put two into yu' before yu' clear leather."

"Wishful thinkin'. This ain't no pansy-blossom mustache yu' see me wearin'."

"Maybe three," Lin said, and without warning he threw the Winchester high into the air. The ruse worked perfectly. For a few precious seconds the ring of killers was distracted. All eyes were on the rifle. Lin's right hand swooped to his Colt, and he banged off his first shot at Brazos but missed because Brazos was throwing himself behind the horses. Pivoting, Lin stroked the trigger twice more and with each shot a man dropped.

The rest of the cat-eyed crowd clawed at their hardware. A few of the fastest had their six-guns unlimbered.

Shots boomed as Lin darted past the pair he had slain. Slugs thudded into a tree he skirted. He plunged into a thicket, invisible hornets buzzing madly by, and winced when his left shoulder seared with excruciating pain. Clamping his teeth, he cut to the right, then the left, bullets

clipping branches so close tiny wood slivers stung his
face. He burst from the brush and ran, aware of a clammy
feeling spreading down his chest and back.

"This way!" a gruff voice bellowed.

"He went through hyeh!" yelled another.

Lin sped on, his boots clumping heavily on the hard
ground. High heels were fine for keeping a man's feet
from slipping out of stirrups, but they were a terror to run
in. He did his best, though, dreading the alternative. Ten
yards he covered. Then twenty. He hit a rut, stumbled, and
winced when his foot twisted. Resisting the pain, he kept
sprinting.

The gun-sharks had stopped shooting, which puzzled
Lin immensely until the thud of hooves revealed the reason. They weren't about to waste their breath chasing him
afoot, not when they could ride him down so easily on
horseback. Glancing around, he saw several riders converging.

Another man might have quaked at the sight. Lin
only got madder. He was mad at Balaam for sending
Brazos, mad at Brazos and his killers for gunning down
Limber Jim, and mad at himself for blundering into their
trap. Most of all, he was mad that he was going to die and
there wasn't a damn thing he could do about it. But he
wouldn't be gunned down meekly. Not him. When his
friends talked of the day Lin McLean died, they'd do it
with pride.

Fired with resolve, Lin snapped up his arm the instant
he spied the riders. The nearest was just coming around a
pine. Lin's Colt spat lead and smoke, and twenty yards off,
the hard case clutched at his chest, then plummeted.

The other riders slowed and commenced shooting. So
did some of the men who weren't in the saddle. Ducking
around a tree, Lin listened to the smack-smack-smack of
slugs punching the trunk. He was using his legs as he had
never used them before, doing a fine job, too, and he felt
he could make good his escape if only the vegetation were
denser. But the undergrowth ended at the edge of a clear
tract, compelling him to dash out into the open.

Not two seconds later they spotted him. Lin ran in a

zigzag pattern, the earth all around him erupting in miniature dirt geysers as slugs sought his life. His left shoulder
was hurting so badly he found it hard to think coherently,
but he refused to give up. He was going to try to reach the
safety of his house even though the task seemed impossible.

A pang racked Lin's elbow. His side took a hit, the
bullet digging a shallow furrow. Lin treated them as he
would insect bites: a nuisance but unavoidable. He'd never
been shot before, but he had talked to many who had, including the Virginian, so he knew there had been men
wounded multiple times who had gone on not only to live
but to experience a full recovery. Merely being hit wasn't
enough to shock him into submission. His enemies would
have to strike a vital organ to drop him.

Suddenly a gully broadened out in front of Lin. He
was going over the rim when a slug found his left thigh,
knocking his leg out from under him. Down he toppled,
end over end, to land in a bruised pile at the bottom.
Dazed, he propped a palm on the ground and sat up.

"I lost him!"

"Where the hell did the bastard go?"

Lin grinned as it dawned on him that his fall had
been a blessing in disguise. With an effort he rose and
climbed back to the top. Removing his hat, he inched his
head high enough to see the frenzied hunt going on not
ten yards off. The killers were concentrating on some
saplings, evidently convinced he had gone to ground
among them.

Elated, Lin slid to the bottom and followed the
gully southward just as rapidly as he could move. He remembered to replace the spent cartridges in his six-
shooter, putting six beans in the wheel instead of five as
he customarily did. Now was no time to fret about the
pistol accidentally going off, especially not when that
sixth bean might make the difference between living and
dying.

Lin began to think a miracle had occurred. He just
might elude his pursuers and reach safety after all. Then
the feel of air on his hair reminded him he had forgotten

to put his hat back on. Stopping, he turned and took a stride, but changed his mind. He had gone too far. He would just have to keep jogging along and hope to high heaven none of Brazos's wild bunch found his hair case.

Seconds later that hope was dashed to bits by a harsh shout. "Lookee here! I found his John B.!"

A bend came up. Lin took it at a lurching run, his left hand pressed over the bullet hole in his thigh, and then drew up with a curse. The gully unexpectedly ended. He scrambled up the left side, dived into a stand of brush, and, in a crouch, worked along until some cottonwoods reared before him. They jogged his memory. He hastened through to where a small spring was nestled at the bottom of an earthen bank. Here Lin sank to his knees and greedily took a swallow of the cold, invigorating water.

Perspiration caked him from head to toe. Blood soaked his shirt and his left pant leg. His body throbbed from the gunshot wounds. He wanted nothing more than to sink into the inviting chill embrace of the spring and let the water temporarily relieve his torment, but he dared not slow down. The killers were undoubtedly scouring the gully at that very moment. If there were competent trackers among them, they'd be on his trail pronto.

Shoving to his feet, Lin stifled a gasp as his left leg nearly buckled from the agony. You can make it! he goaded himself. All you have to do is keep putting one foot in front of the other, and you'll be home in no time! He went around the left side of the bank, clambered up a short incline, then straightened.

Not twenty feet away sat a man astride a bay, his attention on high grass to the southeast.

Lin blinked in surprise. A sense of baffled fury dominated him. He had given it his best, but his best hadn't been good enough. Brazos must have ordered men on horseback to spread out and search the area between the meadow and the ranch house. Now here was one of them, and Lin had no cover handy, nowhere to go but back into the arms of those chasing him.

The rider shifted, wheeling his horse.

Recognition came as their eyes met. Lin blurted,

"Horn!" He tensed, his Colt at his side. "Where's your bluster now?"

Only astonishment showed on the burly man's face. He had his revolver in his right hand, resting against his saddle, but he made no attempt to bring it to bear. Instead, he licked his lips before responding, "You're a tricky one, McLean, I'll grant yu' that."

"And I'm a lot more alive than you're goin' to be in about five seconds."

"Now hold on," Horn said, glancing past Lin as if counting on reinforcements to arrive soon.

"What's the matter, yu' polecat? Yu've been pullin' down fightin' wages for months now. It's about time yu' gave Balaam his money's worth."

"I have nothing against yu' personal-like—"

"Make smoke, yu' bastard!" Lin roared, taking a stride. He saw Horn's arm jump, and his own did the same. Both six-guns thundered together, and Lin rocked to the searing impact of a bullet, but so did Horn, and then Lin was firing again, and again, and at each blast Horn jerked as if walloped. Then, mouth agape, Horn pitched headfirst from the saddle and crashed with a loud thud next to his mount.

"I did it," Lin said, his voice not at all like the voice it should be. He was aware of going numb all over and of more blood, this time flowing from his stomach. Swaying, he took a halting step.

"Here he is!"

Lin tried to turn at the strident cry. He glimpsed more gunmen, a lot of gunmen, pouring from the trees like a pack of rabid wolves, and he brought his Colt up. A slug bored through him from front to back, rocking him on his heels. He replied. A man dropped. And all hell broke loose as guns thundered and boomed in a deafening din. Bullet after bullet struck Lin, driving him backward. He tried to shoot again but couldn't. His body was turning to mush inside, his limbs as weak as poor gravy. Futilely he willed his legs to withstand his weight. The next he knew, the ground was rushing up to meet his face. Oddly, there was no pain when he slammed down, no sensation at all except

a peculiar, pleasant feeling similar to that of drifting off to
sleep.

"Damn! He was a tough one!"

Brazos walked to where the cowboy lay, his spurs jin-
gling, smoke rising from the barrels of his fancy pistols. "I
knew he'd chuck a lot o' lead before he cashed in his
chips."

"Yu' almost sound as if yu' admire him," one of the
men commented.

"I admire any man with courage, and Lin McLean
had it in spades." Brazos gave Horn the briefest of con-
temptuous glances, then began reloading. "Have the rest
o' the horses brought and we'll head for the McLean
place."

"What about the ones who've been killed?"

"What about 'em?"

"Shouldn't we dig them graves or something?"

"No time."

"But they're our pards. Hell, Horn was a good friend
of mine. We can't just leave them for the buzzards."

"Buzzards have to eat too." Brazos looked at the
speaker. "We don't have all year to do what needs doin',
remember? Balaam doesn't know how long the Johnson
County affair will keep the law busy, so we have to move
fast. Now get those hawsses or there'll be one more body
for the buzzards to peck away at."

A lanky man whose hair bore gray streaks above the
ears ambled over and asked, "Mind if I air my lungs?"

"Breathin' is free."

"That's not what I mean, damn it."

"Air away, Webber."

"What the hell has gotten into yu'? Ever since they
found Santee and those boys out at the Little Muddy
crossing, yu've been actin' like a cussed mule."

"Have I?" Brazos finished with the left-hand Colt and
twirled it into its holster.

"Yu' know yu' have. Hell, ain't I known yu' longer
than all the rest? Didn't we ride together a while down in

Tombstone when yu' were doin' all that checkin' on the Ringo feller?" Webber asked, and froze when the cold steel of Brazos's right-hand pistol touched the tip of his nose.

"Talk a little louder, why don't yu'? Tell the whole outfit," the man in black growled. He slowly lowered the six-gun, his face as cold as death. "Perk up your ears. I ain't takin' the chance o' word gettin' back to him. He suspects, but he don't know for sure, and he won't until I tell him right before I put a bullet between his eyes. Savvy?"

"Hell, I know all the trouble yu've gone to. I won't let on to a soul."

"Nothin' is goin' to ruin it, not when I'm this close," Brazos went on as if he hadn't heard. "It's taken me over a year! A lot longer than I figured, but it's all been worth the wait. First McLean, then a few o' his other friends, then him."

"And that will clean the slate," Webber said.

"It'll help." Brazos jammed a cartridge into the cylinder of his pistol. "I just wish I'd been able to find where his kin back in Virginia live."

"Ain't him and his friends hyeh enough?"

"Never enough."

The clatter of hooves interrupted their discussion. By a fluke of circumstance the man sent after the horses had met another bringing them, and together they had rushed to where the man in black stood waiting.

Brazos stepped into the stirrups, studied the hired assassins for a moment, and barked, "This will make the fourth place we've hit since midnight. I don't need to tell any of yu', do I? No one is to be left kickin'."

"Don't McLean have kids?"

"No one."

"Whatever yu' want. But I never have cottoned to shootin' sprouts."

"Then close your eyes when yu' pull the trigger," Brazos suggested. With a lash of the reins he led them through the forest and bore down directly on the ranch house. His eagle eyes espied Honey Wiggin ushering

McLean's wife and a boy inside, and he grinned in anticipation. "Like ducks on a pond," he said to himself.

A rifle cracked when they were still a hundred yards out, and one of the men lost his hat. Brazos swerved to the right and motioned for the others to do the opposite. Resembling a loose-knit guerrilla band, they fanned out, forming a ring around the house and the stable, finding cover where it was available and dismounting for the skirmish.

Brazos shucked his Winchester from its scabbard, gestured for those nearest him to do as he did, then raced to the rear of the stable. Two rifles were now firing in the house, keeping some of the men pinned down. Brazos entered through the back, moved past a row of empty stalls, and crouched next to the open front door. From there he commanded a clear view of the ranch house and could see a barrel jutting from a window. Taking careful aim, he fired. A squeal made him chuckle. "Blood ain't cheap," he said.

"What?" Webber asked.

"Nothin'," Brazos replied. He pointed at a small hay wagon parked in a corner. "Fill it and find something to use as a torch. We're goin' to burn 'em out."

Four gunmen hurried to comply. Two slung pitchforks full of hay into the wagon while the other two hunted around until they discovered a lantern.

"Will this do?" one inquired.

"Fire is fire." Brazos took it and checked the tank, which was partially full. "Who's got matches?"

Several were quickly produced. A half-dozen men pushed their ace in the hole into the doorway, the tongue raised so they could steer as they pleased.

"The rest o' yu' cover us on my say-so," Brazos directed as he struck a match to light the wick. Flinging his arm back, he tossed the lantern into the center of the piled hay, waited breathlessly for flames and smoke to appear, then snapped, "Now!"

Rifles and pistols formed a background crescendo as Brazos and the six pushed the wagon out of the barn, gaining speed with every straining stride they took.

From the house poured nonstop rifle fire, which was ineffective; the smoke prevented the defenders from seeing their targets clearly. Wheels rumbling, the wagon went faster, ever faster, and then, with a resounding smash, Brazos and his gunnies sent it crashing into the McLean home.

28

"He's Alive!"

short while earlier a pair of riders had wound
down out of the high timber onto a ridge overlooking the foothills and the pale plain beyond. In
the lead rode the Virginian on Monte. Behind him came
Dapper on a zebra dun. They reined up to give their horses
a breather, and it was then that the Virginian spied the column of smoke far to the east.

"What do yu' make o' that smoke signal yondeh?"

"Sure ain't no campfire," Dapper responded. "A
brush burn, yu' reckon?"

"Doesn't cover a wide enough area. Besides, most
don't burn it off till the fall."

Dapper rested one hand on his saddle horn, screened
his eyes from the sun with the other, and leaned forward
over his mount's neck. "Bless me if there ain't another
one. Do yu' see it?"

The Virginian had to squint to make out the gray tendril miles distant. "Yep."

"Mighty strange."

"I don't like it."

"Yu' figure it has somethin' to do with why the Judge sent me to fetch Lin and yu'?"

"Can't say yet," the Virginian said. He gave Monte a nudge with his knees. "Enough of admirin' the scenery, yu' pie-biter. I'm lookin' forward to some o' Jessamine's fine coffee."

A surprised glance was Dapper's reaction to their shortened rest. Lifting the reins, he followed the Southerner down the narrow trail leading to the valley in which the McLean ranch house was situated. Visible through the cottonwoods was Box Elder Creek, sparkling blue-green in the sunlight. "Did I tell yu' yet," he mentioned, "Mabel and me done picked out a nice little spot over to Willow Creek we're thinkin' o' layin' claim to come next spring. If we get the money saved, anyway."

"I hope it works—" the Virginian began. Suddenly he straightened, his head cocked, as faintly from below wafted light popping reports much like the sound of fireworks on the Fourth of July, only these weren't fireworks and the Virginian knew it. *"Damn!"* he bellowed, applying his spurs.

Dapper did the same. As good a rider as he was, though, he was hard-pressed to keep up with his friend, who took the trail at three times the speed considered safe and in the process took reckless chances no one in his right mind would choose to take. The lower they went, the louder the gunshots grew. To Dapper it sounded as if a full-scale battle were being waged. He connected the gunfire with the two columns of smoke seen from the heights and felt a stab of fear for the safety of the McLeans. After what had happened at Aspen Creek, he wouldn't put anything past those responsible, whoever they were.

Dapper was surprised a second time when the Virginian bore to the south the moment they hit the flatland. He'd expected to head straight for the house. Instead, the Virginian entered the tract of woods that flanked the rear of the dwelling and slowed once they could see it.

And that was not all they saw. Men completely surrounded the place, firing at will, peppering the walls and

windows with lethal hail. At the front of the barn there
was a commotion. A number of men appeared, pushing a
hay wagon into position.

The Virginian had swung down in the shelter of a
dense thicket and let the reins fall. Shucking his rifle, he
moved to a tree and observed the attack for a few seconds.
"I see Brazos!" he said to himself. He snapped the Winchester up, but the hay wagon came between them.

"What?" Dapper asked, joining him.

"Never listen to your wife when yu' know you're
right."

"What?" Dapper asked again, totally confused as to
the connection between their running mates and the violence being directed at the ranch house.

"If they have any brains, and Jessamine does, they'll
come a-runnin' out the back when the wagon hits the
front," the Virginian guessed. "They'll never make it without help. Come on!"

Once again Dapper had to strain to keep up. He was
amazed when the Southerner made no attempt to conceal
himself but rather ran directly toward the line of gunmen.
To his relief the killers were so intent on the house that not
a single one looked around and spotted them. There were
three clustered directly ahead, shooting as rapidly as they
could work the levers of their rifles. Expecting the Virginian to order them to toss down their hardware, he elevated
his own rifle to cover them.

But the Virginian simply ran up close behind them,
shouted "Hey!" and when the three hired killers started to
swing around, he shot them dead. *Blam-Blam-Blam,* one
shot on the heels of the next, and all three dropped where
they were. Another man, farther east, glanced over his
shoulder, saw his slaughtered companions, and attempted
to train his gun on the Southerner. The Virginian shot him,
too.

"Sweet Jesus!" Dapper breathed as he stepped over
one of the bodies. All of them, he noticed, had been shot
smack between the eyes. "And I figured I could shoot!"

They sought cover behind the same trees the killers
had been using. The Virginian scanned the tree line, seek-

ing other riflemen. None were in sight, although puffs of smoke scattered here and there told where they were concealed.

Out in front of the house the firing had attained a fever pitch. The splintering of wood mingled with the shattering of glass, adding to the racket. Seconds later a thunderous crash rent the air, drowning out everything else, and thick smoke rose from the northeast corner of the structure.

"Watch my back!" the Virginian directed, dashing toward the rear door. He hadn't gone a yard when it unexpectedly opened. Out hustled Jessamine McLean, her youngest, Nate, clasped tight to her bosom, her oldest, Billy, at her side with a rifle in hand. Urging them on was Honey Wiggin, one arm tucked to his side, the sleeve stained crimson.

Billy McLean was the first to spot the Southerner. The boy showed teeth from ear to ear, screeched, "Uncle Jefferson!" then made a beeline for him.

Rifle at the ready, the Virginian ran to meet them. His quick eyes detected a skulker to the west, moving through the undergrowth in their direction, and he halted long enough to fire the Winchester twice. The gunslinger disappeared. By then the mother and her children had reached him. "Keep goin'!" he cried. "Don't stop until I say so!"

"The varmints fired the house!" Honey declared.

"Where's Lin?" the Virginian asked.

"Missin'."

Frowning, the Virginian backpedaled in their wake, constantly swinging from right to left, seeking threats to eliminate. A man wearing a red wipe appeared to the east and received a head wound of the same color. Another popped out, took one look, and popped into his hole again. If there were others, they didn't show themselves or try to stop the fleeing family.

The volume of gunfire out front assured the Virginian the rest of Brazos's bunch were still pouring lead into the house and had no idea their quarry was escaping. Once under the trees, he rushed the frightened boys and their mother to where Monte and the dun waited. "Climb up and ride!" he urged.

"What about you?" Jessamine asked, hesitating.

"We'll make do. Worry about your kids."

"I won't," Jessamine said. "I can't, not without my Lin."

"What happened to him?"

"He went east to find Limber Jim. We heard shots, then Brazos and his killers showed."

Uncertainty made the Virginian waver. His first impulse was to go search for his pard, but he had Jessamine and the boys to think of. They had to be spirited to safety on the two horses before Brazos became aware they had flown the scene. He took her elbow, about to make her climb up whether she wanted to or not, when the thud of hooves brought him around in a flash, the Winchester leveling.

"It's just me," Dapper said, "and these horses I found. I don't think anyone will raise a fuss if we borrow 'em."

No words were necessary. The Virginian boosted Jessamine up and handed up young Nate. He made sure Billy and Honey were mounted, then swung onto Monte.

"Which way?" Dapper asked.

"Southeast," the Virginian said, looking at Wiggin. "If yu' can hold out until we find Lin and Jim."

"If yu' hear me screamin', pay me no mind. Those boys and me go back a ways."

At a trot they made their getaway. Flames were dancing on the roof of the house and licking at the window frames. The gunfire had slackened but not yet tapered off completely.

"What does it all mean?" Jessamine inquired when her burning home was out of sight. "How does Balaam expect to get away with an atrocity like this in broad daylight? It's as if he doesn't care if anyone connects him to it."

"Maybe he doesn't," the Virginian said.

"He'd have to be plumb crazy."

"Or clever, like a fox."

"How do you mean?"

"Balaam never takes a step without thinkin' it through first. If he's bein' this bold, there has to be a good reason, somethin' we don't know about."

"Once word gets out, the whole country will rise up in arms against him."

"If there's anyone *left* to rise up," the Virginian said, thinking of the columns of smoke. Brazos and company had been busy during the night, evidently. In light of the comments Balaam had made at the Cheyenne Club, the Virginian figured that Balaam had decided to drive every last nester out of the territory. Which didn't explain the attack on his place or on Lin's. Did Balaam fear they'd side with the homesteaders because they were homesteaders themselves? Or was there a darker motive?

"Limber Jim was headed for the east meadow," Honey Wiggin spoke up, "and that's where Lin was goin' last we seen him."

"Guide us," the Virginian ordered, hoping to get there that much sooner. While he had visited the McLean spread a number of times, he had never traveled it from end to end and didn't know the layout half as well as Wiggin.

They hadn't gone half a mile when a solitary buzzard wheeling high in the azure sky caught the Virginian's attention. He watched its black pinions beat the air as it slowly descended, and all of a sudden he angled toward the spot where the ugly bird would alight.

"What—?" Jessamine said. Then she saw the carrion eater, too, and a low groan passed her trembling lips.

Ducking under low branches, flashing around every bulge of ground and vagrant bush, vaulting logs and low boulders, the Virginian rode like one possessed. He knew buzzards, knew how they worked. They always pecked at the soft spots first, usually going for the eyes right off. He tried not to think of Limber Jim or Lin lying wounded, too weak to move, while the hungry bird gulped their eyeballs down.

High grass enabled the Virginian to bring Monte to a full gallop. The buzzard appeared, not twenty yards away, plummeting toward a still form. The Virginian whipped off his hat and waved it wildly, yipping Indian fashion. A shot would have done the job, but it also might have brought Brazos on the run.

With the horse and rider bearing down, the buzzard arched its bald head and, with frantic flapping of wings, swept up into the sky to circle with several others that had arrived.

Sliding to a halt, the Virginian sprang down and ran to the body. He could have whooped for joy when he recognized Horn. Then he gazed past the burly killer and spotted more prone men, among them one he knew all too well. "No!" he cried.

Horror mixed with rage shook the Virginian like a fit of ague when he saw the bullet holes and the dark stains—so many, they had blended into one another. McLean was deathly pale, his mouth cracked in a grin of defiance. From the number of dead it was obvious the foreman had gone down fighting. "Oh, Lin," he said softly.

The Virginian barely heard when the rest arrived. Footsteps brought him out of his daze, and he whirled to catch Jessamine in his arms. "You don't want to see," he advised.

"He's my *husband*!" she responded, fighting him. "Who has a better right?"

Truth is impossible to resist. Bowing his head, the Virginian stepped aside and tried to shut out Jessamine's sobs of despair as she threw herself onto Lin. He thought of the boys and looked to find Honey holding them back. Their blanched faces were terrible to behold. They reminded him of a day long, long ago when another small boy had stood neglected while his parents buried his uncle and the uncle's pretty young wife, both victims of a pro-slavery faction. Were they feeling the same awful terror, the same cringing dismay, that small boy had felt? Would their whole lives be shaped because of it? Because of one incident of ruthless brutality?

"He's alive."

The Virginian heard Jessamine, but the words didn't quite register. "What?" he said blankly, turning.

"*He's alive!*"

"You must be—" The Virginian's words choked off in his throat when he saw Lin's eyelids flutter. Instantly he was by her side, Lin's wrist in his hand as he probed for a heartbeat. It was there, sure enough, but weak, oh so weak, no more than a feeble twitching of the vein. "Well, I'll be!" he exclaimed joyously.

Honey Wiggin was hurrying up, a boy at the end of each arm. "What's this? What's all the fuss?"

"We need the sawbones," the Virginian said. "One of us has to ride hell-for-leather and fetch him here. He won't pull through, otherwise."

"I'll go," Dapper volunteered from atop his dun. "Be back before dark, too, if I have to sling him over my shoulder."

"It can't be yu'," Honey said. He nodded at the Southerner. "Nor yu', either. I'm the one has to do it."

"Why you?" the Virginian asked, so overwhelmed to find his dearest friend hadn't made the big jump that his thoughts were all addled.

"You're forgettin' somethin'."

"I am?"

"Brazos."

"Oh."

"That polecat will come sniffin' around onced he figures out what happened back there, and knowin' him, he won't leave Box Elder until he's tracked us down." Honey headed for his mount. "The two o' yu' know what yu' have to do."

"I reckon we do," the Virginian conceded, locking eyes with Dapper.

"Tend him the best yu' can, ma'am," Honey told Jessamine. "And don't yu' fret. Clipped wing or no, me and the doc will show. Yu' can put money on it." With a grim nod he was gone, swinging to the east.

Tilting his head back, the Virginian gazed at the buzzards, now five in number, then at the nearby corpses. He wished he could get Jessamine and the boys away from them, but moving Lin was unadvisable, and they weren't about to leave him alone. Rising, he walked to the horse

Billy had ridden, stripped off the saddle, and took the saddle blanket to Jessamine. "Hyeh. Yu' can keep him warm with this." He also gave her his rifle and ample ammunition. "Just in case."

"Won't you need these?"

"I still have my pistols," the Virginian said. In two strides he was back on Monte. "Keep the horses tied handy. If someone yu' don't know comes by, shoot first and make small talk afteh." He pulled first one Colt, then the other, and spun the cylinders of each, verifying they were both loaded. "Yu' shouldn't have much to worry about, though. Dapper and me are fixin' to show Brazos why Wyoming is no place for amateurs."

"Please be careful. Both of you."

"Ain't I always?" the Virginian responded with his deceptively nonchalant grin. Touching the brim of his hat, he rode westward, toward the billowing smoke visible above the pines, but he hadn't gone a third of the distance when he abruptly reined up. "She shouldn't be alone."

"Who? Jessamine?"

"Neither o' them." The Virginian faced the bronc-buster. "I have a favor to ask o' yu'."

"Anything."

"Ride to Aspen Creek and bring Mary back hyeh to be with Jessamine, then stay with 'em until Honey shows with the sawbones."

"And where will yu' be while I'm doin' all this?"

"Brazos still has ten to fifteen hombres in his bunch, too many for one man or even two to handle alone. I figure to lead 'em to Sunk Creek. The boys there would give away their saddles for a chance to nail his hide to the wall."

Dapper shook his head. "Meanin' no disrespect, but she's your sage hen. Why shouldn't yu' go afteh her?"

"Because, yu' blamed doorknob, I know this hyeh country a lot better than yu' do. I've ridden every inch of it, so I know every trail there is. I have a better chance o' stayin' ahead o' Brazos."

"I won't deny that," Dapper said, "but I ain't afeared o' Mr. Brazos nor his gun outfit, neither." He glanced at

the mountains, rearing glorious in the distance, then back
the way they had come.

"If that's the way yu' want it, I'll go along," the Virginian said. "But hyeh's somethin' to think about. If yu'
take the wrong trail and Brazos catches yu', it'll just be
that much longer before he can be stopped. How many
more homesteaders will he burn out?"

"Yu' have a point," Dapper admitted. His itch to tangle with the man in black battled his common sense. "This
is what I get for stickin' so close to Sunk Creek all the
time." Cursing, he jerked his reins and started off to the
southwest, saying, "Just save a few for me. I'm gettin'
plumb sick and tired of always missin' out on all the lead
slingin'."

Wasting no more time, the Virginian galloped off.

Brazos was fit to be tied. He stood with his pistols in
hand, glaring at the bodies littering the ground behind the
burning building, and turned the air blue with his oaths.
Only when his spleen was vented did he swing around,
causing a nearby hard case to shrink back. "Yu' say yu'
saw them? Ringo and the darky were right hyeh?"

"They sure were."

"Then why the hell did yu' let 'em get away?"

"What was I supposed to do? Show myself and let
that damned Southerner blow my head off like he done
poor Riley? He's hell on wheels, I tell yu'. Walkin' out o'
the trees as brazen as brass and just shootin' men down
like they was turkeys at a shootin' match." The hard case
swallowed, then swallowed again when he saw Brazos's
eyes narrow and the pistols rise. "Besides," he added
quickly, "didn't yu' tell us that yu' want the honor o' putting him under for yourself?"

Whatever retort the man in black might have made
was curtailed by the arrival of a short, stocky man who
was exceptional on two counts. First, he wore beaded
buckskins and moccasins instead of typical cowboy attire.
Second, he had a bow and quiver slung on his broad back.
"I found their trail," he announced.

"About time, Little Wolf," Brazos snapped. "I thought you're supposed to be the best tracker in these parts. Isn't that why Balaam hired yu'?" He motioned sharply. "Show me, yu' damn breed, and be quick about it. I'm in the mood to kill someone and it might as well be yu'."

They covered only a few yards when another newcomer raced onto the scene, a gunman half out of breath. *"It's him!"*

"Him who?" Brazos barked.

"Him! Ringo!"

"Where?"

"Yu' won't believe it. He's right out yondeh. Sittin' there as big as life, just watchin' us."

The skeptical Brazos ran around the house to where the rest of his men were gawking at a lone figure on horseback who was just beyond rifle range.

"Is that really him?" one of the men asked.

Brazos took a few more steps, his brow creased in puzzlement. "Yep," he said softly, unable to credit his own eyes.

"What's he up to?" another gun-shark wondered.

"Why'd he come right out in the open like that?" questioned someone else.

"He must be loco," stated a self-styled shrewd judge of men.

"No, not loco," Brazos said.

"Then why?"

Brazos laughed lightly. "Don't yu' see, boys? The son of a bitch is challengin' us."

"And yu' don't think he's loco?"

"No. His craw is just full o' more sand than any ten o' yu' put together." Grinning in delight, Brazos shoved his six-shooters into their holsters and ordered, "Get the horses and the rest o' the men. If he wants us to burn the breeze, we'll accommodate him."

"I don't like it. Maybe he's fixin' to lead us into an ambush."

"So what? Balaam is payin' top money to each and every one o' yu' peckerwoods. The risk of bein' lead poisoned comes with the territory." Chuckling, he waited impatiently for his mount to be brought.

"If yu' don't mind my askin'," ventured the shrewd judge of men, "why in the hell are yu' so happy?"

" 'Cause I'm havin' a good time. Ain't yu'?"

And when Brazos saw the other's look of amazement, he threw back his head and roared.

29

Converging Forces

The Virginian stayed right where he was until he saw the assembled killers spur their sweaty horses in his direction. Not until then did he bring Monte to a gallop and flee. He had chosen wisely his spot to wait, and within moments he was on the trail he wanted, the same old Indian trail he had used previously, a winding ribbon that brought out the best in the best of riders and taught the worst they needed definite improvement. Soon trees closed around him, and none too soon at that, for some of the eager bloodhounds on his trail had opened up with their rifles despite the range.

Once the Virginian was comfortable with his lead, he slowed a bit. He saw no sense in running Monte to exhaustion, especially since the horses of his pursuers had to be tired after being on the go since before dawn or earlier. He had the freshest mount, and he was going to pace Monte so the horse would have plenty of stamina left when and if the time came for desperate riding.

For over an hour the Virginian forged on. Presently

the trail crested a bench and there he stopped to mark the progress of his enemies. He spotted them a quarter of a mile behind, winding up a switchback. In the lead was a figure in black.

"Keep a-comin'," the Virginian said.

From the bench the trail grew more and more difficult. Monte, having been over it so recently, had the course fresh in mind and could have traversed it blindfolded. All the Virginian had to do was relax and enjoy the scenery.

When another hour had gone by, the Virginian drew up on a bluff that offered a sweeping panorama of the territory he had just covered. The badmen were much farther behind, but not so far they couldn't see his silhouette nor appreciate the gesture when he methodically took out his pipe and made a grand show of lighting it. He stayed put for a full five minutes, puffing and blowing smoke rings into the air.

At length one of the killers lost his head and fired a single wasted shot.

"Definitely amateurs," the Virginian grinned, emptying the pipe bowl. Northward he rode, hour after hour, and eventually he came to the junction with the trail that would take him to Sunk Creek. By then it was late afternoon and the blazing sun had burned the western sky a vivid red.

The Virginian thought of one last taunt. He opened a saddlebag and took out a dirty neckerchief he had crammed in there days ago. Dismounting, he tied it to the limb of a bush, where it would easily be seen.

"I wouldn't want 'em to lose me," the Virginian explained for Monte's benefit as he climbed back up.

Stars speckled the firmament by the time the light of the Henry house beckoned invitingly. The Virginian galloped straight to the corral. "Oats and hay will have to wait, old hawss. I've got work to do."

Chalkeye was crossing from the stable to the bunkhouse, and on seeing the Southerner, he altered course to intercept him. "There yu' are! What did yu' do, lose your way? The Judge was gettin' a mite worried."

"He should be."

The veteran puncher noted the lather on Monte and the dust caking the Virginian's clothes from hat to boots. "I don't see Dapper."

"He's fine," the Virginian said. "Lin's not, though. They shot him."

"Who?"

"Balaam's bunch. And this time I saw 'em with my own eyes."

"That tears it, I reckon."

"It sure as hell does. Collect all the boys. We ride when I'm done repawtin' to the Judge." The Virginian hurried to the front door and entered without knocking. He found the Henrys seated in the parlor. One glance at his face brought both of them to their feet.

"My word! What's happened?" Judge Henry asked. His arm was no longer in a sling, but he still favored it and hadn't been on a horse since the mishap.

Concisely as possible, the Virginian relayed the day's events, finishing with, "I'm goin' to have Chalkeye take three men and bring back Lin and the women. I'll take the rest and meet Brazos on the trail. With any luck his killin' days will soon be over."

Mrs. Henry set down the copy of *Pilgrim's Progress* she had been reading and came over to put a gentle hand on his arm. "Shouldn't you be the one to go after Molly?"

"Yes, ma'am, I should. But I'm the most gun-wise man in the outfit. It ain't brag when I say I'm the only one who can stand up to Brazos and maybe walk away breathin'."

The Judge had a more serious consideration. "What will you do if Brazos has gone on to Butte Creek?"

"Go afteh him and finish it."

"You can't. You're not a lawman."

"They tried to kill Lin. They deserve what they have comin'."

"They deserve to be punished by the legal arm of the law. Send Stringbean into Medicine Bow and have him wire for a United States marshal. We'll file formal charges against Brazos and those who were with him and have them brought to trial." The Judge grew grave. "But I won't have any of my men charging over to Balaam's and shooting up the place. In the eyes of the law they would be just as guilty as Brazos and his pack of paid assassins. Two wrongs don't make a right."

"And what about Balaam himself?"

"Did you see him at McLean's too?"

"No."

"Then we have nothing to tie him to the murder of Limber Jim and the attempted murder of the others. The law can't touch him."

Shoulders slumping, the Virginian began to turn, then stopped. "Yu' talk about right. Where's the right in lettin' Balaam go on with his schemin' ways? We both know he's the head of that bunch. Without him and Brazos they'd light a shuck for tamer parts pronto."

"Need I remind you that in this country a person is innocent until *proven* guilty? That's the cornerstone of our legal system, or at least it was until a few years back when some Eastern lawyers started claiming the burden of proof should be on the accused."

"I don't know much about burdens of proof," the Virginian said defensively. "But I'm not so all-fired ignorant I can't see that the law is a mighty weak sister when it protects those who break it from those who don't."

"Every system has its flaws."

"And some are awful final for those caught with the short end o' the rope." The Virginian could scarcely hide his disgust. "First Mary, now yu'. If it had been up to me, Balaam and Brazos both would have been pushing up sagebrush a long time ago."

"The days of the law of the gun are over. You should know that."

"I'm trying mighty hard to learn it. Too bad Brazos and Balaam ain't doin' the same." The Virginian was again about to leave when he suddenly checked his stride. "Say, why'd yu' send Dapper afteh Lin and me, anyways?"

Judge Henry crimped his lips. "Nebrasky got back from town late last night and passed on some news he had overheard. Apparently Ira Balaam had bought up practically every box of ammunition there was to be had. I wanted to talk it over with the two of you and see what action we should take." He bowed his head. "I learned it too late to do any good."

"Maybe we should be takin' stock of our own ammo," the Virginian advised.

"You're not suggesting Brazos would attack Sunk Creek?" Mrs. Henry asked, aghast at the thought.

"I wouldn't put anythin' past Balaam, ma'am."

"Oh, come now!" the Judge broke in. "Driving off homesteaders is one thing, but Balaam wouldn't be insane enough to unleash his hired killers against a fellow Association member."

"Why not?" the Virginian demanded. "He's got land fever in the worst way, and Sunk Creek is prime property."

"Your dislike of the man is tainting your perception," Judge Henry said. "Why, I've known Ira for over twenty years. And as much as I dislike his attitude sometimes, I don't view him as totally ruthless."

"Lin would disagree. And so do I, afteh what happened at my place." The Virginian shook his head. "No, seh. It's yu' who has blinders over his eyes. Why do yu' reckon Balaam's hired an army o' gunmen? He has four times as many as he needs to drive off every nester within a hundred square miles. And why do yu' think he was so involved with rustlin' our stock last year? I'm afeared he has his sights set on a bigger slice o' the pie than he already owns."

"We don't have proof he was behind the rustling," Judge Henry said.

"There yu' go again," the Virginian said, not without a tinge of disgust. "Yu' can keep buryin' your head in the sand like one o' those ostriches I heard tell of, if yu' want, but don't say I didn't warn yu' if Balaam comes along and takes your head off at the neck." He pivoted and tromped out and over to the corral, where eleven punchers had congregated.

"This is all that's handy," Chalkeye said.

"It'll have to do." Again the Virginian related Lin's

fate. A minute later Chalkeye and two men were raising dust as they sped toward Box Elder while the Southerner led the rest back along the same circuitous trail he had used earlier that day. He went as far as the junction without encountering a soul, and there he swung down to light a match and bend low. The tracks told the story. Brazos had gone on to Butte Creek.

"What now?" Nebrasky asked.

Straightening, the Virginian coldly scanned the trail northward. For long moments personal desire waged battle with law-abiding conduct, and proper conduct won. "We go back," he snapped. "And hope to hell we're not makin' the biggest mistake of our lives."

Ira Balaam loved to read his Eastern newspapers. The accounts of orchestra concerts, the operas, the ballet recitals, they all filled him with an ardent longing for the life of a cultured gentleman. Many times he had cursed the fate that had sculpted him into a wealthy Western rancher when an Eastern railroad magnate or a captain of commerce would have been more to his liking. If the truth were known, he disliked the ranching life, the long hours of hard toil day in and day out, year after year. He despised the constant struggle with the elements and other factors over which a man had no control. And, too, he hated horses. Positively loathed them. Yet the dumb brutes were an indispensable part of maintaining a successful ranch, so he could no more do without them than he could his own legs.

Many was the time Balaam had been strongly tempted to sell out, take his money, and go to New York or Boston or somewhere he would never have to sit in a saddle again. There was a hitch to his dream, though, it being the fact that his money wouldn't last forever and eventually he'd be right back where he had started when he initially ventured to the frontier: penniless and with no prospects worth mentioning.

Several years ago Balaam had concluded that the core of his problem was that he wasn't rich *enough*, that between the large sum he had hoarded and the price he could get for his land he wouldn't be able to set himself up in fine princely style for all the rest of his days. Once the notion took root and festered in his devious brain, he had cast about for ways of increasing his wealth. He sold the timber rights to the trees on his spread and didn't care a whit that the loss of nearly all his timber would increase erosion and cause other problems. He sold mineral rights, what few there were, and made no bones of the scars left by the miners and their blasting powder. He even sold some of his water to a neighboring rancher whose springs had gone dry—at a hefty price. But all he did was not enough.

Balaam needed more money, lots more. He had taken to viewing anyone who was richer than he was with blatant envy and not a little hostility. Why should they have so much more than he did, he reasoned, when he worked just as hard or harder? Life had played a cruel joke on him by giving him just enough of the material things to make him comfortable but not enough to give him his heart's desire.

Balaam was a true rarity, a successful Westerner who hated the West, a man who was good at something but who hated what he was good at. He couldn't bear the thought of spending the rest of his life at Butte Creek, and in his desperation he cast about for a means of reaping the rewards he deserved and the happiness he craved.

Ironically, Balaam owed to the squatters the inspiration that promised to line his pockets with more money than he would ever need. When they had first swarmed onto the scene, with their clinging families huddled in rickety wagons, and set up their rawhide outfits, he had been outraged by their gall. For people to lay claim to something they didn't rightfully own struck him as being not only outrageous but practically un-American. They were like flies, flitting here and there across the Wyoming tableland and mountains, swooping down on choice morsels as the whim struck them. In no time at all they had overrun the land.

Balaam had hired range detectives, both to prevent

any of his stock from being rustled and to drive off squatters on his huge range. Shortly afterward Balaam had his run-in with the Proctors. He had tried to be reasonable when he learned they had children. He had ridden over there personally and told Robert Proctor how things were. He'd explained that Proctor was using water Balaam needed on occasion and that Proctor had started laying fence on pasture Balaam called his own even if he rarely grazed his cattle there. And how had the homesteader reacted? Proctor had laughed in Balaam's face and told Balaam in no uncertain terms that he wasn't leaving. Adding injury to the insult, Proctor had pointed out that Balaam had failed to file on that section, so Proctor could do as he damn well pleased.

Balaam had no regrets about sending Brazos to deal with the stubborn bastard. Later, when Balaam realized how easy and how final his solution had been, he applied it to other squatters. Then to two or three old-timers whose small spreads he had long coveted. At the same time he began to do a little rustling of his own, adding cattle to his herds as he added acreage to his ranch. Somewhere along the way, and he could never pinpoint exactly when, a bold stroke of genius had given him the final solution to his problem.

There was only one other outfit in the territory that rivaled his own, one other spread that was as large or larger, one man who was his social and financial equal. The ranch was Sunk Creek, the man Judge Henry.

What if—Balaam had asked himself and tingled with glee at the thought—what if Judge Henry could be eliminated and Sunk Creek added to Balaam's already vast holdings? The combined incomes would enable him to wallow in luxury, if he kept the land and hired a manager to oversee day-to-day operations. Or he could sell the land outright, take his millions, and retire to the cultured East.

The idea became an obsession. Balaam plotted day and night about how he could achieve his goal. In the meantime he took delight in having his men rustle large numbers of Sunk Creek stock. And since he was shrewd enough to realize there was one man, more than any other, who threatened to ruin his scheme, he had let his men know that a large bonus would go to anyone who made wolf meat of the Virginian.

Killebrew had tried and failed. No one wanted part of the Southerner after that. He was hell with the hide off, they claimed, a wildcat with lightning for hands and nerves of steel.

Balaam had pinned his hopes on Brazos. He knew of the man-in-black's reputation, knew Brazos had a longer string of kills to his credit than the Virginian did. Yet Brazos had danced around the Southerner as if the two were doing a quadrille, avoiding a direct clash again and again until finally Balaam, in exasperation, had demanded to know what in the hell was going on. The answer had stunned him.

Now, as Balaam sat reading one of his papers and reviewing the sequence of events that had led to the fateful step he had taken just twenty-four hours ago, he heard the thunder of hooves. Moments later his front door slammed open, and in stalked the deadliest person in the entire state.

"Are Grimes and Hancock back yet?"

"Hello to you, Brazos," Balaam said quietly, turning the page. "I expect them back shortly. You, however, I didn't expect until closer to midnight. Don't tell me you burnt out both McLean and Ringo already? *And* took care of those other homesteaders I had on your list?"

"McLean is dead. Ringo—" Brazos stopped, his face flushed. "The son of a bitch rides as good as he shoots. He made it to Sunk Creek."

"No matter," Balaam said. "When you hit there the day after tomorrow, his riding days will be over."

"We're ridin' to Sunk Creek just as soon as the rest o' the boys get here."

"My schedule calls for—" Balaam began patiently, and was rudely cut off.

"I don't give a damn about how yu' worked things out, Ira. By midnight me and the men will be on the trail.

By noon tomorrow Jeff Ringo will be fit for a stone slab. It's as simple as that."

Balaam closed the newspaper and folded his hands on top of it. "Let's discuss this like intelligent men, shall we, Trampas? I—" Again Balaam was interrupted, but this time in a manner that caused his heart to beat wildly. For the man in black had bounded around the corner of the desk and seized him by the front of his shirt. Balaam was an enormous man, yet his foreman plucked him out of his chair as if he were a feather, and the next instant Balaam was looking down the barrel of a cocked Colt.

"Don't *ever* call me that!" the man in black hissed, his face distorted by elemental fury. "I gave up the family handle when I heard about my younger brother. And I won't be fit to use it again until I've earned the right."

Exerting supreme self-control, Balaam kept his temper and said, "My apologies. I forgot. But it seems to me you're taking out your feelings on the wrong person. I'm not the one who gunned down your brother. Shouldn't you be saving your wrath for *him*?"

Tense seconds ticked by. Gradually Brazos relaxed. He lowered the pistol, carefully let down the hammer, and spun the Colt into its holster with a reverse flip. "I reckon you're right. It's just that I've waited so damn long for this, I'm as high-strung as telegraph wire."

"Understandable," Balaam said, smoothing his shirt. "And to show you I'm not unreasonable, I'll agree to the change if you can give me one good reason why I should."

"You're doin' it backwards," Brazos said. "When a man wants a grizzly head to mount on his wall, he don't go afteh cubs. We can wipe out the nesters anytime. But Sunk Creek is special. Yu' said so yourself. If you're serious about addin' the Judge's holdings to your own, now's the time while the law is busy with that business over to Johnson County."

A sly smirk lit Balaam's face. "My good friends in the WSGA played right into my hands without knowing it. When I first heard of their plot to import Texan gunmen by train and unleash them on the rustlers in Johnson County, I thought I would die laughing for joy." He leaned back and pressed his hands to the back of his oiled hair. "They handed me the moment I'd been waiting for on a silver platter. The law will be so busy sorting things out down there, no one will investigate the bloodshed in our neck of the woods for weeks."

Brazos nodded. "And by then the whole blamed country will be yours."

"A quarter of a million acres," Balaam said dreamily. "All mine." He sat entranced by the mental vision of his empire for a bit, until a rough cough brought him back to the matter at hand.

"Yu' can't say for sure how long the Johnson County affair will last," Brazos pointed out. "So don't it make sense to take care o' Judge Henry and that damned Virginian now? We can burn out the small fry later."

Balaam had been set to insist on sticking to his original timetable, but he realized he was being unduly stubborn. The gunman had a point. For all he knew, the Association assault on the good citizens of Johnson County might go awry, even though the cattle barons had the support of the governor. And he was counting on the distraction down there to keep the authorities busy while he attended to business locally. He really should attack Sunk Creek next. Once Judge Henry and the Virginian were removed, he would send a wire claiming nesters had done the deed in reprisal for the Judge driving some of them out. Sunk Creek would be his, if his lawyer had everything arranged properly at the legal end. Should any heirs show up, they would be dealt with accordingly. Balaam had it all worked out to the smallest detail, and he was proud of his plot.

"What'll it be?" Brazos asked testily. "I hear hawsses comin'. It must be Grimes or Hancock."

"Very well," Balaam said, rising. "Change mounts, stock up on all the ammunition you need, and ride for Sunk Creek as soon as the men are ready." He paused. "And this time, I trust, you will put an end to Ringo once and for all?"

"Don't yu' worry on that account," Brazos responded, patting his Colts. "I've been playin' him for a fool long enough, doin' everything I could to make his life miserable. Now I aim to do to him like he done to my little brother. Come noon, there won't be no more Virginian."

30

The Law of the Gun

Dawn broke crisp and clear at Sunk Creek. In the bunkhouse slept the punchers who had not gotten back until the wee hours of the morning. In the corral and stable dozed their weary mounts.

Over in the great house, hands clasped behind his broad back, the Virginian anxiously paced back and forth in front of a certain bedroom. Repeatedly he glanced at the door as if willing it to open. Now and again he pressed an ear to the panel to listen, but if his expression was any indication, he heard little to calm him down.

"You keep on like this and you'll wear a rut in my new hall carpet."

The Virginian looked at Mrs. Henry, seated in a nearby chair, and commented, "If I don't hear soon, I'm likely to bust. The doc should know by now."

"They had a long, hard ride from Box Elder. How Lin held up I will never know."

Outside, a rooster crowed. Down the hall appeared

Judge Henry bearing a tray laden with three steaming cups of black coffee.

"Me neither," the Virginian said softly. "Nine slugs in him and he's still breathing. Either he has the constitution of an ox or he's part sieve by nature."

The feeble joke elicited a sympathetic smile from the wise matron. "The two of you have been friends for ages, haven't you? He's your—what's the term?—pardner?"

"Yes, ma'am. You might say he stepped into Steve's boots when Steve learned the hard way that tossing a rope over another man's stock is a sure invitation to a necktie social." The Virginian faced the door for the umpteenth time, then realized what he had said and whirled. "Begging your pardon, ma'am. I wasn't thinkin' straight. I didn't mean to—"

"No harm done," Mrs. Henry broke in. "Goodness! Why must men always feel they're doing women a favor when they try to spare us from the grimmer realities of life? We can bear up under the bad just as well as you can." She laughed gaily to relieve his embarrassment. "And did you think I wouldn't know all about that horrid business? My husband and I share everything."

"Except the recipe for making truly great coffee," Judge Henry said, arriving at the chairs. "Hers is always better than mine, and I can never figure out why."

"It's an old family secret," Mrs. Henry said with a grin. "Passed from mother to daughter, generation after generation. We're pledged never to reveal it to anyone except our own daughters." Her eyes dropped. "And we never had a girl."

"Since you won't share, don't blame me if this isn't to your satisfaction," Judge Henry said, offering her a cup.

All three of them jumped when the door suddenly opened and out stepped Molly. She put a finger to her lips, eased the door shut again, and smiled as she leaned against the jamb. "Lin will live."

The Virginian spun on a boot heel and shook both fists in elation. "Hallelujah!" he exclaimed quietly.

"There's more," Molly said. "The bad news is that the doctor fears spinal damage. One of the bullets he took out was lodged against it." She put a hand on her husband's arm. "Lin might not walk again."

"Oh, sugar," the Virginian said.

"Jessamine will stay by Lin's side until he comes around," Molly went on. "I'd better get downstairs and relieve Mabel. She's been watching the children since we arrived."

"Anyone for breakfast?" Mrs. Henry asked. "I can whip up some scrambled eggs and toast. Tea, too, if anyone would prefer that to coffee."

"We're low on water," Judge Henry said.

"I'll fetch it," offered the Virginian. Eager to enjoy some fresh air, he gave Molly a peck and hastened down the back stairs to the kitchen. The bucket was in the sink.

Outside, a typical Wyoming morning was unfolding: The Eastern sky had been painted a brilliant pink, the cool westerly breeze gently rustled the trees, and the high grass rippled like waves on the ocean. Off in the pasture horses frolicked, and a few cows the Judge had kept to provide milk were grazing contentedly.

Idly swinging the bucket, the Virginian ambled to the pump. As he bent to lift the handle, he caught a flash of light beside a tree in the pasture. Instinct flattened him at the pump's base a fraction of a second before the blast of a rifle reached his ears and the slug whined off the pump instead of off his skull. He flung the bucket aside, twisted so he could draw his right-hand Colt, and lifted to return fire.

From several directions at once poured more lead, so much the Virginian had to hug the ground or be riddled. He heard windows shatter, heard bullets smacking into the walls of the house. To his dismay he realized gunfire had erupted out in front, too, and on both sides.

Somewhere a woman screamed.

The Virginian came up off the ground in a rush, his left-hand Colt leaping clear, both pistols speaking with one voice as he sped to the screen door. By the trees a figure dropped but another promptly took its place. Slugs thudded into the grass and buzzed by. He squeezed off one more shot and slammed into the door like a human batter-

ing ram, not breaking stride for a heartbeat, since to do so
invited certain death.. The frame cracked under the blow,
the top hinge snapped loose, and the whole door caved in,
bearing him with it.

Thunder boomed in some of the rooms. The Virginian
scrambled upright, checked to make certain no enemies
were charging the rear, then raced to the room where the
children were being kept. Slugs were punching through the
windows and doors like leaden hail. As he passed the front
room, he had to jerk aside to avoid a volley. Over in a corner the Judge and his wife were returning fire as best they
were able.

Rounding a corner, the Virginian drew up short at the
sight of a female form lying in a patch of deep shadow on
the floor. For a moment he thought it was the one he
loved, and his breath caught in his throat. Another stride
revealed his error, revealed the creamy dark complexion
and the two neat holes high on her blouse. Pausing, he felt
for a pulse, found none.

"Stay down, Billy!"

The shout drew the Southerner to the room beyond,
where Molly had their baby and Jessamine's children flat
on the floor. She was gazing in horror at Mabel's legs, visible through the doorway, her cheeks streaked with tears.

"There was nothing I could do. It all happened so
fast. The shots came through the window."

"We have to get yu' and the kids out o' hyeh," the
Virginian said, fearing they might be the next casualties.
"There's a way into the root cellar from the kitchen. You'd
be safest there."

A lull in the shooting gave them an opportunity. The
Virginian hustled the youngsters along while Molly
brought Johnny. All went well until they had Billy and
Nate huddled next to burlap sacks of potatoes and Molly
was placing the infant on a blanket.

"Find me a rifle."

"Yu' won't need one down hyeh."

"I will if I'm to help the Henrys," Molly declared as
she placed a lantern on top of a crate. "Don't touch this,

boys," she directed the McLean offspring. "And don't fret. I'll be back for you just as soon as I can."

The Virginian grasped her elbow. "Yu' can't."

"You'd try to stop me? *Now*, of all times?" Molly said, the Grandmother Stark in her veins surging to the fore. "Don't I have as much at stake as you do? This isn't between you men any longer. They're trying to wipe us all out, women and children included. And a woman has just as much right to defend those who are closest to her as a man does. How can you even think of opposing me?"

Properly chastised on that score, the Virginian was about to try another approach and point out that the children would need her to comfort them if the firing intensified, when the firing did just that. Objects were breaking and shattering all over the house. Alarmed for the Henrys, he cried, "Do as yu' please," and jogged for the front room. He got there just as the door buckled inward.

Dapper catapulted across the floorboards and crashed into a rocking chair. His hat gone, his shirt torn, a crease mark on his cheek, he rose into a crouch and fired his six-shooter twice at an elusive target out by the corral. Whirling, he spotted the Southerner. "Where's Mabel?"

All the Virginian could do was gesture.

"No!" Fear rampant on his features, Dapper shot past, and seconds later a drawn-out wail testified to a soul in acute torment.

If not for two things that occurred simultaneously, the Virginian would have gone to his friend. But Judge Henry suddenly shouted, "They're rushing the bunkhouse!" at the selfsame moment Molly came up behind him. Taking her hand, he ran to where the Henrys were crouched.

"What do we do?" Mrs. Henry cried.

"Give Mary a rifle," the Virginian said. A glance out the broken window showed a large group of men converging on the bunkhouse while pouring in a withering fire. Chalkeye, Nebrasky, and the rest of the hands were doing their utmost to hold the killers off, but they were sorely outnumbered, and there was a limited number of windows.

Digging in his heels, the Virginian launched himself for the front door. Molly yelled his name as the sunshine caught him in its glare, and there in front of him stood a gaping dark-haired man, part Indian by the look of him, armed with a shotgun. The Virginian's Colt blasted once.

Other gunmen were at the corral, shooting at the bunkhouse. One of them turned, saw the Virginian, and bellowed a warning to his fellows. They all spun, they all worked the levers of their rifles or the triggers of their pistols.

The Virginian, caught in the open, replied in kind, his Colts spitting lead and smoke. Pain scorched his upper arm. A bee stung his thigh. Two of the gunnies fell. A third twirled and pitched against the rails. The final pair fled.

In long bounds the Virginian reached the dubious sanctuary of a sturdy post and dropped to his knees to reload. Peering through the rails, he saw the fight at the bunkhouse had reached its critical point. Five or six hired killers were nearly to the door, which hung off its hinges. Once they gained entry, the defenders would be swiftly wiped out. Then Balaam's assassins could concentrate on the ranch house.

A fierce *"No!"* was torn from the Virginian's throat as he flicked the hinges on both Colts closed and dashed around the corner of the corral. This time none of his enemies saw him; they all had their backs to him. It would have been so easy for the Southerner to gun down three or four before they even knew he was there. And these were men born to the gun, who lived and died by the law of the gun, the law of the quickest, where the deadliest might made right. They would show no mercy to anyone else, and they deserved none in return.

But the Virginian had never shot anyone in the back; it was "a coward's brand," as his cousin had often said. Instead, he yelled "Try me!" and when they began turning, he gave them their full measure. In cracking cadence his six-shooters sang their lethal litany. Advancing a stride with each shot, he fired alternately with his right and left gun, and at each shot a hard case dropped. Six were down when the rest, like panicked fowl, scattered in all directions.

That was the trouble with hired guns. Their bravery often lasted only as long as they had the upper hand. Once the tide of battle turned, and they realized they might have to pay the price of their hire with their lives, they chose the better part of valor so they could live to hire out another day.

Magically the area between the house and the bunkhouse was cleared of moving forms. Gunsmoke swirled on the breeze, but the gunfire itself had stopped.

With only a single shot left, the Virginian reached the bunkhouse and slipped inside, his back to the wall. The floor was covered with debris from the windows and broken furniture. Wounded men lay in sheltered nooks. Honey Wiggin, Chalkeye, Nebrasky, Bokay Baldy, and others were still in the fight, some sporting wounds.

Honey came over as the Southerner reloaded. "Sweet Jesus! I've never seen the like! Where did yu' learn to shoot like that?"

"My cousin taught me."

"Who the hell was he? Wild Bill Hickok?"

"Johnny Ringo."

Wiggin laughed, thinking it was a joke. When he perceived the truth, his mouth went slack and he said, "That sure explains a lot!"

"Can yu' hold 'em?"

"Now we can."

"Any of ours down at the stable?"

"Curly went to feed the horses about daylight, and he hasn't come back."

"Give 'em hell, boys," the Virginian said to the others. Then he bolted outdoors once more, making for the stable instead of the house. No shots greeted his appearance. Unscathed, he attained the shadows at the southwest corner and slipped on silent feet to the front door. Spooked by the constant racket, the horses were acting up, nickering and fidgeting in their stalls. He darted to the nearest, seeking sign of Curly. He did not have far to look. The cowhand was sprawled by the hay, a pitchfork jutting from his chest.

The Virginian started to rise, to turn, to head for the

house and his loved ones and friends, when cold steel touched the nape of his neck and a metallic click rooted him where he stood.

"Don't yu' so much as twitch!"

Not about to ask for a bullet in the brain, the Virginian imitated a hitching post and said casually, "I was wonderin' where yu' got to."

"Been right hyeh, just waitin' my chance."

"And this is it? You're goin' to shoot me in the back?"

"Don't insult me or I just might."

"How will it be, then?"

Hardly a heartbeat elapsed and the cold steel was pulled away. "Put your hardware in your holsters. But be sure and do it real, real easy-like, or my itchy trigger finger might need scratchin'."

Every nerve jangling, the Virginian complied, his movements so slow a tortoise would have seemed speedy by comparison. At last both Colts were in place and he lifted his arms to show he was not about to do anything rash.

"Take three steps. Then yu' can turn around."

"Is this how Balaam wants it?" the Virginian asked, taking measured strides and rotating. He stared at the leveled pistols of the man in black and willed his body to relax.

"Do yu' think I give a damn?" Brazos responded. "I didn't sign on with him to spend the rest o' my days doin' his dirty work. I just needed money to tide me over until I paid the debt I owe."

"To who?"

"Everyone says you're so blamed smart! I thought yu' would have figured it out by now."

"Oh, I reckon I'm not as dumb as you'd like to believe. I've knowed yu' was kin of Trampas's since Drybone. Which is it, though? Brother, cousin, what?"

"He was my little brother."

"Well, now. There ain't much resemblance in the face." The Virginian had not lifted his eyes from those revolvers. "So yu' rode in hyeh pretty near a year ago lookin' to dig up the tomahawk. Must've bothered yu' some waitin' this long."

"Some," Brazos said. "But I've been doin' my best to make your life miserable." His cruel mouth twisted in a sneer. "How's McLean, by the way?"

"The sawbones says he'll pull through."

"Really? Damn, he's a tough hombre!"

"I'm proud to call him my pard," the Virginian said, continuing to put on the same amiable air as his enemy, though he knew both of them were keyed to kill.

Brazos backed up a few paces and glanced at his pistols. "Yu' do know, don't yu', that I could've done it at any time. A Winchester makes revenge awful easy, but it don't make it sweet."

"So there's honor in the Trampas clan after all," the Virginian commented, and recognized his mistake when the other bared his teeth like a mad wolf.

"I've heard the stories! I've heard it claimed he shot Shorty in the back and tried the same with yu'. But don't think I believe it! He might've been a long rider, like me, and like yu' were onced, but he wasn't plumb despicable."

"Yu' hadn't seen him in a while, had yu'?"

"Not in five years," Brazos said. "Not that it matters. There ain't never been a back-shooter in our family, and there never will be."

"I feel sorry for yu', Brazos. Or should I say Trampas? Goin' to all this trouble to erase the blot on your family name, when yu' should've knowed all along that some stains don't come out in the wash no matter what yu' do."

A feral gleam lit the man-in-black's eyes as he abruptly slid both of his six-guns into their holsters and poised his hands for the draw. "I'll tell yu' what I didn't do," he growled. "I didn't go to all this trouble to tire my tongue. Fill your hand, yu' son of a bitch!"

At that juncture shooting broke out in the vicinity of the ranch house, exploding into a tremendous din punctuated by the roar of a shotgun.

The Virginian, prompted by fear for his family and

the others, involuntarily took a half step, but a sharp gesture by Brazos stopped him.

"You're not goin' anywhere, not until me and yu' end it. If yu' want to save that filly o' yours, yu' have to go through me."

Four hands flashed, four guns crashed.

Only one man hurried away.

Not an hour later the clatter of wagon wheels heralded the return of Scipio le Moyne from Medicine Bow with the supplies he had gone in for almost a week ago. Nebrasky had gone with him, but when they heard of Balaam stockpiling ammunition, Scipio had told the hand to get the word to Sunk Creek right away. Now, as the weary cook set eyes on the familiar buildings he called home, he chuckled and told the team, "Wait until those jokers see the meal I'm fixin' tonight! Fresh bread, sowbelly, and peach pie for dessert! Why, they'll think they're eatin' at Delmonico's!"

Scipio hauled back so hard the whole wagon lurched to a halt. He gawked at the bodies he saw lying near the corral, then at more in front of the ranch house. Grabbing his rifle, he vaulted down and dashed madly to the corner of the stable. From there he commanded a full view of the corral, the bunkhouse, and the Judge's residence. Bodies were everywhere. He tried counting and stopped at sixteen.

"Oh, Lord! Oh, Lord! Oh, Lord!" Scipio breathed. Scooting to the front of the stable, he sought shelter inside and tried to stop his knees from quaking. "Yu've seen worse, damn yu'," he chided himself. "Remember the war?"

Calming his nerves, Scipio wiped a hand on his pants and went to race to the house when he spied Curly dead by the hay and another body lying in the center aisle. Curious, he dashed over, took one look, and gasped. Then, taking a deep breath, he burst into the open, certain he would be set upon by a horde of gunmen. Amazingly, he reached the house without drawing attention.

Low voices murmured within. Scipio cocked his rifle, braced the stock to his shoulder, and barged in. By the bullet-riddled table, on which rested a body draped with a blanket, stood a sad Judge Henry and a sadder Jessamine McLean. "What—" he blurted. "Where—?"

"Scipio!" the Judged exclaimed, brightening. "Can we use you! The doctor, Molly, and my wife are at the bunkhouse tending the wounded. Your help would be appreciated."

"Sure," Scipio said. "But how bad is it? Who did we lose? Where's—?"

Through the far doorway came the Virginian. He was holding one of the Judge's fancy English shotguns, which he placed in the gun rack.

"There yu' are!" Scipio cried. "I saw Brazos! Reckon he didn't have no use for those snake-mean eyes o' his anyway."

"Did yu' see Dapper on your way in?"

"Dapper? No. Should I have?"

"He's missin'."

"Dead somewheres?"

"Not likely," the Virginian said, tapping the shotgun. "He used this scattergun to hold off the last attack. There are five bodies out by the pump."

"Then where could he be?"

Moving to the table, the Virginian lightly rested a hand on the blanket. "Mabel," he said simply.

"Oh. Damn."

The Virginian walked to the entrance and grimly surveyed the carnage. "This is enough for me."

"What?" Scipio asked.

"I'm hanging up my Colts for good. Never again."

"You'd better hope Brazos doesn't have any kin," Scipio quipped, but his humor was wasted. The somber Southerner made no comment whatsoever. "You're serious about this?"

"Never more serious."

"Molly will be pleased."

"Very."

"And how about Balaam?"

"What about him?"

"You know he was behind this. Are yu' just goin' to let him get away with it? Are yu' goin' to let him go on breathin' to maybe try again? Where's the justice in that?"

The Virginian stopped and smiled at his friend, a strange sort of smile that seemed to answer the question of its own accord. Then he clapped Scipio on the back, mustered a wan grin, and declared, "Come on, yu' orn'ry cowpoke. Let's go make Mary happy by lettin' her boss us around some. There ain't nothin' a wife likes better than givin' her husband orders."

"Maybe we should have her examine yu'. Are yu' sure yu' weren't shot in the head?"

"Course I wasn't. Why ask?"

"Because I've never seen anyone get so darned foolish in a week's time."

"Life does that to a man," the Virginian declared, and, squaring his shoulders, he went out.

31

⊘╫⊘

Rainbow's End

While the Johnson County War and its aftermath
received considerable attention from the press,
the Sunk Creek Gunfight, as it was branded,
was accorded only a few paragraphs in a Cheyenne newspaper, and then in connection with the death of one of the
state's leading cattlemen.

"Cattle Land lost a true friend with the passing of Ira
Balaam, who was found in his study dead. A revolver on
his desk told the story. It had been widely known for some
time that Balaam was distraught over the passing of his
wife, who died after a lengthy illness. His own death
comes on the heels of a gunfight involving hands from his
ranch, those from the Sunk Creek outfit, and certain elements of the rustling fraternity."

The newspaper went on to list the number of those
slain and to lament the fact that one of them had been a
woman. "When will all this gunplay stop? How long before Wyoming can lay claim to being civilized? How long

before the forces of law and order prevail? Before reason and integrity are the guideposts of conduct?"

Which was an odd question coming from an editor who knew the truth of Balaam's passing, but who creatively altered the facts at the personal request of several of the most prominent members of the Wyoming Stock Growers Association. The cattle barons had suffered enough embarrassment because of the Johnson County War fiasco. They wanted to avoid further tarnishing of their image, so they exerted all the influence they could bear to keep the public from learning that two of their own members had locked horns.

As for the truth about Ira Balaam, he was found on the porch of his house, shot to ribbons. Someone had put a slug into each of his knees and both elbows. Then, methodically, they had shot him several times in the stomach and in the groin. There was evidence Balaam had tried to crawl away and been flipped onto his back, then finished off by having a pistol barrel jammed into his mouth and the trigger squeezed until the cylinder was empty.

Of the other principals involved, I can relay the following:

Lin McLean recovered fully and went on to become a successful rancher in his own right. In later years travelers who stopped at his spread were treated to the stirring tale of how he heroically survived nine bullet wounds—whether they really wanted to hear it or not.

Sunk Creek prospered. When the influx of homesteaders became too great to resist, Judge Henry displayed his ingenuity by lending money, at hefty interest, to some of the small ranchers and nesters who had nibbled away at his holdings, and then setting up a commission firm in the Chicago stockyards so he could sell their beef and reap even heftier commissions. In addition, within a few years he was breeding fine horses sought by fanciers everywhere.

Scipio le Moyne eventually left Sunk Creek to be a chef in San Francisco. His specialty became known as "frogs' legs à la Jefferson."

Dapper was never seen again. No one ever knew

what became of him, although subsequently a noted black hand going by the handle of Jessie, who looked enough like Dapper to be his twin, made quite a name for himself on the rodeo circuit.

The Virginian and Molly molded Aspen Creek into a thriving concern with lucrative mining and ranching enterprises. Eventually their family boasted three boys and two girls, and in later years their grandchildren could be seen near the gurgling stream, gleefully playing with their wooden six-shooters and stick ponies under the watchful eyes of the Southerner and his lady, who stood hand in hand on the bank as the setting sun blazed the western sky with golden glory.

ABOUT THE AUTHOR

DAVID ROBBINS's Pennsylvania birthplace is about thirty miles away from Owen Wister's—but nearly a century separates their births. Robbins has lived in the West for more than twenty years, in Texas, Montana, Colorado, and Kansas. He now lives and works in Oregon. David Robbins has published more than seventy books.